FAST
and the
DEAD

Praise for Anuja Chauhan

'One of the most readable writers in the country. Fun. Fearless. Fabulous.'—COSMOPOLITAN

'… One of [India's] funniest and most entertaining novelists. The only Indian writer of popular fiction really worth buying.'—MINT

'Chauhan is something of a rarity. A writer of comedy, in an expansive, life-affirming sense of the word, her influences being as much Vikram Seth as Joseph Heller.'—THE INDIAN EXPRESS

'Delightful. Wickedly accurate. Her ear for dialogue is one of Chauhan's strengths.'—INDIA TODAY

'A distinctly Indian flavour.'—FIRSTPOST

'The brazen style of humour, the settings, and the amusing concoction of Hindi and English make her stories richly Indian.'—THE HINDU BUSINESSLINE

'If there's one word that describes [Anuja's] writing, it's chic.'—THE TELEGRAPH

'Anuja Chauhan is the literary popstar of our time.'—VOGUE INDIA

'A bestselling author with instantly likeable characters and relatable settings.'—ELLE INDIA

Also by Anuja Chauhan

The Zoya Factor

Battle for Bittora

Those Pricey Thakur Girls

The House That BJ Built

Baaz

Club You to Death

ANUJA CHAUHAN

The FAST and the DEAD

HarperCollins *Publishers* India

First published in India by HarperCollins *Publishers* 2023
4th Floor, Tower A, Building No. 10, DLF Cyber City,
DLF Phase II, Gurugram, Haryana – 122002
www.harpercollins.co.in

2 4 6 8 10 9 7 5 3 1

P-ISBN: 978-93-5699-537-6
E-ISBN: 978-93-5699-538-3

Typeset in 11.5/15 Adobe Garamond at
Manipal Technologies Limited, Manipal

Printed and bound at
Thomson Press (India) Ltd

Here's to you, **Eppa D'Souza!**
Mere bacchon ki Ma, aur hum sab ki Baap

❤

Prologue

The old lady peers down the barrel of the wicked-looking shotgun and gives a satisfied cackle.

'Still in perfect working condition!'

She places it carefully across her knees, her frail veined hands shaking slightly, then winks at the huddle of onlookers standing uneasily beside her wheelchair. 'Just like me, no?'

'Oh, yes,' they all agree nervously.

Today is Vijay Dashmi. In Bangalore it is also, more importantly, Ayudha Puja—the day when machines, tools, weapons and vehicles are worshipped by those who earn a living through them. The puja has been performed, the offerings made, chunks of freshly 'sacrificed' watermelon glisten blood-red upon the potholed road like shattered heads, and the denizens of Habba Galli are now just eating the snacks provided by the shopkeepers' association and generally chill maadi-ing.

'Isn't it a bit heavy for you, auntie?' asks one young man. 'What about the recoil and all?'

'No, no!' The old lady shakes her head decidedly, making her white candyfloss curls dance. 'We're used to each udder, men!' Saying which, she bows her head reverentially and applies a dab of vermilion to the glinting barrel.

'You hate to be shut up, don't you, gunny boy?' she croons. 'You like being polished and loaded and bam-bammed about! And you loves de gush of warm, sweet blood, yeessssss!'

A thin balding man with a pumpkin-sized paunch steps forward anxiously and clears his throat.

'Um, mummy doesn't really shoot any more,' he clarifies to the group at large. 'We keep this shotgun securely locked up. It's just been taken out for the blessing today.'

The old lady snorts. 'What blessing, men? I just wanted gunny boy to have an outing!' She shakes back her curls and smiles short-sightedly at her audience. 'I just gave deese boys and guls a shooting lesson, Peter!'

'Oh, mummy,' her son says uneasily. 'Why?'

'So dey can protect demselves!'

'From what, mummy?'

'From danger, men! Crooks and robbers and all dat! And from te pettae! Deese bloody street dogs! Look at dem! Look at dat one, showing me her damn teeth! Let me have a go at her with gunny boy, Peter. Please, Peter!'

He releases the handbrake on her wheelchair and firmly starts to wheel her away.

Immediately, the street dogs start to bark. It is a harsh, unpleasant sound.

1

No Groom for Jhoom

'Madum? Are you wet?'

The voice on the phone is breathless and slightly panicked. Jhoomar Rao yawns, stretches and pushes her heavy dark hair out of her eyes.

'I'm the vet, yes,' she replies. 'Problem yenu?'

The problem turns out to be a cat. Its owner has flown off to Pondicherry for the weekend, leaving her driver to house-sit in her stead. The kitty has neither eaten nor pooped for the past two days, and is generally acting listless.

Pulling on a loose jersey, Jhoom requests the clearly out-of-his-depth driver to switch to video.

Squinting into the screen, she recognizes the cat. It belongs to Antara Reddy, one of her ex-schoolmates, who pampers it silly. An orange tabby, inevitably called Santra, he tends to get super anxious and gnawy whenever his mistress is away for too long.

Santra is lying on his side on an expensive Persian rug, panting haughtily. His belly looks distended and his huge eyes are glazed over.

Jhoom frowns.

'What's behind him? Show me the room.'

The driver flips the phone camera. Antara is fabulously wealthy, a fact made evident by the glowing wooden floor and the sumptuous French cane bed with matching dresser. The bed is neatly made, the room scrupulously clean. There is a magazine stack on the carpet, and on the dresser a hairbrush and the usual clutter of cosmetics—glass bottles in all shapes and sizes, a trinket box, powder compacts, Ziploc bags, claw clips, scrunchies…

Scrunchies.

Chewy and elasticky and redolent of the back-of-the-neck sweat of Santra's beloved mistress.

Damn, it's gonna be a long night.

'Kelu, anna,' she says in her most reassuring vet-voice as the driver flips the screen back to himself and looks at her with apprehensive eyes. 'Do you happen to remember how many scrunch—uh, big colourful rubber bands there were on that dressing table two days ago? Are any of them missing?'

Jhoom spends several hours bent over the operating table, extracting four slimy velvet scrunchies from Santra's belly: two ruby-red spangled with gold, one lime-green and pearl-encrusted, and one a glowing turquoise-blue. It is almost four a.m. when she finally steps onto the terrace, leans against the cement jaali and inhales the scent of woodsmoke and freshly fallen, tiny orange-stemmed white parijat flowers.

The late October air feels cool on her hot cheeks. The street lamps are still on, but birds have begun to chirp drowsily in the few-and-far-between Ashoka trees on Habba Galli.

This iconic one-kilometre stretch runs right through the heart of Bangalore's commercial business district. Known in the colonial era as Festival Street, it starts off as a hundred-feet road at the MG Road end—boasting a Starbucks, a gold souk, lehenga/gown boutiques, fabric stalls, bartan shops and posh kebaberies—but gets narrower, twistier and more congested as it passes the Shivajinagar bus stand before ending ignominiously at a garbage dump. Two-storeyed houses are crammed in tight on both sides, their protruding balconies practically nose-to-nose above the higgledy-piggledy parked cars and the single lane of traffic. The street is dotted plentifully with tiny eye-wateringly colourful and hectically multi-tiered temples, one white-and-green dargah, one Roman Catholic church, several demolishers-cum-antique stores, ugly three-storeyed modern flats and, every once in a while, a historic gem of a townhouse built in the Iraqi kasbah, Marwari or Chettiar style.

Jhoom's home is one such.

It is crumbly, pale-yellow and rectangular, with a heavy carved wooden door that opens right onto the street, a straggly enclosed garden within and several pigeon-infested, jharokha-style balconies. Three generations of the wealthy Rao family have grown up, bickered and parted within its walls, most of them eventually migrating to various countries. The only remainders are Jhoom and her mother, Jaishri, for years a full-time homemaker and, more recently, reluctantly employed as an assistant professor at Bangalore University.

'If they had any shame they would just leave the city,' snooty 'old Bangaloreans' had whispered after Jaishri's marriage ended with her husband absconding to the UK, leaving huge debts unpaid all over the city. 'Wealth illa, reputation illa, but Jaishri Rao ge parwah gilla! It's so awkward to invite that abrupt, uncompromising woman to parties! As for Jhoomar—such a crack name, it means chandelier because "the first time she smiled, the sheer incandescence of it lit up the entire maternity ward", it seems! Only that mad Jaishri Rao could have picked such a name! Jhoomar is pretty enough, but she couldn't hold on to her fancy fiancé, could she? Perhaps he panicked when he found out how extra-feminist both mother and daughter are. Maybe he slunk away when he discovered that the house is personal-guaranteed to the banks! Or maybe it finally sank into his besotted skull just *how* obsessed with animals his Jhoomar is. Anyway, the chandelier bulbs are all fused now, and the long line of admirers has turned into a long line of creditors! She even had to drop out of the Royal Veterinary College in London and complete her degree from a local agricultural college in *Hebbal*, of all places, like some hullar from a halli! She can't afford a monthly waxing even, and is getting full kappu in the sun, chasing nais and bekkus and doing their nasbandi! There will be no fairy-tale groom for Jhoom, that much is certain!'

Like Jhoom even *wants* a groom! Jhoom shakes her sweaty dark hair loose from its surgical net and thinks darkly. When he had slipped that (really rather pretty, it must be admitted!) flower-shaped diamond ring on her finger, she had thought that Takshak Vasudeva would always be in her corner, share her triumphs and disasters and dreams, but when the going got tough, the soul that slid out of the black chamois velvet pouch of his body was not diamond, but turd. Like the man said in the movie, 'Sir, yeh toh tatti hai.'

The voiding of tatti always leaves one feeling light and energized (though it sucks about the diamond flower ring) and that is how Jhoom feels about life post-Vasudeva. It helps that her mother is more or less in the same boat or, rather, in the same untethered raft, bobbing cluelessly through the choppy seas of daily living without any societal or spiritual mooring. And it's true, they have both gone a bit feral in the maintenance department, but it isn't *only* because they can't afford the monthly parlour visit but also because at the moment it feels so liberating not to pander to the pretty police by depilating, getting honey-blonde highlights, sucking in their stomachs, holding in their farts or minding their tongues.

All in all, they're doing okay.

Well, she just hopes her mum is.

Jaishri Rao has become alarmingly nocturnal and wanders around the house at odd hours, vaping sneakily or sipping wine, dressed in a series of brighter and brighter kimonos, but she *is* seeing a therapist regularly and seems to be holding on to her job.

As for Jhoom, she has lost faith in everything but dogs. Sure, their breath doesn't smell as fragrant as Tatti Vasudeva's, but their love is just so... *unconditional.*

She slides her hands into the plastic-lined pockets of her baggy much-patched 'vet-pants', loaded as usual with bacon bits and fresh green peas to offer the animals she treats, and watches a green-and-orange-jacketed pourakarmika work her way across the potholed street with steady strokes of her long bristly broom.

What she really needs, she thinks tiredly, is proper equipment for her clinic. A truly state-of-the-art small animal surgery with robotics and cameras so she can operate on cataracts and blockages of the heart, and earn enough money to clear the mountain of debt this house is buried under. Oh, and some free time to do some specialized courses would be nice. And, most vitally, twenty-four-hour power back-up, so she doesn't have to be on tenterhooks every time she operates, petrified that her wheezy old invertor could die any moment. Habba Galli has started getting a lot of power cuts in the evenings.

A sonorous aarti rises from a small Manjunath temple and, at the same time, an azaan warbles up companionably from the minaret of the green-domed dargah opposite, reminding Jhoom of why, power cuts notwithstanding, she loves her neighbourhood.

She glances somewhat wistfully at the house directly opposite. While the Rao family's star has faded, the Saits' sitara has risen in the sky. Old Musa Sait was pretty much a nobody, but his son is a major movie star in Mumbai now, and Ayesha Sait is in the enviable position of being a legit 'Bollywood mom'. The narrow building, a cheap, modern construction of no historical consequence, glows like a polished jewel within its tiny but immaculately maintained garden.

I wonder what it's like to have an upward trajectory in life, Jhoom thinks glumly. To get richer and richer, instead of poorer and poorer, and be able to encase your mother's home in Carrara marble and flood it with central air-conditioning.

At least Ayesha auntie doesn't gloat, and is genuinely nice. And she's refused to move to the fancy new villa her son bought for her in the far posher district of Sadashivanagar, because she prefers the hustle and bustle of Habba Galli.

A husky voice sounds cheerfully from behind her.

'Chai chai!'

It's her mother, wrapped in her deep maroon dressing gown, with her short curly hair—expensive honey-almond fudge at the ends, natural gunmetal grey at the roots—sticking up in a crazy bedhead. Her eyes are slightly gummy and she's carrying two cups of steaming hot shunti-tea.

'You shouldn't have got up, amma!'

'I couldn't go back to sleep,' Jaishri says, thrusting one of the cups into Jhoom's grateful hands. 'Here, I bunged in enough ginger to grow hair on your chest. How much was the emergency case good for?'

'Eighteen thousand bucks,' Jhoom reports happily. 'For Antara's Santra.'

'*Noice!*' Jaishri clinks cups. 'Childhood friends coming in clutch, huh.'

'They know I need the money.' Jhoom shrugs. She doesn't add that Antara and she aren't really friends any more. It's too awkward hanging with the old gang—she can't afford their lifestyle, for one, and their priorities are very different from hers now. All they seem to do is play poker and drink and smoke up and stalk each other on dating apps or bitch out each other's marriage photographs on Insta. Not that some of that stuff isn't fun, once in a while, but most evenings she'd rather just eat a whole Cadbury Dairy Milk and Netflix a nice light show with her mother.

Jaishri sips her tea thoughtfully. 'Maybe I could train that cat to eat scrunchies on the reg.'

Jhoom raises her eyebrows over the rim of her cup. 'Ai, amma, you can't even train your strays not to piss on the tyres of Sushi Kedia's Mercedes.'

Jaishri's kohled eyes widen indignantly. 'They're not *my* strays, magu,' she protests. 'They're community dogs. The whole pilla party feeds them—and you keep them all healthy and neutered and vaccinated. What is that gandu even grumbling about?'

'Maybe about the fact that you were recently heard sneering at people who adopt pedigreed dogs?' Jhoom yawns tiredly. 'And that you *specifically* said that "only people who aren't confident of their own pedigree shell out vast sums of money to buy pedigreed dogs in a bid to pimp up their status and social cred"?'

Jaishri looks conscience-stricken. 'I said that?'

'Yes.'

'That's obnoxious.'

'Yes.'

'Well, he *deserved* it!' Jaishri makes an abrupt about-turn. 'Bloody Sushi Kedia! Damn, that name fits him well! He's *exactly* like a tight little ball of cold raw fish and boiled rice, overpriced and overhyped. Anyway, he shouldn't park that guzzler of his in front of our gate. One of these days I'll take a piss against it too. Good morning, Lakshmi-amma!'

This to the pourakarmika who has now reached their massive front door and is prodding the pack of battle-scarred black-and-yellow street dogs slumbering there with the long end of her broom.

'Shubodaya, amma!' Lakshmi calls back. 'Ai, naigalu! Shoo shoo shoo!'

The dogs move accommodatingly out of Lakshmi's way, yawning and stretching like ancient yogis, their curling tongues very pink in the white light of the street lamps. They watch with patient, unwinking eyes as Lakshmi sweeps their patch of pavement and, once she is done, curl up again on their designated station with contented sighs.

'Good babies!' Jaishri calls down to them loudly. 'You're worth a dozen Sushi Kedias!'

'Amma, shush, you'll *wake* him!' Jhoom shoots an agonized look at the well-maintained townhouse to their right. 'Cut it out! It's gotten so nasty on the WhatsApp group already!'

Jaishri looks unrepentant.

'I'm going to back to bed,' she announces. 'You sleep also, Jhoom.'

'In a bit,' Jhoom says, somewhat distractedly. The exhaustion from the all-nighter is kicking in. She needs to shower and sleep. But she's still too wound up to relax.

She lingers on the terrace.

It's been years since she saw the sun rise over Habba Galli...

On the cold, unyielding surface of a massive boulder, halfway up a scrubby hillock in Ramadevarabetta, with an almost-full moon hanging low in the purple sky behind him and a swathe of slumbering grassland below, Haider Sait is staying awake by doing push-ups.

One simple, one wide-arm, then a diamond, then a clap, then a superman, then back to simple. It's a complex sequence but, as all the choreographers in Bollywood will assure you, Hadi Sait can kill complex every single time. In one wildly memed sequence from his insanely popular comedy *Majnu Mechanic*, he had changed a tyre, flipped a masala omelette perfectly, catapulted through the air and plucked a coin out of the female lead's navel with his teeth, all in thirty seconds.

He finishes his push-ups and springs to his feet, reaching for the water his ancient, bandy-legged spotboy is holding out. As he glugs it down, he checks his look in the mirror being held up by his make-up man. White kurta, tattered jeans, shotgun carelessly slung over one muscular shoulder by a banjara embroidery embellished strap, mussy dark hair, lashings of kohl under his laughing dark eyes.

'This look is gajab, Hadi baba!' declares the spot. 'Sweaty, dusty, hundred per cent natural! You are looking Bandit-like-Beckham!'

Hadi grins tiredly. 'This bandit's ready for bed—how many more shots to go?'

'Just this last big one,' comes the cajoling reply. 'Then you can go home, meet your ammi and sleep in your home bed!'

'God alone knows when the rest of us will meet our mothers and sleep in our home beds again!' grumbles a disgruntled grip in a throaty aside. 'It makes me sick to think we could have shot this in Aarey Milk Colony just outside Bombay!'

'This is where *Sholay* was shot, you ignoramus!' a lighting assistant retorts. 'Bongo sir never compromises—he's a perfectionist! This location is practically a pilgrimage spot for him, it's so correct, it's so authentic.'

The grip starts to mutter something coarse about where Bongo sir can put his obsession with authenticity when a walkie-talkie crackles to life in the hands of an earnest young assistant director.

'Ready for take,' squawks the walkie. 'Wake Hadi. Wake Cake.'

'HS in the house,' replies the AD. 'Check frame, please.'

Everybody moves back and Hadi steps into the artfully lit frame, alive with dappled moonbeams.

'Hadi, you sexy animal,' the walkie clacks. 'You look incredible in the chiaroscuro. Step forward a bit so the light hits your eyes. Where's Cake?'

'Cake, c'mon!' Hadi calls out over his shoulder. 'Rise and shine!'

A pile of plush cashmere blankets stacked on a deck chair behind them stirs and comes to life. The cashmere slides away to reveal an adorable pouting face, squinting mascaraed eyes and a delectable body dressed in classic village belle couture.

'Don't shout, ya, Hadi,' complains Kakoli 'Cake' Roy. 'Ugh, have you been doing push-ups? At five in the morning? Chhee, psycho, freak!'

Hadi blows her a kiss.

'Come na, Cake,' he says persuasively. 'It's the last scene of the shift. Let me look into your eyes and tell you how much I love you, just as the sun rises behind us after our long magical night of passion.'

She blushes. Hadi's voice, even when he's being jokingly ardent, is dangerously heart-quickening. Then she holds out a slender hand triumphantly and flashes a massive solitaire at him. 'Taken, bitch!' she crows.

Hadi mock-clutches his heart and groans. 'Damn!'

'Remove the ring, it's not in continuity,' squawks the walkie.

Cake pouts. 'Can't I just twist it inward, Bongo?' she calls. 'It's bad luck to take it off.'

'Oh, FFS…'

The walkie is turned off abruptly.

And Bongo Banerjee comes stomping up the hillside, past the long line of vanity vans, food vans, generator vans and the general extensive paraphernalia of a mega-budget Bollywood location shoot. He is bundled up in woolens and a monkey cap, and looks like a bad-tempered baby in a bonnet.

Cake and he have an animated discussion and some sort of consensus is reached.

'Nail it, Hadi,' Bongo says to his leading man before he heads back down the hill to where the monitors are set up. 'Nail it for the sighing schoolgirls and bashful aunties and the panting diaspora, and all the hopeful young people who're staying alive just to see you two in a fresh love scene written by Bongo Banerjee! I know Cake's a pain in the ass, but just pretend she's that mysterious hometown hottie of yours again, na? And Cake, pretend Hadi's your pimply fiancé and that he just hit a World-Cup-winning six! Surrender to the dappled moonlight… and the scent of mogra… and the thandi-thandi purwahi and… *action*!'

Easier said than done, Hadi thinks ruefully as he grasps Cake's hand (the oversized solitaire, turned inward, digging into his palm) and looks with determined sincerity into her elaborately made-up eyes. He allows his mind to relax and slide back, and the feels start to flow…

God knows he'd been no monk growing up. There had been the usual number of hook-ups, one-night stands, girlfriends. But Jhoomar Rao? She'd been special.

Every time he was getting ready for football practice, he'd glance over to the sun rising behind her huge cream-coloured mansion and imagine her slumbering somewhere within.

Every time he lounged in the doorway of his mother's tiny silver shop on Commercial Street, it was with the hope that she would walk by, so he could inhale her hair as it trailed past his chest in a perfumed, unattainable cloud. Or—an *even* more daring hope, this—that she would stop, pick up a pair of the dainty, beautiful earrings his mother so painstakingly arranged in the shop window every morning and smilingly ask him how much they cost.

But that had never happened.

Instead, on every single weekday morning, Jhoomar Rao would emerge from the door-within-the-massive-wooden-door of her fancy mansion dressed in the khaki pants and red/blue tee of the posh Mallya Aditi International School, get into a chauffeur-driven Range Rover, and drive off to the wilds of Yelahanka. Weekends she would spend at the Bangalore Club. And holidays, abroad.

Even though it was a recorded historical fact that once Haider Sait turned eighteen and started assisting at Your Wish, it became almost mandatory to shop there. The quaint little store, with its smiling, curly-bearded genie and the *Your Wish... is our command!* signboard had always done decent business, but once customers discovered Hadi's calm, deft touch and his laughing dark eyes, reports of his off-the-charts attractiveness spread like wildfire through the central business district, causing gaggles of giggling girls and women, irrespective of age, faith, class and marital status, to throng to Your Wish to get their flesh pierced by him in all sorts of regular and highly irregular places.

It was a video a grateful father took of Hadi calming down a sobbing two-year-old and then charming her into letting him pierce both her ears that went viral and got him an audition for the reality show *Chance-pe-Dance*, which catapulted him into a film career beyond his wildest dreams.

Sure, Jhoomar was uber-rich and engaged to that smug bastard Vasudeva by then, but how could she have not even *known*? Hadn't she read the articles? Not even the one that came out right after his debut, a stylized *Filmfare* cover of Hadi in jeans and V-necked tee, his arms thrown wide open in the middle of Habba Galli?

The Fresh Prince of Ben-galuru!

In the heart of Bengaluru's shopping district lies a fairy-tale Disney bazaar where, so goes the urban legend, you cannot fail to find your heart's desire.

It teems with cheerful hawkers peddling juicy strawberries, nylon lace panties, tinkling glass bangles and plastic cuckoo clocks all at marvellously cheap prices.

Nike and Dior can be had on Habba Galli; so can Neki and Doir. There is pizza chettinadu and pasta manchurian and chocolate momos. There are harem pants in Kanjeevaram silk and prom gowns in Benarasi brocade. There are cows and cats and dogs. And above all the mayhem, there is fragrant incense smoke curling up from altars of all faiths.

Perhaps it is only fitting that bang in the middle of this hectic desire-fulfilment factory, inside a tiny silver shop called 'Your Wish', before the poster of a smiling blue genie, the Bollywood dream machine has found a young prince whose wholesome charisma may yet save its fast-fading soul.

Haider Sait is a phenomenon. Neither fair nor conventionally good-looking, nor the bearer of a famous Bollywood surname, his warm sparkling eyes and tight, well-knit body exude energy and decency in such lethal quantities that ladies everywhere are rendered weak-kneed. He's the 'street rat with the heart of gold' at whose cheerful, audacious 'khul ja simsim!' the notoriously choosy gates of the Bombay film industry have swung right open.

But the notoriously choosy gates to Jhoomar Rao's heart had remained resolutely closed, much to Hadi's regret.

'You just have a bad case of "Yeh kaun hai jisne Poo ko mudd ke nahi dekha",' a celebrity talk-show host had scoffed when Hadi owned up to his unrequited teenage crush on a Hotstar interview, years later. 'Of course she knew! It's the oldest trick in the book, to ignore somebody in order to catch their eye. I bet she's watching this interview right now and wishing she had let you pierce her flesh while she had the chance! Reveal her name on national television, c'mon!'

But Hadi hadn't. What was the point, anyway? Jhoom was happily married to Takshak Vasudeva, Prince of Choots, bringing up a couple of perfect little Brahmin babies and playing Queen-of-the-MILFs in one of those exclusive gated townships her in-laws were always busy developing around Bangalore.

His childhood friend Krishnan Chetty insists that Hadi had never really *liked* Jhoom. She'd just been the resident goddess, the hottest girl in the neighbourhood, studying in a snooty school, not one of the cluster of Christian schools in the CBD that Hadi and his friends all went to. Rich, Brahmin, forbidden, unattainable.

Hadi has attained many Jhooms since those far-off days.

Still, each time he has to do a big romantic scene, he finds himself reaching out for memories of Jhoomar Rao. The pulse-quickening thrill of catching sight of her. The jagged pain of seeing her climb into her boyfriend's car and driving away. Her sweet, heart-shaped face below the middle-parted waves of dark billowing hair. Her steady focused gaze—it's all grist to Hadi's romantic mill.

And so it is to her and not to Cake that he speaks the beautiful lines that Bongo gives him to say. And when Bongo calls cut, satisfied, Hadi has to force himself to shake off the wistfulness, the restlessness, the sense of some vital road not taken, which always grips him when he thinks of her.

He's still moody as hell as he rattles back in the chopper to town, then puts on a full-face-covering helmet and rides on an inconspicuous-looking motorcycle between his two strapping security men through the early morning traffic to Habba Galli.

As the guard outside his parents' narrow house opens the little gate and Hadi dismounts, raising his helmet's visor, years of muscle memory cause his eyes to swivel automatically to look at the large cream mansion opposite.

It looks… dilapidated. There's crazy amounts of seepage, for one. The paint is peeling, and the shutters on the wooden jharokha windows have all been taken over by roosting pigeons.

Maybe her folks sold it and moved out, Hadi thinks. Went to America like the rest of their fam-jam.

And then, with a queer little shock, he realizes she is standing right *there*. On the terrace.

Jhoomar Rao, in the flesh. The same queenly stance, the same wide shoulders, the same middle parting, the same tilt of her chin. Frozen in time.

He draws an uneven shuddering breath and drops his visor quickly, hiding from her line of sight, his heart thudding in his ears.

Fuck.

Inside her kitchen, whirling from counter to counter in an ice-blue anarkali, Ayesha Sait is mixing food for her street dogs. Naturally, she loves her son Haider the most in the whole wide world, but the raggle-taggle pack of canines currently licking their chops in anticipation of their dinner outside—all descendants of the great spotted dog Phoenix, now long gone and sorely missed—comes a close second.

Third place goes to her pride and joy, Your Wish, the little silver shop she had sold her wedding jewellery to start soon after her marriage, with the full support of her husband,

Musa. ('You have a quick, creative mind, chanda, and it's best for all of us if it is kept occupied.')

Musa had been a large, quiet, perceptive man twenty-two years her senior. There had been no filmy 'love' in their marriage—the kind Hadi showcases in his movies—but there had been affection and respect in plenty. When he had died unexpectedly of a heart attack in the middle of their European holiday, three months ago, Ayesha had felt her bones buckle, like she was a piece of collapsible furniture and somebody had pressed the lever that made her cave in and fold up really small. Hadi had flown down at once to Ajvatovica, the biggest pilgrimage site for Muslims in Europe. They had held a private funeral and buried Musa there itself, on incredibly sacred land.

After the funeral, worried by the blank, adrift look in his mother's eyes, Hadi had suggested she come live with him in Mumbai.

'You're not even fifty, ammi,' he told her. 'This is the beginning of your second innings! I'll set you up in a gorgeous apartment—above or below mine, so you'll have your own separate establishment—and visit you every day for Sulaimani chai.'

Ayesha had gone very quiet.

'But my shop, Hadi,' she'd murmured finally, carefully. 'You want to support me, but I didn't even let your abba support me. I've always been financially independent.'

He'd leaned forward and taken her hands, his wide, dark eyes, so like her own, looking at her persuasively.

'We'll hire somebody really trustworthy to run it for you.'

She hadn't doubted the sincerity of his offer. He hadn't been swept up by the drama of the situation, nor had he been trying to 'act' the part of a dutiful son. Hadi never acts. That's why he's everybody's favourite actor.

But…

'What about my dogs?'

Hadi had sighed.

'Ammi, they're not just your dogs—the whole pilla party looks after them, don't they?'

The residents of Habba Galli have long been divided into three informal groups: the pilla party, a small band fiercely committed to doing the legal and humane thing and coexist in harmony with the descendants of the great spotted Phoenix; the haters, an equally small, equally passionate group who think stray dogs are pests, like cockroaches and rats, and should be exterminated; and a large group who don't give a damn either way about the whole wretched business.

All three factions manage to get along more or less amicably, apart from the odd flare-up involving a chewed-up scooter seat, ripped packets of Nandini milk, or dog poop where no dog poop should be. But that's the magic of Habba Galli.

Ayesha had explained to Hadi that her life was here and that she would heal much better in the narrow, three-storeyed house Musa and she had lived in all their married lives.

'I need the continuity, ma,' she had told him. 'Same shop, same dogs, same house, same neighbours.'

And so Hadi, busy with work, had had no option but to return to Mumbai and just phone her as often as he could to get all the Habba Galli news.

Lately, it has all been dog-oriented.

One year ago, Harsh Kedia, the older son of jeweller and mongrel-hater-in-chief Sushil Kedia, had bought a gorgeous little Weimaraner puppy as a wedding present for his brand-new animal-loving wife, Sona. Entranced by the elegant golden-eyed, long-limbed, silver-grey creature, the new bride had named her Tiffany. This had swiftly changed to Tiffinni because she was so fond of eating.

It didn't take the family long to fall besottedly in love with Tiffinni. Even Sushil Kedia had been seen to crack a sour smile at the sight of the pretty, prancing puppy.

Time passed, Tiffinni grew into a fine young lady, ready to socialize with males of her own class. A handsome young suitor was brought in for mating purposes and all seemed to go off well. But two months later, Tiffinni produced not the slender, silver-grey, golden-eyed litter the Kedias had been expecting, but a plump, snub-nosed brood in variegated patches of brown, yellow, black and white, with shrill yippy voices and piebald spots upon their plump pink bellies, a sign that damningly proclaimed blood ties with the great spotted Phoenix.

'That sounds like the work of either Bachchan or Darponk,' Hadi had told his mother during one of their phone chats. 'They both inherited Phoenix's cow-patches. What's this, ammi, your dogs are indulging in straight-up love jihad.'

'Excuse me, Bachchan and Darponk are both neutered,' Ayesha had sprung to her pack's defence at once. 'Obviously that fancy Weimaraner groom had bad blood in his DNA!

Or maybe Tiffinni isn't as much of a pure-blood as they thought she was.'

'Ammi,' Hadi had sighed.

'What ammi-ammi?' she had demanded.

'You've been throwing your weight around the neighbourhood,' he had accused her. 'Rubbing in the fact that you're a big shot now. *That's* the real reason you don't want to move to Sadashivanagar.'

'Don't talk rubbish,' she had replied. 'I'm not a show-off and you're not that famous! I've fed the street dogs for years—this isn't some sudden, shallow obsession.'

'It is for Sushil Kedia, though.'

'Yes,' she'd agreed. 'Before he'd just glare at them from afar, but after this incident with Tiffinni, he's become rabid. He almost ran over Roganjosh the other day.'

'Roganjosh is still around? She was Phoenix's main babe, no?'

'She's around, but she's old, ma—she can't dodge car wheels as easily as she used to. She got hit, and naturally she squealed the place down. Aiyyo, that dog's squeals are louder than a car alarm! So Jaishri Rao ran out and gave Sushil a piece of her mind.'

He had chuckled. 'I can imagine. So who are the other leading lights of the haters' group these days?'

'All of Sushil Kedia's Marwari chamchas up and down Habba Galli,' she had replied. 'And old Dondi Pais.'

'Pais? Oh, that old ajji with the curly hair?'

Ayesha had nodded. 'She's started making evening appearances on her balcony nowadays, like she's the Pope or Shah Rukh Khan, and heckling the dogs till they bark at her. And when they do, she threatens to put a bullet through their brains.'

'Aiyyo, so she's completely gaga.'

'Yes.'

'And she lives alone? With a *gun*?'

'It's a huge gun, Hadi! From her coffee estate in Sakleshpur, it seems! It's for killing wild boar and other large animals. She brought it down to the street on Ayudha Puja and gave everybody pointers on how to use it!'

There had been a rather stunned silence at the other end.

'Ammi, I'm getting worried,' Hadi had said finally. 'If that baldie Sushil Kedia is taking this on his ego, things will get unpleasant. He's a full-on asshole. You know what, I've got a month-long schedule coming up just outside Bangalore—I'll come stay with you for a while.'

'*Come*, baba!' Ayesha had said delightedly. 'You haven't been to Habba Galli in eight years!'

And now he is really coming! His chopper has landed and he's driving towards her!

She picks up two big steaming thaalis of dog food and hurries out with them only to find Hadi chatting with the guard at the small gate outside.

'Alhamdulillah!' Ayesha gasps. 'How lovely to have you home at last, ma!'

'Ammi!' He holds out his arms. 'Here I've entered on a chopper to meet my mother, just like in the movies, and you're greeting me with thaalis full of dog food?'

She hands the thaalis over to the guard and hugs him hard.

'You're too thin, ma,' she frowns, worriedly feeling his ribs through his shirt with her fingers.

'It's called shredded,' he says lightly, sinking his chin into her hair.

She pulls back and studies his face. 'And why do you look like you've just seen a ghost?'

'Maybe I have.' He grins. 'Come, let's feed the great spotted Phoenix's descendants together, shall we?'

He nods at the guard, who opens the gate.

'Darponk! Bachchan! Pyari!' Ayesha calls. 'Tintin! Gudiya! Gigi! Rogu!'

They're sleeping in front of the heavy wooden door-gate across the road, but they uncurl and lope up at once, wriggling their bums and wagging their tails as they enter the gate.

'Whoa.' Hadi laughs. 'That's quite a battalion!'

Ayesha takes the thaali from the guard and wheels around, her anarkali swishing about her heels.

'Sit!' she commands.

Six out of the posse of seven sit down at once, chests out, chins raised, docked ears erect, as straight as soldiers.

'Well done, guys!' Hadi applauds.

But one frisky, tan-and-white spotted fellow continues to stand, dancing a little, staring up at them with bright, impudent eyes.

'Sit, Bachchan,' Ayesha repeats sternly. 'Sit! Sit, or no chicken–rice for you.'

Bachchan continues to prance about, barking and yelping.

'No food for anybody till Bachchan sits,' Ayesha declares. 'I can do this all day, you know.'

Low whines and tiny growls are heard from the throats of the other dogs.

Cowed, Bachchan finally gives his ears a conciliatory waggle and sits down, as erect as the others. He stares up at Ayesha with his pink tongue hanging out and thumps his tail good-naturedly on the ground.

Ayesha smiles. '*Good* dogs!'

In one smooth, practised move, she places the steel thaalis down and the dogs leap forward, three to one thaali and four to the other. They start eating voraciously but companionably, going round and round the thaali.

Hadi watches, both amused and impressed.

'Where's Roganjosh?' he asks the guard.

'Some ladies fed early in the morning that side also today, sir,' the guard, overwhelmed at speaking to a movie star, says bashfully. Then he adds, 'The Karwa Chauth sargi. Our wife is also keeping the fast, in Uttar Pradesh...'

He shoots a furtive look at Ayesha, then trails off, embarrassed.

Ayesha supposes this is because Karwa Chauth is essentially an all-day fast married women keep for their husband's long life, and mentioning it may make her, a new widow, more painfully conscious of her loss. Which is stupid, because how much more conscious of her loss could she possibly be? A wave of intense sorrow washes through her, making her feel almost giddy. Sudden, stupid tears sting her eyes.

And then a wet snout is thrust into her hand.

Looking down, she sees Roganjosh's bristly black face raised to hers in a friendly hello. She is wearing a marigold necklace and somebody has drawn a bright orange teeka on her forehead. Ayesha laughs and bends to pull one clipped black ear.

'Hadi, look!'

Hadi bends down and grips the sturdy paw solemnly.

'Shubhodaya, Rogamma!'

Roganjosh blinks her rheumy, yellow-flecked brown eyes and yawns lazily, exposing a curling tongue that looks (to the besotted Ayesha) exactly like the petal of a pink Oriental lily.

Then she rolls over, revealing toughened black nipples that have nursed several litters of puppies now settled, through the efforts of the pilla party, all over the Bay area and southern California.

Hadi squats easily on his heels and strokes the exposed tummy. Roganjosh thumps her tail in ecstasy.

'Oota aitu, Rogu?' Ayesha smiles. 'Yen oota?'

'She's had some good prasadam, madam!' the guard grins. 'See how tight her stomach is! Mrs Pooja Kedia fed her.'

'You mean Mrs Sona,' Ayesha corrects him.

But he shakes his head. 'No, no, madam, Mrs *Pooja!* Mrs Sona's *mother-in-law*. She has become quite fond of Roganjosh these days!'

Ayesha scans the old dog anxiously. The anti-stray dog feeling in the neighbourhood has grown so much recently that poisoning has become a legitimate fear.

Lately, she's even started to think that someone is actively encouraging the ill-feeling, fanning people's apprehensions as busily as the bhutta lady fans the coals below her corncobs—posting alarmist, misinformed videos here, teasing the dogs there, winding up people's fears to hysterical pitch everywhere.

But no, she shakes her head, nobody would have the guts to actually *poison* the dogs—it's a crime that can get you put behind bars in India.

Unless poor Pooja Kedia, under express orders from her horrible husband, is befriending the street dogs with the intention of doing them harm?

Ayesha sucks in her breath sharply at this thought.

Hadi looks up, concerned.

'Ammi?'

'Nothing.' Ayesha smiles.

'Roganjosh looks well enough!' he says. 'The vegetarian food doesn't disagree with her, clearly.'

'She's become *too* fond of Pooja Kedia, sir!' the guard volunteers. 'And Pooja Kedia madam has become *too* fond of *her*. This morning, they both sat together on that bench, leaning on each other, and watched the Karwa Chauth sun rise into the sky. Like a pair of lovers, like. Mr Kedia may get jealous, I think so!'

'Don't be silly,' Ayesha says uneasily.

The guard sticks to his guns.

'Well, madam, you know Kedia sir doesn't like the street dogs.'

'All that has changed under the new daughter-in-law's influence,' Ayesha replies firmly. 'She's a sensible girl, shukranallah!'

Sona Kedia stares down at her puja-ki-thaali. The fat little Karwa doll, shaped out of atta dough and dressed in a lehenga hand-stitched from a scrap of her wedding sari; the vermilion; the orange kanakambaram flowers; the grains of raw rice; and the blob of fresh creamy dahi. Everything looks perfect for her first Karwa Chauth.

Her girlfriends at work had declared her keeping of the fast as 'too cute' and 'madly exotic'.

'I hear post-KC sex is the best,' somebody had said, giggling. 'Because your stomach's so flat, you don't feel conscious or bloated and end up getting super adventurous.'

'And guys get super emo about it,' somebody else had chimed in. 'The fact that you woke up early and did sixteen shringaars and fasted devoutly for them to live longer ends up making them *last* longer—in the bedroom, I mean!'

'Harshu already lasts quite long, thank you very much,' Sona had defended her husband. This had been met with good-natured oohs and aahs and exhortations to enjoy maadi.

'It *is* kinda regressive, though…' somebody had suggested hesitantly. '*If* he's forcing you to keep it.'

But Harshu isn't forcing Sona. Harshu is the best thing to have ever happened to her, restoring her faith in all things sunny and decent after a nightmarish break-up with an unfaithful stoner boyfriend. He has booked them a night's stay at a fancy suite at the Leela Palace Hotel in honour of their first KC, and he is keeping the fast along with her.

'I'm keeping it to bond with my MIL,' Sona had explained to her girlfriends. 'Warring DILs and MILs are *such* a cliche! And *so* anti-feminist. I want a chill relationship where my mother-in-law and I banter back and forth, and have nicknames like Saucy Saasu and Bindaas Bahu and invent fusion recipes like mango salsa and rasam ramen and all.'

Her friends had looked slightly sceptical at this and tactfully changed the subject.

But mummyji and I *are* friends, Sona now thinks determinedly. And we would be even better friends if papaji wasn't such a...

Well...

Such an asshole, really.

He's always taking snide little jabs at mummyji. Her plumpness, her frizzy hair, her drab wardrobe choices, her dislike of air-conditioning, her lack of general knowledge, the poorness of her English. Harsh and his brother barely seem to notice, and as for mummyji herself, she just blinks and smiles vaguely.

Indignant on her behalf, Sona had started rushing in to defend her mother-in-law whenever she was in earshot. But then she had heard papaji talking to mummyji in their bedroom one night.

'They say a man and a woman can never be friends.' He had snickered. 'And maybe that is true—but what's *even* more true is that a woman and a woman can never be friends! They are essentially rivals, competing for the attention of their men around them! So don't get too excited about your new daughter-in-law!'

And still mummyji had ignored him.

Seething in the corridor, Sona had wondered for the first time if her mother-in-law was mentally deficient or something, and immediately felt horribly guilty.

But today, Pooja Kedia has finally struck back at her husband with a vengeance.

Sona isn't sure *what* exactly triggered the turnaround, but she suspects KLPD has something to do with it.

Kedia Lakshmi Pooja Designs is the name of mummyji's first ever jewellery collection. She'd had so much fun shopping for Sona and Harsh's wedding that, encouraged by the newly-weds, she had enrolled in a jewellery designing course once the celebrations were over. An enthusiastic student, she had attended every lecture, kept meticulous notes and posted respectful, gratitude-filled messages to her teachers on Teachers' Day. At her graduation function, she had glowed almost girlishly—'more than I glowed during my pregnancies!' she had confided in Sona laughingly.

Armed with her brand-new degree, she had spent months carefully creating the new line, with the hope of launching it during this year's festive season.

Sona and Harsh had been both surprised and grateful to papaji for being so supportive of his wife's hobby, but then…

Sona's pretty eyes harden as she recollects how papaji had swept up with his team of designers, taken one look at mummyji's creations and pursed his thin mouth in finicky distaste.

'No no no no,' he had murmured, shaking his narrow bald head. 'The Kedia promise is four-pillared—every single ornament has to deliver hundred per cent on Kwality, Kosmopolitanity, Kreativity and traditional Kulture. These... crude... *baubles* deliver on none of the above! Approving them would be nepotism—and blatantly unfair to more talented designers!'

'None of those promises even begin with a K!' Jhoom had said indignantly when Sona had confided in her. 'And Kosmopolitanity isn't even a word! Sorry, but your FIL is a cruel, crude-ass choot, Sona. Or should I say Kchoot. Actually, a full-blown sadist.'

'You're right,' Sona had agreed miserably. 'In fact, I'm pretty sure he *never* intended to approve her designs. He was toying with her all along for fun! Suppose my kids inherit his genes?'

'Oho, your kids will get Harshu's nice genes,' Jhoom had replied. 'What did Harshu say, by the way?'

Of course, Harshu had suggested that mummyji's designs be displayed at the store.

'Let's give them a chance, at least, papa,' he had pleaded. 'Surely mummy knows the popular tastes?'

But papaji had overruled him.

'Melt it all down at once,' he'd said.

'But the wastage, and the making charges!' Harsh had exclaimed, appalled.

'We'll absorb it,' Sushil Kedia had heaved a long-suffering sigh. 'What else can we do? At least your mother cannot say that I did not give her a chance-to-dance!'

And, as the inevitable tears flooded Pooja Kedia's eyes, he'd added tersely: 'Don't make a scene, Pooja. I'm only trying to protect you from embarrassment and heartbreak.'

'Ma, I told you KLPD is an inauspicious name!' Harsh's sixteen-year-old brother Sparsh had told his weeping mother that evening. 'What else did you expect? Forget about it and fry me a nice aloo parantha, na!'

And mummyji had resignedly gone back to rolling paranthas.

But there has been an odd hostile gleam in her eyes ever since.

That had been about a week ago.

Now Sona wrinkles her pretty brows and fast-forwards mentally to the latest episode in the daily TV serial that is life in Kedia Kutumb.

It started last night when the teenaged Sparshu, a human tapeworm who needs to eat every forty minutes, had wondered aloud how Harsh, Sona and mummyji would have the willpower required to complete the Karwa Chauth fast successfully.

Papaji had waded in at once to scoff at their efforts.

'Nil by mouth for twenty-four hours is hardly a hardship! Think of Irom Sharmila who fasted for years! Or Gandhiji! Harsh is clearly keeping tomorrow's fast to lose a little weight. As for these two, they will spend the whole day parading through the mall in those sleeveless kurtas that suit Sona but make your mother look like a wrestler! The attention they attract will be enough to fill their bellies! Where is the hardship in any of this?'

He had ended this nasty little speech with the snide laugh that Sona has come to hate.

Stung, she had retorted that it was all very well for papaji to talk, but had *he* ever kept a nil-by-mouth fast for twenty-four hours straight?

This had goaded both Harsh and Sparsh to challenge their father to keep the fast, a challenge he had accepted with a confident sneer. Mummyji, who was still barely speaking to him post the KLPD incident, had remained wooden-faced and merely taken another helping of peas pulao.

She hadn't spoken much when they ate their sargi together at dawn either, pretty much ignoring her 'best friend' Mrs Tomar as well as Sona, and lavishing all her attention on the old mongrel-matriarch, Roganjosh.

In the afternoon, all three fasting ladies had gone malling together. Sona could have done without Tomar auntie, a large lady with skinny hands and feet positioned at four corners of a massive, square trunk, whom she finds aesthetically displeasing. Besides, she has narrow eyes that match her narrow outlook, and her shapely nose, sandwiched between high, meaty cheekbones and festooned with a thin flashing gold hoop, is always stuck in other people's business.

But Sona had been given no choice.

They'd planned to shop, catch a movie to distract themselves from their hunger pangs and generally have fun.

And it *had* been fun. They tried on daring cocktail dresses, beachwear and lingerie in store after store, under the tolerant gaze of experienced store attendants who had identified them at once as a Karwa Chauth hen party. Then they got fancy acrylic nails. Finally, they made their way upstairs to the cinemas to watch a movie.

And that is when things had started to unravel big time.

As Tomar auntie and Sona argued over which film to watch—Sona was keen on the new Haider Sait release while Tomar auntie was being all #BoycottMuslimActors and pushing some fail Akshay Kumar film—mummyji had turned around and walked off purposefully towards the food court.

They had assumed that she was headed to the restroom. But when she didn't come back after a while, they had gone looking for her, worried she may have fainted out of hunger and thirst, and been utterly gobsmacked to find her sitting at a table in the food court, her eyes glittering with a queer, defiant fire, chewing with steady determination through:

1) One plate of chola bhatura
2) Ten steamed chicken momos
3) One spicy Twistato with dollops of mayonnaise
4) Four assorted Krispy Kreme doughnuts
5) A packet of spicy nippattus
6) A plate of dahi bhalla
7) A can of diet Pepsi

'Om-ji Gods!' Tomar auntie had gasped. Sona too had been horrified. The sight of a married woman, dressed in full suhagan glory, slurping through a seven-course meal on such a day, that too in full public view, had been a shocking one.

Silently, she had sunk down beside her mother-in-law, who had smiled at her kindly while continuing to steadily munch. For one insane moment, Sona, sniffing the piping hot bhaturas, had wondered if she should eat one too, but Harshu's sweet face had swum before her eyes and she had managed to stop herself.

But Tomar auntie had fully lost her shit. Letting out a loud hiss, she had hurtled around the table, her hawkish cheeks aflame, her eyes narrowed to slits, her gold nose-hoop gleaming like a scimitar, and stood glowering before mummyji like Yamdoot himself.

'What are you doing, Pooji?'

'Eating,' mummyji had replied indistinctly through a jammy doughnut.

'Well, then, stop eating. Go to the bathroom and make yourself vomit.'

'Shan't.'

'Do you want your husband to die?'

A careless little shoulder shrug. 'Maybe.'

Sona had sucked in her breath, half awed, half horrified.

'The wrath of Matarani will come down on your marriage!' Charu Tomar had thundered.

Mummyji had got to her feet, moving slowly, perhaps because of all the food she had ingested. She had burped delicately, then laid a (sticky) hand upon Tomar auntie's massive silk-encased shoulder.

'You know, Charu, I'll tell you something my younger son Sparsh is always telling me.'

Charu Tomar had drawn herself up to her full height. She had towered. Clearly, it was a cue for Pooja Kedia to cower.

'What?'

But mummyji hadn't cowered. Her eyes had been kindly, defiant and a little bit crazy as she leaned in and enunciated clearly:

'Get a life.'

And the mighty Tomar, weakened by a day of fasting, had just stood there, opening and shutting her mouth like a landed fish!

Pooja Kedia had turned majestically to her daughter-in-law. 'Tell them to parcel the last two doughnuts, Sona. And bring the car to the porch. We are going home.'

Sona had bobbed her head and bowed, like one does before royalty.

'Ji, mummyji.'

Thinking about it now, Sona gives a shaky little laugh.

But it hadn't been funny then, and it certainly isn't funny now.

Her phone rings suddenly, startling her.

Pati Babe.

She picks it up slowly.

'Heyyyy! How's my fasting beauty? Ready for a big dinner at the Leela?'

Sona can't help it. The sound of his voice, so cheerful and sane, makes tears roll down her cheeks. In a rushed, choking voice she updates him on what has happened.

Harsh is caught up at work—the rush of women buying jewellery today is insane—but he listens to her carefully, making concerned clicking sounds till she is done.

'*Good* for mummy,' he says finally. 'I hope she enjoyed the momos and the bhaturas and everything else.'

'Harshu, you're missing the point! She broke her *KC.*'

'Who cares, Sona?' he replies distractedly. 'It's a stupid regressive ritual.'

'Well, I'm concerned for her mental health,' Sona replies. 'She's menopausal and overwrought and I think it's all becoming too much for her.'

'Maybe you're right.' He sighs. 'She's kept that dumb fast for as long as I can remember. It's definitely unusual.'

'*That's* what I'm saying!'

'Poor mummy.' Sona imagines him raking his hair off his forehead tiredly. 'Where is she now? And where's papa?'

Sona shakes her head. 'She's in her bedroom, asleep, I think. And he… he's holed up in his bloody atelier, with the AC cranked down to freezing.'

'Atelier, indeed!' Harsh snorts. 'Why can't he call it a workshop like everybody else?'

'Harshu, please focus.'

He sighs again.

'Where's that idiot Sparsh? Can't he pour some oil on these troubled waters?'

'He has a full-day seminar with some American university tonight. He's prepping frantically.'

'Of course. How convenient.'

Her voice rises, there is a slightly hysterical edge to it. 'Don't ask me to go knock at either door, Harshu, please! I haven't eaten all day and it's all too unpleasant, and I *won't.*'

2

Gunny Boy

Nestled neatly inside their triangular rack, the colourful pool balls gleam like a pack of patakas upon the green baize table. Then a chunky brown hand lifts the rack away with a flourish and Krish Chetty steps forward, cue stick in hand. He leans in, takes aim unhurriedly and taps smartly at the ball, sending it shooting across the green baize to break the formation with an inimitably sexy *click*! Balls bloom out in all directions like a Diwali cracker, five of them hitting the rails and one striped ball rolling obligingly into a corner pocket.

Bhavani Singh, a comfortable-looking man with a square brown face, rounded nose and grey crew cut, waves the triangular rack about like a cheerleader's pompom and beams genially.

'Jai ho! Excellent break, Krishji!'

Krish straightens up, smiling and slightly flushed. Superhost of consistently five-star-rated Airbnb The Hub@HabbaGalli, he is twenty-eight years old, tall, slightly flabby, with a handsome but jowly face, curly hair and large, languid eyes.

Krish is Bangalore-born-and-bred, and The Hub, a tiny jewel of Chettiar architecture, a hundred and twenty years old, is his family home. His slow, deep drawl is at its most animated when he's telling visitors about the origins, culture and unique pluralism of his beloved 'Uru. He's picky, though, and if he doesn't like his guests he takes a backseat and lets his staff handle them.

But he has warmed to Bhavani and his elegant wife Shalini from their first interaction.

They are a well-adjusted sixty-plus couple—Delhi-based, but with a preference for the quaint eastern UP 'we/our' pronouns. They had confided to him on a video call that they had decided to take an 'annual honeymoon' to a new destination every year.

'It is a sixtieth birthday resolution, you can say,' Bhavani had explained. 'And as our senior Gautham sir has invited us to his daughter's wedding in Bangalore...'

'We're going to make our very first attempt at this late-in-life honeymooning there!' Shalini had chimed in. 'We will come two weeks before the wedding, spend Diwali in Bangalore and escape the Delhi pollution, which troubles Bhavani so much.'

'An excellent choice of destination!' Krish replied warmly. 'Have either of you visited before?'

'We were born there, in the military hospital,' Shalini said. 'Our father was in the army, you know, and we have a very clear memory of being walked in our pram by our parents there, on a cold winter morning, through lush green lawns, past a stone statue of a fat lady and down an avenue with huge, soft, pink flowering tree canopies.'

'That's Cubbon Park,' Krish said at once. 'And that's Queen Victoria and, if it was winter, those are *Tabebuia avellanedae* or Pink Trumpet trees. You must come ASAP; they are blooming at the moment.'

For almost a week now he has watched over them, advising them on which areas to visit, which heritage walks to sign up for, which pubs and restaurants to frequent, and assisting them in the serious business of picking out a present for the wedding: should it be a simple twenty-four-carat gold Lakshmi–Ganesh coin, or a bone-china tea set? A Benarasi silk saree or a baby Krishna figurine rocking in a cradle of the purest silver? Their budget is limited, but in shoppers' paradise Habba Galli, their choices are certainly not.

Krish is used to paying attention to people—it is his job—but the Singhs are the first who seem only too happy to return the compliment. Neither of them ever glances at their phone and both seem deeply interested in the challenges and dreams of a young man in the hospitality business.

And so, over sips of chilled Vat 69 (for the Singhs) and pulls of garden-grown weed (for Krish), and many games of amiably competitive pool in the parijat-scented courtyard, Krish has poured his heart out to Bhavani.

Of course, he is unaware that hundreds of people before him—criminals, tricksters, murderers and regular folk—have done exactly the same thing in the presence of ACP Bhavani Singh, Crime Branch, Tis Hazari, New Delhi.

Because listening is Bhavani's superpower. He exudes sympathetic attentiveness from the spread of his chunky shoulders to the tips of his interlaced fingers, and his kind, attentive eyes never look away from you till you want them to, in which case they swivel away obligingly and only come back when you are composed enough to handle eye contact again.

His twin homilies—'Hitting people will loosen their tongues, listening to them will open their hearts' and 'Never overthink, never strain, all that will give you is haemorrhoids in the brain'—are iconic at the Tis Hazari headquarters.

Basically, everybody at the Crime Branch agrees that when ACP Bhavani starts to exude that nuclear-level sympathy and attentiveness, he is like a latest-model Dyson for the soul. The interrogatee gives a heave and a hiccup, and then woooosh, out comes all the dirt: fears, secrets, childhood crushes and the places where the bodies are buried.

And so Krish has told the Singhs about how Bangalore used to be such a chikka town, with just the cantonment and the clubs and the level-crossing train tracks. He has told them how he used to cycle to Russell Market on empty, rain-tree-shaded roads to do the shopping for his mother. He has mourned the fact that the city's famous lakes are choking in sludge; ugly buildings have come up where weathered, creamy villas used to slumber in the shade of banana and breadfruit trees; and everywhere there are flyovers rising into the air like the curved stings of steel scorpions. He has told them how he and his best friend Hadi, who is a hugely successful actor in Bombay now, had a two-member band called Love Sachet (Sait-Chetty) and how they'd been world-famous in Bangalore city. And he has told them in great detail about the unnamed lady whom he has loved and lost. Basically, the Singhs are *intelligent* people, Krish, an erstwhile school and college topper, has concluded approvingly. Really, so few people are intelligent nowadays.

'Auntie doesn't keep the Karwa Chauth fast for you, uncle?' he asks now as Bhavani readies to play his shot. 'How come? Couldn't you do with the extra life insurance?'

Bhavani, very natty in his holiday uniform of floral shirt, Bermuda shorts and ghastly purply-blue Crocs, looks up from the baize table with a smile.

'Shalini kept the Karwa Chauth fast when we were younger. But her daughters made her stop. All three of them are atheists now—they only believe in hard work, kindness, trees and puppies.'

He doesn't seem perturbed by this set of clearly pagan values. But Krish is. He lowers his joint with a frown. 'But it's a bit sad, no, uncle? When old customs and traditions get lost that way?'

Bhavani plays his shot. The cue ball collides with a solid ball and sends it rolling to a pocket. 'We are nat particularly traditional, Krish.'

Is there a hint of reproof in the gentle voice? Krish isn't sure. He's about to ask, when Shalini enters the veranda, bearing a tray upon which stand two highball glasses, clinking with ice and 90 ml pegs of Vat 69.

'Shalu, did you know today is Karwa Chauth?'

'Oops,' is her rueful reply.

Krish gets to his feet.

'Arrey, why did you take trouble, auntie! I would have made the drinks for you.'

She gives him the tray and sits down. 'So hand them around now,' she says placidly. 'Here, give ours first. And tell us please, who even keeps KC in south India?'

Krish gestures towards the street beyond the courtyard. 'A lot of people. All the Marwaris, for one, and there are thousands of them in Shivajinagar. It's basically a commercial district, you know. And some of the blame goes to my friend Hadi too.' He laughs. 'He's made the tradition trend this year, with that cringy "Ae chaand, don't be lazy, I wanna break my KC" song.'

'We're more KFC than KC people, frankly,' Shalini confesses smilingly. 'By the way, we heard your friend has just arrived here? The whole bazaar was very excited about it.'

'Yes,' Krish confirms. 'The cast and crew are putting up at a hotel near the location, but Hadi's staying at home and taking choppers daily so he can hang with Ayesha auntie.'

'And you.'

Krish looks gratified. 'And me. We grew up together, right here on Habba Galli, he used to play a mean lean guitar... We were *bros*.'

'And now?' She searches his face.

'He still plays well, dude.'

'No, we mean, are you still bros now?'

There is the smallest of hesitations before Krish replies: 'Yes.'

Bhavani puts down his glass with an approving grunt.

'That is good. A young man in Haider Sait's position, surrounded by sycophants, has need of honest friends who tell him what's what.'

'Of course, he is very busy now,' Krish continues. 'I don't see him that often. Ayesha auntie says he's become an Eid-ka-chaand. Speaking of which, where *is* the chaand?'

Because tonight the moon is dawdling like a Bollywood diva and refusing to make an appearance at the time predicted by the weather app.

Outside, on Habba Galli, the usual restive, hungry KC murmurings—about pollution, smog, climate change and the unreliability of apps—have started doing the rounds. Hadi Sait, sneaking out of his house with an N-95 mask hiding his famous features, hears 'I wanna break my KC' play for what feels like the nth time tonight and shakes his head at the moon's lack of consideration.

Up on the terrace of their plush bungalow, Harsh and Sona Kedia are waiting for the moon too.

'Partly cloudy sky.' Sona sighs as Tiffinni rears up and rests her forepaws upon the railing, wagging her tail interestedly. 'The weather app predicted rain also. But later in the night. Look, Harshu, I got the big gate-lights turned off, so we'll see the moon better when it rises.'

'It helps that most of the streetlights don't work,' Harsh replies. 'The BBMP is a total disaster.'

'Don't be so negative, Harsh, it's KC.'

'Sorry,' he says contritely. 'I'm just hungry, I guess.'

There is a cry from the terrace of a scaffolded building. A gang of teenage boys has been stationed there to conduct a moon vigil, fortified with a goodly supply of dal-vada, chutney, Old Monk and Thums Up.

'Bandidde bandidde!' one yells triumphantly. 'Chandra! Nodi!'

'I see it, I see it!' chimes in another, jumping up and down excitedly.

A flurry of excitement ripples through the balconies and terraces, everybody looking eagerly in the direction of the boys' pointing fingers. The street dogs, excited by all the yelling, start to bark as well.

'Where, where?'

'There!'

But nobody else can see it yet.

'The boys are just having some fun, we think,' says ACP Bhavani Singh, chuckling and squinting up at the skies from the courtyard of The Hub. 'We cannat see anything rising in the east just yet.'

'Maybe they made a genuine mistake,' Shalini replies. 'But it's a little mean to play such a trick on the poor women who've been starving all day!'

Everybody continues to scan the skies.

And then Sona sees it. Through the mesh of cable wires, above a ridge of pinkish-grey cloud. A huge, glowing, cream-red disc, almost perfectly circular, beaming down at her benignly.

She gives a small glad cry and clutches Harsh's shoulder. 'Look, Harshu! Chaand!'

'I see it,' he replies smilingly, but he is looking at her face.

She punches him laughingly. 'Chhee, so cheesy!'

He lifts his phone and clicks pictures as she raises her steel tumbler and pours out a stream of water as an offering to the moon god.

'Om shri chandrakantah namah!' Charu Tomar rattles her brass prayer bell aggressively from across the street. 'Om shri som namah!'

'Poor Mr Tomar.' Harsh winces. 'She's probably deafened him!'

'Om shri shashi namah! Om shri rishi namah!'

'She's just making up shit now,' Harsh murmurs.

Sona starts to giggle, then frowns.

'Chup, I'm praying for your long life…'

Reverentially, she raises her thaali and performs her aarti. Then she lifts her sieve and looks through it, first at the moon and then, with a very full heart, at her husband's beloved face. Tears prick her eyelids.

Harsh winks at her. Smiling, she winks back.

In the courtyard of The Hub, Bhavani and Shalini clink their whisky glasses.

'A long life to you, Bhavani,' says Shalini.

'Oh, yes,' he replies comfortably. 'A long life, with you.'

Across the street, Charu Tomar smiles at mild Mr Tomar, the glow of her prayer lamp softening the harsh lines of her face.

'Happy KC, Tomarji,' she says, and there is genuine tenderness in her strident voice.

'Thank you for fasting for me, Charu,' he replies. 'You are a good wife.'

On the Kedia terrace, Sona and Harsh finally slake their day-long thirst with a glass of water.

'Done!' Sona lowers the glass and wipes the back of her mouth with a satisfied sigh. 'I really wanted to do this properly for mummyji! Come, we'll check on her and then leave.'

They start to go in, but right then, the window of the tiny house opposite theirs is thrown open aggressively, and old Mrs Dondi Pais peers out into the street, her curls backlit like a halo around her slightly wobbly head.

'Wort you looking?' Her voice is shrill and combative. '*Wort you looking at me for, men?*'

She follows up these interrogations with a loud hiccup.

The young boys sitting atop the scaffolded building nudge each other knowingly.

'Ajji has put.'

'Ajji has *properly* put, da.'

'Full tight she is, it seems.'

Dondi Pais leans further out of her window.

'*I said*, don't look at me!'

'Is she talking to us?' Sona wonders.

'She's talking to the dogs, I think,' Harsh replies resignedly. 'It's the same old tamasha.'

This is confirmed when the old lady rests her elbows on the windowsill and continues her shrill harangue.

'Ai shaitana cho petto! Whole day whole night MaryAnn, you bark!'

'That's a bit unfair,' Sona tells Harsh. 'Everybody was yelling chaand-chaand so they barked a little. Why's she so *mean*?'

Outside the Raos' massive carved door, the dog pack looks up. Old Roganjosh's tail begins to wag steadily. She utters a low, warning growl.

Outraged at this insolence, Dondi Pais's voice rises to a shriek.

'Don't show me your eyes! Oho, don't you *dare* show me your eyes, you damn darkie-barkie-sharkie bitch, who d'you think you are? Maddum president of our RWA, archbishop of Bangalore and de queen of England to boot? Well, de queen is *dead*, and you should be too!'

Responding to the hostility in her voice, Roganjosh springs to her feet, bares her teeth and starts to bark. It is a harsh, unpleasant sound.

In The Hub, the shouting and the barking have brought the three pool players out into the front porch. Leaning against a pillar, Shalini Singh looks out anxiously into the darkened street and makes a distressed sound.

'She sounds mentally unwell. Doesn't anybody live with her?'

'Her son does,' Krish replies. 'The bugger's a saint. *And* a bachelor. He's a Josephite too, about thirty years senior to Hadi and me. The entire congregation at St Joseph's Church agrees that he looks after her beautifully. He'll quiet her down and put her to bed in a bit, you'll see.'

'How old is she?'

'Past ninety, I think. Quite gaga. Recently, she's become completely obsessed with Roganjosh and gang. That's the stray dogs. She and that jeweller Sushil Kedia. The fellow's loaded and one assumes he would have bigger fish to fry, but no, they're both absolutely rabid on the topic and keep harping on about it on the neighbourhood WhatsApp group and everywhere else!'

'Really?' Shalini's eyes widen. 'But is your stray dog situation very bad? They seem so sweet! Have they bitten anyone?'

'Aiyyo, no, auntie! They're peaceful buggers, only. Eight of them, all vaccinated, neutered and socialized.'

'Then why…'

'Stray dogs incite extreme emotions all over urban India,' opines Bhavani. 'People become either fierce protectors or rabid haters. We think it is because stray dogs have a total lack of respect for established human hierarchies—they tend to grovel before beggars and bark impudently at billionaires.'

Krish chuckles. 'You've hit the nail on the head, uncle.'

'It's not funny,' Shalini says, distressed. 'Just listen to that woman—she's going to make herself ill.'

The old woman's ranting has intensified.

'Insolence! Nothing but a pack of non-stop pissing, shitting, humping squatters giving rabies to our babies! *Shut up, men!*'

Her voice rises to a shriek on the last three words, electrifying the dogs, making them all spring to their feet, hackles bared. They bark louder, their docked ears pricked, their tails wagging aggressively.

Old Dondi Pais's voice escalates to a shrill scream.

'Showing so much cock, eh? You wait… I'll pop you! I'll have you castrated! I'll have you arrested! I'll make skipping ropes wid your tails! I'll pull out your tongues! You bad, bad devil-rascal-pigs... you wait, I'll pop you, I'll jusst now pop you—'

Two terrific bangs ring out in the darkness.

They are followed almost immediately by the high-pitched, blood-curdling screaming of an animal in pain.

'WTF!' The boys on the scaffolded building put down their bottles in shock. 'Ajji's actually packing! Put on your phone torch, macha.'

As Habba Galli watches in horror, Jhoomar Rao bursts out through a heavy carved wooden door, her long dark hair streaming wildly about her vivid, fearful face.

'Roganjosh?' she screams, looking about wildly. 'Rogu! Ro... oh, *shit*!'

She dashes towards the downed dog, even as two more deafening bangs ring out in quick succession.

Ignoring the shots, Jhoom rushes towards the small black form writhing in the middle of the dusty road and falls to her knees beside it. As she feels the dog's body for injuries, two more bullets whiz by her, the last one making her gasp and jerk forward in pain.

'Stop shooting!' a voice thunders in the darkened street. 'There are people there! What you're doing is illegal! Stop it at *once*!'

Further down the road, inside The Hub porch, Krish Chetty swears under his breath.

'That's Hadi's voice. He's out there. What the hell is happening?'

'Were those gunshots?' Shalini says in disbelief.

Bhavani nods grimly. 'A shotgun, we think.'

Krish swears. 'Must be that ancient thing she made a big show of worshipping on Ayudha Puja. She calls it gunny boy.'

'And it hit one of the dogs!' Shalini is horrified. 'She's screaming. Let's go to her!'

Bhavani restrains her. 'Wait, the old lady could still be shooting. Can somebody nat go to her house and stop her?'

People are leaning out from gates and balconies, exclaiming and murmuring. Phone torches flicker on, as well as balcony and porch lights, and finally the gate-lights of Kedia Kutumb come alive, illuminating the tableau in the middle of the narrow, empty street.

The huddled black dog, the girl with waves of messy black hair on her knees beside it, and blood flowing freely from both.

'Rogu!' Jhoom gasps at the dog. 'Look at me, Rogamma!'

The dog finally looks up at the girl, panting heavily. Her rheumy old eyes are full of pain. Her grizzled chin is wet with blood. More blood is starting to collect in an inky pool below her belly. She whines weakly and shudders when Jhoom touches her.

'I need more light,' Jhoom mutters worriedly. 'I need to see where the bullet went. Jesus, a *bullet*! That *fucking* crazy old crone! Yes, Rogu, yes, good girl, good girl, can you get up? Rogu, can you move?'

Roganjosh thumps her tail weakly and lies back, whimpering. The sour, rusty smell of blood rises from her heaving flanks in hot waves. She tries to lick Jhoom's fingers but can't. Her eyes roll unseeingly towards the shimmering Karwa Chauth moon above.

Panic thrashes its hairy wings against Jhoom's ribs. She fights to keep it down.

'Can I help?'

The voice is deep, slightly out-of-breath and vaguely familiar.

Jhoom shakes back her hair and looks around to find a brown, muscular figure in a lowered mask squatting down easily on the ground a little way from her.

'I'm a vet,' she tells him, relief making her voice curt. 'I need you to lift her. Quickly, please!'

'Done, doc,' he says calmingly. 'But you're hurt too, I think. Is it bad?'

She looks confused. 'Me? No, I'm good. Please just *lift* the dog, *will you?*'

Her voice rises hysterically at the last word and he decides not to argue with her.

'Sure, just tell me how so I don't fuck it up.'

She nods.

'Okay. Come closer. Slide one hand here… and one there. Careful!'

Because Roganjosh has raised her hackles at his touch. Her yellow-flecked eyes glint, and a nasty snarl sounds through her bared, pointy teeth.

He backs away. 'Wow.'

Jhoom strokes the tense snout.

'Hush, Rogu, friend idde. Be nice.' To the new arrival, she adds, 'I think she's hurt there, be careful.'

But it's no use. The moment he comes closer, Roganjosh scrambles and tries to sit up, barking aggressively, teeth bared, foam flying from her black lips.

'Oh, come *on*, Roganjosh!' Jhoom says despairingly.

Hadi studies the dangerously panicked animal for a moment and then gets to his feet.

He's going to walk away, Jhoom thinks hopelessly, and who can blame him if he does?

But he doesn't. Instead, he pulls off his tracksuit top, drops it over the snapping snout, and double-knots the sleeves securely around the powerful neck. Then he scoops up the dog in one deft move and grins at Jhoom. 'Where to, doc?'

'Well done!' She gives a shaky laugh. 'Careful with her underbelly! Come.'

'Jhoom, you're hurt!' says another voice beside her.

Jhoom takes a second to recognize her friend in her Karwa Chauth finery.

'Yeah, Sona, apparently I am, but it's just a graze. Can you calm the rest of the pack down? Be careful of your good clothes.'

'Never mind those chootiya dogs.' Jaishri Rao has arrived too, drawing her maroon dressing gown over a rather sexy negligée. 'Or Sona's clothes. Show me your arm.'

Jhoom shakes her head and shifts from foot to foot in a fever of impatience.

'Ma, please, *Rogu*!'

'Whyn't you let your mother look at your arm while the guard shows me the way to your clinic?' Hadi suggests gently. 'We won't lose any time that way.'

She nods, her face growing marginally less worried, and then, gawked at by a growing crowd, some in lehenga-cholis and some in skimpy night suits, Haider Sait carries the limp, bleeding body of old Roganjosh through the heavy carved wooden door into the Dr Rao Small Animal Clinic.

Wearing surgical scrubs over his clothes, staying out of her way but standing close enough to provide her with any help she may need, Hadi watches Jhoomar Rao fight to save Roganjosh's life.

She has shaved the bleeding animal's chest, swabbed it with antiseptic, given her a quick anesthesia shot and secured her fore and hind legs into restraints. The dog is now intubated and out cold, her mouth and eyes slightly open, her tongue lolling. To Hadi, uninitiated in such matters, she looks dead. 'Have we lost her, doc?' he whispers and she gives her head a fierce shake, a gloved finger pointing at the flanks of the beast moving faintly in and out with every breath, before throwing him a withering look that clearly says: 'Are you stupid?'

Abashed, he goes silent and lets her do her thing.

She looks… same-same but different, he thinks. Her eyebrows are thicker than he remembers, her hair darker, without highlights and pulled back into an unflattering askew knot. Her movements seem surer than before—strong, deft and economical. The tightly tied gauze bandage around her left arm doesn't seem to be slowing her down in any way. And she clearly knows her way around an operating theatre. She switches on an X-ray machine and signals him to wheel up the operating table upon which he had laid the dog.

Hadi does as he is told.

The X-ray machine makes a low whirring sound and a few minutes later, Jhoom is studying a sheet.

'Fux.'

'What?' he asks, worried.

'It's bad,' she says crisply. 'One of the bullets just glanced off her, but the other one's lodged between the first rib and the manubrium. I have to get it out or it could embolize.'

This is Greek to Hadi, but he nods readily enough. 'You're the boss. What can I do?'

'D'you have your phone?' she asks, and when he holds it up she says, 'Play some eighties rock, please.'

'Sure,' he replies, surprised into smiling. 'You got it!'

His heart lurches as her eyes smile briefly at him above the mask, and then she bends over Roganjosh.

Hadi steals a look over the sterile drapes drawn across the dog's torso, but it is all too bloody to watch.

So he focuses on the music, choosing each song carefully, rejecting 'Another One Bites the Dust' as too pessimistic and picking 'We Are the Champions' as more suitable, while standing ready to hand her anything she points at.

Twenty minutes later, he hears the chink of metal being dropped on metal and looks up to see a bloodied roundish chunk of steel in an enamel pan. Jhoom is still bent over the belly of the beast, working.

'A ball cartridge,' he whispers, surprised.

She looks up sharply. 'What?'

He shakes his head. 'Nothing. It's a bloody whopper, that's all. Enough to kill three dogs. Is that it?'

'Yeah,' she says shortly. 'But there's a lot of internal bleeding. I'm gonna have to—'

A strangled moan rises from the slack black lips, a sound so ghastly it makes the hair at the back of Hadi's head stand on end. The dog stirs and begins to struggle.

He stops the music.

'Hold her down,' Jhoom snaps. 'She mustn't move. We need more anesthesia. I'll get it.'

He moves in, holding the dog down, murmuring soothingly. Roganjosh struggles weakly, her grizzled head turning this way and that. Her eyelids flutter.

Jhoom comes back, holding a syringe. 'Just keep her there,' she says. 'This'll take just a sec…'

And then there is a deafening thunderclap and the clinic is plunged into pitch darkness.

Roganjosh moans again, a guttural, despairing howl.

'Shit,' says Jhoom tightly. 'Now what?'

'Don't you have power back-up?'

'I can't afford it.' Her voice is defensive. 'The electricity only ever goes at night, so I never schedule surgeries then, but this, as you can see, is an emergency.'

'O... kay... I've got this,' Hadi says in as reassuring a voice as he can manage. 'Nobody panic.'

'I'm not panicking.'

'I'm talking to myself, obviously,' he replies placatingly. 'Could you put your syringe down somewhere and hold her for one nimsha? I'll switch on my camera torch.'

'Okay.'

A second later, he feels the cool, light touch of her hands on his shoulders. As he breathes in the unexpected scent of fried bacon, they slide searchingly down his arms, all the way down to his hands, and take over the holding of Roganjosh's squirming body.

'Gotcha.'

'Great,' he breathes. 'Now lemme just... *here* you go.'

The torch light comes on, illuminating the little scene. The girl, the dog and the operating table.

He restarts the music; then, carefully slipping the phone into the front pocket of his tracksuit jacket, he regains hold of Roganjosh's flanks and gives a quick nod.

'Do your thing, doc.'

As the lead guitar riff of Dire Straits's 'Money for Nothing' kicks in, Jhoom picks up her syringe again.

When the lights come back about seven minutes later, she looks up at him, her eyes fever-bright above her mask.

'Still taking requests?'

He nods. 'Yeah, tell.'

'"I Will Survive" by Gloria Gaynor.'

'Should've thought of that one myself. Coming right up.'

Jhoom continues to work steadily, clamping, tying, dissecting, suturing, her focus absolute. Half an hour passes before she finally puts down the needle, looks up and says, with a little sigh, 'Done.'

She steps away from the table, removes her mask and stretches out her stiff body, unselfconsciously massaging the back of her neck. Watching her, he thinks she looks plainer than she did back then, less glossy, more ordinary, or maybe it's just because the understated flash of incredibly high-grade diamonds at her throat and ears is gone. She wears absolutely no jewellery now.

'She should start stirring in about two hours' time. I didn't give her too strong a dose of anesthesia because she's like a hundred years old, and has lost so much blood. That's why she started moving about in the middle.'

'You did great,' he reassures her. 'If I ever need a surgeon you're the one I'm gonna call.'

She has released her hair from its top knot and is raking her hands through it tiredly as he speaks, but at this she turns to look him full in the eyes and smiles.

It's a sudden, wide, somehow wild smile. It causes her spikily lashed eyes to crinkle up in a manner that is utterly adorable, it blooms out like the moonrise all the fasting aunties had been waiting so hungrily for and makes nonsense of her ordinariness.

Dazzled, he holds out one sinewy hand and utters the words he's been waiting to say to her for sixteen years.

'I'm Haider Sait, by the way.'

She takes it. Her grip is firm, friendly and utterly unaware of the momentousness of the occasion.

'Of course you are! And I'm Jhoomar Rao.'

3

The Serpent in the Garden

'Ma, the whole thing was just like a Bollywood movie. *Better* than a Bollywood movie! How could you sleep through it?'

Thus sixteen-year-old Sparsh to his mother the next morning.

Pooja Kedia grimaces. Measuring three heaped spoonfuls of Bournvita into a mug for him, she says listlessly, 'Uff, must you talk so loudly, Sparshu? You sound like a cheerful crow. Kraw kraw kraw!'

The comment is not unjustified. Sparsh's young voice still wobbles and breaks whenever he gets excited, which is often. He is dark and lanky, with bright eyes and a trick of cocking his head sideways. He is dressed in a sharply tailored dark jacket, a meticulously ironed white shirt, a deep red tie, Batman pyjama bottoms and Havaianas flip-flops.

Not at all offended by the comparison, he continues to hold forth, 'Hadi Sait was looking at Jhoom like she was an actress from one of his movies, and she was looking at him like he was an actor fro—'

'He *is* an actor.'

'He looked so heroic carrying Mutton Curry in his arms!'

'Roganjosh.'

'And his eyes were all glazed…'

'Must be nasha,' his mother replies darkly, pouring hot milk into the Bournvita. 'Drugs. They all do drugs in Bombay.'

'*Ma!*' Sparsh exclaims in reproach.

'First toh you call me mummy,' she retorts. 'Always trying to be stylish! And secondly, that old woman is a crack! She could have killed somebody! Arrey, she could have killed Roganjosh! I've been praying for her ever since I got the news—*such* terrible news to wake up to, it was! That sweet dog…' Her voice breaks, a tear drops into the cup she is stirring. 'She is so independent, yet so loving! Better than most human beings I know.'

Sparsh, not accustomed to snappiness from his mother, looks at her in slack-jawed surprise.

'Aiyyo, the dog is fine. She'll recover fully! I was only trying to tell you that romance is alive and well!'

She stirs the milk more violently.

'Why would I need to know that? What do I care about romance?'

He spreads out his hands. 'Well, bhabhi said that yesterday you…'

She cuts him off at once. 'Don't try to act too grown-up, Sparshu!'

'Wow.' Sparsh hunches down into his chair. 'You spend the whole night kissing up to a bunch of Americans so you can make your parents' dreams come true and this is how they talk to you!'

'Sparshu!' Pooja Kedia looks conscience-stricken. 'Your big interview! How did it go?'

'*Seminar*, ma, not interview.' Then he smiles. 'It went well, mostly. I did some solid networking.'

She puts down the cup with a thump. 'It went well! Thank God! Why didn't you tell me that first instead of chattering all that other rubbish?'

'Because it isn't rubbish!' Sparsh says earnestly. 'Shots fired over Habba Galli! By our very own Dondi auntie! I'm kicking myself for missing it!'

'Who told you all about it then?' she asks.

'The same people who told you,' he shrugs. 'The car cleaner, the paper guy and the milkman! Accha, give my Bournvita, na. Simply you're stirring and stirring it.'

She slaps his hand away. 'There are still lumps in it. I'm dissolving them.'

'Where's Sushil?' Sparsh looks around. 'Overslept, has he? Tsk tsk. No discipline.'

'Don't take your father's name with your cheeky mouth.'

'And where're bhaiya–bhabhi?'

'Your bhaiya–bhabhi are at the Leela Palace Hotel,' she replies. 'Don't you remember? For their first KC?'

'Of course!' Sparsh smirks knowingly. 'Let's hope Horny Harshu got lucky last night! Should I go give your husband his tea?'

'Saraswati will take it,' his mother says shortly. 'You drink your Bournvita and go to sleep.'

Saraswati chamchamms into the room just then, very bright in an orange-and-pink salwar-kameez, scenting the room with the parijat flowers in her hair.

'Shubhodaya, amma!'

'Yes, hello,' says Pooja Kedia, not very encouragingly. She knows what Saraswati will ask next and she is not looking forward to replying.

'How your Karwa Chauth fast was, maydaam? You did-it all your prayurs nicely?'

'Give saar's tea,' sniffs Pooja. 'You talk too much.'

Sparsh hands the teacup to Saraswati.

'Did you hear what happened last night, Saraswati?' he asks her chattily. 'Did your sister tell you? She works in Dondi bai's house, no?'

Saraswati promptly leans her back against the wall and gets comfortable.

'Aiyyo, saar, Dondi bai's son Peter Pais phoned my sister in the night, shouting and abusing! Telling that he is driving back to the house and Bhagya should go there at once! Poor Bhagyalakshmi ran without taking oota or tea or anything! She has a key so she let herself in and there was the old lady peacefully sleeping, her whisky glass by her side! And Peter saar breathing fire and so angry and telling that it is all Bhagyalakshmi's fault! How it is Bhagya's fault if Peter saar's mother is a mad?'

'Don't talk so much, Saraswati,' Mrs Kedia replies. 'Give the tea. It'll get cold.'

Saraswati looks at her inquiringly.

'Saar yellidare? Bedroom? Garden? Aafis?'

'Check all three,' says Pooja indifferently.

She slides Sparsh his milk and goes back to stirring her tea. The dining room grows silent, except for the sound of Sparsh slurping his Bournvita, and the chamchammimg of Saraswati's anklets as she moves from the master bedroom to the small, enclosed garden, then further to the front room which Sushil Kedia insists on calling his atelier.

This is a sunshiny space looking directly onto Habba Galli, where his most exclusive clients can meet him one-on-one and design bespoke pieces of jewellery. Except for a row of dove-grey heavy-duty reinforced metal safes lined up against a back wall, the rest of the room looks as spartan and industrial as a high-end New York studio. There is a glowing wooden floor, a wide glass-topped worktable, crayons, thick art paper, strings, beads, several high-tech office chairs on castors and a massive rectangular mirror. Saraswati likes sweeping and swabbing here because except for a single narrow Persian runner in deep blues and reds and greens that lies in front of the desk, the decor is minimal.

She is surprised to find the door shut. She has never figured out how to use it, so saar leaves the door open for her in the mornings. Hesitantly, she presses down on the handle of the Yale smart lock. It doesn't budge.

She knocks on the hard wood with the solid end of her stainless steel mop.

'Saar.'

There is no reply.

She knocks again.

Silence.

Frowning, she tries the handle again.

The door doesn't budge and the automated female voice with the American accent she finds so intimidating says something in git-pit English. Saraswati wheels around and chamchamms back to the dining room.

'Saar not opening-it the door,' she announces.

Pooja Kedia and Sparsh look at each other, confused.

'Did you knock?'

She nods. 'Many times. He not opening.'

Pooja looks at Sparsh, who gets to his feet with a yawn.

'He probably fell asleep on that daybed of his. I'll go rouse him.'

He thrusts his bare feet into his Havaianas and shuffles down the corridor with both Saraswati and Tiffinni at his heels.

'Pa!' He knocks sharply on the door.

There is no reply.

When he tries the handle, the animated female voice asks him to '*Enter code.*'

'Code yenu?' he asks Saraswati, who shakes her head.

'Ma!' Sparsh hollers. 'Do you know the code for the atelier door?'

His mother appears in the doorway, her eyes apprehensive.

'No, Sparshu,' she says. 'Try your father's birthday.'

'Don't look so worried, ma,' he says soothingly. 'He's probably just fast asleep.'

He hunkers over the door lock screen and squints. 'Err, what is it?'

Her eyes widen in disgust.

'You don't know your father's birthdate, you horrible boy?'

'Just kidding,' Sparshu grins. 'Zero-nine, zero-three, sixty-one! Okay, that should do it!'

Only it doesn't. The door remains stubbornly shut.

Mother, son, maid and dog eye one another uneasily.

'Let's go around to the window,' Pooja suggests. 'Maybe if we knock on the window he'll wake up.'

In a little procession, they troop out into the garden and walk along the leafy hedge and clumps of birds-of-paradise to the glass windows of the atelier.

'Paaaa!' Sparsh starts to thump on the glass. 'Pa, wake u—'

His mother clutches his arm sharply and he stops mid-holler. 'Sparshu, look.'

Beside her, Saraswati's dark eyes dilate in horror. She starts to moan softly: '*Aiyyo devre…*'

As Tiffinni growls uncertainly, Sparsh drops to his heels to look at what his mother's finger is pointing shakily at.

There is a small hole in the glass window.

A thin stream of extremely cold air-conditioned air is coming out through it. A tiny web of cracks radiates outwards from the hole itself, irradiating the glass around it. As Sparsh watches, the glass crackles faintly and the web of cracks spreads further.

'Saar,' Saraswati moans. '*Maydaam!* Dondi bai's bullet must have hit saar and now saar is… sattho gidaare! Dead! Finished! Illa!'

Pooja Kedia gasps and sags against her son's lanky frame.

'I've killed him,' she says in a tiny, shattered voice. 'The fast—I broke it before time—and he died.'

Saraswati responds to this utterance by sinking to the muddy grass, lowering her head to her knees and rocking back and forth.

'Sattidaare!' she moans. 'Dead, gone, finished!'

'What rubbish you're both talking!' Sparsh says angrily. 'Maybe he's just injured. Or it missed him entirely and he's simply asleep!'

He flattens his hands against the glass. His mother's hands cling to his entreatingly.

'No, Sparshu, don't look, you're a child—*I'll* look!'

Gently, he pulls his hand away. Then, grim-faced, his milk moustache still wet upon his upper lip, he leans in resolutely, put his eyes to the glass and scans the room.

The line of bulletproof metal safes against the far wall…

The Persian rug in front of them…

The wide glass-topped table…

And in front of the table, facing him, a still figure in a wheeled office chair, slumped to one side.

Sparsh shuts his eyes and spins around quickly to meet his mother's apprehensive gaze.

'Is he…?' she asks faintly.

Sparsh draws a deep breath and turns back to peer through the glass again.

The neat spare figure in the white kurta-pyjama is still sitting slumped in the chair.

Like it has been all night.

Filled with dread, Sparsh's young eyes take in the horror in full detail. The hard little potbelly. The narrow ascetic face. The bald head and the naked forehead, in the middle of which is a neat bullet hole and a small coagulated trickle of blood.

Sparsh gives a convulsive gulp and turns to face his mother.

Her arms are ready and, as he falls into them, they are steady as rock.

His shoulders shake against hers. His knuckles rise to slam into his teeth. All his cocky teenage snark deserts him. He suddenly seems much, much younger than his sixteen years.

'Pa-pa-papa!' he falters. '*Papa!*'

Tiffinni sits down beside the little group, raises her long silver-grey snout and lets out a mournful howl.

Leaning over the railing of her strawberry-pink balcony, Mrs Charu Tomar has been sipping the green tea that helps with her water retention and watching Kedia Kutumb avidly. She has observed Saraswati exit the house through the back gate, weeping hysterically, and then watched Sona and Harsh tumble out of their blue BMW, still in their nightclothes.

'Something is Up,' she tells mild Mr Tomar (of Tomar Hardware and Tools, Dispensary Road) as he feeds papaya peels to the squirrels on the balcony. 'They're back too early. The checkout time at the Leela is noon. I don't think they've even eaten the complimentary breakfast! And I told you na, that Pooji broke her fast before moonrise yesterday?'

'You told me five times.'

'I was waiting to see if she would come out onto the balcony with her daughter-in-law last night, but she didn't! Sushi wasn't anywhere to be seen either! She is angry with him about KLPD.'

Mild Mr Tomar chortles, 'Usually *men* are angry with women about KLPD!'

Mrs Tomar shoots him a disgusted look, then glances down towards Kedia Kutumb and utters a shrill cry. The squirrels scurry away, chattering, and Mr Tomar clicks his tongue.

'You've scared away my pets, Charu! They didn't even finish their breakfast.'

She shakes her head in an agony of excitement.

'Ambulance!' she gasps, leaning further out over the balcony. 'Look, Tomarji! An *ambulance*—driving into the front driveway of Kedia Kutumb!'

'Oho, that's not good.' Mr Tomar gets to his feet slowly, shaking his head. 'I hope nobody has been taken ill ... I don't know what's going on in this neighbourhood, there seems to be one tension after another... How loudly that Tiffinni is howling!'

'And now the street dogs have started to bark too,' Charu says, continuing to peer down the street. 'This must be their fault only!'

'Now that's unreasonable,' he counters. 'What could the street dogs possibly have to do with the ambulance?'

'I don't know,' she says obstinately. 'But they're horrible, violent creatures—one of these days they'll kill your squirrels, then you'll see!'

Mr Tomar sits down rather suddenly, his face troubled. 'The squirrels are too quick for the street dogs—aren't they?'

But Charu is too busy arranging her dupatta across her broad chest. 'I'm going down to find out who's been taken unwell.'

'Don't barge in just like that, Charu.'

She turns to him at once, bristling indignantly. 'Why ji? Pooji may need me. I'm her best friend!'

'I know,' he says soothingly. 'But… why not… just phone her?'

'I did, earlier this morning. She didn't pick up.'

'Then wait for her to phone you back. Don't interfere in her private business.'

'*Hainn?*' She straightens up belligerently, tightening her ponytail. 'So much is happening right in our back side, and we should just ignore? I toh cannot! I am not so hard-hearted! I'm going down to get *all* the details.' Belatedly she adds, in a more sensitive voice, 'And to help in any way I can.'

Downstairs at Kedia Kutumb, things are moving at a blurry pace. A stunned Harsh, after calming down his weeping brother and dazed mother, remembers that Kedia Jewellers recently created the trousseau jewellery for the daughter of Karnataka's top cop. He calls the DG's office, explains the situation and is assured that 'the best possible person' would arrive very soon to take charge of the situation.

Meanwhile, a police team arrives and forces open the door of the atelier. Doctors from the team declare Sushil Kedia officially deceased.

'But why do we need police in the house, Harsh?' Sona asks him as he paces up and down inside his mother's bedroom.

'You *have* to call them, Sona,' he replies. 'It's standard procedure in such cases.'

'But it was an accident,' she says. 'You aren't planning to get such an old woman put behind bars, are you?'

'That old hag won't get away with this,' Harsh says grimly. 'Her son has been criminally neglectful, leaving her alone with access to a loaded weapon. I mean, what the hell?'

Sona shakes her head in bewilderment. 'It all feels so unreal—to think that a stray bullet from her shotgun shattered the glass of papaji's atelier window, caught him bang in the middle of the forehead and *killed* him!'

Harsh sits down heavily.

'He must've been watching what was happening,' he says. 'You know how obsessively he'd started hating those dogs, Sona. He would've pulled his chair to the window the moment the barking started.'

She nods wretchedly. 'Yes. I wish we'd realized. It was odd of him not to come out and react to the situation.'

Harsh gives a short mirthless laugh. 'He would've been cheering Mrs Pais on!'

He was too cunning for that, Sona thinks bitterly. *He would have acted all disapproving while cheering on the inside. Oh God, is it horrible of me to feel no sorrow that he's dead? Am I completely callous?* She realizes with a start that Harsh is talking.

'The old woman is a hazard! She should be in an asylum!'

Sona pats his back.

'But would papaji have wanted that? I mean, Dondi Pais and he were comrades-in-arms. I don't think he would want her penalized, Harsh.'

'Perhaps.' He sighs. 'Anyway, the DG's man should be along soon.'

'Well, that's good,' she says soothingly. 'Just the sight of police uniforms will shock Mrs Pais into good behaviour.'

'I wish Tiff would stop barking the place down,' Harsh says impatiently.

'She's *mourning* him, Harsh. So are Roganjosh and party.'

'Those bloody street dogs should be drowned in a lake!'

Sona, wrestling with a lot of emotional ambivalence internally, feels a surge of disproportionate anger at these words. What had those poor dogs even done?

She takes a deep breath and says quietly, 'Mummyji fed Rogu with me yesterday morning. She *likes* her.'

Harsh rakes his hands through his hair. 'Mummy thinks that damn bitch is Germaine Greer or something!'

Sona doesn't reply.

He looks up at her with tormented eyes. 'I just keep thinking that maybe, if we had found him earlier, we could have saved him. Instead we left, went to a hotel, made love, watched a movie, drank champagne! While he lay dying in that room all night! God knows how long he suffered!'

She sinks down beside him on the bed.

'Harsh, don't do this yourself,' she entreats, her eyes troubled. 'Please. It's not your fault...'

He squeezes her hands. 'Mummy should've checked on him...'

'You know she was too angry with him to do that!'

'And whose fault is that?' he demands. 'You've been upsetting all the family dynamics ever since you came to live here, Sona! Saying that for years there's been a gender imbalance with three men against one lone woman and you're here to correct it! Cracking jokes about being Team Mummyji and making her feel dissatisfied with her life!'

Sona pulls her hands away, anger flaring in her pretty eyes. 'She was already dissatisfied with her life!'

He throws up his hands. 'She should've checked on him when he didn't come to bed that night!'

Sona looks a little guilty. 'As to that, I'm sorry, but I slipped some sleeping meds into the haldi-doodh I gave her before we left for the hotel.'

He stares at her, stunned, starts to speak, then stops again.

'I wanted her to sleep well while we were out,' Sona continues. 'She wasn't in the best place mentally, as you know.'

'You did the right thing,' he says heavily. 'You meant well. But at least that idiot Sparsh should've checked on papa!'

Sona strokes his arm.

'Harshu, be fair. Sparsh is a teenager and entirely self-absorbed. And anyway, how could either of them have even imagined that such a freakish accident could take place?'

Besides, you know how much easier this makes things for you. It's practically a blessing in disguise.

She doesn't say the words aloud, but he reacts almost as if he has heard her.

'He was my *father*, Sona,' he says wretchedly.

Good riddance to bad rubbish, she wants to say but all she says before leaving the room is: 'I'll go check on mummyji.'

Bhavani Singh's stubby brown index finger moves unhurriedly down the dessert menu and comes to a firm stop at a photograph of an impossibly large beer mug, made of thick bubbled glass, filled with three differently coloured ice-cream scoops, layered with fresh fruit, dry fruit and raspberry jelly and topped with a pineapple wafer triangle, cashew nuts and ruby-red pomegranate pearls.

'We will have *this*. What do you say, Shalini?'

She laughs.

'How marvellously extra! We want one too. But how do you pronounce it, Bhavani?'

'It's pronounced "free"!' Mehta bhai, the tall, golden-skinned and glamorously handsome proprietor of Wonders of Kashmir holds out his hand for the menu with the flamboyance that characterizes his every gesture. 'Because-for it's a treat for you and Shalini beni from your younger brother!'

Cornered, the Singhs smile and protest weakly.

Mehta bhai had greeted them like old friends on their first day in Bangalore, bursting out of his exotic showroom in Safina Plaza and immediately claiming kinship in this southern city because 'Delhi and Srinagar are *next-tu* each other!'

'Is it Mehta or Mehtab?' Bhavani had murmured to his wife, to which Shalini had replied with an already charmed smile, 'Shhhh, it's Mehta with a B, obviously!'

In his lilting Kashmiri-English, Mehta(b) bhai had warned them to beware of the fast-talking cheats and rogues that operate in the Shivajinagar area—'They'll sell-it to you all cheaps, made-in-China maal. But they'll have to go through me first!'

Now he clicks his fingers—a gesture that shows off the stack of bracelets at his wrist, some leather, some metal, some beaded—and strides off to place their order. 'Maga! Yerudu gadbad, eega!'

'It's no use, Shalu,' Bhavani whispers. 'This man will nat rest till he does us so many favours that we are *obliged* to buy a Tree-of-Life carpet from Wonders of Kashmir! Let us pray for the stamina to push back enough to end up nat with the ten-by-twelve foot version but the four-by-six one.'

'But Bhavani,' she says mischievously, 'you know that no tasteful Indian home is—'

'Complete without one,' he finishes Mehta bhai's sales patter wryly. 'We know. Perhaps Gautham sir's daughter will like it as a wedding present.'

'Maybe we can get away with just buying some shawls,' she says hopefully. 'His and Hers pashminas? We could give *those* as a wedding present. Or we could just ask Krish to send Mehta bhai packing.'

'*You* could send him packing anytime you want.' Bhavani twinkles. 'You just don't want to.'

'Oh, but…' She looks conflicted. 'He comes from such a troubled homeland na…'

Bhavani snorts. 'We have nat seen a less troubled man in our whole life!'

Mehtab hurries back just then, bearing two massive beer mugs. He places them on the table and sits down, beaming with the sheer joy of treating.

'Bavani boi, Shalu beni, this is-a Gadbad. You must be knowing Pop Tate's Triple Sunday? This is the local version of it!'

'Gadbad!' Shalini chuckles as she picks up her spoon. 'What a name! Will it cause a gadbad in our tummies?'

Mehtab half rises to his feet, looking concerned. 'No, no, gadibadi means "quickly", beni!'

They are halfway through the second layer of ice cream when Bhavani's phone rings. He eyes his loaded spoon longingly, but perks up when he sees the name on the screen.

'Gautham sir, hullo! We are in your city, sir!'

'Jai Bhavani!' says the deep familiar voice. 'Yes, of course you are. I received that detailed itinerary you sent. You've started quite a trend with this annual honeymoon business! Revathi is demanding one too.'

'We are glad, sir,' Bhavani replies seriously. 'At this stage in life we must savour our health and the company of our life partner. How are the wedding preparations going, sir? Can we help with anything?'

'They are going well enough, I suppose,' Gautham says a bit grumpily. 'My duties seem to consist of saying, "That looks beautiful, my dear," drinking buttermilk or rose sherbet in shop after shop, and liquidating my entire provident fund.'

Bhavani chuckles. 'You have that entirely correct, sir!'

There is a short pause.

'Bhavani.'

The DG's voice has a different ring to it now and Bhavani reacts to it immediately.

'Yes, sir.'

'There has been a freak accident on that street you're staying on.'

Bhavani puts down his spoon.

'Habba Galli? You mean yesterday's incident, sir? An old lady shooting at dogs?'

'Correct—did you see it happen?'

'We are staying just a little away, sir. The road twists and turns a lot so we couldn't see; besides, it was dark. But we heard the whole tamasha. The dog is out of danger. We inquired in the morning.'

DG Gautham's voice grows grim. 'Well, she hit more than just a dog, it seems.'

Bhavani's voice grows sharp. 'She hit a person?'

Shalini sucks in her breath.

Mehtab's eyes widen.

Gautham responds, 'Apparently. Sushil Kedia of Kedia Jewellers, who lives directly opposite the old lady's house, was discovered dead early this morning.'

'The jeweller!' Bhavani exclaims. 'We were just talking about him last night—he dislikes the street dogs too. How ironic that a bullet meant for them went through him instead.'

'Well, yes, and he was our family jeweller, Bhavani, so its feels rather personal—our wedding shopping happened there only.'

'We're so sorry, sir.'

'It was a clean single shot to the head.'

'Very convenient, sir. But to whom?'

'My thoughts exactly. It *seems* like a genuine accident, but could you go have a sniff around?'

'Certainly, sir.'

'I've got a bright chap in position there already. You hit it off with him quite well at that witness interrogation workshop we had at the Academy, in Hyderabad. You remember?'

Bhavani's forehead creases. 'Hyderabad…'

Then he snaps his fingers. 'Naik! Manu? Madhu?'

'Manjunath Naik. He will meet you at the house. Thank you so much, and apologies for intruding on your annual honeymoon.'

'Nat at all, sir.'

Inspector Naik's face lights up when he sees ACP Bhavani striding down Habba Galli in his bright blue shorts, floral shirt and purply-blue Crocs.

'Sir! An honour to be working with you, sir!'

He is a conscientious-looking young man, very neat in dress and manner.

'Good to see you, Manju.' Bhavani smiles. 'How's the family? And your new baby?'

Naik smiles boyishly. 'You remembered, sir!'

The rest of Naik's reply is drowned out by the terrific barking of a large lean silver-grey dog straining at the end of a strong leash on a bedroom balcony upstairs.

Bhavani winces.

'The family dog, sir,' Naik supplies. 'Tiffinni.'

'Ah!' Bhavani shades his eyes with his hand and gazes up.

'So there are dog lovers in this family, also? We thought… but come, let us see the body. A lot of people are staring at us; has the news spread?'

Manjunath shakes his head regretfully. 'Couldn't be helped. It's such a narrow road. Everybody can hear and see everything. And the cleaning lady did so much galata. Come this way.'

Ignoring Tiffinni's barking, he leads Bhavani into the house, raising his voice to fill him in on the domestic set-up. Bhavani listens, nodding.

'Two sons, one daughter-in-law. And the wife is in a bad way, you say?'

'Yes, sir.'

'What a magnificent home. One would nat think it would be so big and quiet from the dusty, noisy street outside.'

'There are several homes like this on Habba Galli, sir.'

'Yes, our Airbnb is similar, but this Kedia Kutumb is shaandaar! Very well-maintained.'

'They're a wealthy family, sir. One of Bangalore's biggest jewellers.'

As they walk from the living room into the street-facing front room, Bhavani's eyebrows rise.

'He had a home office?'

'It's a sort of design workshop, sir, for very premium clients who like to sit in quiet comfort and consult personally with the designer.'

'Ah, we understand. With buttermilk and rose sherbet and the discreet liquidation of provident funds, we suppose.'

Naik smiles.

'You have been talking to DG Gautham, sir! He is very tensed about how much the wedding is costing! But the victim didn't have any clients visiting, sir. It was a Saturday— he was here just for some peace and quiet, I think. According to the maid, Saraswati, he retired to this room at around two p.m. He has been here since.'

Bhavani bends down to look at the Yale lock.

'A smart lock. Quite an expensive one.'

'Yes, sir. Only the victim knew the access code. We've had the memory chip examined. It was last used around seven p.m.'

They enter the atelier.

'Everything has been left just as it was found, sir.'

They stare at the scene. Bhavani's skin goosepimples in the cold, expensively spartan space; his genial round face grows gradually grimmer above his jaunty floral shirt. He scans the room, his eyes flickering from the glass window to the leafy hedge beyond, to the first floor of Dondi Pais's house above, to the dead man in the revolving chair, to the big table in the middle of the room.

And so the forehead of Bangalore's biggest jeweller has met with the business end of a bullet, he muses. No more business-class travel to the jewellery capitals of the world; no more fall, spring, festive or wedding collections; no more locked safes with secret combinations; no more fervent perambulations of the puja-ki-thaali at the altar of Lakshmiji. The goddess gave, and the goddess has taken away, all in one hot excruciating moment of contact.

'You found his phone?' he asks.

Naik nods. 'It was beside him, sir. Last message sent out at five p.m. A forward about the menace of stray dogs. He sent it to several groups.'

'And he was found in this exact position?' Bhavani asks. 'With his back against the desk, facing the street?'

'Yes, sir. I'm theorizing that he heard the commotion and rotated along with the chair to see better—he had a strong opinion on the dogs, apparently, and would have wanted to know what was going on. It's possible to see through the hedge if you really want to. And then the bullet hit him square in the forehead.'

'The ballistics people will have to do a test when it is dark,' Bhavani says. 'Point a laser tracer from the old lady's first-floor window to his ground-floor window across the road.'

'Yes, sir.'

'Look at that entry wound. She must have used a ball cartridge, at least. Bloodthirsty old lady. Strong, too.'

'Yes, sir.'

'Only one bullet, Manju?'

'Yes, sir. And one hole.'

Bhavani's eyes go to the walls. 'There are switches here, but no light fixtures.'

'It is all concealed lighting, sir, European-style. He was fond of hi-tech things.'

'How many lights were on when he was found?'

Naik nods towards the table. 'Just the one desk lamp, sir.'

'So the room was dimly lit, then.'

Bhavani approaches the desk. 'And what do we have here? An AC remote? This looks hi-tech as well.'

'Yes sir, it has many modes and features. The AC was turned on full blast when we forced the door in. He liked the room to be very cold, apparently.'

'How does the lock work?'

'There's a six-number code known only to him, sir. He can open it from inside anytime, but no one can enter from outside unless they have the code.'

'But there must be a key also?'

'That key was inside his wallet, sir. Inside the room with him only.'

'A very neatly organized desk…' Bhavani muses, then bends to the floor sharply. 'What are these?'

He kneels beside a slim sheaf of white tracing paper covered with pencil sketches. They are lightly splattered with blood.

'Perhaps he was holding them and they fell out of his hands, sir?' Naik suggests.

'Perhaps,' says Bhavani, looking at the top sheet more closely. 'It appears to be a chain design, Manju, rather snake-like.'

Naik bends to the floor as well. 'Flat herringbone links,' he reads the labelled sketch. 'Onyx. Sapphire. Diamond. Pt. That would be platinum, sir.'

'A rather masculine design. Expensive. And it's drawn by hand, too!'

Naik shines a torch. 'Sir, there is a lightly etched signature in the corner there.'

'Devika Johri,' Bhavani reads. 'So it was nat drawn by Mr Kedia—by one of his designers, perhaps.'

He sits down on one of the chairs.

'These are extremely comfortable.'

Pushing off with his toes, he rolls the chair across the room. The castors move smoothly, soundlessly. When the chair is halted by the worktable in the middle, Bhavani pushes off against the table and glides smoothly through the room again, his expression placid.

Naik looks at him in confusion, slightly embarrassed by this juvenile rolling-about.

'It is a very smooth floor,' Bhavani remarks.

'Yes, sir,' Naik replies uncertainly.

Eyes closed, hands in his pockets, Bhavani muses.

'When Sushil Kedia heard the altercation, he would have pushed with his hands against the edge of this table and glided on his very hi-tech chair towards the window. When the bullet caught him in the forehead, *thhaaaaan,* the impact would have made the chair roll backwards again, till it came to rest against the desk, *thhupp!*'

'Yes, sir.'

'There's nothing on the desk, though.' Bhavani frowns. 'What was he working on?'

'It seems like he was just sitting there, sir.'

Bhavani walks over to the window. 'Nobody in the street noticed he'd been shot because of the hedge. It blocks the view completely if you are on the street level.'

He is silent for a while.

Finally he asks, 'How many bullets did that lady fire last night? We counted six, but we could be wrong.'

'We're figuring out, sir. Luckily, there were several eyewitnesses, because of the Karwa Chauth ritual happening on the street at the same time. Unfortunately, because of the ritual, most people had dimmed their lights, so that the moonrise would be more magical.'

Bhavani looks up. 'Did somebody suggest dimming the street lights?' he asks.

'We'll find out, sir. And we have one promising eyewitness—he was crossing the street at that very moment, and would have seen the whole incident unfold…'

The living room of the Sait house has been taken over by a massive wire cage, inside which is a big black dog, curled up, with bandages strapped across its midsection and rump. There is a white plastic cone around its neck—to prevent it from biting at its bandages, Bhavani assumes—which, coupled with the long snout and bristly grey beard, gives it the look of a mangy wolf dressed in Red Riding Hood's grandmother's frilly nightgown.

As Naik and Bhavani enter, the dog throws back its head and emits a long mournful howl.

'Rogamma, hushhhh,' a slender lady in a mint-green anarkali says soothingly. She has fair skin and the delicate features of a Mughal miniature, but when she looks up at him, Bhavani immediately knows who she is. Her warm playful eyes are so much like those of her famous son.

'I'm Ayesha Sait.'

They introduce themselves, and she invites them to sit with a graceful gesture.

The living room is cozy and unpretentious. It does not look, Bhavani thinks, like the home of a movie star. There are simple white curtains of the Fabindia variety, a lot of plants, wide, comfortable couches, and a large photograph of a smiling man with the bluish permanent forehead bruise that proclaims the regular namazi, set in an ornate silver frame.

'You're here about the shooting last night, is it?' she asks as she takes the sofa closest to the cage. 'Poor Roganjosh! She's lucky to be alive!'

'So this is the famous Roganjosh!' Bhavani beams at the be-frilled beast. 'Beautiful!'

Roganjosh thumps her tail at him sociably, then continues to yowl.

Naik shoots a horrified look at the expensive Persian carpet the cage has been placed upon. In the far plusher Kedia house, Tiffinni had been leashed upon bare vitrified tile.

'Your carpet, madam! And it looks so new!'

'It is.' Ayesha admits. 'But look, inspector, there's a sliding plastic tray at the bottom of the cage. If she soils herself, it won't affect the carpet.'

'Er, yes.' Naik clears his throat. 'Ma'am, we are not sure whether you are aware of the happenings at the home of Mr Sushil Kedia.'

'Aiyyo.' Ayesha pulls a face. It is a childish gesture but she succeeds in making it look charming. 'That Sushil Kedia! *Now* what is he angry about?'

'He is not angry at all, madam. He is—'

'Allow us to offer our condolences on the death of your husband,' Bhavani cuts in to say smoothly. 'He looks like a good person.'

'Thank you, he was,' she replies simply.

'And what a handsome silver frame!' Bhavani continues. 'Designed by you?'

Ayesha flushes with pleasure. 'Yes. I have a small silver-design business. I started it almost three decades ago.'

Bhavani nods. 'We read about it. You sold your wedding jewellery to chase that particular dream, did you nat?'

She laughs. 'Yes.'

Then, noticing Naik's scandalized expression, she adds, 'I'm a very practical woman—and I've more than made up the money since, you know!'

Naik smiles uncertainly.

'Your Wish is very famous,' Bhavani says. 'Deservedly so. And so is your son.'

'Allah has been kind.' Ayesha says contentedly. 'Hadi has *such* good energy... it's his best quality, the fact that he is so *hundred per cent* about everything. When he was a toddler my neighbours used to keep borrowing him to dance in baraats, because he was such a showstopper!'

'It sounds like a nice neighbourhood,' Bhavani replies.

She sighs. 'It was.'

He tilts his head. 'Was?'

'It still is, I suppose,' she says slowly. 'Only recently, say for the past few months, it feels like…' she raises one delicate hand, curling the palm so it looks like a snake's hood, 'like a serpent has entered our garden!'

'What sort of serpent?' Naik's voice is sharp. Too sharp. Ayesha's expression changes. She sits back, looking self-conscious.

'Maybe I'm just being fanciful,' she says with a small embarrassed laugh. 'Or paranoid, because, oh, because of the mood of the nation, these days! People are thinking more about their religion and caste and loyalties than they have ever done before…'

She shivers.

'But it is more than just that, is it nat, Ayeshaji?' Bhavani prods gently.

She nods, crossing her arms across her chest.

'Well, take this anti-stray dog sentiment, for instance! It's *completely* disproportionate. There are just eight dogs on the road, all neutered, vaccinated, socialized. They've never bitten anybody and the BBMP has no issues with them, but my God, the level of animosity against them on the WhatsApp group!'

'What sort of things are being said on the group?'

She raises her hands, and starts to count off on her fingers:

'One, stray dogs poop, pee, bark, howl, copulate, overpopulate and spread rabies.

'Two, they should be eradicated like cockroaches or snakes.

'Three, all dog feeders are rich frustrated women who seek love and validation from dogs because no sane man will give it to them.

'Four, rich women are safe from rabid dogs within their fancy houses, but what about ordinary people like vendors, cyclists and pavement dwellers who risk getting bitten?'

She looks at them mock-interrogatively, her hands on her hips.

A pleasant male voice, heavy with sleep, speaks up from behind them, making them all turn around.

'Five, one of these rabid roadside Romeos impregnated the high-born Tiffinni and her owner went batshit nuts.'

Haider Sait has entered the living room. He's barely awake, his hair is mussy, he is dressed in tracks and a loose tee. Yet, muses Bhavani, he manages to make it seem like sunshine has flooded the room.

'Hadi, don't talk rubbish. You know our strays are neutered.'

'Are you sure? I'm not certain when exactly young Darponk went under the knife. He could've had time for one last glorious night under the stars with his pedigreed haseena.'

'Everything is not like in your stupid movies.' His mother sniffs. 'Officers, please ignore my foolish son.'

'Just like you should ignore Sushil Kedia!' he retorts. 'He just has a pathological need to prove he's the biggest rowdy on this street. Let him do it, ammi.'

Her jaw thrusts forward pugnaciously. 'He's not the biggest rowdy on this street. *I* am.'

'Ammi!' Hadi half laughs, half groans. 'You can't go around saying things like that.'

'Chupp!' She scowls darkly. 'Just because you've become a little famous, and your father is no more, you're whole day trying to shush your mother! That man tried to run over Roganjosh with his big car—'

'There are several versions of that story.'

'So people can just pull out a shotgun and kill our dogs, is it?' Her voice trembles.

Hadi's face softens. 'No, no, of course not.'

Roganjosh, perhaps sensing the stress in the room, whines plaintively and thumps her tail.

Hadi walks over to the cage and squats down easily to stroke the black head. 'Hey, sweetie! Who's a battle-scarred badass? Who took a bullet? Who took a big bad bullet and lived to tell the tale, huh? Good girl, good girl...'

His voice, Bhavani thinks, is one that all women, bar none, would describe as incredibly sexy.

'Hadi!' Ayesha Sait says imperatively.

Haider Sait looks up. 'Hello, gentlemen, I assumed my mother would get around to introducing us finally.'

'This is Inspector Naik,' Ayesha says. 'And this is...?' She looks inquiringly at Bhavani.

He inclines his head. 'ACP Bhavani Singh, Crime Branch.'

Hadi's eyebrows fly up. He rises to his feet. '*Crime* branch? Wow, why? What happened?'

'I didn't realize…' Ayesha is taken aback too. 'I assumed you're here to ask if the pilla party want to file a case of animal cruelty against Mrs Pais. And bloody Sushil Kedia too, for good measure. Not that we would want to, because it is, eventually, just a neighbourhood matter!'

'So why *are* you here, officers?' Hadi asks.

Naik tells them. Rather baldly. Bhavani, watching closely, feels that both mother and son look genuinely distressed.

'Y'Allah, what a ghastly thing to happen!' Ayesha says in a low stunned voice. 'Has anybody told the Paises yet? Poor Peter!'

'Not yet.' Naik shakes his head. 'Do you know them well, ma'am?'

'Peter is a good man.' Ayesha continues, looking troubled. 'And a dutiful son. He is extremely attentive and hands-on, which is why it is so surprising that this happened. And that poor Pooja! She'd just kept that Karwa Chauth fast for her husband's long life! She fed Roganjosh her sargi! It's just *too* sad. What a strange, pointless thing life is.'

Her voice trembles.

Her son's arm drops around her shoulder in a protective side hug.

'Yes, ma'am,' Bhavani says gravely.

'But you're definitely the biggest rowdy on the street now,' Hadi points out comfortingly.

Ayesha shudders. 'I'm the biggest *witch* on the street. The poor man is dead—he was a horrid man, but…'

'Make up your mind, ammi!'

Bhavani leans in. 'Ayeshaji, you were saying earlier that a serpent has entered Habba Galli?'

Ayesha stiffens slightly. Her eyes stray towards her son and she quickly shakes her head.

'Oh, that! I was just being fanciful.'

Bhavani leans forward. 'But when did you start feeling that somebody was instigating people one against the other, Ayeshaji? Because that is what a serpent does in a garden, does it nat?'

She hesitates, then says in a rush, 'Well, I suppose it started when Tiffinni delivered those perfectly sweet puppies.'

'And Sushil Kedia blamed the strays?'

'Without *any proof* !' she says heatedly. 'Well, yes, maybe it *was* Darponk, but Tiffinni shouldn't have been out on the streets when she was in heat.'

Hadi gets to his feet.

'Ammi gets fanciful sometimes,' he says easily. 'Don't listen to her conspiracy theories, unless…' He looks from one cop to the other, '… you have any reason to suspect foul play?'

Bhavani gives a shrug. 'Maybe, maybe nat. We are examining all the possibilities. You do agree that it is rather a freakish accident?'

'Oh, yes.'

'Ayeshaji.' Bhavani turns to her. 'If you could just tell us what all happened yesterday evening, from your point of view.'

Ayesha frowns. 'I was cooking dinner at the other end of the house and missed the entire incident. But Hadi had quite the starring role!'

Hadi sits forward.

'Yes, I did see the whole thing. They'd been playing really loud music all evening—Karwa Chauth songs, you know, all the usual cheesy numbers…'

'Ae chaand don't be lazy, I wanna break my KC,' Bhavani says with a smile.

'That one too.' Hadi rolls his eyes. 'But finally things got quiet and I figured the auntie brigade had dispersed to get dressed for the chaand-sighting, so I put on my N-95 mask and snuck out to go to The Hub—my friend's Airbnb—just down the road.'

'No bodyguards, nothing?' Naik raises his eyebrows.

Hadi grins. 'It *was* a little chancy, perhaps, but I've come home to Habba Galli after eight years.'

'Why?' asks Bhavani.

Hadi blinks. 'Sorry?'

'Why did you suddenly decide to visit The Hub?'

'Oh.' Hadi's expression clears. 'I, uh, I had to ask Krish—my friend—something, and I figured we could have a game of pool. Anyway, I was on the road for just a couple of minutes maybe when the first floor of the house opposite Kedia Kutumb lit up. A curtain was drawn back, a window thrown open, and then the old lady started yelling at the dogs.'

He shakes his head and gives a short laugh.

'Man, was she pissed! And the dogs weren't taking her shit lying down. They started barking even louder, so she left the window and huffed off somewhere, and I thought, wow, she's conceded defeat—and then she came back, lugging gunny boy.'

'Gunny boy?' Naik repeats.

'Her shotgun,' Ayesha puts in. 'We all saw it on Ayudha Puja. Even I saw it; in fact, she showed me how to use it!'

'It looked like an ancient twelve-bore double barrel,' Hadi says. 'She was holding it like a pro—leaning forward, weight on the left leg, butt stock snug in the collarbone of her right shoulder.

'Textbook posture! I'm shooting a period dacoit film currently so I know what's what.'

'Oh yes,' Bhavani smiles. 'On the *Sholay* locations, we heard.'

Hadi grins. 'You're remarkably well-informed, ACP. Anyway, she fired two quick shots. The recoil made her stagger back a good bit, or maybe she was just startled by the high-pitched *kaaaun-kaaaun-kaaaun* yowling Roganjosh let out the moment the shot ploughed into her. It sounded horribly painful, and of course that's what made the vet come racing out.'

He pauses, and the expression on his face changes. Bhavani recognizes the new expression immediately. The boy is obviously nursing a solid crush.

'Dude, what a girl. She looked around wildly at first, then got her eye in and started racing straight to the dog! Another couple of gunshots rang out and I yelled at her to stop, but she didn't even slow down; in fact she ran faster—I think the fourth shot hit her, or maybe it was the fifth or sixth— which, I think the old lady fired just out of spite, because by that time all the dogs had fled, except for poor Josh who was immobilized with pain in the middle of the road. Then finally the old lady stopped, let go of the gun with a sort of a mic drop flourish and shut the window, just as I reached the fallen dog.'

Bhavani's eyebrows fly up. 'She *dropped* the gun? Where?'

Hadi blinks. 'Uh, I don't know. In the garden below, I guess. I remember hearing a sort of a thump and thinking finally ajji has come to her senses.'

'I'll get the men to check at once, sir,' Naik says crisply.

Bhavani continues to question the actor. 'How many shots were fired, Hadiji? Five or six?'

'Six, I think. But I could be wrong. It all happened pretty fast.'

'Was the old lady wearing glasses?'

Haider wrinkles his brows. 'I don't think so—but maybe I was too far away to see…'

'Did you hear a crash? Like the sound of glass being pierced?'

'Not really, no. But there was so much yowling and barking I could've missed it.'

'How about Sushil Kedia? Was he visible at all?'

Haider shakes his head, his expression grim. 'No, sir. There's a hedge around their house. To think we were just a few feet away! He could've been saved if we'd known earlier… What a shit show.'

'And then?' Bhavani prompts.

'Well, then I carried the dog into the clinic. Jhoom—the vet, that is…' His cheeks pinken again. '… was bleeding. One of the shots grazed her arm. Her mother bandaged it up, and then she came in and did the surgery. I thought the dog was done for, TBH, the projectile was lodged in real tight, but Jhoom really knows what she's doing and she got it out clean. It was huge for a shotgun—a ball cartridge. The old lady does *not* mess around. Have you spoken to her yet?'

'All in good time,' Naik replies officiously. 'Thank you for your inputs.'

GOD BLESS ALL WHO ENTER THIS HOME, says the pretty cross-stitched sign above the entrance of the Pais home. Naik rings the bell.

'She shouldn't have been left alone!' he says disapprovingly. 'I mean, this is India—we are not *Americans*! What kind of son allows a ninety-three-year-old lady to be unsupervised and have access to a shotgun?'

The door is opened at this unfortunate moment by a thin dark man with balding hair and a pumpkin-sized paunch, probably in his sixties. He eyes them warily.

'Yes?'

Naik steps forward. 'Inspector Manjunath Naik. I've been phoning you, but you weren't answering.'

The man licks his lips. 'I have, uh… a new phone. The old one went missing two months ago. I got a replacement SIM but I am still unfamiliar with its functioning…'

His voice trails away.

Naik ignores this feeble excuse. 'This is ACP Bhavani Singh.'

The man wilts a little. His voice drops to an agonized whisper.

'Mujhe Jezu! So it has come to this! I'm Peter Pais—I apologize in advance for what mummy did. How is that poor, poor dog? I will pay all the expenses for its treatment!'

'Dog, what dog?' Naik swells a little. 'Are you not aware that your mother has also—'

'Manju.' Bhavani puts a restraining hand on the younger man's shoulder. 'One minute. Sir, please step outside.'

Confusion and then dread seeps into Peter Pais's eyes as he looks around furtively, then steps out, half shutting the door behind him.

'What is it?' He licks his lips again. 'Nai sattidya? Is the dog dead?'

'Sir, the dog is alive.' There is a wealth of sympathy in Bhavani's voice. 'And well on the way to recovery, we believe. The lady-vet has saved his life.'

'God bless her!' Peter Pais throws up his hands devoutly. 'An angel from heaven, that girl!'

Naik curls his lip at this excessive display of emotion.

Bhavani shoots him a quelling glance.

'Unfortunately, there is one more victim,' he says.

The colour drains out of Pais's face. He staggers back.

'What! Another dog?'

Bhavani shakes his head.

'Your neighbour,' Naik says flatly. 'Mr Sushil Kedia.'

This seems to be a complete shock to the already reeling man. He turns deathly pale, whimpers, covers his eyes with his hands and starts to rock back and forth like a child.

Bhavani pats Pais's back gently.

'It is nat your fault, sir. It is nobody's fault.'

Pais's eyes peer at them from between his fingers.

'There is no mistake?' he asks brokenly. 'You are sure?'

Naik nods. 'The bullet passed through his forehead. We are sure.'

Pais crosses himself. 'Mujhe Jezu.'

'Who's dere, men?' a querulous voice calls from within the house. 'Who are you talking to behind my back, men? Peter! Peter!'

The voice seems to galvanize Peter Pais. He moves a little closer to the two policemen.

'Are you going to arrest her?' he demands. 'Will she have to be put into assisted living?' He squares his narrow shoulders resolutely and speaks with more strength. 'Because I will *never* allow her to be put away like that! I keep telling my sisters and brothers-in-law that. They're all nicely living abroad, sending money home to assuage their conscience, but she needs her own flesh and blood to look after her. I'm her oldest son and it's my duty not to abandon her. She needs—'

'Can we talk inside?' Naik's voice has thawed a little. Perhaps Peter Pais is not such a villain, after all.

Pais shakes his head frantically.

'Mummy mustn't know. Please! She's so shaken up about hitting the dog, you can't tell her that a man got shot, too. The shock may be too much for her.'

Bhavani raises his eyebrows, then nods. After the smallest of hesitations, Naik nods too.

Pais continues to speak rapidly: 'I had some urgent work at the estate, so I drove there for just one night. I was halfway there when Jaishri Rao called me saying that mummy had somehow managed to load her old shotgun and had shot a dog, and that I should come at once. So first thing I did was, I phoned Bhagya to go to the house and see if mummy was okay. She complained so much, you won't believe, but at least she went. Then I U-turned and drove back as fast as I could. It's a four-hour drive—and the state of the roads is wretched! I reached early in the morning to find mummy sleeping like a baby with her whisky glass beside her.' He gives a high little titter of laughter. 'Whisky–soda is her Gaulish magic potion, we always say!' Then he sobers up, shuddering. 'But this news about Sushil Kedia is too much. Perhaps…' He scans the two men's faces hopefully. 'Perhaps there is some confusion?'

'There is no confusion,' Naik says stolidly. 'The man is dead, and we have several eyewitnesses who saw your mother shoot him. I am sorry but if, like you said, she has mental health issues, she may benefit from psychiatric treatment. Where is the shotgun?'

Pais licks his lips. 'That, actually, is a very good point. Neither Bhagyalakshmi nor I have been able to find it. In fact, when I returned and couldn't find it, I started hoping that perhaps there has been some sort of mistake…'

'There's no mistake,' Naik reiterates for the third time. 'Our eyewitness says your mother dropped the gun after she finished shooting.'

'Perhaps,' Bhavani suggests gently, 'perhaps when your mummy realized she had shot Mr Kedia, the gun fell from her hands out of fright.'

'She couldn't possibly have seen that far!' Peter exclaims. 'Her eyes are very weak. Unless she was wearing her glasses— was she wearing her glasses?'

Bhavani shakes his head. 'The eyewitness could nat tell from so far away.'

'Well, then!' Pais looks vindicated.

'Have you looked outside her window yet?' Naik is getting impatient.

Peter Pais's face falls. 'If it fell out of the window it must be in the garden. We haven't actually looked there.'

Naik snorts. 'We'll look now, don't worry. Is it licenced?'

'Yes, yes,' Pais assures him eagerly. 'Gunny boy. Been in our family for years.'

'Naming it doesn't make it legal, sir. We'll need the licence.'

'Of course. But I beg you, don't tell mummy she's murdered somebody by mistake—she's a very pious woman and she will never be able to forgive hersel—'

'Peeeeeter!!!!'

The voice is a thin wail, coming from inside the house. Peter Pais's lips tighten.

'Do come in.'

He leads them into a sparsely furnished living room. There is a basic 3+1+1 sofa set, a glass-topped table, some family photos and a flat-screen television. Looking around, Bhavani counts five crucifixes on the walls. Alternating with the crucifixes are the stuffed heads of a jackal, a barasingha deer, two snout-nosed boars and a sort of low-browed bison. Their large glassy eyes stare down at Bhavani accusingly.

A wide-eyed young girl, armed with dustpan and broom, emerges from a bedroom door. She has a small flashing nose-stud and a string of fresh orange kanakambaram flowers in her long hair.

'Hello, saar!'

'Go do the other rooms,' Pais says shortly.

The girl's eyes kindle with resentment but she ducks her head respectfully and leaves the room.

'Which is the window she would have shot from last night?' Naik asks.

Peter Pais walks forward, pushes apart the curtains between the two boar heads and throws open a window.

'This one.'

The two policemen peer out.

The window is directly above Habba Galli. The heavy carved door of the Rao mansion is off to the left. Directly opposite, and clearly visible above the leafy hedge, is the glass frontage of Sushil Kedia's atelier, no more than thirty feet away.

'So it is nat very far away at all,' Bhavani murmurs. 'And look, Manju…'

'I see it, sir.'

There is a bank of dried leaves and faded pink papery bougainvillea flowers below, swept up all along the edge of the tiny garden. The leaves have been disturbed recently, and visible through them, at the very bottom of the pile-up, is the faint wicked glint of metal.

Naik punches a number on his phone and starts giving instructions in Kannada.

'Peeeeeeter!!'

Pais starts, then looks imploringly at the two policemen.

Bhavani inclines his head. 'Come, we will both go and meet mummy.'

Pais squares his shoulders and leads the way to the master bedroom. Bhavani follows.

Old Dondi Pais is sitting in a wheelchair by the bedroom window. She is a tiny stooped old woman with fluffy white curls, dressed in a soiled floral nightgown, holding a knobbly-looking wet towel to one frail shoulder. There are ice cubes inside the towel and one slips out and falls to the floor as she raises her head, painfully, to look at them. She looks, Bhavani later tells Shalini, like the Queen of England gone bankrupt and browner.

As her beady little eyes travel from her son to the men behind him, her voice changes from querulous to cooing.

'Kaale zaley, Peter puta? Wort 'appened? Who are dees nice people?'

'Mummy, they want to talk to you about what happened last night.'

A cunning look slides into the ancient eyes.

'Wort 'appened last night?'

'Arrey! The dogs were hassling you, no? Te pettae maka kitle dosstat! You're always saying, no?'

'Aaah, te pettae!' Her tone is practically caressing. '*Those* dogs! So cute and cuddly. Wort about dem?'

This statement stumps all three men. They look at each other. Then Bhavani pulls up a chair, sits down in front of the wheelchair and takes one wrinkled, twitchy hand, as hard and cold as ice, into his.

'What happened to your shoulder, madam?' he asks kindly. 'You have hurt yourself.'

Dondi Pais sniffs. 'Nort as strong as I used to be,' she mutters. 'It's dis rubbish pish-pash food dey serve me!' She directs a bitter glance at her son as she massages her sore shoulder. 'Chicken stew and mashed potatoes and boiled peas! Wort I need is a good sorpotel with a lot of pig blood in it! And some beef cutlets!'

'Mummy, Dr Colaco said no red meat…'

'Te Colaco old woman asa! And so are *you*. Dat's why no one wants to marry you. All de time at dat estate, planting planting… you've become a damned plant! Liza and Suzy are right: your only culture is agriculture.'

'Well, I don't see Liza and Suzy here, looking after you,' Peter lashes out suddenly. The acceleration from mild to wild is alarming. His breath comes fast, his thin hands open and close, his paunch trembles. 'For all their big talk, where are they? Where? Here is only boring old Peter, doing his duty by his mother and being laughed at for doing so!'

'Dey have work, men!' Dondi Pais lashes back. 'Important-important jobs dey have! And *children*! Dey love me, dey phone me every day…'

He draws a deep, shaking breath. 'I *live* with you! And my job is important too!'

'Oh, *your* job!' She dismisses it with a contemptuous gesture and Naik is surprised to find his sympathies shifting to the hapless Peter.

'I leave you alone for one day and what do you do?' Peter Pais's voice rises to a thin scream. 'Pull out gunny boy and have yourself a shooting party!'

'Enough, men!' She throws out her tiny chest defiantly. 'I already told you, I dint do anyting! It's all lies! I ate my pishpash chicken conjee and went to sleep at eight p.m.! I dint do *anyting*!'

Her eyes skitter imploringly between Bhavani and Naik. The towel at her shoulder slips, revealing an angry blue bruise on her shoulder.

'Mrs Pais.' Naik's voice is grave and heavy. 'How did you hurt yourself?'

'It's the recoil from the shotgun, of course,' Peter Pais says bitterly. 'She fired six shots last night! Reloading twice! Bhagya put the empties in the dustbin.'

Bhavani makes a clicking, sympathetic sound. 'That is too bad. Your mummy will need assistance for a few days...'

'Wort's dat?' Old Dondi Pais struggles to her feet, madness blazing out of her eyes. '*Assisted*? Assisted living? Dat is an old-age home! Dis Peter wants to throw me into an old-age home! I won't go! Assisted-pissisted! You can't make me *go*!'

'I know what has happened. My sister Saraswati phoned and told already, but I did not have the guts to tell Peter saar. Peter saar is not a bad man, saar. He is a good devoted son. Ask anyone! Jushtu shy but, and quiet, like. She is difficult, but not bad either. It is jushtu the situation that is bad, saar!'

Bhagyalakshmi, having accepted Bhavani's invitation to share her thoughts with the police, is standing with Naik and him by the stairwell, and proving to be extremely chatty.

'He makes breakfast for her before he goes to church. He brings her fruit. He programmes her TV shows and he combs her hairs, even! Never she lets me touch-it her hairs! Verry vain she is of it. And also very independent. Goes to the toilet by herself, only wants me to stand outside and keep singing a song—so she knows I'm there to help if she needs me. She misses Pais saar, talks about him every time! He taught her to shoot on their honeymoon, it seems, and she killed her first pig then, the one whose head hangs above the bedroom door. Sarr Francis Bacon she calls him. Because sarr means head, you know, it is a joke Pais saar used to make!'

Bhavani chuckles. 'That's very funny.'

Bhagya shudders. 'Aiyyo, I don't like dusting Sarr Francis or any of the others! But I do every day, without fail!'

'The house is very clean,' Bhavani says. 'You are a good worker.'

She looks gratified.

'But you can't tell her no, sir. Last year, when I had jushtu newly come and she and Peter saar were fighting about something, I don't know what, he told her *No*, directly, straight, just like that, and she pulled out gunny boy and starting putting bullets in it! I got so frightened!

'And then her daughters from America started phoning and telling that she must be put into assisted living but Peter saar refused. He loves her too much, he has made her his whole life, even the Fathers from the church who come to give her that round white prasadum, they are also telling that Peter saar is a saint! So what Peter saar did to make her happy, he got her a really big TV and all the OTT channels and she got hooked on *The Crown* and *Mere Sultan*, and then she found *Anupama* on Hotstar and forgot about being angry with him and didn't even notice when he hid the bullets and the gun.

'If he had been there this would never have happened, but he had to do a quick trip to the estate and I went off home after giving her her drinks and chakhna.'

'Why don't you just live at the flat twenty-four-seven?' Naik asks her. 'Surely she needs round-the-clock monitoring?'

Bhagyalakshmi shakes her head.

'Peter saar does not like me staying there at night. He says people will talk about me and him! Can you imagine, he must be sixty-five years old at least—*who* will think I could be interested in such an old ajja?

'Anyway, I was just sitting down to my oota with my sister when Peter saar phoned me and started shouting that Dondi bai is killing dogs and asking what-for does he pay me so much money? So I came running back, and she was asleep with her whisky glass beside her. The window was shut, no gun, nothing, anywhere, but near the window I found the six covers of the six bullets she had fired. Smelling like firecrackers and still warm! I threw them in the dustbin.

'What you are telling about Kedia saar is very sad but Dondi bai did not mean to shoot him! She is a harmless old lady, but yes, when she takes-it the whisky she becomes a loony-crack. A *dangerous* loony-crack. Too dangerous for me! Now, please excuse me, I'm going home to take-care my sister—she has had a very big shock! Maybe we will both look for new jobs in a new neighbourhood—with all these barking dogs and shooting guns, Habba Galli is becoming thumba risky!'

4

Chengez on a Scatter-Shooting Spree

In the ornately decorated living room of Kedia Kutumb, ACP Bhavani Singh and Inspector Manjunath Naik sit in a carved loveseat like a pair of unlikely lovers and sip tea out of delicate bone-china cups.

The tea tray, a pretty découpage piece in turquoise and pink, is loaded with hot chips and suji biscuits—not out of a packet but home-baked, with jeera and butter.

Bhavani bites into one while taking note of the fact that, even though it has been only six hours since the body was discovered, a large framed photo of the dead man already sits centre stage on a console table. It is garlanded in jasmine and small battery-operated fairy lights. The tiny bulbs twinkle bravely but cannot soften the angular bald head and the thin nose, nor warm up the smirking lips and the assessing eyes.

Munching on a bite of buttery goodness, Bhavani wonders if it was the cold-eyed Sushil Kedia who had demanded such a high level of efficiency in the running of the house.

The only incongruous note is the gnawed legs of some of the furniture, markers of Tiffinni's teething phase.

'Sir, what did you make of Mrs Pais?'

Naik's tone is reverential. He is clearly hoping for some penetrating, illuminating observation from the great man.

Bhavani chews his biscuit stolidly, a thoughtful look upon his homely face.

Naik waits.

'She has very thick hair, Manju,' Bhavani says finally. 'Pity the son hasn't inherited it.'

Naik is wondering how to respond to this when a loud abrupt voice speaks up from the door.

'Policeji! I can tell you everything!'

A large woman enters the room with an air of tremendous self-importance.

Bhavani gets to his feet to greet her.

'Hullo, hullo,' he says. 'You are Mrs Pooja Kedia?'

'I am poor Pooji's best friend!' The woman comes forward, thrusting out a hand dyed up to the elbow in complicated looping henna patterns which makes Bhavani think of meats marinating in aggressively orange Amritsari masalas.

'Ah!' He shakes it tenderly. 'It is so good that Mrs Pooja has you by her side.'

The lady swells with gratification.

'And your name...?' Bhavani inquires.

'I am Mrs Charu Tomar,' she replies. 'Of Tomar Tools and Hardware on Dispensary Road.' She sits down on the sofa, folding her arms across her broad chest with the air of one who plans to sit for a while.

Bhavani resigns himself to the inevitable.

'It is a famous shop! Charuji, please, tell us everything!'

She shakes her head, sighing lugubriously.

'Life is very sad, policeji, you never know ki what terrible event is lurking around the next corner like a whack-in-the-box! Poor Pooji woke up at four-thirty yesterday morning to eat the pre-dawn meal of Karwa Chauth, least knowing that is was going to be her last day as a married lady. We performed puja in her garden together, she and me and Sona, her daughter-in-law. *My* daughter-in-law lives in Baroda and the less said about her, the better!' She gives an eloquent sniff.

Bhavani produces the expected sympathetic murmur.

'We ate our sargi, then went back to our own homes, and at around four in the afternoon... Do you know anything about fasting, policeji?'

'No,' Bhavani admits.

Her gaze flickers to his mid-section.

'You don't do intermint fasting or anything?'

'We simply do our 5BX workout every day.'

She sniffs again, not particularly impressed.

'Yes, yes, it is easy for men to be fit, they have enough free time to exercise. We women are busy morning, noon and night. I myself barely eat at all, and am too thin—see how delicate my wrists and ankles are! But I have *terrible* water retention, it started during my menopause—'

'Madam, about the fast,' Naik murmurs.

She gives him a slightly resentful look.

'Ya, so, as someone who has kept KC for thirty-plus years, let me tell you ki the four o'clock bhook is the worst. No matter what movie you are watching, or which facial you are getting, or what jewellery you are buying, the four o'clock hunger pangs strike you like a serpent's fangs. And yesterday, at four o'clock, Pooji just... surrendered to the bhook! I am so ashamed to say this about my closest friend, but the truth is the truth—momos, doughnuts, nipattu, twistato, chheeee!' Mrs Tomar shudders. 'I told her then only ki Pooji, with every bite and swallow you are signing Sushi's death warrant!'

Bhavani's eyebrows rise. 'Are we to understand that Mrs Kedia did nat complete her Karwa Chauth fast?'

Charu Tomar nods vigorously. 'Yes, ji! Ask her daughter-in-law if you do not believe me! She fully and shamelessly broke it, and when I told her it was a sin, she told me to *get a life*. Get a life indeed! And see now, Sushi bhaisaab has *lost* his life!'

She pauses to let that sink in, breathing heavily.

Naik makes to speak presently, but she silences him by holding up a peacock-festooned palm. 'Don't give me any logic-pojic! Any rational-passional! I know what I know—Pooji desecrated her fast and not even three hours later Matarani's trident flew through the air,' she makes a graphic throwing gesture, 'and struck Sushi bhaisaab dead.'

'Actually, he was shot,' Naik clarifies. 'By Mrs Pais.'

'Charuji is speaking metaphorically, inspector,' Bhavani says reprovingly. 'She knows Matarani did not actually *hurl* her trident at Mr Sushil Kedia like Neeraj Chopra at the Olympics. Is that nat correct, Mrs Tomar?'

A thousand expressions flit across Mrs Tomar's meaty face. She looks, Bhavani thinks, like she is standing before a lavish buffet holding an empty plate, mouth watering, savouring all the delicious options. What-what to pick, what-what to eat, how to wring the maximum value from the opportunity?

'I fear for Pooji's mental health,' she says finally. 'I fear for her spiritual health, and that of her family's. And I am also wondering,' she pauses delicately, 'if there is any chance that this was *not* an accident?'

She looks up at their impassive faces with guileless eyes, and continues to feel her way in.

'Because when I asked Pooji, "Do you want your husband to *die*," she replied, "Maybe."'

'We see,' Bhavani murmurs. 'Tell us, Charuji, from your privileged position as the best friend of the suffering lady, what reason Mrs Kedia could have had to break her fast early? Was she angry with her husband? Had they argued about anything?'

'I will say one word and one word only on that subject,' Mrs Tomar says.

'We are listening,' Bhavani replies invitingly.

She leans in, breathing hard.

'KLPD.'

Bhavani's eyebrows shoot skyward.

The non-Hindi-speaking Naik repeats, confused, 'KLPD?'

Mrs Tomar nods. 'Yes, ji, and...' She hesitates, her eyes skittering to Bhavani's.

'Yes?' he presses gently.

'Mahatma Gandhi,' she says unexpectedly. 'You know Mahatma Gandhi? His sons hated him. For the nation he was father, but in the home he was Babur! A hated oppressor. Arrey, Gandhiji's own sons pleaded with the government to spare the life of his assassin, Nathuram Godse! They knew Godseji was in the right and Gandhiji was in the wrong!'

'So Sushil Kedia was like Gandhiji?' Naik hazards. 'Loved everywhere but hated by his sons?'

She sighs gustily. 'Wealth is no guarantee for happiness in the home, policeji. The boys and the father fought all the time, in fact…' She pauses, then claps a hand to her mouth in shock. 'Om-ji Gods, I just remembered something!'

Not very well done, thinks Bhavani. The shock is clearly artificial.

'Yes?' he nods encouragingly. 'Tell us, Charuji.'

Charu Tomar leans in, her nose-hoop aglint.

'There was a really nasty scene last week. That Sparsh has just come to class twelve, na, with his boards next year. But instead of focusing on his studies, he started spending time with Krish Chetty and Peter Pais—all three of them were whole day around the pool table in Krish Chetty's Airbnb. Now, one–two games for relaxation during studies is okay, but they were betting also! With the winner winning big-big sums of money! Naturally, Sushi bhaisaab did not like that. Krish Chetty is a charsi who has to rent out his family home to strangers to earn a living; his only claim to fame is that he is Haider Sait's childhood friend. And Peter Pais, always running to the church for confession—arrey, I want to know ki what-what sins does he *do* that he has to keep going to confess them all the time? He's either a drug peddler or a homosexual! So Sushi bhaisaab came around to talk to Krish and Pais about it, and there was a nasty fight and Things Were Said. And nasty fights can lead to murders,' she finishes meaningfully.

'Where did this fight happen?' Bhavani asks. 'Did you hear what was said?'

But Mrs Tomar is on a scatter-shooting spree. Rather like Mrs Dondi Pais, she has decided to unload a whole lot of random bullets into the air and doesn't seem to care where they land or whom they hit. Moving on to her next insinuation, she leans forward and whispers, her nose-hoop gleaming like a curved sword: 'That terrorist Mehtab has been making all sorts of threats against Sushi bhaisaab lately.'

'Terrorist?' Naik's voice is sharp.

'The carpet seller?' Bhavani says mildly.

'He barged into Sushi bhaisaab's Commercial Street store and created a huge scene. Ask anybody! Ask Harshu! He was there when it happened.'

'What was he making a scene about?' Naik asks her.

But she has moved on.

'Actually, the whole of the pilla party could have got together and killed Sushi bhaisaab! Mehtab and that divorcee Jaishri Rao, and that widow Ayesha Sait and all! Hypocrites all of them—non-vegetarians claiming to be animal lovers, is that not contradictory? Antisocial elements who think themselves to be too great for the rest of us! They all hated Sushi bhaisaab. *And...*' She lowers her voice.

'Please continue.'

'Musa Sait spoilt his wife rotten! When she got married, she was *obsessed* with jewellery! Kedia Jewellers designed her bridal sets, and she kept going there every day to get this one adjusted and that one restrung and another one exchanged till Musa bhai got fed up and told her to open her own jewellery store.'

'You mean twenty-eight years ago?' Naik asks.

Mrs Tomar shoots him a dissatisfied look and starts to address Bhavani exclusively.

'Such an indulgent husband he was, and see how she repaid him!'

'How?' Bhavani asks.

'Arrey, the man just dropped dead on a holiday in Europe! Miles from anywhere! With nobody but his much younger wife by his side! And they buried him there only! You think that is normal? Ayesha Sait boasts from the treetops that her son is a self-made hero, but *hides* the fact that she is a self-made widow! Sushi bhaisaab found that out, so mother and son got together and...' She makes a violent slashing gesture, '... ended him.'

This seems to be her climactic statement.

She sits back, panting heavily.

Bhavani reaches out and grips the luridly orange hands.

'Thank you for all this information, Charuji,' he says sincerely. 'You have been too generous. We will seek you out for a more detailed interview soon. Manju, take Mrs Tomar to her friend. She has need of her.'

Naik has just shepherded the reluctant Mrs Tomar away when a fair bespectacled young man, slightly pudgy, with clean features and thick dark hair, enters the room.

'Sorry to keep you waiting.' He has a low pleasant voice. 'I'm Harsh Kedia.'

Bhavani rises to his feet and offers his condolences. Harsh accepts them with folded hands and gestures for him to be seated.

'The DG spoke of you, I think? You're the ACP from Delhi Crime Branch?'

'Yes.'

'Thank you so much for interrupting your holiday.'

The polite words and the steady voice combine to create the impression of a young man who has it all under control. But Bhavani notices the slight tremble in the hands and the pulse beating at the temples.

'Nat at all, Harshji,' he replies.

Harsh sits and stares fixedly at the floor. Then he looks up and meets Bhavani's sympathetic eyes.

'Have you seen the scene of the accident?'

Bhavani nods.

'Yes. And we just have a few simple questions. Tell us, please, that road-facing room was your father's private uh... atariya?'

'Atelier.' Harsh rolls his eyes slightly. 'He was invited to lecture at the Paris School of Design once and has called his workshop an atelier ever since. He consulted privately with clients there.'

'He was a talented man,' Bhavani says appreciatively. 'With refinement and taste and an obsession with perfection.'

'Yes,' Harsh replies, his tone colourless.

'We heard the ads for Kedia Jewellers on Indigo FM!' Bhavani continues to wax lyrical. 'Your commitment to the four Ks—Kwality, Kreativity, Kulture and what was it…?'

'Kosmopolitanity,' Harsh supplies woodenly.

Father and son clearly had some differences, Bhavani thinks. But that is only natural. Having no differences at all would have been odd.

'That is kay-rrect!' Bhavani smiles. 'We passed the big showroom on Commercial Street also. Being a policeman, we could nat help observing that the showroom has excellent security! What sort of security provision was there in this home atariya?'

Harsh shakes his head.

'None. I mean, we have no gunmen or guards there. The atelier is a design space, so mostly it's stocked with iMacs, and resin gemstones, and yellow and white metal mock-ups. We do store some precious stones for colour reference, but not too many, because mummy doesn't like to keep valuables in the house. They're in a row of solid steel safes lined up against the back wall. Bulletproof, fireproof, waterproof!' For the first time, Harsh looks mildly curious. 'Why do you ask?'

'Just to understand the general background,' Bhavani replies. 'So papaji would often sit in his atariya, dreaming up jewellery designs? Perhaps listening to some music? Or sipping a drink?'

Harsh's mild eyes kindle. 'He wasn't an alcoholic.'

Bhavani throws out his hands.

'When did we say that! We are only trying to understand his schedule and how it came to be that—please don't mind—he had been in there from eight-ten p.m., when the shot was fired, till seven a.m., when the body was discovered, without anybody missing him?'

Harsh's face grows dark. 'My wife and I were not home last night. My mother retired early. We have no live-in staff. Anyway, the only person eating at home yesterday was my brother Sparsh, who is Swiggy-obsessed. And he had a college interaction all of last night. So.'

Bhavani reaches delicately for another biscuit.

'Why were you and your wife nat home?'

'It was her—*our* first Karwa Chauth. We had booked a suite at the Leela.'

Bhavani hails this statement appreciatively. 'Your missus kept Karwa Chauth! So many ladies do nat keep it any more. You are a lucky man, Harshji!'

'I kept it too,' Harsh says somewhat defensively.

Bhavani's beam broadens. 'And a modern man, also!'

Harsh grins. It's a shy likeable smile and takes years off his face.

'It was pretty tough though,' he admits. 'No water, no tea–coffee.' He adds feelingly, 'I really missed the coffee!'

'And your mummyji? Your mummyji kept KC for your papaji?'

The smile vanishes from Harsh's face.

'No. I might as well tell you, because I am hundred per cent sure Chengez Khan has already told you, that my parents had an argument.'

It is a tribute to Mrs Tomar's protruding cheekbones, narrow flashing eyes and general take-no-prisoners vibe that the old policeman knows know exactly whom he is referring to.

'Hmm.' Bhavani grimaces philosophically. 'Well, you know, they say that Karwa Chauth is like the matrimonial year-ending. A complete balance sheet is prepared for that day—better than anything a chartered accountant can prepare—what-the-husband-did-right during the assessment year, what-the-husband-did-wrong during the assessment year, an exhaustive stock-taking is conducted! When the ladies speak with empty stomachs and full hearts, with the moral high ground in their firm possession, then the poor men are in trouble!'

Harsh says wryly, 'That's why I kept the fast.'

'If you can't beat them, join them!' Bhavani chuckles.

'Papa didn't beat mummy,' Harsh says quickly. Too quickly.

There is an awkward pause. Harsh's face reddens.

'I'm sorry,' Harsh mutters finally. 'I misunderstood your meaning. I'm—'

'Grieving.' Bhavani nods understandingly. 'You have suffered a huge loss, if you do nat want to talk now, we can always…'

Harsh shakes his head. 'I'm fine.'

Bhavani nods. 'Very well, so what was the argooment about?'

'It was about, well, it was more a disagreement really…'

'Or discussion,' Bhavani offers.

Harsh seizes upon the word. 'Yes! A discussion!'

'Mrs Tomar mentioned the phrase "KLPD",' Bhavani says delicately.

'Well, of course she did!' Harsh gives a wry nod. 'That would be Kedia Lakshmi Pooja Designs. It's the name of the collection designed by my mother Pooja Kedia, which my father rejected. He has a horror of nepotism.'

'So your father took a professional decision, but your mother reacted to it in an emotional manner. That happens sometimes.'

Harsh's forehead creases. 'Well, yes, I suppose so.'

'Her designs were nat up to his high standards,' Bhavani suggests.

'Perhaps,' Harsh says unwillingly.

'They were childish... or impractical?' Bhavani pushes. 'Lacking the four Ks, perhaps?'

His head comes up.

'No!' The denial is almost violent.

Bhavani's eyes gleam.

'So they were good designs. And your papaji was unfair in his assessment?'

'Yes... no, I don't know.' Harsh looks desperately unhappy.

Bhavani leans in comfortingly. 'Harshji, do nat torture yourself. We have seen your papaji's mortal remains. Death was instantaneous—even if your mummyji had been on cordial terms with him and you had been home, and you had all discovered the incident minutes after it happened, nothing could have been done to save him.'

Harsh's face lightens. 'Really?'

Bhavani nods. 'Yes.'

'Hullo,' a husky adolescent voice sounds uncertainly from the door. 'The other cop—Naik, I think? He said I should come here.'

Bhavani looks towards the new entrant with great interest. He is gawky, perhaps still growing, about sixteen years old.

'My younger brother, Sparsh,' Harsh gestures to him.

'You found the body?' Bhavani asks as Sparsh Kedia slopes into the room, dressed in an odd combination of clothes— formals on the top half, pyjamas below.

'We sort of found it together,' Sparsh replies. 'Saraswati, ma, Tiffs and me. I collapsed utterly and was of no use at all.'

'Rubbish!' Harsh says affectionately. 'He held the fort, ACP—comforted mummy, calmed down Saraswati, phoned me.'

Bhavani notices that Sparsh's pale face pinkens a little at his older brother's words of praise.

'Thanks, Harshu bhaiya.'

'Usually young people do nat wake up early,' Bhavani remarks.

Sparsh shakes his head.

'I hadn't gone to sleep yet.'

'He had an eight-hour Zoom interaction with a top American university last night,' Harsh says proudly. 'Their days are our nights, you know.'

Meanwhile, something has just occurred to Sparsh. 'OMG, d'you think this gives me some kind of compassionate edge? Should I write to them and be all, while I was in your seminar, unbeknownst to me, my father lay dying…?'

Harsh smiles tolerantly. 'Don't try to shock us, kiddo. Come sit here.'

He pats the sofa beside him. Sparsh drops down upon it obediently.

'You must focus on your goals, Sparshji,' Bhavani says seriously. 'All these interviews and preparations! Staying focused in hard times is a real test of your character.'

Sparsh nods. 'I'll do a Virat Kohli! He was batting on forty overnight, during a Ranji Trophy match, when his dad popped it. The next morning, he came back, scored ninety and saved Delhi from a follow-on.' He tilts his head thoughtfully. 'Hmm, d'you think that means Kohli hated his dad?'

'Oh, shut up, Sparsh.' Harsh's tone is exasperated.

Bhavani smiles at the young boy.

'We think that some talented people have the ability to take excesses of emotion and channel them in a focused manner to fuel their productivity. Like Virat—or you. And the excellent marks and admissions you will certainly get will be a tribute to the memory of your late father.'

Sparsh's young face works. Tears brim in his eyes. He blinks them back, turns his face into his brother's shoulder and asks gruffly, 'Are we going to sue old Dondi Pais? Let's not. I like her.'

Harsh looks over his head at Bhavani. 'What is your read on the situation, ACP? Should we file a police case against Mrs Pais or her son? *And* her son? Do you think it was a genuine accident?'

'We are awaiting the official forensic report,' Bhavani says gently. 'But an accident is clearly indicated. Haider Sait is a key eyewitness and he said Mrs Pais was nat even wearing her long-distance spectacles. And your father was working with just a single white-light lamp, which could have spotlit him and made the job easier, *or* it could have made it hard for anybody to judge distances and perspectives. These are tests our ballistics team will run tonight after it is dark. But either way, she would have had to be a really expert markswoman to pick him out from across the road in such unusual light. That too while she was intoxicated.'

Harsh nods. 'Besides, they were a mutual admiration society! They saw eye-to-eye on the whole stray dog issue. Despised all the dogs and the dog feeders even more!' He gives a bitter laugh. 'It's too ironic that he got caught in what he would have classified as friendly fire.'

Bhavani raises a mental eyebrow at this speech. Charu Tomar's remarks about Mahatma Gandhi and his sons seem to be ringing true. How accurate had the rest of her 'information' been?

Naik enters the room with a dark-eyed young woman in tow.

'Sir, this is Saraswati.'

Bhavani leaps to his feet at once.

'Ah yes, Saraswati! Come come.'

But she continues to hover in the doorway.

'Banni, Saraswati,' Harsh says kindly. 'Koothkoli!'

Saraswati looks more composed than she did in the morning, but her face is still puffy, and there are tear stains on her smooth brown cheeks. She sits down gingerly in the chair indicated—a chair she is clearly more used to dusting than sitting upon—and looks at them with anxious eyes.

Naik nods at her encouragingly.

'Saraswati, you gave lunch to saar yesterday?'

She shakes her head.

'Illa, saar. All were keeping the fast, except Sparshu baba who said he would Swiggy,' she gulps. 'Actually, I was worried that Sushil saar was little bit angry with me yesterday. Sometimes my younger sister Bhagya comes over during her lunch break from Mrs Pais's house and we eat together, and if we chat loudly and Sushil Saar is working in his home aafis, he gets disturbed. So I said, "Sorry, saar, if we were too loud," and he smiled at me kindly and it was all right. Aiyyo, I am so happy he said that, otherwise I would still be feeling bad about it! So I just did my cleaning and went-it my home.'

'Did he seem the same as usual?' Naik asks. 'Or was there anything different about him yesterday?'

She shakes her head.

'He was jushtu like every day, saar. Same only. Never did I think it was the last time I would see him alive!'

'Now tell us, in your own words please and taking as much time as you require, what happened this morning?'

Her response is halting at first, but slowly gains speed and confidence.

'Thummmba cold morning it was, but at least it wasn't raining! My slippers weren't muddy, I didn't have to do scrapping-scrapping on the mat as thoroughly as I usually have to. I put my slippers away, hung up my umbrella, used the hand sanitizer and rang the bell. Sona didi wasn't home so maydaam let me in. She had already prepared-it the tea and Bournvita and taken it into the dining room. So I picked up my dusting cloth—I do dusting first, only after that sweeping and swabbing—and started my work. Then maydaam asked me to give-it tea to saar, and I walked with it to his aafis. But the door was locked.'

'Have you been inside that room after it was opened?'

'Yes, saar. This saar,' she says, nodding at Naik, 'asked me to go inside and tell if anything was out of its usual place.'

'Because she's the only one who goes in there every morning, sir,' Naik explains. 'The family didn't disturb him there very often, it seems. So I thought it was a good idea for her to look around.'

'And?' Bhavani asks the young woman. 'Was everything in its usual place?'

She shuts her eyes and wrinkles her forehead.

'It was cold, saar,' she says. 'Saar liked a room to be very cold. He even had a remote to make the room cold one hour before he entered it! Sitting *anywhere* he could do it! But at the same time very sunny, because the sun was coming through the window. The room was neat only, saar. Sometimes things would be moved around, crayons, papers, mugs with leftover coffee or tea. But not today. I *did* think, though…' She pauses doubtfully.

'Yes?' he says encouragingly. 'What did you think?'

'It seemed…' She pauses again, then says apologetically, 'When I walked over it, I mean—it seemed as if the carpet had faded.'

'Faded?' Bhavani frowns.

She nods. 'Howdu. But when I turned back and looked at it, it seemed absolutely fine. It must have been a cloud passing over the sun.'

'Yes, probably,' Bhavani says softly. 'Manju, were the lights on in the room?'

'No, sir.' Naik shakes his head. 'Just one lamp at the desk. It must have been on all night.'

Saraswati's lower lip quivers.

'Saar, when we all walked out of the house and looked through the window, I got suchu strange feeling, saar, suchu strange strange feeling! Like birds were inside my chest, flapping-flapping their wings like anything, anxiously-like! I knew something was wrong but I didn't know what! And then, and then Pooja maydaam saw the hole in the glass and then we saw—I saw—*him, there, dead… Aiyyo!*'

Her voice rises hysterically, her eyes open. Tears roll down her cheeks.

Bhavani pats her shoulder. 'Well done, Saraswati,' he says kindly. 'You have done well, very well, go home now.'

'Harshu?'

Sona Kedia has entered the living room. Even in her simple salwar-kameez she is an attractive woman—tall, slender, olive-skinned. Her kohl-rimmed eyes are slightly pink, but her voice and manner are otherwise composed.

Harsh Kedia looks up. To Bhavani it seems that the worry lines on his face relax a little as he looks at his wife.

'They're calling from the stores. The news has leaked out and the managers want to know what to say if anybody asks.'

'Oh God.' Harsh rakes his hair back from his forehead helplessly. 'What should I tell them? Should we shut down the shops?'

A slight crease puckers her smooth brows. 'For how long? It's Diwali season. We make our maximum sales on these days. Papaji would say we're insulting Lakshmiji.'

Sparsh chuckles. 'Way to go, Sona bhabhi! Munafa before papa.'

'Shut up, Sparsh.' Harsh frowns, then turns back to his wife. 'Just for today then,' he says decisively. 'Let them attend to the customers who are already in the stores, but not allow new people to enter. And Sona, we'll need framed copies of this photograph to be displayed everywhere…'

'I've already ordered hi-res prints,' she replies. 'Two feet by three feet on canvas paper. And rose-sandalwood garlands. You should spend tomorrow visiting every store and doing shraddhanjali in front of every framed photo.'

He smiles at her gratefully. 'How's mummy?'

'I left her with Tomar auntie,' is Sona's neutral reply. Then she looks beyond the brothers to the two men squashed into the loveseat. 'Hello, you must be the police? I'm Sona Kedia. Do you require anything? More tea?'

So this is the competent presence behind the well-run household, Bhavani thinks. Not much would escape this young woman.

He smiles at her.

'A few minutes chatting with you would be good, Sonaji.'

'I'll go sit with mummy.' Harsh gets to his feet. 'And send that Tomar woman packing. I don't want her filling mummy's ears with rubbish. Come, Sparshu.'

The brothers leave the room. Sona sits on the couch and looks at Bhavani and Naik with polite inquiry.

Bhavani leans forward. 'Sonaji, at the moment, only an accident is indicated but…'

Her eyes widen. 'Of course it was an accident! The old woman couldn't possibly have shot him on purpose. She can barely see ten feet in front of her! Frankly, I'm surprised she managed to shoot a dog as well as a man!'

'Her husband taught her on their honeymoon, we were told,' Bhavani murmurs. 'Clearly, he taught her well.'

Sona's eyebrows rise.

'They must have been quite the couple!'

He nods in agreement.

'Like you and Harshji!' He smiles at her. 'Did you two get married recently?'

She nods, smiling faintly. 'Yes… Yesterday was my first Karwa Chauth.'

'Mrs Tomar mentioned.' His manner is avuncular, almost jovial. 'And how did you and your young man meet? It was arranged?'

'It was arranged by *Sparshu*!' She laughs. 'I met Harsh through a Marwari matchmaker, in the usual conventional manner, but he was so stiff and unfriendly that I thought he was either a snob or had a girlfriend tucked away somewhere and was being forced into a match by his parents. That happens so often, these days.'

'Oh, yes,' Bhavani agrees. 'We have two daughters. We know.'

'But apparently, he was just struck dumb by how beautiful and vivacious I was!'

'Like in *Pride and Prejudice*,' Bhavani produces the reference not without a little pride.

She looks surprised. 'Yes! Exactly! But luckily Harsh had a better wingman than Mr Darcy did! Sparshu, who is *such* an enterprising child, got hold of Harsh's phone, opened WhatsApp web, scanned Harsh's WhatsApp QR code on his laptop and started sending me all these sweet messages.'

'And you replied?'

She smiles reminiscently.

'Yes! I thought he sounded a little immature, but sweet, so I agreed to a second meeting at a coffee shop. And Sparshu brought Harsh there and left us alone together. That's how it all began. He was quite our little Cupid.'

'An intelligent boy! And you are happily settled now with your new family?' Bhavani asks her, all paternal solicitude.

Sona's expressive eyes grow troubled. 'Well, I love Harshu. He's…' She makes a graphic all-encompassing gesture. 'Oh, he's everything I ever dreamed of! And Sparshu is precocious but sweet overall, and mummyji is kindness personified…'

'And papaji?'

Words seem to tremble on Sona's tongue, but she bites them back.

'Papaji is—was a *dry* sort of man. Some people are.'

'You mean that he was nat likeable?'

'Well.' Sona pauses.

She looks up at the homely brown man before her, sitting with his hands folded, not saying much but somehow exuding non-judgemental sympathy and hundred per cent attention.

'I think the biggest problem is that papaji indulged in *reverse*-nepotism,' she confides. 'Matlab he went out of his way to be nicer to other people's families than he was to his own. He claimed he did it because he's so scrupulously honest and fair, but it's one thing to be impartial and quite another to actively take a dump on your family members on a daily basis, don't you agree?'

'Oh, yes,' Bhavani says at once. 'Some misguided parents do this kind of thing to "toughen up" their children...'

'What he did to mummyji's KLPD collection was downright *sadistic*. And he never praises his sons! Never ever! Even though both of them are such good boys. Toppers at Joseph's, clean, obedient, with no bad habits, *and*—I feel like a complete chudail for saying this...'

'Good,' Bhavani says cheerfully. 'All the modern psychiatrists say you must embrace your inner chudail, Sonaji!'

'I think he was *jealous* of how Harsh has taken the stores from strength to strength. He was always belittling him, and hinting that all of Harsh's marketing initiatives for the business are just textbook and unoriginal while Sparshu is a chip off the old block, and fresh and ingenious! He kept going on about how Sparshu's grades are going to be so much better than Harsh's were, even though we all know that ICSE results have become completely insane and nobody, not even a donkey, gets below 90 per cent nowadays! And at the same time he's always low-key taunting Sparshu about how successful Harsh is!'

Bhavani's face has become very stern. 'That is *very* bad parenting.'

'And these stupid boys can't even see that he sets them one-against-the-other! They're both obsessed with winning a "shaabash" from their dad! He's got them jumping like … like two dogs for one marrow bone!'

She's speaking like her father-in-law is still alive, Bhavani notices. Clearly, the hold he had on the family remains strong.

'The whole thing is super toxic,' Sona continues. 'And *another* thing…'

'Do tell us, Sonaji.'

'He dismisses everybody's successes by saying they must have compromised somewhere. Like if you're a woman, you must've slept with someone; if you're a man, you must have bribed someone or accepted a bribe.'

'That is indeed cynical.'

'And whenever somebody tremendously successful hits a bad patch, he gloats over their failure. Like he actually starts humming Carnatic ragas and his face becomes all saintly and glowing. You should see him when big businessmen get caught in a tax net, or when a big cricketer gets out for a duck. He lights up from inside.'

'What the Germans call *schadenfreude*.'

'Yes!' She is pleasantly startled, again.

'Our wife is a literature teacher,' Bhavani says modestly.

'Ah, that explains…' She stops, apologetic. 'Sorry, I didn't mean…'

'We are nat at all offended. Please continue.'

She passes a hand over her face. 'What was I even saying? What was the point of it?'

'We think the point you were making was that your father-in-law was nat a very nice person and that he had sadistic qualities that might have made several people want to murder him.'

She grimaces. 'I was?'

'Mrs Sait mentioned an incident involving your dog Tiffinni.'

Sona's pretty face darkens. 'Oh God, yes. He wanted us to cull Tiff's puppies, can you imagine? Simply because he'd promised pure-bred Weimaraners to some of his ghastly relatives and friends! He said he'd become a laughing stock if people saw that his expensive dog had had mongrel puppies.'

'His prestige was important to him.'

She nods vigorously. 'Oh, yes, tremendously important. And, of course, his obsession with what he called "scrupulous honesty". What a scam.'

'Why do you think he objected so strongly to your young brother-in-law playing pool with some neighbours?' Bhavani asks.

'Oh, that.' She shrugs. 'He's terrible at pool himself, and it pinched him no end that the boys were such naturals. We used to have a table, you know, but both Harsh and Sparsh kept beating him on the reg, so he sold it on the internet. He claimed it took up too much space. The boys were quite cut up about it and Sparshu flat-out refused to part with his cue sticks. He's very possessive about them.'

Harsh pops his head into the room.

'Who's possessive?' he asks mildly. 'Me, about you? You know that's not true.'

Sona laughs. 'No, silly, something else entirely.'

'Okay.' He turns to look at the policemen. 'My mother is asking to see you. She's being quite insistent, actually.'

On their way to Pooja Kedia's bedroom, Naik speaks hesitantly into his senior officer's ear: 'Sir, I have a theory.'

Bhavani halts, nodding vigorously, and gestures for him to speak.

'Sir, let us, for argument's sake, say that it was a murder.'

'Let us!'

Naik steps closer to the ACP.

'Sushil Kedia seems to have made it a habit to sit at that particular table at that time of day. So if somebody happened to know, in advance, that Mrs Pais was planning to shoot at the dogs that night...' He trails off to a halt. 'Perhaps it is too far-fetched.'

'No, no.' Bhavani shakes his head. 'Let's think it through! How, if Mrs Pais herself did nat know that she was going to shoot at the dogs and did it on the spur of the moment, could this person have known *that she was going to do it*?'

Naik clears his throat. 'Perhaps, sir, the killer did some kind of complex psychological button-pressing? To make her shoot when she did.'

Bhavani nods. 'Carry on...'

The younger man eyes Bhavani self-consciously. 'It's just that I recently attended a workshop on criminal psychology, sir...'

'Very good!'

Naik continues diffidently, 'You know what Mrs Sait was saying about how some serpent has recently slithered into this peaceful garden and is making everybody fight? Maybe somebody primed the old lady for many days, stoking her hatred for street dogs, and wound her up like a clockwork toy, so that yesterday evening when they barked, she burst out like a cuckoo from its clock, and *bam bam bam*!'

'And the killer was waiting, lurking in the next balcony perhaps, and fired at the same time?'

'Yes, sir.'

'It is nat a bad theory, Manju,' Bhavani says. 'Let us share it with ballistics and see if the shot could have been faked in the manner you say.'

'Officers!' Sona comes hurrying up the corridor to them. 'Mummyji is waiting. Please come!'

Mrs Pooja Kedia's pretty plump face is very pink and the tip of her nose decidedly red. She is sitting ramrod-straight upon a wingchair, looking hyper-alert. When the policemen enter the room, she nods politely at them, but her eyes are on her daughter-in-law.

'Mummyji, the police are here,' Sona says gently.

Pooja Kedia gestures graciously with her hand.

They take their seats.

Pooja Kedia smiles regally. 'I'll talk to them, Sona.'

'Okay,' Sona says uncertainly.

'You wait outside.'

Comprehension dawns on Sona's face.

'Oh!'

'Good girl.' Pooja Kedia waves her hand in a dismissive gesture.

With the tiniest of eyerolls, Sona withdraws from the room, closing the door firmly shut behind her.

The moment she is gone, Pooja Kedia turns to Bhavani.

'She dropped the gun after she finished shooting, I heard?' she whispers.

Slightly taken aback, he nods.

Pooja Kedia sits back, satisfied. 'Then I know who did it.'

When this announcement is met with a rather nonplussed silence, she adds, for extra clarity, 'I know who committed the murder, I mean.'

Naik can't help giving a small surprised gasp even as Bhavani's hand closes warningly upon his arm.

'Excellent,' Bhavani says calmly. 'We have come to the right place and the right person, Manju! Would you be willing to share this information with us, Poojaji?'

'Well, of course I would!' she replies with some asperity. 'I don't want to be murdered next, do I?'

Bhavani leans forward. 'Who committed the murder of your husband, Poojaji?'

Pooja Kedia leans forward too, till they are practically nose-to-nose. Her pupils look slightly dilated.

'A madwoman,' she whispers.

Bhavani makes a small sympathetic sound. 'Yes, it does appear like poor Mrs Pais…'

But Pooja Kedia is shaking her head decisively.

'*Not* Mrs Pais.'

'Oh?' asks Bhavani.

'Then who?' Naik bursts out from the sidelines.

Pooja Kedia turns to look at him.

'First I thought it was Matarani herself,' she whispers. 'That I had angered her by breaking my fast early, so she cursed my husband with instant death. But then, because I am an educated woman, with a gold medal in geography and an intelligent daughter-in-law, I knew this cannot be true! So then I thought this is what she *wants* me to think!'

'Who, Matarani?' Naik asks, slightly at sea.

'No, obviously *not* Matarani!' Pooja Kedia shoots him a withering look and turns to look at Bhavani again. 'My so-called best friend. Charu Tomar. If you talk to her for fifteen minutes you will understand ki the poor thing has mental health issues. She thinks she is Matarani ki number one representative upon this earth! And because I broke my fast early and displeased the goddess, my husband must die. Please do your proper tehkeekaat and see—*hundred per cent* she has convinced herself that Matarani has decided to use her as a tool (her husband's shop is called Tomar Tools and Hardware, after all!). And then, in her avatar as the Tool of the Goddess, she tiptoed down the stairs, picked up that fallen gun from Dondi Pais's garden, pointed it across the road and shot Sushi dead through the glass in his revolving chair to teach a lesson to me and godless women everywhere! You should arrest her immediately.'

5

Chance-pe-Dance

'Mad,' Naik says with bitter relish. 'All these north Indians are mad. Marwaris, Punjabis, cracks, all of them! They've taken over our city and they've taken over our rituals. What is this peculiar fast, this obsession with dogs, this picking up a dropped gun and running amok, I've never heard the likes of it!'

'Manju, chill maadi.' Bhavani's Kannada accent is atrocious. 'We got a lot of useful information today. Go home, take a nice bath, drink a glass of warm milk to help you go to sleep, you have seen a lifeless body today—it is always difficult to sleep after seeing that.'

Manju looks at him with wild hope in his eyes. '*Is* it murder, sir?'

'It might be,' says Bhavani neutrally.

'Is it very bad of me to want it to be murder? It would be my first big case.'

'It is only natural for you to want to test your training and skills on a big case, Manju,' Bhavani replies. 'Many things in this case seem to point towards an honest accident and yet some things, *some* things seem to indicate otherwise… Chalo, we have put all the evidence in the hands of Dr Krishnan. He has more experience than any one of us! Let's see what he has to say. Go home now. And do nat forget the glass of warm milk.'

'How did it go?' Shalini calls out from the bathroom when Bhavani gets back to The Hub. 'With the dead jeweller? We passed the showroom on Commercial Street and everybody was talking about how he had been shot dead because of the stray dogs! They were openly cursing them.'

Bhavani has not thought of this development at all. He wonders if the pilla party has, and if they're taking any steps to keep their dogs safe from the general public's ire.

Shalini comes out a little later, wearing a pretty waffle-weave dressing gown, to find him nursing a large drink and staring pensively out of the window at the street outside.

'Bhavani?'

He looks around and his eyes light up. 'How nice you look, Shalu.'

She twinkles. 'It's new. From Commercial Street today. We went shopping with Mehta bhai after you abandoned us.'

'A date of sorts.'

She grins. 'Yes.'

'Did he shed any tears for his rich jeweller neighbour?'

'He pretended to, very briefly.'

'Ah!'

She sits down. 'It was a little horrible, actually. People were throwing stones at the strays sleeping peacefully on the street. Mehta bhai roared like a lion and rushed up to defend them. Then the crowd slunk away, cowed.'

'That makes sense. He is a member of a group called the pilla party, we heard.'

'A founding member, *we* heard! *But…*' Her eyes sparkle. 'We got the definite impression that his affection for stray dogs has its origin in his affection for a lady who has an affection for stray dogs!'

Bhavani chuckles. 'That is natural enough! Do you know who the lady in question is, Shalu?'

She shakes her head. 'Not yet, but I have a hunch. What was the Kedia clan like? Were they shattered? What a dreadful thing to happen! A freak accident, like in the movies!'

He tells her. Everything in extensive detail. The police department may frown upon this free sharing of information in the marital bed, but Bhavani and Shalu have split everything evenly for over thirty years now—bank accounts, home loans, baby duties, pizzas, vegetarian thaalis, wedding expenses for their two daughters and problems at their workplaces. She listens intently, laying out sliced vegetables and a garlicky yogurt dip for them to eat along with their drinks.

'Why do you think she dropped the gun after she finished shooting, Bhavani?' she asks when she sits down beside him finally. 'Isn't that odd?'

'One theory is that she saw, from her window, that Sushil Kedia had been shot. That frightened her and she dropped the gun. The other theory is that because she is such a frail lady, the recoil must have been too much for her, so the gun fell. The bruising on her shoulder was quite bad.'

'Hmmm.' Shalini swirls a cucumber slice in the dip thoughtfully. 'Or maybe she just did it for *ishtyle*, like Hadi Sait said. What Pooja Kedia said was interesting, though. About somebody picking up the smoking gun and shooting Kedia through the glass with it. Later.'

'Yes,' he agrees as he sips his drink. 'That theory opens a big field of possibilities. *Suppose* there was, on Habba Galli last night, a quick-witted person with the guts to seize an opportunity if it suddenly presents itself. What is called chance-pe-dance...'

'That's the name of the reality show that Haider Sait participated in.' She sits up, interested. 'The one that catapulted him to fame. How strange that you should use the same phrase!'

'Very strange,' Bhavani agrees. 'So, suppose this somebody, called X, has a grudge against Sushil Kedia. From what we can tell, he was certainly nat a well-loved man. X is drawn onto the street by the commotion below, notices the fallen shotgun and also notices, through the gaps in the hedge, the jeweller in his study—a sitting duck! X realizes that this is a brilliant opportunity to finish Sushil off without any suspicion falling on himself. So he or she sneaks back onto the street later in the night, praying that Kedia is still at the window. He is! X grabs the dropped shotgun from the heap of dried leaves and, under cover of the thunder now rumbling above, aims through the leafy hedge, shoots Sushil Kedia through the glass window, then simply drops the gun back into the leaves and walks away!' Bhavani concludes, his face glowing with excitement in a manner that makes his blunt features appear, suddenly, almost handsome. 'It could have been done like that, Shalu!'

'By a crack shot,' she adds thoughtfully. 'Somebody who was a highly trained marksman.'

'Or by somebody desperate enough to take such a risk,' Bhavani pushes back. 'Who had maybe received lessons from Dondi Pais on how to operate gunny boy on Ayudha Puja.'

She tilts her head to one side.

'There *was* a bullet left in the gun, then?'

He tilts his head to the side opposite hers.

'There would have to be.'

They sip their drinks, imagining, one by one, all the people Mrs Tomar had made insinuations about, picking up the shotgun from the pile of dead leaves on that dark thunderous night and shooting through the glass.

Mehtab.

Krish Chetty.

Haider Sait.

Peter Pais.

Pooja Kedia.

'Charu Tomar didn't spare anybody, did she?' Shalini says.

'Oh, she did nat!' Bhavani agrees. 'She suggested a motive for absolutely everybody. And we're sure she would've come up with one for the vet and her mother as well, but Harsh came in and she had to stop. A thoroughly nasty woman.

Usually people have some redeeming quality in them, but we found none in her. Her own so-called best friend told us she must be the killer.'

Shalini sucks thoughtfully on a celery stick.

'Why are they all so convinced there even *is* a killer? And that it wasn't just a genuine accident?'

'That is a good point,' he replies. 'The whole neighbourhood almost seemed to be bracing for something horrible to happen. It seems that things have been building towards some sort of explosion.'

'A serpent in the garden. Who said that again?'

'Haider Sait's mother, Ayesha.'

'Hmm. But Bhavani, in your chance-pe-dance theory there is no serpent slithering through the garden, slowly stoking the fires.'

'That is nat necessarily true.' Bhavani sticks out his lower lip. 'Also, the serpent could be a figment of Ayesha Sait's imagination. Her son seemed to think so.'

'But she's a pragmatic woman,' Shalini points out. 'Not given to fancies.'

'Because she sold her wedding jewellery to start a business?' he asks.

She nods. 'Yes. Of course, maybe her wedding jewellery was just ugly, or not to her taste…' She trails off thoughtfully, then asks, 'So what was Haider Sait like? Arrogant? Charming?'

'He is what you and your daughters would call "devastatingly attractive",' Bhavani produces the phrase with a flourish. 'But a pleasant boy. And fit. Very fit.' He adds with a chuckle, 'He seemed very impressed by the girl who saved the dog—the vet.'

'Ooooh, a romance!' Shalini looks pleased. 'How nice! Mehta bhai said the vet's mother is extremely eccentric, by the way. She recently called Sushil Kedia socially desperate for adopting a pedigreed dog. He said that lately the topic of the street dogs has intensified into a full-blown battle.'

'With Hindu–Muslim overtones?' Bhavani suggests.

'I don't think so,' she says doubtfully. 'The vet and her mother are the highest level of Brahmin, and they are firmly in the pro-stray camp.'

'So perhaps it is a men-vs-women dynamic?' Bhavani muses. 'But no, Chengez Khan—we mean Mrs Charu Tomar—is firmly in the anti-stray-dog camp. And your Mehta bhai is a man too.'

'Most definitely.' She grins. 'So it's the usual ideological split then. Patriarchal traditionalists against the liberals, the feminists, the LGBTQ and the young ones.'

He nods tiredly. 'Yes, but you know, Shalini, stray dogs *can* be dangerous. Rabies is an issue. And sometimes they attack small children…'

'Because they're scared, starved and diseased,' she retorts hotly. 'And anyway, one biting case doesn't mean *all* stray dogs are biters. Any more than one male rapist means all men are rapists. That's straight-out discrimination.'

He rubs his eyes and yawns. 'Yes. Yes.'

She hugs him.

'Anyway, nobody got bitten in Habba Galli!' she says. 'It was probably just an accident, Bhavani. Enough now. Come to bed.'

'And what did you say after she said, "And I'm Jhoomar Rao"?'

Krish Chetty is cooking chicken ghee roast in The Hub@ HabbaGalli kitchen, while his friend Haider sits atop the kitchen island, swinging his legs and chewing a massive carrot.

Hadi looks a little sheepish. 'I said goodnight.'

'Wuss.' Krish bends down to sliver onions finely.

'I know!' Hadi groans and mock-hits himself on the head with the end of his carrot.

Then he puts it down and asks, 'So listen, is she, like, poor now?'

'Why d'you ask?'

'Coz the house looks like shit!' Hadi says, his dark eyes troubled. 'And she used to wear this flower-shaped diamond pendant on a thin gold chain, with matching earrings…'

Krish shakes his head. 'All that's gone, bro. Even the house is hanging by a thread. Her dumbfuck dad gave it as personal guarantee.'

'What a *choot*,' Hadi says feelingly.

'Ai, cut him some slack. I've heard the mom's a total psycho.'

'I liked the mom,' Hadi replies. 'She was always nice to me, in a vague sort of way.'

Krish doesn't reply.

Hadi rakes his hands through his hair, making Krish cover his wok hurriedly.

'Ai macha, keep your goddamn DNA away from my ghee roast!'

'I should have asked to see her again, right?'

'You're never gonna do that, Hadi.' Krish drops the onions into the hot sputtering ghee. 'Don't kid yourself.'

'Andre?' Hadi looks puzzled.

Krish shoots him a knowing look.

'Andre, you and your Bombay Bengali bestie Bongo Banerjee have built this whole Jhoomar Rao thing up to ludicrous heights! You like the *concept* of being in love with Jhoomar Rao. You like the *state* of being in love with Jhoomar Rao. You probably even *think* of her whenever you have to do a romantic scene, and that's the source of your knicker-dropping superpowers… but you don't really want to *get* with Jhoomar Rao.'

Hadi is suddenly, disproportionately angry.

'WTF?' he demands. 'How can you even say that?'

Krish shrugs. 'Because if you really did want to get with her, you wouldn't be sitting in my kitchen, singing the same sad "Twenty-four years I've been living next door to Alice" song. You're a go-getter. You would've *gone* and *got*.'

'And how do you suggest I could have gone-and-got when she was clearly end-gaming with that choot Vasudeva?' Hadi asks in a dangerously even voice.

Krish looks around, surprised.

'Wow, you remember the bugger's name?'

'*Yes!*' Hadi exclaims, louder than he meant to.

Krish raises his eyebrows.

'I mean, I remember his surname,' Hadi continues in a more controlled voice, 'and the fact that his dad is the Pledge Group. And that he's the exact same variety of whatever highest level of Brahmin *she* is.'

'Glad you remembered *that*,' Krish mutters, rolling his eyes.

'How could I not?' says Hadi. 'I know her dad's super-conservative! But he's out of the picture now, and so's Vasudeva…'

Krish stirs his ghee roast.

'Musa uncle wouldn't have approved either.'

Hadi's jaw tautens. 'That wouldn't have bothered me.'

Krish sighs and shakes his head.

'What?' Hadi demands. '*You* also don't approve? Is that why you never mentioned even once that she's still single? That's what I was coming over to ask you that night, by the way, when I almost got shot! Why'n't you tell me, Krish?'

Hadi glares accusingly at Krish, who calmly sprinkles water into his sizzling wok before turning around.

'Hadi, we've pulled several drunken all-nighters discussing this over the years, haven't we? We agreed that you never *liked her* liked her, you just liked her because she was the local trophy, the hottest girl around.'

'Uh-huh.' Hadi shakes his head. 'That was always *your* theory, bro. Never mine.'

'I don't think so,' Krish maintains steadily. 'And stop talking like you've been pining for her. I've lost count of the number of women you've been with.'

Hadi's eyes widen. 'Bro, you're the last person on the planet who should be slut-shaming anybody.'

Krish stares at him for a moment, then says stiffly, 'I'm aware I fucked up bad with Sona. I'll never get a girl that good again. But it hasn't made me cynical or resentful of other people's happiness, I promise.'

Hadi shoots him a sympathetic look. 'She's happy with the jeweller? He was a few batches senior to us, no? Dull, but decent. Where'd she meet him?'

'On the arranged circuit,' Krish mutters. 'Pretty poetic, huh, Sona and the sunhaar? And in a savage, turn-the-knife-into-the-wound twist they decided to live happily ever after on the same damn road as me.'

'Maybe it's the universe at work,' Hadi suggests, straight-faced.

Krish flushes. 'Don't talk bloody Bollywoody nonsense like Bongo Banerjee,' he growls.

'Aww.' Hadi grins. 'You're jealous of Bongo! Don't be, you know you're my OG.'

'You're such a piece of shit, Sait.'

There is a short companionable silence.

'D'you bump into her often?' Hadi prods curiously.

Krish shakes his head. 'The younger brother comes over to play pool sometimes. He's a good kid.'

Hadi studies his friend's face.

'Any plans to slide into her DMs with a sympathetic message about being "sorry for her loss"?'

Krish gives a rather mirthless laugh. 'She's blocked me everywhere, bro.'

'Wow, okay, she was always a thorough girl.'

Krish lowers the heat on the stove and turns around.

'So you want to marry Jhoomar Rao now?'

'Huhhhhh?' Hadi's jaw sags in utter shock. 'Where'd the Em word come from?'

Krish crosses his arms across his chest.

'Shat your pants, huh?' he says sardonically.

'Chill maadi, bugger.' Hadi edges away. 'She could still be into Vasudeva. Do you know why they broke up?'

Krish starts pulling curry leaves off their stem and tossing them into his wok.

'Are *you* serious about her? Or not?'

'I'm not unserious.' Hadi looks torn. 'When we met that night, the vibe… it felt… fated. And so, *yes*, I'm open to exploring the possibility of a serious relationship, *if* she isn't hung up on Vasudeva, of course. But I can't commit to more than that at this moment, obviously!'

Krish turns around.

'Look, if the desire in your Em-for-Mossie heart is to Em-for-marry her, then all's well that ends well. But if it's gonna be some random hook-up to get closure on your pathetic crush, then it could potentially start Hindu–Muslim tensions in the galli.'

Hadi's face tightens. 'You're mad,' he says bluntly. 'And fuckin' regressive. And *obsessed* with this stupid neighbourhood. You've started talking like some ball-scratching shopkeeper.'

'I *am* a ball-scratching shopkeeper!' Krish shoots back. 'And you keep giving interviews about how much you love

Habba Galli, but now you're calling it stupid. You're a bloody hypocrite!'

'Really.' A dangerous glint enters Hadi's handsome eyes. 'Look, Krish, if this is about that girl—I forget her name—whose dad is some hot shit in the Central Muslim Association of Karnataka, and whom you've been low-key pushing at me as a possible wife, you can forget about it. I know you want to kickstart your political career, but find some other way to curry favour with the local big boys.'

They eyeball each other for a long, tense moment.

Then Krish looks away to raise the lid on his wok.

'Okay, motherfucker,' he says lightly. 'I'm Team Jhoomar, starting now. What d'you want me to do?'

Hadi's boyish grin flashes, making it seem like sunshine has flooded the room.

'No, bro. First, we're gonna talk about *you*. We were gonna live together in Mumbai, remember? When the fuck you gonna get your CA degree?'

Krish scowls.

'When you gonna act in a South movie? The whole world is in love with our cinema, but you go around acting like Hindi is your first language!'

'Uh, because it is?' Hadi says. 'I speak Hindi at home, Krish, FFS. And I will do a South movie—when they write me a good one!'

Krish shakes his head.

'Look at you, calling all the shots! Well, I *still* haven't cleared the CA finals. You think, just because it worked out that way for you, that if somebody works really hard things will eventually happen for them. You don't understand that some people can do their bloody *damnedest*, give something *everything* they've got and *still* be unsuccessful.'

'No!' Hadi slams his palms down on the granite counter and glares at his friend. 'Dude, you're a goddamn topper! You can ace that exam!'

'I don't have *time*!' Krish throws up his hands. 'It's a full-time job running this place!'

'No,' Hadi contradicts him flatly once again. 'This place pretty much runs itself now; you don't need to hang about playing superhost and probably stalking Sona and smoking up around the pool table.'

Krish's face grows dark.

'I do *not* stalk Sona! And stop pissing all over me in the name of friendship. You think I don't know that you do it just so your fans can wank off to how grounded you are on Reddit threads and the 'Gram? *Such an unspoilt regular guy, so unaffected by fame and wealth, still so tight with the friends of his youth?*'

Hadi has gone very pale. 'Don't change the subject, bastard,' he says in a low voice. 'You gonna pound that CA final or what?'

Krish sticks his jaw out obstinately. 'Don't show up after a hundred years and tell me what to do.'

'Oh my God.' Hadi is angry now. '*I've* shown up after a hundred years, is it? *I'm* the one who keeps in touch with you!'

'I don't have a team to aid me,' Krish says sarcastically. 'Make-up man, manager, bouncers, bodyguards, court jesters... I'm busy.'

'No, you're not,' Hadi shoots back frankly. 'Stop stoning and get some exercise. You look sad and fat.'

'*You* look like a hyper-sexualized gigolo,' Krish growls.

Hadi looks furious for a moment, then chuckles. 'Thanks.'

Krish bangs the lid over the wok and turns to glare at him aggressively.

Hadi meets his gaze unperturbed, laughter brimming in his eyes.

Silence simmers along with chicken in the kitchen for a while.

Then Krish grins, looking heartbreakingly handsome.

'Fuck you, Sait.'

'That chicken smells done, Chetty. Let's thulp it.'

'It's for my guests.' Krish waves him away. 'ACP Bhavani and his elegant wife.'

'Ai, but I need the protein! How'm I gonna maintain my gigolo form otherwise?'

'*Bounce*, bugger. Get lost.'

'I could go over to Jhoom's,' Hadi says uncertainly. 'What do you say?'

Krish raises his hands and flashes him a double thumbs up.

Hadi looks petrified.

'I'll go?'

Krish nods, laughing. 'Hogi, macha.'

'But what'll I even say to her?'

'You'll find something to say.' Krish rolls his eyes. 'You always do. I know, convey the hot goss that Sushil Kedia got iced as an ice-breaker.'

Hadi's eyes brighten. 'Good idea. That gandu Kedia should come in clutch for *something*.'

Dr Rao Small Animal Clinic and Surgery

24-hour emergency
Consultation (Rs 800) from 10 a.m. to 6 p.m.
Free for strays and rescues

Curled up in their sand pile, the strays thump their tails at Hadi in a friendly manner as he strides up to the huge carved door of the Rao mansion.

'Hey guys,' he greets them. 'Your ammi's doing good. She should be back on the streets in a week or thereabouts.'

They look at him intelligently, then blink, yawn and look away.

Eighties rock comes faintly to Hadi's ears. Jhoom is within.

'Here goes everything,' he mutters and leans hard on the buzzer beside the sign.

No answer.

He stares uneasily at the massive door, which has intimidated him since childhood, then presses the buzzer again.

No answer.

Third time lucky, he thinks and gives it one more shot.

The music is turned off and a few seconds later, a smaller door opens within the massive door frame and her head pops out.

'What?' she says belligerently.

Her middle-parted waves are pulled off her vivid face with a bright red headband. A bandage bulks up one of the sleeves of her loose, ragged-edged maroon jumper. Her collarbones shine, their bareness hitting him like a personal rebuke. She has a bottle of Sprite in one hand and a toilet brush in the other.

His mouth grows dry. He whips off his mask. 'You're cleaning your commode with Sprite?'

Surprise replaces the glower on her face as she recognizes him. Not particularly happy surprise, he notes with misgiving.

'Obviously not,' she replies. 'I'm cleaning out the animal cages and drinking at the same time. It's Sunday.'

'Sprite is your Sunday drink?'

'I don't drink alcohol.' She waves the toilet brush about vaguely. 'I mean, I did too much of that shit when I was younger, and now I'm good with this.' She shakes the bottle, 'But why're you banging my door down? Fuck, is Rogu not okay?'

'No, no, she's good,' he assures her.

'Thank God! So you've come for her meds, then?'

'Er, yes.' He looks at her carefully. 'Wait, you mean you don't *know*?'

She looks confused. 'Know what?'

He steps closer.

'Seriously? Nobody told you? Maids, helpers? The Habba Galli grapevine?'

Her chin comes up defensively. 'We don't have any maids. My helper doesn't come on Sunday. And as far as I know, amma and I are the hottest items of discussion on the Habba Galli grapevine. Why, what even happened?'

'Wow, okay.' Hadi pauses, then continues in a gentler voice. 'So, um, the old ajji managed to take down Sushi Kedia by mistake while she was shooting the dogs.'

Jhoom almost staggers. '*What*?'

'Yeah.' He looks at her, concerned. 'I hope you weren't too fond of him or anything—coz he's... kind of... dead.'

Jhoom blinks. 'Fuck.'

'Yeah...' Hadi nods. Then he holds out his hand for the toilet brush still dangling from her hand. 'You, uh, want a hand cleaning up?'

But she wards him off, waving the brush, causing a few droplets to hit his face. 'No, no, I have to call Sona and find out how everybody is. Shit, Pooja auntie must be shaken up! Maybe I should go over.'

She continues to stand at the door, her mind clearly reeling.

Hadi dabs his face dry with his mask and leans in.

'Jhoomar, would you please let me in? People are starting to circle—these selfie-seeking crowds build up damn fast.'

She looks startled, then smiles. The moonrise smile. Sudden, supreme.

'Sure, get in here, movie star. I'll provide sanctuary.'

They sit down on a couple of plastic chairs in her tiny enclosed garden, a gunky cobblestoned space half full of steel cages, flooded with sunshine and thick with sweetly decomposing parijat flowers.

Jhoom is more composed now, even curious.

'So!' she prods him. 'Give me all the details! How, when, why?'

He tells her everything the cops have told him. She listens wide-eyed, hanging on his words.

When he finishes, she sits back and says candidly, 'You know, Hadi, I'm sorry to speak ill of the dead, but your mom probably told you this: Sushil Kedia was an A-grade asshole.'

He stares at her witlessly for a moment because he can't believe it's really happening.

You know, Hadi.

So casual, so natural, so easily uttered! Unspooling effortlessly like music into his happy ears!

You know, Hadi.

You know, Hadi.

'Um, yes, but Jhoom …' (Hah, he's matching her chill for chill, somebody give him a goddam Filmfare Award already.) 'That doesn't mean he deserved to die by a bullet in the brain.'

She shakes her head firmly. 'Last month, he deliberately tried to run over Roganjosh in that big fat Merc of his. And when my mom came running out to yell at him he told her, "What are you complaining about? Now that rich Bollywood mother will give your daughter lakhs to treat this dog!"'

Hadi frowns. 'Why doesn't ammi tell me all this?'

'She probably doesn't want to think about it any more than she has to.' Jhoom shakes her head. 'Even *I* don't want to talk about him. The guy is—*was* a total pill.'

'Okay,' he says obligingly.

There is a small silence.

'So tell me about yourself then, doc,' Hadi says finally. 'We've never actually spoken, though we lived opposite each other for years.'

'Ya, that *is* strange!' She laughs, then adds ruefully, 'But probably for the best—you wouldn't have liked me back then.'

This is so ironical that Hadi is actually silenced. It takes him a while to clear his throat and casually ask: 'Why?'

She shrugs. 'Oh, I was a clueless, stuck-up idiot. I'm much nicer now.'

'No, you weren't.' His denial is immediate. 'You were just part of a different crowd, and also very much in love, if I'm not mistaken.'

She rolls her eyes. '*Yeah*, whatevs.'

They stare at the wall for a while. The silence doesn't feel awkward at all.

'So why'd you become a vet?' he asks presently.

'Because I was too dumb to become a proper doctor,' she says, grinning.

He laughs.

'Actually, when I was ten, my mum and I found this injured dog. His jaw was dislocated, all his teeth broken, and one eye was smashed to pulp. He was lying in the lane, too weak to even cry out, just gasping soundlessly… ' She shakes her head. 'How can people be such choots?'

His eyes are soft as they rest on her face.

'Good thing for him that you came along.'

'Ya, well, amma and I nursed him back to health and we named him Phoenix to inspire him to heal himself.'

'Ai, Phoenix!' Hadi exclaims. 'All the dogs in the lane today are his descendants.'

'Yes.' She nods proudly. 'And that's how I knew what I wanted to be.'

'Well, your set-up looks great to me,' he says sincerely. 'Though, NGL, you should probably invest in a no-lag switchover generator.'

She rolls her eyes.

'Those cost a bomb.'

'And a pet ambulance.'

'Those cost a bomb, too.'

He grins.

'And twenty-four-hour CCTV surveillance for your medicine cabinets and convalescing animals.'

She throws up her hands. 'Yet another bomb! I don't have access to bombs, Haider Sait, I'm not a fucking terrorist!'

'Wow, neither am I. Islamophobic much?'

She looks startled for a moment, then bursts out laughing.

Encouraged, he leans forward, pokes a finger through a hole in her ragged jumper and taps her wrist meaningfully. 'Kelu.'

She smiles at him. 'Helu.'

'You're better off without Tatti Vasudeva. I assume that wasn't his real name?'

She giggles. 'Close enough.'

'Why'd you dump him anyway?'

The question is so unexpected that she stares outright at him.

Hadi takes a deep stealthy breath and dares to stare back.

And it is so… easy. An easy surrender. Like taking off your shoes and falling backwards onto fluffy white five-star-suite pillows. He could do this all day and never call cut.

'Wow,' she says finally. 'You're the first person who has ever asked me that.'

'Really?' It's his turn to look surprised now. 'Why?'

She shrugs. 'Everybody just assumed he dumped me.'

'And the real story is?'

'Oh God,' she mutters, hunching her shoulders. 'Look at me flexing to the big movie star about how *I* did the dumping! Basically, I couldn't take how fuckin' noble he got about the whole thing. *Noble* and *bossy* and *masterful* and okay-your-dad-turned-out-to-be-a-choot-so-now-I'm-gonna-be-your-new-dad. And expecting me to be *grateful* for it!' She looks up suddenly. 'You've seen *K3G*, na?'

'Not a big fan,' he admits. 'But sure, I've seen it. You mean the scene where Anjali's dad is lying there dead in the rain with cotton wool up his nose and she and her little sister are crying and Rahul comes up and randomly lays his palm on her head.'

'*Exactly!*' Jhoom looks at him with stars in her eyes. 'Like, WTF, bro? Who needs *you*?'

'So you've given up on human beings entirely, then?' Hadi has to draw back a little, as naturally as he can, because his heart is pounding so hard in his ears. 'Marriage, kids?'

She thinks about this for a long time, her expression wistful. 'It's not so much marriage and kids I object to as it is prescribed social mores that ensure your lovely nangu baby grows up to be a judgy auntie or a furtively horny uncle.'

'Okay, so *definitely* not up for marriage.'

'And you?' She raises her eyebrows. 'You really believe in the shit you're selling? "Ae chaand don't be lacey, I wanna break my KC"?'

'Lazy,' he corrects her, looking a little hurt.

She waves her hand dismissively.

'Ya whatevs, it doesn't even rhyme properly.'

'I want kids, I think,' he says after a pause. 'And a long-term relationship. Something to ground me.'

Jhoom snorts. 'What are you, a fluttering chiffon sari? Learn to ground yourself!'

His eyes widen in mock alarm.

'Wow, okay.'

'My practice grounds me,' she offers, a little apologetically. 'The daily parade of little critters. And my mom. It's all good, really, worse things happen to people every day than breaking up and going bankrupt. I mean…' she pauses dramatically, 'I could be ugly.'

He bursts out laughing.

'So, on the significant-other front,' she continues, 'the only position I am interested in interviewing applicants for any more is…'

She stops, hesitant.

He grins. 'Helu, helu.'

Jhoom grins back.

'A lover who lives down the lane,' she whispers.

He tilts his head. '*In*teresting! Which lane? *This* lane? Any lane?'

She winks at him. 'Geographical proximity is kinda vital to the plot.'

Hadi's eyes start to dance.

'What else is vital to the plot? A ba-ba black sheep? Three bags of wool?'

She gurgles.

'Well, notice I said lover. I demand long-term emotional involvement. And exclusivity. And lots of space. Oh, and he must be able to coherently *and* convincingly explain why he likes me.'

His eyebrows rise.

'*Why* he likes you? You mean why he likes specifically *you*?'

She nods. 'Ya. It's a standard interview question, na. Employers always ask it. They're like, "Why this company and no other," and you have to give a convincing answer.'

Oh, what an answer I could write to that question, Jhoomar Rao. Truly a one-of-its-kind answer. But would it be convincing? Or disqualifying? That is the real question.

Out loud he says, banteringly, 'Well, nobody ever gives the honest answer, which is, "I'll take anybody who wants me, if they pay me enough."'

Anger kindles in her eyes so he quickly adds, 'Is there a word limit?'

'Two hundred words,' she says. 'Answers may be given in writing, or declaimed oral.'

Hadi's face brightens.

'My oral game is *solid*.'

'Good,' she says demurely.

'I mean I'm good at speaking!' he hurries to clarify, his ears reddening. 'I'm an actor, na, so I'm good at like, saying stuff out loud. That's *all* I meant! Jeez!'

But Jhoom has moved on. 'Look, I'm not saying one should mate for *life*—like wolves or gibbons...'

Hadi struggles to keep up.

'They mate for life?'

'Ya, but out of love, not like the black vultures, who are obsessed with conventionality and brutally shame any vulture who tries to stray from matrimony. Kinda like the Akhil Bharatiya Brahmin Mahasabha of the animal kingdom.'

He blinks. 'Okay.'

'But I'm not some raging bonobo either.'

'Bonobo?' He is now fully out of his depth.

'A sort of pygmy chimpanzee,' she explains. 'Wildly promiscuous.'

'Who's wildly promiscuous?' a husky voice demands.

A lady with transitioning curls and a maroon dressing gown has stepped into the tiny garden, radiating angst.

Hadi leaps to his feet.

'Auntie, hello!' he says eagerly, then adds, because she's looking so stern, 'I'm Ayesha's son, Hadi.'

'The hero of the hour.' Jaishri's tone is withering. 'Talking to the *heroine* of the moment. I feel like giving you both one hard kick on the backside.'

'Amma!' Jhoom is horrified.

'Don't amma me!' Jaishri's voice shakes a little. 'Ayesha just told me that Dondi bai's bullets took down Sushil Kedia!

You could have died! And this one over here thinks he's acting in a movie! Your mother just lost her husband, how do you think she'd've coped if something happened to *you*?'

'Auntie…'

'Don't auntie me!'

'Ma, we're okay, na!' Jhoom tries to hug her. 'Nothing happened! We're fin—'

Jaishri throws up her hand. 'Just *shhhhush* for a moment please, Jhoom.'

There is silence. Hadi stares fixedly at the ground, his expression penitent. Jhoom, looking at him, has a sudden vivid memory of a much smaller browner Hadi, with exactly the same expression on his face, standing amongst the debris of a shattered windowpane, holding a cricket bat and letting a massive lecture delivered by her apoplectic mother simply wash over him.

'You guys know each other,' Jhoom realizes.

Hadi grins warily at Jaishri. 'Mostly by sight.'

'Yes.' Jaishri rolls her eyes. 'Your war film was riddled with historical inaccuracies. Didn't you know, or didn't you care?'

'Er, both, I suppose, if I'm being honest,' he admits, 'but its heart was in the right place; at least that's what all the knowledgeable reviewers said.'

'There are no knowledgeable reviewers,' Jaishri growls dismissively. 'And Jhoom, you shouldn't be cleaning with that shoulder.'

'Auntie, I was just telling her to let me help!'

Jaishri ignores him.

Jhoom gets to her feet.

'I'll give you Rogu's meds, Hadi, come.'

Hadi, come.

Hadi, come.

Hadi, come.

He smiles happily and starts to follow her.

Jaishri Rao snorts. 'He isn't coming anywhere. He is *going*. His mother called me to tell him to come home.'

'Oh.' Hadi is startled. 'Damn, I must've left my phone at Krish's. I didn't even notice! Peace then, I'll go. Jhoom, just drop off the meds later, na? At my place?'

There is an odd little pause. Hadi's tone is correctly, carefully casual, and yet utterly loaded.

Her cheeks very pink, Jhoom says, equally offhandedly, 'Sure.'

Jhoom wanders into the living room in a state of dazed chaotic shock. Has she just been conversing easily with a movie star? Maybe she should've gotten an autograph!

Jaishri is frowning down at her term papers but she looks up as Jhoom enters.

'We should send over some food,' she says worriedly. 'What d'you think they'd like? Sambhar-rice? Puliyogare?'

Jhoom immediately feels guilty for forgetting all about her bereaved neighbours.

'I'll take it across once you've made it,' she offers.

Jaishri pulls a face. 'Aiyyo, I'll have to cook now. Jhoom, put the rice in the cooker at least. I'll check one more paper quickly. Should we send a box of laddoos also—because honestly, how is this even bad news? Nobody will mourn that horrible man!'

'The whole thing is just so unreal.' Jhoom shakes her head as she walks to the kitchen. 'The way she came out last night and starting yelling and shooting! It felt like a movie!'

'The movie star likes you,' Jaishri calls from the living room, causing Jhoomar to stop with her hand poised on the lid of the stainless-steel rice container.

'Amma! *Simply!*'

'What?' Jaishri calls loudly.

Jhoom strides back into the living room.

'He just came for the medicines,' she says uncertainly.

Jaishri snorts. 'Ayesha Sait has a staff of eight. Any one of them could have come for those medicines.'

'You're mad,' Jhoom says decidedly. 'I don't have low self-esteem or anything—and I know my hair curls prettily and my legs are hot, and even if we don't count Tatti Vasudeva—'

'May he rot for ever,' Jaishri says devoutly.

'… I've had *some* admirers—Antiseptic Gaurav, Weird Rajeev, Stoner Vishnu and Hairy Mandeep—but I definitely don't possess the lusciousness required to pull a Hunky Haider. Do I?'

Jaishri cocks her head to one side, looks at her without speaking for almost a whole minute, then admits with a shrug: 'No.'

Disappointment surges through Jhoom in such disproportionate quantities that she is appalled.

'*Thank you!*' she manages to reply. Then she straightens up and pushes her hair away from her face. 'I'm going to soak the rice.'

'What did you think of him, Jhoomie?' Jaishri asks. 'We didn't pay much attention to him before the glow-up, did we?'

Jhoom's eyes widen guiltily.

'It sounds bad to say, amma, but I really do not remember him at all!'

'Blinded by the tawdry dazzle of Tatti Vasudeva!' Jaishri grimaces.

'And brainwashed into a Brahmins-only cockblock!' Jhoom shoots back. 'Imposed by *you*, by the way!'

'Agreed,' Jaishri says with a sigh. 'But I'm wiser now. I know assholes abound in *all* castes and religions—and so do sweet boys. Did you like him?'

Jhoom rolls her eyes. 'I think I'm guilty of looking at him and the whole time only thinking, *wow, movie star*! As if he were a ticketed exhibit, like the Taj Mahal, or a zoo animal.'

'So you objectified the poor boy. Very bad.'

Jhoom sinks to sit cross-legged on the shabby living-room carpet. 'He's clearly kind, because he rushed up to help Roganjosh,' she says. 'And he's brave also, because he faced the bullets *and* he picked her up even though she was snarling and raising her hackles like Varun Dhawan in *Bhediya*.'

'He's cuter than Varun Dhawan,' Jaishri says decidedly.

'I think I talked too much.' Jhoom looks worried.

Jaishri tilts her head inquiringly. 'In what way?'

Jhoom is starting to look more and more sheepish. 'Like I over-shared, I think. I talked so much rubbish! Oh God, I'm pathetic! I meet absolutely no glamorous people, so when I did, I got all giddy and babbled like a fool! And he must meet beautiful successful women who know how to keep it together every single day! He must've thought I'm a gauche little idiot.'

Jaishri rolls her eyes and shrugs. 'Or maybe he thought you two share a special spark.'

Jhoom is silent. She has stopped believing in special sparks. But there *had* been a hot moment in the surgery. Specifically, it had been the moment when she had placed her hands on Haider Sait's tee-shirted shoulders, then run them down his sinewy arms and forearms to land on his strong, steady hands and take over the holding of Josh's wriggling body. For just a single, stupid second there, her knees had almost buckled and her mind had split into two. She'd been fifty per cent business-like super-surgeon, fifty per cent shallow bimbo having foolish, skittering thoughts.

Ugh.

Of course, that had just been her poor ignored hormones running amok.

'Well, I've certainly given you something to think about!' Jaishri's eyes sparkle. 'Are you gonna trot across with these famous medicines later?'

Jhoom looks petrified. 'Well, I suppose so... oh God, who am I kidding? Of course not.'

'Come on, it's only Ayesha auntie's house, you've been there before.'

Jhoom scowls. 'Ma, modern etiquette is quite clear on this—as *he* is the more famous and successful person, it falls upon *him* to make the move, if any.'

Jaishri sniffs.

'Hoity-toity.'

Jhoom gasps. 'Who even uses words like that? *Hoity-toity?*'

'And anyway, you aren't that unfamous and unsuccessful. People come all the way from Gauri Bidnur to get their buffaloes looked at by you.'

'Thanks, amma, but I think Haider Sait's fame stretches further than Gauri Bidnur.'

'D'you think he *knows* that?' Jaishri leans in to ask earnestly. 'Like, *really*? Because in spite of all his fame and fortune and fabulousness, he essentially seems like a *suchu* nice clean Shivajinagar boy. Like Aladdin after he rubbed up a genie and entered the city pretending to be Prince Ali.'

'You're just extrapolating from the logo of Ayesha auntie's shop.'

'Maybe,' Jaishri admits. 'Anyway, the next time he comes around radiating his little street-rat charm, try and see him as a person, not as the Taj Mahal, okay?'

'Aiyyo, what is this sudden obsession?' Jhoom pulls away. 'You're acting weird. I thought we were living full happy lives without men, amma!'

'*I* am living a full happy life without men. You're too young for that! Besides...' Her mother pauses, looking conflicted.

'What?' Jhoom demands.

Jaishri looks agonized. 'I don't know if I should tell you this. Should I tell you this?' She throws her hands up into the air and addresses the sky: 'Solo parenting sucks!'

'Spill, amma, you know you'll burst otherwise.'

'I need a smoke.' Jaishri looks about the room restlessly.

'You do *not.*'

'Okay, fine.' Jaishri takes a deep breath, then says, all in a rush: 'He used to like you.'

Jhoom's eyes bug out. 'Who?'

'He liked you for years.'

'*Haider Sait?*'

Jaishri nods.

Jhoom laughs shakily. 'Amma! *Simply!* What evidence do you have?'

Jaishri's eyes widen.

'Evidence? Why are you talking like a policeman? My evidence is Amma's Antenna. Aka Maternal Radar. Besides, I'm not blind and, as you may have noticed, he has extremely expressive eyes. He would stand in that little window across the road and look at you through the bars like a lovesick pony. Sometimes he even licked the bars. Okay, maybe he didn't lick the bars. But you get my drift.'

Jhoom's cheeks grow hot. 'What rubbish! I know people are partial to their daughters but this is ridiculous!'

'It's true,' Jaishri insists. 'Of course, I Did Not think it a suitable idea At All. And later you seemed so happy with—'

'Tatti Vasudeva.' Jhoom sighs gloomily. 'Wow. Not that I believe any of this. You're just making it up because…' She pauses, frowning. 'Actually, why would you even make such a story up?'

'Exactly,' Jaishri replies. 'So the next time he—'

'There isn't going to be a next time,' Jhoom cuts her off, overwrought and feeling rather fed-up. 'I'll never have the guts to go over with the meds, ancient crush or no ancient crush. And soon he'll go back to his fabulous life and continue to do fabulous K-pop stars and lingerie models. That there? That was our one and only fated interaction.'

'No.' Jaishri sticks to her guns. 'In fact, I would bet big money on you guys ending up together.'

'You don't *have* any money,' Jhoom says crossly. 'Go cook your sambhar-rice.'

Meanwhile, Hadi lets himself out of the heavy door-within-the-door of the Rao house and collides with a wall of beefy, black tee-shirted chests.

'Bheema, Luther.' He pulls back. 'What are you guys doing here—*holy shit*!'

Because, from under their armpits, he can see Habba Galli. It had been pretty empty a while ago, but now it's packed chock-a-block with news vans. Horns are beeping, cameras recording and journalists pushing towards him, yelling his name, their microphones massed and waving like ears of corn in a surreal chrome cornfield.

'Walk to the car, HS.' Luther's voice is clipped. 'It's just up ahead. Yeah, that's it, get in, good.'

Once the doors of the black Q7 have slammed reassuringly around them, Hadi bursts out, bewildered, 'The fuck? What happened? Is ammi okay?'

Bheema hands Hadi his phone. 'It's all good.'

'So then what's up? Why is everybody suddenly screaming my name? Did I randomly win an Oscar or something?'

Luther takes off his dark glasses. 'You just got accused of murder.'

Hadi's eyes widen. 'Murder!'

Luther nods grimly. 'Some fat auntie has given a statement to the newspapers that at ten o'clock last night, she saw you pick up the dropped shotgun and nose it through the hedge into Catacomb.'

'Kedia Kutumb,' Bheema clarifies.

Hadi's jaw sags.

'Huh? To do what, exactly?'

'Bump off the Bling King.'

'But he was already dead! It was an accident!'

Bheema takes up the explanation. 'The press's theory is that somebody with a grudge against the jeweller guy saw the old lady shooting wildly and then ditching the smoking shotgun, and got the bright idea of quickly grabbing it and bumping him off and making it look like the old lady did it accidently.'

'Dude!' Hadi says indignantly. 'The cops didn't even *know* she'd dropped the gun till I told them! Why would I draw attention to it if I'd done all this?'

Both security men shake their heads.

'Were you in the street at ten p.m.?'

Hadi rakes his hair off his forehead. 'Maybe, yeah, I would've been crossing the road and walking back home after the surgery around that time, I guess. It was storming AF. Thunder, lightning. Hey, that's probably why the current went off in the clinic!'

'Did you stop and pick up a shotgun?'

'No! And I have literally nothing against this jeweller! I've never even *met* the guy.'

They shrug.

'Dunno, HS.'

'She's swearing it was you.'

Hadi indulges in a little swearing himself, then realizes his phone is ringing. He snatches it up.

'Bongo! All okay on set?'

'Bro, it's Sunday, this is Bangalore, everybody's chilling, *nobody's* on set. But why're you trending as #HadiSlays? Who's the dead guy?'

'He's my mom's neighbour. I've never even met him.'

'Insane. You okay?'

'I guess. There's a pile-up of news vans outside my car though.' He gives an incredulous laugh. 'This whole thing is fucking hilarious.'

'Hadi.' Bongo's voice grows stern. 'The one thing this is not is hilarious. Take it seriously. Call your lawyers, scare the pants off the cops, sue the fatso for slander. And move your ammi out of that crowded neighbourhood and into your other house. The one with the high boundary walls.'

'Correct!' Bheema, who has been listening in keenly, nods.

'The higher the better.' Luther also nods.

Hadi groans.

'But ammi hates Sadashivanagar!'

'Arrey, it's only a temporary shift,' Bongo says. '*Do* it. You know the state of the nation, and how insanely this kind of thing can blow up.'

'Okay, *okay!*' Hadi says with bad grace. 'You're right. I'll do it.'

6

Definitely Murder

It is a truth universally acknowledged that every cluster of human habitation must possess one highly self-motivated person who makes it their business to know what-what is going on with who-who in the neighbourhood, and avidly juice and judge the same.

Habba Galli is no different. As the anchor from the NationNow! news channel sits across an ornately carved Kashmiri coffee table, under a massive photograph of a shirtless and very hirsute old Babaji, and gazes into Charu Tomar's eager, slanting eyes, he silently congratulates himself on having once again unerringly tracked down the resident busybody.

A make-up artist is briskly at work on Charu Tomar, smoothening out the circles beneath her narrow eyes and accentuating her chunky cheekbones. Finally, he steps back, satisfied.

'Ready, sir.'

'Good, good. Ready, Charuji?'

Mrs Tomar nods composedly. 'Kahan dekhna hai? Where to look?'

'Look at me please, not into the camera. Ekdum natural! Ready?'

She dabs delicately at her eyes. 'Yes.'

'Excellent!'

He turns around, flicks an errant kiss-curl off his forehead, takes a deep breath and stares into the camera sternly.

'We live in a corrupt society, ladies and gentlemen. The canker of corruption has eaten into the soul of our civilization, crimes are being committed with impunity and covered up with the collusion of the highest power in the land. The minority appeasement never ceases, never! Here, in the heart of Bengaluru, a major movie star, currently shooting a controversial film which is already under fire for its sympathetic portrayal of a heartless gangster, is not being investigated as severely as he should be for his role in a brutal crime that has *shocked* the nation.'

He pauses to breathe heavily and stares, outraged, at the nation at large.

'We have here a brave, *brave* lady, the only one in this circle of privilege who has *dared* to speak up against this *monstrous* cover-up and conspiracy!'

He flicks his curl off his face again and turns to her dramatically.

'Charuji!'

Charu Tomar closes her eyes and lets out a low wordless moan. It extends for a good eleven seconds, and only then does she open her eyes to say in a tiny, broken, choked voice, 'The moment I saw her. The very moment I saw her, chewing away, that too with so much enjoyment, my heart contracted in my chest, saying, *oh dhak*!'

'Oh dhak,' he repeats respectfully. 'I see.'

Charu Tomar nods.

'Pre-motion,' she says with gloomy relish. 'I get them, you know, I saw the *entire* pandemic in my dreams. I saw Cyclone Tauktae. And the night before demonetization was announced, I just *felt* I should deposit all my money in the bank. Everybody thinks I had inside information, and I *did*. From my *inside*.'

She points a skinny beringed finger at her massive bosom.

'So, Charuji, did you feel something bad would happen because Pooja Kedia broke her fast before the prescribed time?'

She shakes her head. 'More than that. I felt that Sushil Kedia's time was up. Very clearly I felt it. I *knew* he would not live out the night. Such is the displeasure of the goddess!'

'Yes, yes. But Charuji, setting aside celestial displeasure for just a moment—'

'No no no no no.' She waggles a stern finger in his face. 'You cannot set aside celestial displeasure even for a moment!' She raises both hands into the air and twirls them, one clockwise, one anti-clockwise. 'It is celestial! It is the Will of the Goddess!'

'The Will of the Goddess!' The anchor copies her gesture with gusto.

'Yaiss.' Charu Tomar eyes him critically, as though she would like to give him tips on technique but is setting aside this urge to focus on larger issues.

The anchor leans forward. 'Madam, let us come to the point. The point our viewers are eager to hear.' He pauses meaningfully.

She responds with a theatrical shudder, 'Bhai, I toh do not eat non-veg.'

He looks a little confused. 'Oh, really?'

'Nor does my mister.'

'Please go on.'

'Because eating flesh makes you violent. And *these* people...' She lowers her voice. 'These emmz, Om-ji Gods, you know, they eat so much flesh it makes them brutish... and then murder is nothing to them! Nothing at all!'

'Emmz?'

Reluctantly she says, as if the very word is sullying her lips: 'Muslims.'

'I see.' He nods sagely.

'And they are very adept at bribing people—did you know the handling of this case has been hijacked away from our honest Bengaluru Police? A *special* policeman—some halkat-jawani Bhavani—has come from Delhi and got the true facts of the case hushed up, and is shifting all the blame on that poor old Dondi Pais!'

'A *special* policeman?' The anchor is outraged. 'This is breaking news, ladies and gentlemen! Collusion, evasion and cover-up! Only on NationNow! But please tell our viewers, Charuji, who is doing this cover-up? Who is the evil face behind it all?'

She sniffs.

'Some would call it a handsome face. But I am not so shallow.'

She prims up her mouth and presses a finger to her lips.

'Whose is it?' he asks, breathing heavily. 'Don't be afraid of telling the truth, Charuji! This is India! Ordinary citizens and celebrities are equal before the law!'

There is a long pregnant silence.

Then she leans forward, her cheeks all pink and flushed with pleasure.

'Haider Sait.'

Almost instantaneously, the words *HAIDER SLAYS!* start to flash across the bottom half of the screen, blinking rapidly enough to make one nauseous. Above them, the anchor pounces upon this statement like a cheel upon a chicken nugget, his voice hysterical.

'Haiiiider Sait, ladies and gentlemen! Haider Sait! But why do you say this, madam?'

Her eyelids flicker.

'The thunder woke me up. Half asleep, I looked out of my bedroom window and saw a man in an N-95 mask bending over the pile of leaves beneath Dondi bai's window. Then there was a flash of lightning, and I saw it was Haider Sait.'

The anchor's eyes bug out.

'You actually *saw* him? At ten o'clock in the night? Almost two hours after the supposed accidental shooting?'

Her eyes flicker slightly, but her nod is firm enough. 'Yes, ji. And then he straightened up, holding something long, and pointed it through the hedge.'

'Ah!' The anchor ducks his head. 'But let us be fair, let us be unbiased, we are often accused of being biased against certain communities—which of course is a *diabolical, diabolical* lie—but if it was so dark and he had on a mask, how did you know it was him?'

She snorts. 'We are lifelong neighbours! Why, you see this nose-hoop? He only put it in for me! I have seen Haider Sait at *this* close distance! I think-so I can recognize him!'

'Yes, but madam, if Haider Sait had murder in his heart, why would he pick up the gun so openly? Would he not be worried that he might be seen?'

'Bhai, all that I do not know,' she says primly. 'I cannot claim to understand the mind of a murderer, but like I told you, these people eat so much flesh that it makes them…'

'Violent!' The anchor nods understandingly. 'And then, a little later perhaps, you heard something? A gunshot?'

Her eyes flicker again. 'Perhaps.' She shrugs. 'But of course, there was a big thunderstorm happening. Loud enough to drown out the sound of a shot being fired.'

The blinking graphics on the screen change immediately to scream *HAIDER SLAYS WITH SHOTGUN???* in a blood-red font.

The anchor shouts over the blinking words, now semi-covering him.

'Murder! Murder most galore in Bangalore! *Bloodshed* most galore in Bangalore! Thank you, Charuji! So, ladies and gentlemen, Haider Sait, who you may recall is expert in the working of handheld weaponry after the intense training he put into the films *'71* and the under-production *Bittoo: From*

Lover to Lootera, was seen aiming a long object through the hedge at ten p.m. on Karwa Chauth night! His neighbour Mrs Charu Tomar saw *everything*!'

'Yes, with these eyes.' She points at her bright little piggy eyes. 'And at that very moment,' her voice rises zealously, 'at that *very* moment I had the *strongest* pre-motion that he had cold-blooded murder in his heart and the ground slipped from beneath my feet and my whole heart contracted inside my chest, *so* violently, and every cell of my body cried out—'

'*Ohhhh dhak!*' the anchor bellows, spraying spittle freely. 'So you're saying in that *one* impulsive moment, black-hearted murder entered Haider Sait's heart and he *leapt* upon the gun! What madness! What hatred! What a diabolical *diabolical* deed!'

'Ye-es,' says Charu Tomar slowly. 'That is what I think happened!'

The anchor nods. 'As you say! Thank you, Charuji. This story will be trending number one tomorrow. You have dared to speak up to expose a murderer when everybody else was too scared and your courage will rightly make you famous! On behalf of every patriotic, responsible Indian, thank you very, very much!'

He flicks his errant curl out of his eyes and looks sternly into camera.

'Shame! Shame! Shame! NationNow! has laid bare a devilish attempt to cover up a cold-blooded murder! Bengaluru Police must act on these findings immediately. The video footage must be meticulously scanned and the brazen, opportunistic murderer nabbed. The blood of Sushil Kedia, patriot, father, husband, designer and patron of the arts, cries out for justice! May it soon prevail!'

'Jai Bhavani.'

'Daaktar sa'ab!' Bhavani's face lights up. 'We have been waiting for your call. What news?'

'You're the one in the news,' is Dr Krishnan's laconic reply. 'Think that actor fellow did it?'

'The lady giving evidence against him certainly thinks he did it. But she seems personally motivated.'

Krishnan grunts.

'Doesn't like Muslims? Or doesn't like attractive young men in general?'

'We think it is more a case of liking the spotlight too much. In our initial conversation with her, she seemed to be scatter-shooting in every possible direction in a hope to hit something, anything! Clearly the press have explained to her that Haider Sait is the most eyeball-grabbing target. But he insists he went straight from the veterinarian's surgery to bed by ten p.m. He spent three hours texting his film director subsequently. He's shared all the time-stamped screenshots.'

'Those can be faked.'

'Yes, but it isn't easy. Besides, he has no motive to kill this man. He has never even met him. Yes, there has been some khit-pit on their colony WhatsApp group about the stray dogs—the actor's mother feeds them and the jeweller didn't like that, because they impregnated his Weimaraner and they routinely make number one on the wheels of his expensive car…'

Krishnan's voice grows animated for the first time. 'Same damn debate in every blessed RWA, Bhavani. In my colony too! They keep trying to embroil me in it, asking me to weigh in with my professional opinion either for or against, but I have told them politely that life's too short to socialize with neighbours; I prefer to spend it cutting up corpses in a cold sterile basement.'

'You are wise, duck sa'ab! Indeed, in life one should focus on what provides one with happiness and recharges one's batteries. Shalini, for one, gets tremendous joy from feeding stray dogs. And we get joy from walking under beautiful flowering pink trees like these ones in Cubbon Park. Accept our request to switch to video, and we will show you. You will think ki we are in Japan!'

'Control these artistic excesses, Bhavani. I have to tell you something important.'

Bhavani stops walking, causing an overeager golden retriever and his out-of-shape minder to almost collide into him.

'What?'

'Your jeweller was murdered.'

Bhavani is very still. Candy-pink Tabebuia flowers drift down slowly around him, one of them landing lightly on his shoulder.

'Oho…'

'Yes,' Krishnan says severely. 'Rejoice. You now have an excuse to let GOI pick up the tab for your very first annual honeymoon.'

'Arrey! The news of our honeymoon has reached even your cold sterile basement?'

Krishnan chuckles. 'The whole department is talking about it, Bhavani!'

Bhavani's cheeku-brown cheeks grow as pink as the flowers dropping around him.

'How do you know it was murder?'

'Because you said the old biddy went on her shooting spree at moonrise—eight-fourteen p.m. But from the core body temperature I'd say he died some time around ten p.m.'

'*That* late?'

'Yes, both the cleaning lady and the younger son say in their statements that the room was ice-cold when they found him...'

'Yes, he always kept the AC on maximum cooling apparently. Probably to harass his wife, who catches cold fast.'

'A pleasant fellow. So, to repeat, the room was ice-cold, but the deep rectal temperature readings were on the warmer side. He hadn't been dead for more than a few hours when they found him. I'd even say time of death could be as late as eleven p.m. last night, if not later.'

'Then Charu Tomar's accusations need to be taken seriously.'

'Yes,' Krishnan says. 'It's likely that she did see somebody, you know, and wishful-thunk it into being the most famous person in that pincode area. It's the sort of thing a lot of sensation-seekers would do. Are there any other contenders who could've been lurking around there at that time of night?'

Bhavani furrows his forehead.

'The mother's bedroom and balcony are visible on the CCTV cameras and there is no movement on those at all. The older son and his wife checked into the Leela at around nine p.m., and the footage from the hotel restaurant and corridors rules them out. And the younger son interviewed with the admissions panel of a top American university the entire night. He is on camera from eight p.m. to six a.m.'

'So it's not an inside job by the loving fam, then.'

'The shot would have had to be fired from the road. It was probably the serpent.'

'Serpent? Nothing in the gent's innards points to poisoning, Bhavani, either by snakebite or anything he ingested.'

'We mean a metaphorical snake, duck sa'ab.'

Krishnan continues like he hasn't heard Bhavani. 'In fact, he ingested nothing the whole day! Pity, otherwise the contents of his stomach would have provided double confirmation of the time of death.'

'He was keeping the Karwa Chauth fast. To prove to his wife that it is no big thing to go without nourishment of any sort for a whole day.'

'Seems an argumentative sort of fellow.'

'He was thoroughly unpleasant by all accounts, and with this new time-of-death confirmed, the list of people who might have killed him really lengthens.'

'What does ballistics say?'

'They found nothing suspicious in the path of the bullet. According to them it flew out of her gun, across the road, through the glass and *bam* into his forehead.'

Krishnan laughs dryly. 'A hole-in-one, in other words!'

'You have certainly punched a hole into that theory!' Bhavani replies.

'Now, make sure this fat lady who loves the spotlight doesn't get bumped off too,' Krishnan says. 'With all the noise she's making on national television, she may attract the killer's attention.'

And on this encouraging note, he disconnects the call.

Bhavani stands under the gently drifting Pink Trumpet flowers for a while, a vacuous look on his homely face.

So it is a deliberate killing, after all.

Not a random accident.

Everything he has thought so far will have to be—to use Dr Krishnan's phrase—rethunk.

The news that the police have ruled out accidental death as the cause of Sushil Kedia's demise explodes like a bomb on news channels and social media by the next afternoon. Public feeling against Hadi whips up to hysterical levels, with the result that the denizens of Habba Galli have to pretty much barricade themselves within their homes to avoid the crush of press people and vans outside. Foiled by the fact that the Saits have shifted base to the high-walled villa in Sadashivanagar, the journalists accost any hapless resident who happens to be walking by and want to know if they want Hadi arrested.

Jaishri Rao, coming back from college where she's had several Hadi Sait fangirls break down and weep their eyes out in her class, is in no mood to suffer such foolish questions gladly. So when the journalists assault her with their mics and ask, 'How does it feel to be living next door to a probable murderer?' she gives them what for.

'How does it feel to be a soulless vulture for a puny salary?' she demands.

The journos don't back down.

'Aren't you worried sick about being murdered in your bed, madam?'

'I'm worried sick about the state of journalism in this country.'

'Do you think the curse of Matarani has bought about this death?'

This causes Jaishri to halt in her tracks in disbelief.

'Are you *stupid*?' she snarls. 'You think Matarani reached down from the heavens with her trident and pronged Sushi Kedia like a piece of prawn sukka?'

There is a small startled pause and then they leap forward again, yelling questions incoherently.

'Hatt, gandu!' says Jaishri rudely and slams shut the door-within-the-door of her crumbling mansion.

This unfortunate interaction plays on loop on all the news channels all day. Jaishri, half appalled, half delighted with her sudden fame, listens meekly when Jhoom tells her sternly not to speak to the press again. 'They'll twist everything you say, amma! And Charu auntie will hate us! And the Brahmin Mahasabha will think we're godless atheists!'

Jaishri snorts. 'I stopped giving a damn about those clowns years ago!'

Jhoom throws up her hands.

'Maybe *I* give a damn! I don't want people to think I have a delinquent mother!'

'Oh, magu, don't worry!' Jaishri's face softens at once. 'He'll message you for sure. Ayesha has your number! He's just been accused of murder, give him a little time.'

'Oh my God, I don't *care* what he thinks!' Jhoom explodes. '*You're* the one with Haider Sait on the brain, not me!'

She throws her mother a look of utter exasperation and storms out of the room.

The journalists circle Habba Galli hungrily for the next few days but finally, after scoring nothing but endless videos of Bachchan, Darponk and the rest of Roganjosh's pack scratching themselves, retreat to set up camp outside the Saits' Sadashivanagar residence.

The coast clear at last, Jhoom cautiously pushes open the door-within-the-door and joins the throng of shoppers on Habba Galli.

It feels good to be out. There's a weak sun shining through the clouds, the air is green-apple-crisp and the fruit carts are loaded with the most gorgeously vibrant—and hopefully not too expensive—produce.

'Yeshtu bele?' She stops at a particularly luscious thela.

'The newspaper says it's a very good year for custard apples,' a smiling, homely-looking gent says conversationally as he leans in to pick up a custard apple from the cart. 'There has been a bumper crop apparently.'

'Oh, I can believe that!' she agrees. 'These chaps are huge! Don't they look like hand grenades, only greener? So pretty!'

He chuckles. 'Exactly like hand grenades! Yeh uthaya, yeh maara! But you are the vet who so bravely saved Roganjosh's life that night!'

'And you are night ki naughty kahani, halkat Bhavani!' She gives him a tight smile.

He laughs. 'Your Mrs Tomar has made us famous! But how is your shoulder now?'

'Fine,' she replies shortly. 'How's your investigation going?'

'Saar, beku athva bekilla?' the fruit seller interrupts the tête-à-tête irritably.

'Beku, bhai, beku,' Bhavani responds. 'One kilo of your yeh… this very good custard apple. And Jhoomji, what are you buying?'

'Bananas,' she says wryly. 'And now that you've called my attention to them, I'll splash out on one custard apple too.'

They collect their fruit and walk down the noisy, bustling street together, dodging puddles, potholes and loudly tooting two-wheelers. Then Bhavani stops at the ice creamery and smiles beguilingly at Jhoom.

'We have fallen in love with Gadbad, Jhoomji. Come, let us get some.'

Soon they are sitting across from each other on the tiny formica table, loaded beer mugs between them.

'Is this an interrogation?' She tilts her head playfully. 'Should I be afraid?'

'You should be wary, at the very least,' he replies seriously. 'You must have heard that our forensics team has ruled that what occurred at your neighbour's house is most certainly a murder.'

Jhoom experiences the most peculiar sinking feeling in her belly.

'Well, I've heard, of course,' she says. 'But I guess I was kinda hoping it was a rumour.'

He shakes his head gravely. 'It isn't, Jhoomji.'

She pokes at the Gadbad with her spoon. 'Fuck! Sorry, I mean, *shit*, I mean *damn*!'

'It is definitely all three,' he replies. 'Now, you are an educated, observant and responsible lady. Please help us collect some background and understanding of your neighbourhood.'

Jhoom nods intently. 'Sure, ACP. Happy to help.'

'Is it correct that Dondi Pais did a show-and-tell demo with her gun in the middle of the street on Ayudha Puja?'

Jhoom's pretty chin drops. 'Holy shit, I'd clean forgotten! Yes! My mom was out there worshipping her scooty and she showed *us* how to operate gunny boy too!'

'Very well.' He lowers his voice. 'Next question: in your opinion, who might have wanted to kill Sushil Kedia?'

'Dude!' She gives a wry laugh. 'Me, for one. His wife. His son. His other son. His daughter-in-law. His maid Saraswati. All his employees. Your superhost Krish Chetty. Ayesha auntie. My mother. Mehtab, the proprietor of the shop opposite. *All* the pilla party, in fact. He wasn't a very nice person.'

'You mean Mehta bhai?'

She laughs. 'Yes. He tweaks his name just a leeetle bit according to whom he's hoping to sucker into buying a carpet that day! I've heard him calling himself Meta when he was drunk and telling a bunch of Americans that he owns Facebook.'

'Does he love dogs very much?'

'Arrey, amma and he *started* pilla party! They roped in Ayesha auntie and me later. He's our main source of food. Has lots of butcher-shop friends. Has lots of friends generally!'

She takes a bite of her Gadbad. Bhavani watches her eat.

'Jhoomji, think carefully. Did Sushil Kedia always dislike the dogs so much or did something intensify his dislike of them recently?'

'Duh.' She rolls her eyes. 'Tiffinni's mongrel litter made him totally rabid on the topic!'

'We have been meaning to ask, how did the high-born Tiffinni come to mate with a mongrel?'

Jhoom rolls her eyes. 'Love will find a way, I guess. But he was furious—he actually told his driver to *drown* the puppies! But Sona intervened and Pooja auntie backed her up, and the pilla party ran around and got them all adopted.'

'How did Sushil Kedia take that?'

'Not very well at all. But Pooja auntie stood firm. She's become quite fun recently. It's all because of Sona—she's a stray-dog lover and, under her influence, Pooja auntie is slowly becoming one too.'

'We see. So *after* Sonaji moved in, the acrimony intensified?'

'Ye…es. And maybe I'm being really fanciful here, but I think Roganjosh has a lot to do with it. Pooja auntie draws strength, even inspiration, from Roganjosh. She's always saying ki dekh Jhoom, kitni independent hai, her nipples are as hard as bullets, all the male dogs obey her, see how she snarls back at her tormenters and takes no nonsense! Roganjosh is #Goals for Pooja auntie, basically.'

'We see.'

His expression is so serious that Jhoom starts to look worried. 'Uh, ACP, I really don't think Pooja auntie got inspired by Rogu's wild female energy and bumped off Sushi uncle. If she wanted to, she would've found a less complicated way of doing it. Can she even handle a shotgun? The whole thing is preposterous!'

'We are nat saying she did.' Bhavani shakes his head. 'Ekchully, we are thinking about what Ayesha Sait told us…'

He tells Jhoom about the serpent in the garden.

'Aiyyo, Ayesha auntie is becoming too filmy! You're actually taking this seriously? And you think *Sona* is the serpent?'

'It is a possibility,' he replies. 'Your friend and her husband get to have complete control of the business now. You do know that father and son had very different ways of doing business, don't you?'

'Sona is a *darling*,' Jhoom says heatedly. 'Just because she has a personality and her own opinions, and a life before she met Harshu…'

'A life before she met Harshu?' His eyebrows rise. 'You mean a boyfriend?'

Jhoom pushes her chair back, looking conscience-stricken.

'I've been talking carelessly. I take back everything I've said.'

'Arrey, this is nat some police statement,' he says soothingly. 'We are simply chatting.'

'No no no. I don't want to chat about this. I don't want to...'

Bhavani's face grows grave. 'A man was murdered, Jhoomji, in the house next door to you. Don't you want to help us catch the killer? Won't it make your whole neighbourhood feel safe?'

She shakes her head. 'Not if it means betraying my friends and neighbours! Sushi Kedia was a *horrible* man. I'm *glad* he's dead.'

The girl is genuinely upset. Her eyes are moist, her chest is rising and falling with agitation.

Bhavani nods sympathetically.

'You value your friendships. Your family has been through a bad patch and these people have stood by you?'

Surprise floods her face. 'You understand! Yes, I had a whole set of other friends till about six years ago, but then...' she gestures vaguely, 'everything changed. These are my second set of friends... my *real* friends...'

'You said Krish Chetty has a motive. And Ayesha Sait too?'

'I was joking!' Her voice is shaking slightly. 'You suspect somebody in the Kedia family, don't you? Or Haider. Or...' She sucks in her breath suddenly, her pupils dilating with fear. 'Somebody else?'

'It is our job to suspect everybody,' Bhavani says calmly. 'And yes, it would have been quite easy for Haider Sait to commit the crime. He was at the scene. He saw the whole incident unfold, he rushed up to aid you in your rescue efforts. Suppose, *after* the surgery, as he walked home about two hours later, around the time that Charu Tomar claims to have seen him, he saw the gun lying on the ground and decided, impulsively, to finish off Sushil Kedia?'

'But *why*? He didn't even know the guy!'

'There seems to be no motive,' Bhavani agrees and changes tack.

'What do you know of the younger Kedia boy?'

'Sparshu?' she says incredulously. 'He's a *child*.'

'So? There was a case in Delhi, less than four years ago, in which a seventeen-year-old slit the throat of a five-year-old in the school lavatory because he was hoping to get the final exams postponed.'

'Ya, well, Sparshu is a bloody genius,' Jhoom says triumphantly. 'He'd probably slit somebody's throat to get exams *preponed*, not postponed. He's been a topper all his life.'

Bhavani nods grimly.

'That kind of genius comes with its own psychological challenges.'

She gives a disbelieving laugh. 'Then go arrest him! Do his psychological analysis or whatever! Leave me out of it!'

He lets her rant, quietly eating his ice cream.

She gets to her feet abruptly. 'I'm paying for my own Gadbad,' she says jerkily. 'You pay for yours. Goodbye.'

He nods sympathetically, not at all put out. 'Thank you for talking to us, Jhoomji. Do nat forget your fruit.'

He hands her her shopping bag. Her custard apple falls out as she hefts the bag and rolls across the formica tabletop. He retrieves it and hands it to her expressionlessly.

Jhoom had likened it to a hand grenade, and now, as she takes it, she feels a crazy urge to throw it up in the air, once, twice, thrice, then lob it across the table at the old policeman and see him burn.

I'm losing my mental balance, she thinks chaotically. Oh God, what's *wrong* with me? Why are all these dreadful thoughts even crossing my mind?

She manages a small tight smile for Bhavani Singh. Poor chap, he was, after all, just trying to do his extremely unsavoury job.

'Namaskara,' she says awkwardly, reverting to extreme formality to hide her embarrassment, and then walks away.

Bhavani carries on eating his Gadbad, unperturbed. His brain is busy mulling over one little bit of his conversation with Jhoom.

'You suspect somebody in the Kedia family, don't you?' the girl had said. 'Or Haider. Or… somebody else?'

Raw fear had flooded her eyes in that little pause between 'or' and 'somebody else'.

Jhoomar Rao is worried for someone.

Who?

'Bavani boi!' A lilting Kashmiri accent reaches his ears. 'You have betrayed me!'

A sinewy arm pulls up the chair Jhoom has vacated and a black Pathani-draped figure sits down upon it. Bhavani smiles weakly.

'Huh—how, Mehta bhai?'

The impossibly handsome Kashmiri points a dramatic finger at the old ACP. Bracelets jingle upon his wrist.

'A silak sari!' he says accusingly. 'A Benarasi silak! What is this, Bavani boi? Who comes to Bangalore and buys a Benarasi sari? For that you should going to Benaras, no?'

'Well, for that matter,' Bhavani rallies, sticking his chin out, 'who comes to Bangalore and buys a Kashmiri carpet? For that we should go to Kashmir, no?'

The huge hazel-green eyes grow massive with reproach. 'We would give *anything* to go back to Kashmir,' Mehtab says brokenly. 'You are making fun of a homeless exile.'

Bhavani hastily puts out a hand but it is too late. Mehtab's voice has grown louder and more declamatory. 'What I would *do* to go back to Kashmir! What I would give up, what I would *sacrifice*…'

'We are very much interested in a Tree-of-Life carpet,' says the cornered Bhavani. 'Our wife Shalu and we were discussing it only yesterday; we were saying that no tasteful Indian home is complete without one.'

Mehtab's eyes slowly resume their normal size. 'Ah,' he says with intense satisfaction.

'But we must add,' Bhavani says as he picks up his spoon again, 'that we find it very odd that you are concerned about closing a sale when your neighbour has been so brutally killed.'

This silences Mehtab for a moment. But only a moment. '*You* are sitting here eating Gadbad,' he shoots back.

Bhavani assumes a lofty air. 'We are checking that there is no gadbad in this so-called accident,' he says austerely.

There is silence as Bhavani continues eating. Presently Mehtab says, in a much quieter voice than usual, 'I cannot do acting of being sad, Bavani boi. That man, he was no good.'

'But a murderer running around your neighbourhood cannat be good either.'

There is another pause, during which, with the power of his reproachful hazel gaze, Mehtab contrives to make Bhavani feel increasingly in the wrong. He covers up as best he can, finishing his ice cream and pushing the empty beer mug away.

'Why did you barge into Sushil Kedia's Commercial Street store and threaten him?' he asks. 'And please do nat ask us to call you Mehta any more. Your name is Mehtab.'

'A rose by any other name still smells as sweet, Bavani boi! We are terribly discriminated against. Sometimes dropping that B at the end of our name makes the difference between getting a full meal of goat curry and saffron-scented rice, or going to sleep on an empty stomach!'

'We would nat call you a *rose*, personally.' Bhavani smiles gently. 'You do nat belong to the plant kingdom at all. The animal kingdom would suit you better. A wolf by any other name still hunts for meat, is how we would rephrase that quote!'

Mehtab smiles, showing perfect pearly teeth. 'I do like meat, I cannot deny.'

'Can you deny that you were very upset with Sushil Kedia?'

Anger smoulders in the hazel-green eyes.

'That man was a pig. A sweet NRI lady tourist whose son was getting married asked me where she could buy good jewellery for the wedding. I recommended Kedia Jewellers most highly and, Bavani boi, I am not boasting or exaggerating, bagwaan shapath, she went in there and spent two crore on gold! Am I not entitled to a commission? She could have walked into Bhimas or Jos Alukkas or Tanishq, but I—because I love my adopted home of Habba Galli so much—recommended her to shop at Kedia Jewellers and even *took* her there! He was like my brother, we have exchanged festive sweets for decades! And *jenwinly*, Bavani boi, I *believed* that, from my heart! But Sushil Kedia's people treated me like kachra, they said the lady shopped there because she heard the ads of Kedia Jewellers on Indigo FM and not because I took her there personally! And so, there was no commission for me! I had to be happy with the tea and lassi and two-hundred-rupee dhokla they served us while she shopped! Is that right, is that fair? Should I have not received the market-accepted rate of a one per cent commission?'

'Wealth changes people, Mehta bhai,' Bhavani commiserates sorrowfully. 'And seldom for the better.'

Mehtab exhales gustily. 'That is truly true. He used to have one small showroom and now he has eight big ones, and he has managed to purchase the big mansion next to the Raos, so he thinks he has become a big man! But you cannot become a big man with a small heart, boi!'

'Did you manage to speak to him directly, though?' Bhavani asks. 'Sometimes people in the middle create unnecessary issues.'

Mehtab snorts. 'There was some important white man visiting his office that day. Intricate kolam had been done and flower garlands hung and everybody was on their best behaviour. Maybe that is why Sushil Kedia got extra-angry, because I made him look bad in front of the gora. But why should I keep quiet just because some white man is visiting, eh?'

'Why indeed.'

'A few days later, when my brain had cooled, I went around to the house and spoke to his daughter-in-law. She is a kind person, she understood that I had been wronged and she got me what was rightfully mine.'

'How?'

'She put me on to her husband, who was intelligent enough to know my worth. He met me, gave me full respect, paid my full commission, told me to keep bringing in more customers, and said that I am fifty times better than Indigo FM!'

'Their marriage looks like a happy one.'

Mehtab eyes him quizzically. 'What are you suggesting?'

Bhavani shrugs his chunky shoulders. 'We are just asking an observant man to share his observations!'

Mehtab doesn't reply immediately. 'It is happy enough,' he says finally.

Bhavani smiles. 'You are a romantic, Mehta bhai. How could you nat be? You are Kashmiri, after all! The lake, the lotuses, the houseboats, the snow…'

Mehtab chuckles. 'Maybe, maybe.'

'Let us go back to the Kedia family. What else do you know?'

Mehtab exhales gustily, then wriggles his head about, thinking.

'There was friction between father and son,' he says. 'Harsh is a simple fellow and a hard worker. The father was more political. He liked one client or one employee, he didn't like the other, he played favourites.' The hazel-green eyes look deep into Bhavani's. 'He enjoyed having power, you know?'

'Yes.'

'Naturally, customers preferred Harsh. They asked for him by name when they came in. He is dependable and decent, and when you are investing so much money, you want dependability.'

'That isn't enough of a motive to kill somebody.'

The hazel-green eyes flicker.

'Harsh loves his mother a lot. And things have changed since Sona gobra came to Kedia Kutumb. Harshu has become newly sensitive to the ladies' point of view.'

'I see.'

Mehtab eyes him keenly. 'Succession battles are always bloody, Bavani boi.'

'What about the younger shehzaada then?' Bhavani asks. 'Sparshu?'

Mehtab chuckles. 'He really is quite the shehzaada! He has a beautiful much older fashionista girlfriend! Studying in Europe now, I think. She was an intern at the big Kedia store. I used to see them eating Gadbad together all the time.'

'An intern,' Bhavani says thoughtfully. 'A design intern, perhaps? How long ago was this?'

'A few months ago.'

'Was her name Devika Johri?'

Mehtab draws back, impressed. 'Yes,' he says. 'Now how did you know *that*?'

Bhavani twinkles. 'We are Dilli Police. With you, for you, always.'

'Why is everybody so quiet? I can't bear it! Say something, one of you. I can't eat in silence like this, I'll go mad.'

Pooja Kedia glares around the dining table at her sons and daughter-in-law, all of whom look rather startled at her outburst.

'Arrey, mummyji.' Sona gives an uncertain laugh. 'We aren't keeping quiet on purpose—'

'I am,' young Sparsh admits. 'I'm trying to be sensitive and all.'

'We just don't want to trouble you, mummy.' Harsh reaches out to grasp his mother's agitated hand. 'You've had such a terrible shock—'

Pooja Kedia shakes off his hand. 'I'm fine!'

She says this vehemently, too vehemently. The three others exchange glances.

'There's just so much paperwork to go through and arrangements to make, mummyji,' Sona says soothingly. 'But Sparshu will chat with you after lunch, no, Sparshu?'

The young boy nods. 'Yes, done, we'll chill, Ma!'

'Chupp!' Pooja Kedia's eyes flare with anger. 'I'm not a child. Or a donkey. Or a murderer. But—'

They stare at her, open-mouthed.

Her voice drops to an almost-whisper as she says, her words tumbling out one on top of the other, 'But there was murder in my heart when I broke my fast in the food court that day. And I can understand if there has been murder in your hearts too, at sometime or the other. Do you understand what I am saying?'

An odd silence falls over the table. Everybody looks exclusively at Pooja Kedia as though afraid to look at each other.

'Let's not have secrets from each other,' Pooja Kedia continues to speak with soft urgency. 'Let's not have silences. I am your mother and I will support you and protect you always. Chahe kuch bhi ho jaaye. No matter what you did or may go on to do. Understood?'

'But mummy, we have no secrets—'

'Understood?' Her voice is like a whip crack.

'Yes.'

'Sir, a motive has been found for Haider Sait, sir. It's a peculiar sort of motive, but it may well be the correct one.'

'Does it incorporate the serpent, Manju? We have been thinking more and more about the serpent.'

Naik hesitates. Sometimes he cannot tell when the older officer is being dead serious or slyly pulling his leg.

'It may or may not, sir. I can't say for sure.'

He hands Bhavani a printed sheet.

'But this is a newspaper article! Nat a statement given to the police!'

'Please just read it, sir.'

There is a pink sticky note stuck onto the 'report' to make it look more official.

Bhavani peels it off and starts to read.

Recorded statement of Vidyadhar Khare, age 42, spotboy at the location shoot of *Bittoo: From Lover to Lootera*

Bongo sir and Hadi baba have been arguing a lot during this schedule. I have shot with both of them before also, and it has always been bindaas and no-tension, but this time something is off.

I focus only on my job when I am on set, I never even watch the shooting, except to come forward and help change the set-up when it requires changing, so I can't tell you what exactly the problem was on set that day, but there was definitely a problem. I know this because the scene they were shooting—Scene 52 on the storyboard—had already been shot twice before, but both times Bongo sir rejected it after watching the rushes.

That day, we were shooting it for the third time.

It was a very small set-up, just Hadi baba, blood-splattered and drunk, staring into a mirror in a dirty bathroom.

Scene 52 is an important scene. I haven't read the screenplay and I only have a vague idea of the movie plot—Bongo sir insists on complete confidentiality on his set and we have to sign contracts saying that we will leak nothing—but I know it is an important scene. I've heard them discuss it several times.

Anyway, they were shooting it, just Bongo sir and his first AD, and Hadi baba and his hair and make-up people, and the cinematographer and his team. And me.

There was a long silence after Hadi baba did his take, I think it was his fifth take. You could have heard a pin drop on the set as Bongo sir stood behind the monitor to check the replay. Finally he looked up, smiled, raised his hands in a double thumbs up and said, 'Got it.'

We were all so relieved. That wretched Scene 52 had been hanging over our heads like a noxious cloud!

But then Hadi baba, instead of smiling back and looking happy, said very quietly: 'Don't you fuckin' fake your orgasms with me, Bongo.'

I was confused. Why was he talking about orgasms? We weren't making that sort of movie. I'm a God-fearing man and my mother would throw me out of the house if I worked on that sort of set.

Bongo sir started insisting he wasn't faking, and Hadi baba insisted he was, and they sort of ran towards each other, shaking their fists and yelling loudly, with both of them talking and neither of them listening.

It went on like that for a long time and finally Bongo sir admitted, almost weeping, that maybe it was just the writing that was bad and it was wrong to blame Hadi baba, and Hadi baba said the writing was on-point and needed no tweaking, and Bongo sir said, 'Hadi, you're a serial killer, I need to see raw bloodlust throbbing in your eyes,' and Hadi baba said, 'Behenchod Bongo, how d'you expect me to throb with raw bloodlust, by actually killing somebody?' And Bongo sir replied, very seriously, 'Yes.' And then Hadi baba burst out laughing, and Bongo sir joined in too, then they hugged each other and Bongo sir called pack-up.'

Bhavani pushes away the paper slowly.

'We see.'

Naik looks at him eagerly. 'It's a psychological motive, sir. He's a dramatic, creative fellow, he might have seen the gun fall to the ground and, in the spur of the moment, decided to experience raw, throbbing bloodlust for the sake of his art. Chance-pe-dance, like you said that day, sir.'

Bhavani nods. 'Yes, it is a motive of sorts. The sort of motive the news channels and social media will love. But let us nat get too carried away. It could have been another person. Manju, do nat let the circus distract you. We need to do a systematic investigation of every single person who had motive and opportunity to carry out this crime.'

For the first time in his life, ACP Bhavani is inside a movie star's trailer. He looks around it interestedly.

While he had been making the long drive to Ramadevarabatta, and while he had walked through the crowd of avid onlookers at the location itself, he had been preparing himself mentally for some kind of a dim 'man cave', he realizes. Very chrome and leather and hi-tech. But this space is sunny and functional. There's a wooden floor, a comfortable-looking white couch/bed, a rather fancy juice-and-coffee station, and simple dumbbells and resistance bands.

'The wardrobe and make-up sections are on the other side,' Hadi informs him. 'These are my sleeping quarters, really. What would you like to ask me this time, ACP?'

Bhavani smiles blandly. 'We are here simply so that our people can examine the shotgun you are using in the film, Hadiji.'

'It's pretty similar to gunny boy,' Hadi replies. 'But I could have just told you that.'

'We have to follow procedures,' Bhavani explains. 'Tell us, this scene number 52. Why do you think you are having so much trouble with it?'

Hadi's face darkens. He says, with unusual violence, 'Scene bloody 52 has absolutely *nothing* to do with the murder!'

Bhavani nods, unperturbed.

'You are trying to *grow* as an actor,' he says encouragingly. 'Explore, improve, evolve?'

Hadi stares moodily at the floor for a while, then his head comes up defiantly. 'Yes, dammit. When we read scripts, we're always looking for the character's growth arc—don't I deserve one as well? I *love* entertaining people and I'm grateful for their love, but I'd be lying if I said I don't want to be feted for something other than my energy and my eyes, or win awards, or appeal to people with more refined sensibilities.'

'Like Jaishri Rao,' Bhavani suggests.

Hadi flushes. 'Yes. She said *'71* was riddled with inaccuracies. And of *course*,' his lips twist bitterly, 'she was right.'

'Your eyes and your energy are your biggest strengths, Hadiji.'

Hadi shoots him a decidedly resentful look. 'How d'you know my *acting* isn't my biggest strength?'

Yeh dil maange more, Bhavani muses. Truly, young people are never satisfied! Haider Sait seems to be hankering for fandom from a social class that he considers somehow 'higher' than himself. A class Jaishri Rao and her daughter belong to.

Aloud he says, 'So what will happen to Scene 52 then?'

'Bongo's doing some rewrites,' Hadi says stiffly. Then he smiles, a charming, rueful smile. 'Apologies for my rudeness. Do stay and take some refreshments. My team will look after you. I have to head back into the shoot now.'

'Ai, Bongo, what kind of movie are you and Hadi making? With raw and throbbing bloodlust? What's wrong with jushtu simple lust, huh?'

Thus Ayesha Sait that evening to her son's director in the living room of the house-with-the-high-boundary-walls in Sadashivanagar.

'Hear hear!' Krish Chetty's deep voice chimes in lazily. 'Why are you even attempting intelligent cinema, Bongo? Just stick to the formula.'

A flush spreads across Bongo Banerjee's plump, harassed-looking face. He turns to Ayesha, ignoring Krish entirely.

'Well, Ayesha auntie, an artist should explore his range and all the rasas. Hasya rasa, vir rasa, shringaar rasa, karuna r—'

'Bas bas,' she cuts him off hastily. 'Don't give me all that gyaan, ma! Hadi will never be able to play a serial killer convincingly, he is too sweet, why did you even cast him?'

Hadi, lying crossways across a leather couch and staring at his phone, lazily raises his voice: 'Ai, ammi, don't troll poor Bongo.'

'Then look up from your phone, Hadi! And tell the whole story of this movie, why is he a serial killer, who does he go around killing, give me a full—what's that word you boys use—narration!'

Hadi swings his legs down and sits up.

'No.'

'Y'Allah!' she gasps, her hand going to her breast. 'So rude. Why not?'

'Because you'll leak it,' her son replies bluntly. 'You know you sing like a canary. You'll tell everybody who comes into the store for a pair of earrings, you'll tell the entire pilla party—Mehtab bhai and Jaishri auntie and Jhoom—'

'Speaking of Jhoom,' Krish cuts in smoothly, 'how did your visit to her place go that day?'

His tone is so meaningful that Ayesha's ears prick up.

'What is all this?' She sits up. 'What about Jhoom?'

'Dude.' Hadi shakes his head at his old friend reproachfully. '*Why?*'

'That's the vet who saved the dog and got shot in the shoulder, right?' Bongo sits up too, interested. 'I heard the news report and thought it was an unusual name.'

'It's because the first time she smiled, it was so incandescent it lit up the maternity ward like a chandelier,' Hadi says softly, producing the sentence like one reciting a piece of well-loved folklore. 'Ergo, Jhoomar.'

'Oh my God!' The penny drops in Bongo's brain. '*She's* the girl you were obsessed with, growing up? The one you talked about in that interview!'

'What! *Our* Jhoom!' Ayesha looks delighted. '*Is* she, Hadi?'

Both she and Bongo stare up at him, excited. He stares at the carpet, a series of expressions flitting across his mobile face. He looks, his mother thinks, rather like he does in his ad for Mountain Dew, where he stands at the edge of an immense cliff and talks himself into mountain-boarding off it.

Hadi draws a deep breath and grins sheepishly.

'Yeah.'

'Whooooof!' says Krish, very low. 'Finally. Out and proud.'

Ayesha utters a piercing squeal of delight, leaps up from the couch and flings her arms around him.

Bongo lets out a joyous roar.

Hadi winces.

'Ammi, swalpa control maadi.'

'But why did you never *tell* me?' she demands, slapping his chest.

Hadi's face grows vulnerable.

'She was in a serious relationship. And while you guys gave me everything I needed growing up, the Raos were just so... *rich*! Anyway, you know abba wouldn't have approved. He liked everybody to play nicely and neatly inside their own boxes. Arrey, even his thaali had separate sections for rice and saalan and qurma! He didn't like it when things mixed.'

'He was a real Habba Galli wala,' Krish says fondly. 'I miss Musa uncle!'

Ayesha makes an impatient gesture. 'All the food mixes in the stomach anyway, does it not?'

Hadi laughs. 'Yes it does.'

Ayesha stares at him ecstatically.

'A *local* girl!' she sighs. 'From Habba Galli! Not a Korean K-pop waali! Not a Bengali! Well chosen, Hadi!'

Bongo chuckles. 'Ayesha auntie, remember that all the food mixes in the stomach, anyway! Even Korean food or Bengali food.'

'Calm down, ammi,' Hadi says hastily. 'It's too early to say anything; she may not even like me!'

Ayesha swells till she looks three times her tiny size. 'Nobody,' she says impressively, her eyes aglow with complete confidence, '*nobody* can resist my son!'

'Hear hear!' Krish applauds, laughing.

Hadi turns to glare at him. 'Stop laughing, bastard, you shouldn't have told her. What's wrong with you?'

'Don't shout at him, Hadi,' Ayesha says. 'It's the first sensible thing he's done in ages.'

Krish stops laughing abruptly. 'Wow. Thanks, auntie.'

'So her marriage broke up or what?' Bongo wants to know.

'Her engagement.' Hadi's voice is soft but his eyes are shining. 'It's been over for a while now. She's single.'

'Yessss!' Bongo pumps his fist excitedly. 'Let the love jihad begin!'

Ayesha and he burst out laughing. Hadi shakes his head at them, then looks across at Krish, who raises a quiet eyebrow.

How did it go, bro?

'It went well, I think,' Hadi says cautiously. 'It was just a friendly chat, of course.'

All three of them draw back in collective disgust, throwing up their hands.

'Uff!'

'Useless!'

'Chaman!'

'Or…' His voice softens, grows musing. 'Maybe it *wasn't*.'

Everybody scuttles closer delightedly.

'Is he asking or is he telling?'

'Shhh!'

'Hadi! Helu!'

Hadi continues to speak in the same dreamy voice: 'We talked about *K3G*. She called me a fluttering chiffon saree. And then she said she doesn't drink, and that she doesn't want marriage or kids, and that while she isn't a wolf or a gibbon, she isn't a bonobo either and…'

Ayesha starts to look worried.

'Aiyyo, what is this chootiya conversation.'

'Hush, auntie, let him tell.' Bongo prods Hadi. 'And?'

'… and she would want an exclusive relationship.'

'She seems to have done most of the talking,' Krish drawls.

'Yeah, but it wasn't a competition.' Hadi's voice is faraway. 'I could've traded bants much better if I hadn't just been looking at her and thinking...' He looks up impulsively, his eyes stabbing Bongo's. 'You know that beautiful script you wrote once? About a boy who dreams of buried treasure and leaves his tiny hometown to find it, and travels all over the world seeking, seeking, seeking, and finally realizes that, all this time, the treasure had been buried in his tiny hometown?'

'How beautiful,' Ayesha declares fervently. 'What a lovely story!'

'Ai, that's *The Alchemist*!' Krish gives a low rumble of laughter. 'You've been passing it off as your own writing, have you, Bongo?'

'What's *The Alchemist*?' Hadi demands.

Krish smirks. 'Ask The Plagiarist.'

Bongo goes a little red. 'Well, yes, it's *The Alchemist*,' he admits, looking annoyed. 'But Krish, *The Alchemist* isn't really original. It is based entirely on international folk-tale type 1645, "The Treasure at Home", from the Aarne-Thompson-Uther Index of folk tales.'

'You Bombay walas...' Krish shakes his head, looking amused at the glib defence.

'And Rumi and *One Thousand and One Nights* feature versions of the same story too,' Bongo continues defensively.

'Plagiarizing from multiple sources isn't plagiarizing, eh?' Krish smirks. 'Whyn't you let me have a look at this famous Scene 52? I won't leak it, promise. A fresh pair of eyes may help.'

Bongo rolls his eyes. 'Uff, the arrogance of the ignorant!'

'Can it, you guys.' Hadi springs to his feet and turns around to face them, his shoulders squared. His fond mother thinks privately that he has never looked more attractive. 'I think my treasure is at home, too.'

'Of course it is, ma!' Ayesha says ecstatically. 'What a lovely wedding we will have! All the rituals: a nikaah, and a walima, and a haldi and a fire ceremony… all the dogs can attend too, we'll put flowers in their collars and make Roganjosh carry the ring. It will be so much fun!'

'Ammi!' Hadi looks half delighted, half appalled. 'Would you please *chill*?'

'*I* know.' Ayesha gets to her feet, her eyes gleaming mischievously. 'I've packed Diwali hampers for all our Habba Galli friends. I was thinking of driving over with the maids to distribute them. You can deliver Jaishri's—but for Khuda's sake, Hadi, don't talk about wolves or bonbons!'

7

The Pilla Party Party

'Amma,' Jhoom says, picking forlornly at the rips on the knees of her baggy workpants. 'D'you remember Laiya and Gaiya Padiwal?'

Jaishri looks up, half hopeful, half wary. It is the first time Jhoom has spoken to her in over three days.

They are sitting on the couch of their faded but comfortable living room (more shabby, less chic) with the shades drawn. Jaishri's term papers are finally all corrected and she has popped a bottle of Sula white to celebrate. But it's been a pretty flat celebration, so far.

It's my own stupid fault, Jaishri thinks wretchedly. I shouldn't have blurted out my private hunch about that boy's feelings for her, and got her hopes up. Damn, it hurts when young girls go about looking so pinched and thin and colourless.

She knits her brows.

'Help me, puppy,' she says. 'Are Laiya-Gaiya the fair-and-vapid twins who like to date the same boy at the same time, or are they the sisters who used the economically backward quota to go to Sarah Lawrence even though pappa Padiwal is a multi-millionaire?'

'Both,' Jhoom replies. 'But d'you remember their old golden retriever, Macho?'

Jaishri's face brightens. 'Awweee, he was a sweetie! I used to feed him vast amounts of lychee mousse at every Laiya-Gaiya birthday party! Maiya Padiwal was so proud of her stupid homemade lychee mousse—yuck, it tasted exactly like I'd imagine human placenta to taste.'

'You did *what*?' Jhoom looks appalled. 'Wow, well, thanks to his weakness for rich sweet food, and thanks to irresponsible people like yourself who pandered to it, I had to put him to sleep today.'

Jaishri puts down her wine glass.

'Oh *no*, Jhoomie.'

Jhoom's chin quivers. 'He was such a sweet dog! He had no clue what I was gonna do. He licked my hand trustfully and looked at me with pain-glazed caramel eyes while I injected a lethal dose of ketamine and xylazine into his body.'

Jaishri scrambles over to her, concerned.

'Jhoomie! I'm so sorry.'

Jhoom shakes her head, tears dropping on her knees. 'I have a *shitty* job!'

'Have some wine!' Jaishri urges. 'Sula's not all that bad, actually.'

Jhoom blows her nose dolefully.

'You know I don't drink, amma.'

Jaishri glugs down some more wine herself.

'Well,' she says bracingly. 'Good only you put him out of his misery! Those ghastly girls are totally obsessed with social media. They would've been sharing aesthetically shot pics of his soulful suffering with their 'Gram-fam for months. #BraveTillTheGrave, #MachoTillTheLastMoment, #NotDeadTillYoureDead.'

'Amma!' Jhoom looks revolted. 'Why are you always so…'

Jaishri raises her eyebrows. 'So?'

'I don't know… brutal!'

Jaishri waves her wine glass about. 'It's the life I've led, I guess.'

Jhoom looks at her keenly. 'Are you seeing your therapist regularly?'

'Of course!' Jaishri winks. 'Why? Worried I capered down the road barefoot in my sexy negligée and put a bullet through Sushi Kedia?'

'You're impossible.' Jhoom gets to her feet.

'I'm joking, Jhoomie! Anyway, Macho lived till a ripe old age! And tomorrow, you might help a mummy-dog birth a brand new litter. Go have a bath and shake it off. The geyser's on.'

'Uff, just don't use any more "youthful" slang, okay,' Jhoom says crossly as she flounces away to the bathroom. 'I can't bear it. *On the reg* and *'Gram-fam* and *shake it off*, indeed!'

As she soaps herself under the steaming shower, Jhoom tries to figure out what is getting her down the most. The conversation she had with ACP Bhavani, which has left her feeling uneasy about her mother? Or the memory of the light fading from Macho's melting caramel eyes? Or just how patently fake Laiya-Gaiya's tears had seemed? She's nobody to judge their grief, but honestly it had been fake as fuck. As fake as the hugs the three of them had shared afterwards, and the promises they had made to 'catch up again, soonish'.

Is she doomed to feel bitter and resentful and dissatisfied around rich people for the rest of her life?

But you didn't feel bitter and resentful around Haider Sait.

Aaaand there he is, back to topping the list of things-that-have-been-getting-her-down-all-day.

She scrubs her scalp with fierce shaking fingers.

She has literally met him twice, FFS.

This is ridiculous.

And damn amma too. Where was her stupid Amma Antenna when she'd actively encouraged Jhoom to date Takshak Vasudeva? How come it hadn't warned her that *that* wasn't going to end well?

She steps out of the shower and yanks a towel angrily from the rail.

It is damp, and her mother's wet undies are hanging below it.

Gross, thanks, amma.

Sudden stupid tears sting her eyes. She blinks them away and starts to slather on moisturizer, her eyes searching for her comfiest 'jammies. I'll spend the evening putting nail polish and drinking hot chocolate and watching veterinary clinic makeovers, she tells herself determinedly. I don't care what amma says, I can be perfectly happy by myself—I do *not* need a bloody Bollywood hero to brighten up my life.

When she emerges, finger-combing her hair, she finds that Jaishri has shed her shabby maroon dressing gown, put on a pretty emerald-green silk kaftan, cleaned up the house, dimmed the lights, lit Bath & BodyWorks candles everywhere and is busily simmering a red wine risotto over the gas in a massive orange Dutch oven.

'We still have the Le Creuset?' Jhoom says, surprised. 'I thought you sold it, along with everything else we possess.'

Jaishri winks. 'I kept a few things. I'm bankrupt, not dead, though some might argue that having to drink Sula on the reg *is* dead.'

'You shouldn't be drinking at all.'

'I know my limits, magu. Now where're the sundried tomatoes?'

'We don't have sundried tomatoes,' Jhoom replies testily.

Jaishri chuckles. '*I* do,' she says, patting her breasts affectionately through her kaftan.

'Gross, mother. Also incorrect—your tomatoes are perfectly juicy.'

'Awww!' Jaishri blows her a kiss, then starts scooping out holes in a large chunk of cheese with a melon peeler.

Jhoom gasps.

'Are you trying to make that stale old Amul look like Gruyère?'

'Don't be a snob, Jhoomie, it tastes just as good. And everybody will think that my Goan sausage is imported chorizo, wait and see. Here, juice these little oranges for me— they're borderline rotting, but nobody will know if we stick them into sangria. Oooh, here's a custard apple, how posh! I didn't know we had a whole custard apple!'

'I bought it.' Jhoom looks at her suspiciously. 'Are we entertaining? How come?'

'Oh!' Jaishri waves her hands airily. 'Ayesha Sait called. She's coming this side to drop off some Diwali hampers and wanted to know if we were home. So I told her you're depressed about putting an old dog to sleep and she suggested we cheer you up by having a small send-off for Macho. And then I invited a few happy Habba peeps, for good measure.'

'Nobody says peeps, amma.'

'I do.'

'Who did you invite?'

'The pilla party,' Jaishri replies with dignity. 'They all accepted, which shows that this neighbourhood really needed this little jamboree. So basically, Mehtab bhai, Krish Chetty, Pooja Kedia, Sona Kedia…'

'But there's been a death in the Kedia family!'

'Ya, so they'll wear white chikankari and come, na. That makes it okay.'

Jhoom, wondering how a meeting between Sona and Krish will pan out, doesn't question this nicety of social etiquette.

'Did you call Harsh too or just Sona?' she asks.

'The Dark Lord's son will be at work, I think,' Jaishri replies. 'Thank God!'

'And when did Krish Chetty become pilla party?'

'Well, he was really Ayesha's suggestion, but he's nice only, no? I also called Peter Pais.'

'*Peter freakin' Pais*? Are the Kedias even talking to him?'

'Blessed are the peacemakers!' Jaishri folds her hands virtuously. 'Besides, I'm hoping to emotionally blackmail him into coughing up some funds for the pilla party after his mother pumped lead into poor Roganjosh.'

Jhoom snorts. 'As if! He'll just hand you packets of green pepper and filter coffee from his estate. He's super stingy.'

'And I went a little wild and invited Mr and Mrs Tomar as well,' Jaishri finishes, looking a little guilty.

Jhoom's mouth sags.

'*Chengez?* Why?'

Jaishri Rao wriggles her shoulders sheepishly. 'I was on the balcony, and I saw Mr Tomar walking home from work, his shoulders all slumped, and the bald spot on top of his head looked so defeated and vulnerable that I leaned down and invited him in my gayest socialite voice and he agreed to come at once.'

'But Chengez *hates* our dogs! Why would she come to a pilla party party?'

'Maybe she won't come,' Jaishri says hopefully. 'Mr Tomar might wrangle a stag evening out.'

Jhoom shakes her head at such foolish optimism.

'She'll hundred per cent come. Just so she can take a judgemental dump on all of us.'

'Arrey, Charu Tomar declines all invites featuring meat and alcohol.'

'Well, whatever.' Jhoom bends down to pick up her laptop and charger. 'I'm glad you've planned a fun evening for yourself, but I'm just gonna hang in my room, okay?'

Jaishri eyes widen. 'I need you, Jhoom. We haven't entertained in years, stay and enjoy a fun evening with me!'

'Amma,' Jhoom says patiently, 'I wish you very well with your eclectically curated crowd, but—in the hip slang you favour so much—Imma bounce. This was your bright idea, *you* handle it. Goodnight.'

Jaishri looks martyred.

'Fine, just hand me my vape before you go.'

'Oh God!' Jhoom stops in the doorway. 'Emotional blackmail?'

'You, my girl…' Jaishri points her ladle dramatically at Jhoom, '… are a horrible snob.'

Jhoom gasps. 'I am not.'

'My guests aren't good enough for you.'

'That's not true,' Jhoom replies hotly. 'I'm just not very sure it's in good taste to throw a party…'

'A send-off ceremony! For Macho!'

'… just a few days after a tragic *human* death. Also, none of these people knew Macho, I don't see why they would want to mourn him. It's just hypocritical. And thanks to your weird theories about Ayesha auntie's son and me, I am no longer comfortable hanging with her. So *if* you don't mind—'

The doorbell rings. They look at each other.

'Please, puppy,' Jaishri wheedles. 'My hands are full of cheese.'

Jhoom glares at her.

Jaishri shuts her eyes tight and blows her daughter a series of small pleading kisses.

Jhoom sighs and steps out into the tiny garden to find Pooja Kedia, Sona Kedia and Mehtab entering through the door-within-the-door, which Jaishri has welcomingly left wide open.

'Welcome!' Jhoom beams gamely and leads them into the living room.

'Drinks?' Jaishri warbles from the kitchen as they all enter. 'We have lovely fresh Nagpur oranges and red wine! Jhoom can make sangria!'

'That sounds deliciously decadent.' Sona smiles. 'I'm in!'

They all turn to look inquiringly at the new widow.

As predicted by Jaishri Rao, both Kedia women are dressed in chikankari. Pooja Kedia's face looks tranquil and unlined and the soft pastel hue of her sari makes her glow like a pink-and-white rose. She hesitates, her gaze moving to all of them one by one, before settling on Jaishri.

'Yes,' she says in a soft but firm voice. 'I would like some.'

'Excellent!' Jaishri comes up to give her a hug and bears her away into the living room.

Jhoom grabs Sona's arm.

'Amma's gone and invited Krish,' she tells her in a low voice.

Sona, very pretty in a cream salwar-kameez, stops in her tracks.

'Awwwkward.'

'I'm so sorry,' Jhoom groans. 'She's clueless, and I didn't want to tell her.'

Sona nods, conflicted, and then a fighting sparkle enters her eyes.

'Well, it had to happen some time,' she says. 'It's a small street.'

'Okay, okay.' Jhoom breathes, relieved. 'Come!'

They go into the living room together to find Pooja Kedia and Mehtab oohing and aahing over the living room.

'I love what you have done here, Jaishri,' Pooja Kedia says. 'It's such an incredibly *female* space! I love the energy!'

Jhoom looks around the room which, now that she thinks about it, is indeed aggressively bereft of any 'male' decor. It is all faded rugs and jewel-toned shabby-chic throws, with Georgia O'Keefe prints covering up the empty spaces on the walls where her parents' collection of expensive art used to hang.

'Perks of being a divorcee,' Jaishri smiles happily. '*Or* a widow!'

'Too early for that joke, mother,' Jhoom cuts in hastily. 'What are you doing on the *floor*, Mehtab bhai?'

Because the handsome Kashmiri has dropped to his hands and knees and is busy examining their moth-eaten rug.

'Beautiful!' he breathes. 'Priceless! So rare, so old, so unique!'

The Rao women stare at it dubiously.

'Really?' Jhoom asks. 'It looks so… *done*. I uploaded tons of pics of it on Etsy but couldn't snag a single bidder.'

Mehtab shakes his head. 'You have been photographing it all wrong, Jhoom gobra! The wrap and weft of hand-knotted silk rugs make them appear light when viewed from one side, and dark when viewed from the other!' He smoothens the worn supple material with his hands. 'See, come around this side and look at it.'

Jhoom steps across to look at the carpet from the angle he is recommending.

'Oh!' she exclaims, 'it's so pretty!'

'Life is like a Persian carpet!' Mehtab straightens up to a kneeling position. 'It has a light side and a dark side, and everything depends on how you look at it, yes?'

'Pop psychology, but I'll take it!' She laughs.

His hazel-green eyes twinkle. 'You are too young to be so cynical! But you just *wait*—there's a very worthy and faithful admirer coming your way!'

'What's this?' Sona asks gaily as she comes up to join them. 'Who has a faithful admirer?'

At this inopportune moment, Krish comes through the door with Mr Tomar and Peter Pais.

His eyes meet Sona's across the room and for a moment— to Jhoom, at least—the static in the room is so electric that she glances into the bar mirror to confirm her hair isn't standing on end.

'Drinks?' She smiles at the new entrants with determined cheerfulness.

Mr Tomar smiles back hesitantly and requests a 'light juice'.

Krish makes some laughing response about the choices being alcohol-only and normalcy is restored.

Twenty minutes later, well-plied with sangria, they are all talking animatedly over Jaishri's improvised charcuterie board.

'This Gruyère is divine, Jaishri auntie!' Krish declares.

'Thank you,' Jaishri replies demurely with a ghost of a wink at Jhoom.

'And these nuts are so fresh!' Peter Pais enthuses, shovelling caramelized walnuts into his mouth.

'Oh, Mehtab brought those.' Jaishri smiles at the handsome Kashmiri.

'I've started watching *Anupama* on Hotstar,' Pooja Kedia declares in the meantime, thrusting crackers into a beetroot dip with gusto. 'She is a devoted wife, mother and daughter-in-law, but then she finds out that her husband has been cheating on her for nine whole years, so she divorces him and starts her own business with the help of her college friend, who is a handsome billionaire bachelor!'

'That sort of thing is easy to do when your husband is out-and-out *hundred per cent* trash,' Jaishri muses. 'Problem is, most of them stop short of being *complete* trash, the wily dogs, and that five per cent adulteration of decency creates all the confusion!'

Murmurs of agreement greet this acute observation.

'Divorce is just so final,' Pooja Kedia muses. 'I don't know how Anupama had the guts.'

'Arrey, *marriage* is so final,' Peter Pais chimes in. 'I don't know how *anybody* has the guts!'

He laughs his high thin laugh and raises his glass.

There is a small surprised silence.

Jhoom leans forward hastily and raises her glass.

'Hear hear!' she cheers.

Everybody clinks glasses.

'I thought he was socially anxious?' Sona murmurs to Jhoom. '*Flying* tonight, isn't he?'

'How come *you're* still single, Mehtab bhai?' Krish Chetty demands. 'Are you nursing a secret passion for someone?'

The hazel-green eyes gleam within their curling lashes. 'Perhaps I am.'

'Is it a man?' Sona says at once.

'Or a married lady?' Jhoom guesses.

'Neither!' Mehtab gives a deep rumble of laughter. 'Perhaps it is no one at all!'

'Or perhaps you just… messed up,' Krish says slowly. 'You met the right person but you were too stupid to recognize that they were the right person… and you… let them go.'

Sona stiffens.

Jhoom squeezes her hand.

The other ladies murmur sympathetically.

'Ah!' Mehtab holds out his glass to Krish sorrowfully. 'You have suffered, but perhaps you have also earned a lesson, gobra! Next time somebody walks into your heart, you will be a *super*host!'

'Hear hear!' Krish's smile is rather twisted as he reaches forward to clink glasses.

'It is very common to dream about your spouse dying, I believe,' Mr Tomar volunteers to the group at large. 'Especially a spouse who is not very… nice. So one dreams that they… just… died! Painlessly, of course. It's very common, I have heard.'

He looks around the room hopefully. Almost, Jhoom thinks suddenly, like he wants to start a game of never-have-I-ever. *Never have I ever dreamt that my spouse is conveniently dead.* God, who *are* these people amma has invited over?

'That's just lazy,' Jaishri replies categorically. '*And* cowardly! I mean, if you're having issues, talk it out, *sort* it out, don't go around wishing people dead because you can't be arsed to come to grips with the situation!'

'Some people don't like confrontation,' Peter Pais weighs in. 'It's nothing to do with laziness! And sometimes, the confusion is genuine—people are pulled in two directions, conflicted, anxious to avoid causing pain to the other...'

'Uff, there's nothing more painful than procrastination!' Sona declares rather hotly. 'And *dithering*, and self-indulgent shilly-shallying and not letting people know *where* they stand!'

Jhoom kicks her friend under the table.

'So is Anupama going to marry this billionaire?' Krish's handsome eyes glitter in a face gone oddly pale. 'Coz that would be a case of out of the frying pan into the sacred fire.'

'Well said!' Jaishri raises her glass to applaud this sentiment.

'Arrey, she has *already* married him!' says mild Mr Tomar.

Everybody turns to him, wide-eyed.

'*You* watch *Anupama*, Tomarji?' Sona asks.

He blushes. 'The actress is very beautiful,' he confesses. 'In a dignified lady-wife way, you know!'

There is general hooting and cheering and catcalling.

'Anupama and Tomarji sitting in a tree, KLPPPPD!'

Mr Tomar blushes and laughs and tries to shush them, looking touchingly, almost childishly happy.

'*Such* a nice man!' Sona whispers to Jhoom. 'Thank God Chengez hasn't come! Hai-hai, how she told my MIL to go to the loo and make herself vomit! If I were him, I wouldn't just fantasize about her dying. I would *actively* work to make it happen.'

Meanwhile Pooja Kedia is still holding forth on *Anupama*.
'What is the need to rush into this new commitment?'
She frowns disapprovingly. 'She should have stayed single
and mingled for a bit!'

'Is that your plan now, Pooja auntie?' Krish asks softly.

'You *know*, Pooja,' Jaishri's voice grows chattier—a tone
Jhoom recognizes with some trepidation as her holding-forth,
hobby-horse voice, 'some people would say you are entering
the most exciting phase of your life! You're healthy, you're
gorgeous, you look no older than forty-five, you're well-
provided-for, your children are all grown up—'

'Sparshu still needs me.'

'... so you really have no responsibilities!' Jaishri waves her
glass about expansively. 'The world is your oyster! You could
go *anywhere*, do *anyone*!'

'Anything,' Sona amends hastily.

'We all get just one life,' Peter Pais says with sudden
peculiar fervour. 'We owe it to our Maker to grab it and own
it and live it to the full like the Gift it is!'

Nobody knows quite what to say to this. Probably because
Peter Pais doesn't seem to be practising what he's so fervently
preaching.

'Yes!' Jaishri reaches out and lays a hand on Pooja's arm.
'I know you are devastated that Sushi is no more, Pooja, but
if life has given you lemons, why not make lemonade?'

'Why not make margaritas?' Jhoom rises to her feet.

'If *I* were you...' Jaishri draws herself up and points
a finger impressively at Pooja Kedia, '...I would send
Peter's mother Theobroma brownies and a pitcher full of
margaritas!'

'Mummy's doctor won't allow her to consume either.' Peter Pais gives his small constipated smile. 'And the police have said quite clearly, by the way, that mummy had nothing to do with the terrible fate that befell Mr Kedia. In fact, *I* have a bone to pick with the murderer too, for trying to pin this crime on my blameless mother! If she ends up in assisted living, instead of living with her only son, it will be the murderer's fault! I hope they catch the bugger fast. I'll give him a tight one when they do. A *really* tight one!'

Nobody responds to this longish speech. Perhaps they are all suddenly conscious of the fact that they have been talking too loosely.

Then Pooja Kedia puts her glass down with a sigh. 'Do you *really* think I look forty-five?'

'Kilograms also, and years also!' Krish assures her promptly.

Pooja Kedia glows.

Just then a sturdy lady pushes her head into the living room, holding aloft a massive beribboned basket.

'Humper for Jaishri maydaam,' she says loudly.

Much raucous laughter erupts around the dining table.

'Who sent the humper?' Jaishri calls.

'Ayesha maydaam!'

This causes more inappropriate giggling. The sturdy lady holds out the hamper, looking confused.

'Ignore them, they're just being stupid.' Jhoom smiles at her kindly from the bar. 'Please leave it by the door and tell Ayesha madam thank you.'

Clearly, Ayesha auntie has had second thoughts about delivering the hamper in person. Jhoom hopes her mother won't be too disappointed.

But then a deep pleasant voice calls out: 'Sakina! Hey, no, Sakina, *I'm* delivering that one. You please go deliver the others!'

Mehtab and Krish have been struggling with a wine cork, and it comes loose with a dramatic *pop!* at this moment and flies through the room straight towards Haider Sait, who has just made his entry.

Hadi is holding the hamper now, but he still manages to put up a hand and catch the cork, causing the older women to break out in applause.

'I do my own stunts.' He grins, bowing to all of them before sauntering over to stand next to Jhoom by the bar.

'Hello.'

'Hello.' She gives him a quick smile and goes back to her mixing, appalled by how her pulse has quickened and how hot her cheeks suddenly feel.

He looks around the bar. 'Uh, can I help with anything?'

'You can squeeze lemons,' she replies briefly. 'I'm making margaritas.'

'Nice.' He slides in behind the counter and gets busy with the knife and squeezer.

Ayesha Sait enters the living room, all sparkly-eyed and rosy-cheeked, and greets her hostess effusively.

'Jaishri, this emerald-green looks amazing on you!'

'Does it?' Jaishri smoothens her kaftan. 'I'm kinda missing my famous maroon housecoat. It even has pockets!'

'Amma, please, that thing is a rag.'

'Jhoom, are you in much pain?' Ayesha walks over to the bar to ask. 'Two slaps you should be given for running out into the bullets like that!'

She always talks to Jhoom nicely, but tonight her manner seems more caressing than usual. Across the room, Jaishri quirks an eyebrow in amusement.

Jhoom feels her cheeks redden. Feeling absurdly self-conscious, she says matter-of-factly: 'I'm fine, auntie.'

'You must take care of yourself, chanda!' Ayesha says seriously. 'Thankfully, Rogu is much better too!'

Hadi, who is hovering, worried that his mother may any moment pull out a pair of fat gold bangles and clap them like handcuffs onto Jhoom's wrists, says with an uncertain laugh, 'What's this, ammi, *you* want to slap her and Jaishri auntie wants to give her a tight kick on the backside—'

'Hello, Haider!' Jaishri swaggers up to interject, beaming. 'So happy to have your hamper!' Then her grin widens, and she declaims dramatically: 'Handsome Haider Helps Hottie Haseena Host Henparty, Hoping His Humility Himpresses Her!'

'This is not a hen party,' Jhoom points out. 'If anything, there're more men than women here. They're all in that little group over there, discussing spousal culling.'

'You're definitely a Haseena, though, Jaishri auntie,' Hadi interrupts, causing her to throw him a knowing look, which immediately makes him redden and worry that he's kissing up to her too obviously.

'Are you a man hater, Jaishri?' Pooja Kedia has arrived at the bar too, waving her empty glass. 'Everybody says so!'

'Are you, Jaishri?' Ayesha asks interestedly, as a suddenly subdued Hadi pours margarita mix into all their glasses.

Jaishri takes a big glug and slams her glass down. 'I have *nothing* against the penis-dhaaris,' she says superbly. 'I do not generalize on the basis of gender. I just hate assholes—of any sex, faith, age, class and ethnicity.'

'Hear, hear!' Ayesha raises her glass.

'That's sounds reasonable,' Hadi recovers enough to say.

Pooja Kedia rests her elbow on the bar counter and cups her chin in her hands.

'And what is your definition of,' she pauses, blinks, then continues gingerly, but with great determination, 'asshole?'

'Oh God, there'll be no shutting her up now,' Jhoom groans to Hadi in a soft aside. 'Amma can hold forth on assholery for ever.'

'Do you want some fresh air?' he asks at once. 'Come, we'll go into the garden.'

'Aiyyo, it's *my* garden,' Jhoom flares at him. 'I don't need *you* to tell me to go there.'

'Whoa.' He raises his palms into the air and steps back. 'Okay, Jhoomar Rao, you do you.'

She looks at him, standing there looking so *present* and so warm-brown, and the sharp tense achiness that has had her in its grip all day eases away.

'Grab a margarita,' she says. 'And we'll go into my garden.'

The garden isn't looking its best. There's the usual pile of cages and a faint smell of sewage. But the parijat tree in the corner is trying valiantly to add a bit of romance to the proceedings. Hadi decides to try valiantly too.

He drops down on the bench below the scraggy tree and holds out a hand to her. 'Sit, na.'

She sits down beside him, dragging her loose sweater over her knees and folding her bare legs up to her chest.

'I'm so sorry about Macho.'

She sighs. 'I'm not sure why I'm feeling so shitty about it. I mean, I've done it before, plenty of times, it's no big—if they're old or suffering, it's good to give them their release. But Macho trusted me so much, he was never scared of visits to the vet. He died licking my hand and thinking I was gonna make him well, like always.'

'And you did,' Hadi says steadily.

'Yeeeaaah.' She shakes her head. 'I don't know, dude, like if there's a doggie heaven, or any heaven at all. *And* it also got me thinking about the murderer—*our* murderer, you know, the one who's on the loose.' She shivers.

Hadi frowns. 'Maybe there's no murderer. It could well be an accident.'

She gives a short mirthless laugh. 'Nope. The police have ruled out that possibility quite definitely.'

'Do you suspect somebody?'

She looks troubled. 'No, well, maybe…' She gives a firm shake of the head. 'No.'

'Hey, you don't have to tell *me*,' he replies. 'But maybe tell ACP Bhavani? He seems like a real pro.'

She shakes her head violently and looks away.

'Though, I must say,' Hadi's voice grows lighter, 'I'm a little hurt you won't confide in me, considering we've trauma-bonded and all!'

She tilts her head up to shoot him a sideways smile. 'I never did thank you for running up to help that day, did I? Thank you.'

'Don't be silly.'

He sips his drink, embarrassed. 'Would you be upset if I wanted to offer some financial help to the clinic?' he says presently. 'This way you can treat more street animals? Please let me.'

'Oh, I'm good.' There is a touch of hauteur to her voice, 'We get by. The rich pooches subsidize the streeties. But if there's any special need, I'll reach out for sure.'

'Do that.' His voice is sincere, but Jhoom finds she's kinda pissed. It's a bit irritating to be offered a handout from somebody who from childhood she has always vaguely thought of as... oh, not a source of wealth, let us say! I'm being a classist cow, she tells herself and quickly raises her head.

'Actually,' she says contritely, 'I'd be happy to accept help for the power back-up.'

Delight floods his face. 'Great!' he says. 'Somebody from my team will call you first thing tomorrow.'

'Awesome.' She smiles. 'Thank you.'

'You're welcome.'

She stares at the parijat tree while he sips his margarita.

'What's it like being a big movie star?' she asks finally. 'Do you have to work very hard? Are you always on a diet?'

'Yes and yes,' he replies. 'But entertaining people is my thing. I *love* doing it.'

Jhoom pulls a face. 'You really like people, huh?'

'You don't?'

She looks towards the living room, from where comes the sound of laughter and drunken singing.

'I didn't trust them for a while,' she admits. 'But now, maybe… no, I still don't.'

Hadi has a vivid heartbreaking flashback of Jhoomar Rao, sunglassed, red-lipped and fabulous, dressed in a strappy silver sheath dress, getting into the front seat of a silver Mercedes as Tatti Vasudeva holds the door open for her with a sappy look on his face, and finds himself overcome with a desire to reach out and crush her in a nose-flattening hug against his recently worked-out chest.

With a start he realizes she is speaking.

'Sorry?' he asks.

'Have you always lived in that house?' she repeats. 'Across the road?'

'I was born there,' he says lightly. 'It was a single-storey house. Then my dad landed an extra-big order for cashew nuts and suddenly we could afford to put a second floor. I remember that day so clearly.'

He had run barefoot up the newly cemented steps, so cool and damp and echoing, clasped his hands on the smooth iron grill of the wooden window, looked down into the very courtyard they are sitting in now and been rewarded by the sight of twelve-year-old Jhoomar Rao practising her Bharatanatyam.

'How nice,' she says wistfully. 'Do you miss him?'

For a moment he doesn't know whom she means. Then he nods.

'Yeah… He was much older than ammi, and he was pretty traditional. Conservative, I mean. She had a hard time persuading him to let me go to Joseph's. He'd have preferred Islahul Banath.'

'Are you very religious?'

He looks towards the massive open door at the front of the house. 'Ammi believes in Habba Galli,' he says simply. 'You know, you really missed out, Jhoom. That big-ass door of yours was always shut in the old days. And outside that door, we were constantly celebrating every Habba on the calender! Weddings and births and Eid and Ganapati and Varamahalakshmi Puja and World Cup finals and husbands and wives quarrelling and buyers and sellers all swearing at each other! Peter Pais taught us how to play pool on a scuffed second-hand table, and we spent one entire summer learning to skate on the main road, and somebody leaked the ISC math final paper and we all scored perfect centums… And then there were all these house parties, mostly at Krish's coz he was so handsome and had a fancy house and the best sound system.'

'Krish *was* quite the stud muffin,' Jhoom says. 'I sort of knew him, growing up. But not you.'

'No, we were never introduced.'

Something in his tone makes her glance up at his face, arrested, but he's just looking at the parijat tree, his expression thoughtful.

'I had an argument with Krish about it,' he says slowly. 'I felt he was too attached to the neighbourhood. I told him to look beyond, strike out, widen his horizons... But maybe I was wrong. Living in Habbi Galli rocks.'

'Ai, there's no right or wrong,' is Jhoom's bracing reply. 'He's your childhood friend, it's your duty to give him honest feedback. I'm sure he doesn't spare his punches when he doesn't like your movies!'

He stares at her, feeling much lighter. 'True!'

'Did *he* say something to you?' she asks impulsively. 'That made you think it was me who called it quits with my fiancé, not the other way around? I mean, how did you guess?'

His eyebrows rise.

'Well, it's only polite to work with the assumption that the person you're talking to is the dumper, not the dumpee, isn't it?'

She looks disappointed. 'Ye-es.'

Hadi's eyes start to dance. 'Besides, you're undumpable, Jhoomar Rao,' he drawls. 'No man, having got you, would ever let you go. There, isn't that what you wanted me to say?'

She blushes.

'Yes,' she sighs happily. 'That's *so* much better. Thank you!'

He grins, then says impulsively, 'Hey, you *know* about...'

He checks himself.

She looks up at him questioningly.

'I know about... what?'

Watching her carefully, he says, 'About Krish's old equation with...?'

His voice trails off.

'Sona?' she mouths the name softly.

He nods, relieved.

'Yes,' she says. 'Harsh knows too.'

'He does?' Hadi looks surprised.

Jhoom nods.

'He's chill with it as long as they don't talk any more.'

He nods towards the living room. 'Well, they're talking now.'

'Shit.' Jhoom whirls to look through the grilled windows. Sure enough, Sona and Krish appear to be deep in conversation over the sangria pitcher.

'I should go in.' Jhoom starts to her feet, conscience-stricken.

'Ai, they're consenting adults,' he says. 'Stay.'

Jhoom shakes her head. 'You don't know anything. Sona's sensible—and sorted—and *into* her husband—but Krish has this weird *hold* on her.'

'Not any more,' Hadi replies. 'She's telling him to fuck off—look.'

Jhoom looks. Sona's body language is clearly dismissive. As they watch, she tosses her head, picks up the pitcher and stalks off with it, leaving Krish lounging at the bar and smirking in a foolish sort of way.

'Ouch.' Hadi winces.

Jhoom chuckles. '*Good girl!*'

As she speaks, her hands slide automatically into her pyjama pockets.

Something clicks into place for Hadi.

'*That* explains it!'

Jhoom looks around.

'What?'

'You keep dog treats in your pockets.' He grins. 'You hand them out to good girls and good boys.'

'Yes.' She looks mystified, then self-conscious. 'What does it explain? Why I reek of meat?'

'Not all the time.' He laughs. 'Only if one gets real close, like in the surgery that night, when the lights went off, then yes.'

'Then?' She looks mortified. 'Oh God, not *then*! I thought we were having a mom—'

She stops abruptly.

He raises an eyebrow. 'Having a… *mom*?'

'Oh God!'

He tilts his head. 'A momo?'

She shakes her head, her cheeks flaming.

'A *moment*!' Hadi drawls, delighted. 'You thought we were having a moment, then!'

She tightens her lips, rises to her feet and walks to the front of the garden to bolt the door-within-the-door.

Hadi lounges back and watches her, not bothering to hide the fact that his dark eyes are savouring her every movement.

She's wearing a loose navy-blue jumper over tiny white satin shorts and pink fluffy slippers. Her toes are unpainted and very clean. Her hair is midnight dark, and after years of shooting with actresses under every kind of lighting, he can tell that she's wearing no make-up at all.

She bolts the door and walks back. He's expecting her to come and sit down beside him again, but instead she stands over him, challenge shining bright in her eyes.

'Well, weren't we?' she asks, point-blank.

It is his turn to redden now. His eyes drop.

'We were,' he admits, very low.

'I'm glad that's clear,' she says, satisfied. 'Don't push me-aa, Hadi Sait, coz I'll push right back.'

She turns around to sit but he reaches out and grabs her wrist.

His voice is silky, it is his movie-star voice, his most elemental voice.

'And we're having a moment now.'

He tugs at her wrist. It is a gentle jerk, but it is enough to pull her up short and tumble her neatly into his lap.

'Oh!' Jhoom lands with her back against his chest, breathless, tangle-haired and very flushed. 'You did that so well!'

But Hadi cannot speak. The fact that this girl, this particular, spectacular girl, is sitting in his lap and seems to like it there, has rendered him entirely speechless. Overcome with emotion, he holds her warm slender body to him, his hands trembling, his face buried in her shoulder, half submerged in the masses of her incredibly soft dark hair.

After a while Jhoom says softly, 'Hey? Reek or no reek?'

But he just shakes his head and doesn't speak.

So she lifts his loosely fisted hand and lays her cheek gently against his knuckles.

They are still sitting there when the doorbell rings fifteen minutes later. The Kedia boys have arrived, uninvited, to join the party.

8

Ketamine and Xylazine

When Jhoom wakes up the next morning, she finds her mother wandering around the house in her grubby maroon dressing gown, painstakingly pressing crumbled bits of cake back together, scraping up leftover sausage, pouring out the dregs of juice cartons and carefully packing food into airtight boxes.

'People waste so much food! See, Jhoom, a perfectly good half-eaten chunk of sausage lying under the sofa. Should I have it for breakfast?'

'Amma!' Jhoom rushes over and snatches the plate out of her hand. 'Don't be so dramatic.'

Jaishri rubs her eyes tiredly. 'I dreamed I murdered your appa, buried him in the courtyard, and was doomed to spend the rest of my life crucified by guilt.'

'Not by the fear of getting caught?'

'Nah. I covered up my tracks too well.'

'Oh, well.' Jhoom thumps Jaishri's back comfortingly. 'You must've been happy to wake up.'

'I was!' Jaishri lays both hands on her bosom fervently. 'The flood of relief! It's always exquisite! The moment you realize it's okay, and that you do *not* have blood on your hands, after all!'

She reaches for the half-eaten sausage with animation, but Jhoom wards her off.

'Hey, how about the fact that you just threw an awesome party? It reminded me of the times when you'd casually host magnificently successful parties every weekend!'

'For rather a different sort of crowd, though!' Jaishri's smile is wobbly.

'These are *nice* people!' Jhoom exclaims. 'I don't care that they don't have Bangalore Club memberships. Plus, they will invite us back, which most of those freeloaders never did!'

'Good,' says her mother feelingly, 'because I just blew my entire Big Market budget for the month in one night. It's gonna be curd-rice and papad till the first of next month now.'

'I love curd-rice and papad,' is Jhoom's firm reply. 'And everybody owes us a party now, so we can look forward to that!'

Jaishri sniffs.

'Harsh Kedia is a pompous prick,' she says. 'How he came and gathered up his womenfolk like they were cattle that had strayed! He single-handedly shut down the party.'

'Pooja auntie had fun, I think,' Jhoom says.

'Oh, yes!' Jaishri brightens up. 'And I had frisson with Mehtab bhai! But what's with that Krish Chetty? So grumpy!' After considering the point for a while, she adds, '*And* pudgy.'

'Hot Chocolate Pudge,' Jhoom says wryly, which makes Jaishri snort with laughter.

'His *friend*, though!' She digs Jhoom in the ribs. 'What were you two doing in the garden? Helu?'

Jhoom's face reddens.

'Uff, go check your term papers, amma.'

'Hah!' Jaishri cackles gleefully. 'You can't say that any more. I've checked them *all*! Yay!'

'Are you still mad at me?'

Thus Harsh, softly, to his wife in their bedroom over morning tea.

She tightens her lips and stalks into the bathroom without replying.

Harsh sips his tea and stares out at the garden with unseeing eyes.

When she emerges, dressed for the day, looking heavy-eyed but still incredibly lovely, he says, 'Sona, you took my just-widowed mother to a *party*! How was that wise?'

She shrugs. 'I thought mummyji needed an outlet. She's been behaving so oddly.'

'Yes, but a party hosted by that loose-nut Jaishri Rao? Full of Habba Galli riff-raff? When there's a *murderer* on the loose? *C'mon!*'

She throws him a scornful look as she slips on her earrings.

'You're just angry because Krish was there. At least don't be a hypocrite.'

'Fine.' Harsh's jaw hardens. 'That's a factor too. Chetty's presence there pissed me off big time.'

She sits down on the bed.

'Well then, that makes the two of us,' she says candidly. 'I wouldn't have gone if I'd known he'd be there, believe me. It's much too painful.'

Harsh sets his teacup down abruptly.

Sona winces. 'Don't, Harshu, you'll break it.'

'You're never going to be indifferent to him, are you?'

She shrugs. 'I guess not. But then, I'm not indifferent to snakes either. I just... avoid them.'

'That's not what papa said,' Harsh says, very low.

She looks up, startled. 'What?'

He looks up at her with tortured eyes. 'He told me you guys are still meeting. He said he saw the two of you together at the Westend when he went there for the Jewellery Expo. He said I was a fool to trust you. Am I?'

In the veranda of The Hub, a shirtless Krish Chetty is practising potting shots on his pool table. He moves with the lithe grace of an expert, his eyes narrowed over the smoke rising from the cigarette between his shapely lips.

'You should stub out your cigarette and pick up some dumbbells, Krishji,' calls Bhavani, who has just finished his 5BX workout and is sitting cross-legged in prapti-mudra in the sun. 'With your height and your broad shoulders, it will nat take you more than three months to look like a browner Hrithik Roshan.'

Krish looks up at him briefly, then goes back to focusing on his shot. 'Been there, done that.' He grins wryly. 'I'm happy as I am.'

'Leave the boy alone, Bhavani,' Shalini calls from her chaise longue under the parijat tree. 'Can't you see he's hungover?'

Bhavani clicks his tongue sympathetically.

'You were socializing last night?' Bhavani asks. 'With friends? A special lady, perhaps?'

Krish gives him a quizzical glance. 'Speaking as my guest or as an ACP, Bhavani uncle?'

Bhavani gets slowly to his feet and ambles over to lean against the baize table. 'As Dilli Police,' he says simply. 'You do realize that your past association with Sona Kedia brings you under our scanner? And there is also this argooment between you and Sushil Kedia and Peter Pais?'

'Sona and I haven't spoken in four years,' Krish says curtly, straightening up and leaning on his cue stick. 'As for her dear departed father-in-law, he barged in here accusing me of cheating the kid and indulging in game-fixing—which is ridiculous because our buy-in is pathetically low and it's a standard table, and anyway Sparsh always brings his own cues in that hard case of his.'

'And he believed you?'

Krish shrugs. 'I think so, yeah. He was more pissed off about Sparsh hanging with Peter Pais, actually, which I can understand. Pais is definitely odd. I'm sort of glad our little threesome broke up, really.'

'Odd in what way?'

Krish bends over the table again. 'God-odd.' He rolls his eyes. 'Always rushing off to church.'

Mild Mr Tomar had returned from the pilla party party inebriated, invigorated and ready to defend himself for accepting the invitation to dine at the heritage (albeit crumbling) home of the most glamorous ladies in the galli, but gallingly, his Charu had been unusually disinterested in his doings.

'Bhai, I toh enjoyed myself thoroughly!' he had declared when he burst into the bedroom well past midnight with his chest puffed out. 'Such A-class people! Such high-level food and drink! Mrs Rao, so sparkling and refreshingly frank! So brave too, living all alone and being financially independent! She was even doing all the cooking and serving herself—there were no servants or helpers around. And you know, Charu, I don't know how they did it, there were no air-conditioners anywhere but the house was so cool and airy, with small-small flames everywhere and *such* a lovely smell!'

'It's the smell of divorce, Tomarji,' Charu Tomar had yawned dismissively. 'And imported candles.'

Refusing to be deflated by this tepid response, he elaborated on the topics of conversation that had been discussed, the racy language, all the new ideas that the younger people and the single older ladies had been bouncing back and forth.

'You should have come, Charu!' he concluded. 'You would have enjoyed.'

But all Charu had said rather absently was, 'Can you off-the-light and on-the-AC, please? I have a headache.'

Lying quietly in the darkness, he had replayed the evening in his mind. Jaishri Rao, Pooja Kedia, Ayesha Sait, they were all incredibly pleasant women. It had been the nicest socializing he had ever done, he decided sleepily. And also… Mr Tomar struggled to pinpoint his feelings… he had sensed a sort of freedom and lightness in the Rao mansion. Like their Isht devi or cherished goddess was somebody pagan who didn't damn care about rules or consequences or anything!

He had woken up this morning, fed his squirrels and gone off to work, still in a jaunty mood. Charu had still been a little stand-offish, but he hadn't let that affect him.

Now, as he returns from work, he finds the NationNow! van parked outside his narrow gate.

'Not again,' he mutters as he squares his shoulders and enters the house.

Inside, the mood is subdued. The press team is huddled around the dining table, and he can see on the monitor screens they have set up that the fire-breathing anchor is on standby, but Charu is nowhere to be seen.

'Madam yellidare?' he asks Saraswati, who is serving tea and refreshments to the press team. 'Getting ready?'

She shakes her head. 'Maydaam resting.'

Mr Tomar is impressed. His wife seems to have become Kareena Kapoor, keeping the paparazzi waiting!

'Please, Mr Tomar!' the famous anchor voice sounds, electronically amplified, from his screen. 'Could you ask Mrs Tomar to join us? She had requested a satellite link as she has a major disclosure to make to us.'

Supressing a pleasurable thrill at being addressed so deferentially by a celebrity, Mr Tomar nods.

'I'll check on Charu,' he says and starts to climb the narrow stairs, Saraswati hot on his heels, bearing a tea tray.

They enter the darkened bedroom together.

'Hello, hello, what is this?' says Mr Tomar briskly. 'Charu, NationNow! is waiting for you downstairs!'

But Charu Tomar does not stir.

'Charu,' Mr Tomar repeats as he turns on the lights, 'get up.'

The figure on the bed remains motionless.

The tray starts to tremble in Saraswati's hands. Her eyes fill with dread, she gives a little gasp.

Mr Tomar shoots her a mildly reproving look. 'My good woman, everyone who doesn't get up to drink their tea is not *dead*,' he says. 'I have seen Charu's janampatri and she is destined to outlive me by two whole decades! I understand that you have been traumatized, but please do not create a scene.' He goes closer to the recumbent figure on the bed and pulls back the quilt. 'Charu, come, wake—'

And then he stops.

Because Charu Tomar's body is cold and far too still. Her eyes are closed and her face looks curiously slack, the tongue lolling lightly. He pulls the quilt entirely off her body and realizes there is a small wet patch on the bed below her.

As he straightens up, pale-faced and shaking, Saraswati lets out a long low wail and sinks to the ground.

'Aiiiyyyyyyo… yella janaru heltaare naanu murderer anta! Naanu murderer alla!'

Mr Tomar ignores her. He sits heavily on the edge of the dead woman's bed and pushes back his thinning hair with shaky hands.

The NationNow! crew stampedes their way up to the bedroom, all inquisitive eyes and rolling cameras, and hushes the wailing Saraswati.

'You silly woman, nobody will say you did it!'

But Saraswati's denials only grow louder and more mournful.

'Naanu murderer alla!'

The abrupt demise of Charu Tomar explodes like a bomb on the nation's mediascape, with NationNow! not even bothering to hide its ecstasy about being on the spot, perhaps even the cause of the death.

'What did Charu Tomar *know*?' the anchor thunders. 'What was she about to tell us? *Why* did she call for an interview with *us*, India's most trusted and followed news channel?'

DG Gautham calls Bhavani, sounding hysterical, from the banquet hall of the five-star hotel which is to be the venue of his daughter's wedding.

All the news channels call Bhavani, demanding updates, action, justice and the head of Haider Sait on a platter.

He ignores all the calls, turns off the TV and plaintively asks Shalini for a glass of warm milk.

'Well, that puts an end to the accident vs deliberate murder debate once and for all,' she says as she places it at his elbow. 'Doesn't it?'

He picks up the glass and drains the milk in a series of steady ghut-ghut-ghuts.

'Yes,' he says, putting it down with a sigh.

She looks at him with concern. 'Bhavani, this was supposed to be a holiday.'

He grimaces. 'That silly lady, we dismissed her as a giddy gossip, but there must have been truth in at least one of her wild accusations.'

'Your phone is ringing again.'

He scowls, pushing it away, then sees the caller ID and grabs it eagerly.

'Daaktar sa'ab!'

'I told you to watch out for that woman.'

Bhavani hangs his head.

'You did, you did.'

'Well, don't beat yourself up about it!' Krishnan says gruffly. 'Here's the thing—she had been dead for at least eight hours.'

Bhavani nods several times.

'We found a needle prick in the upper left thigh,' Krishnan continues. 'From the angle it seems to have been self-administered by the right hand, intra-muscularly. Did you find anything in the house that corresponds to that?'

Bhavani sticks out his lower lip thoughtfully.

'The packaging of a Lasix injection was found in the dustbin of the en suite bathroom,' he offers.

'Lasix? That's furosemide, a diuretic. Makes you pee like a horse.'

'Yes, yes, that is what Manju also discovered on Google.'

'Google!' Krishnan scoffs. 'Fine way to conduct research! What else does Google say?'

'That ladies abuse it for cosmetic purposes sometimes. To look sleeker and less puffy.'

'Hmm, this woman was a hefty specimen, could've done with a little de-puffing, I suppose. Then again, I haven't seen her at her best—I daresay she was an attractive woman when animated by the spark of life. She had a nice shapely nose too. Think she knew whodunnit? So the murderer came calling for her?'

Bhavani spreads out his hands.

'Maybe, or maybe this death and that one are entirely unconnected.'

'Trust you to make things more torturous than they are! How did the Lasix reach her anyway? Did she have a stash of the stuff?'

'We found SpeeDart courier packaging in the dustbin. We checked with SpeeDart, and they confirmed that while she did order it via them, their parcel will nat be out for delivery for another two days.'

'So somebody left a fake SpeeDart parcel at her door, and she thought it had arrived early and took it in and consumed it?'

'That's the theory, yes.'

'Well, I can tell you this, whatever there is in her system, it isn't furosemide.'

'When will we know what it is, daaktar sa'ab?'

'We're working on it,' Krishnan says non-committally. 'Checking for all kinds of things. It could take a few days. I'll get back to you as soon as I can.'

'Hello.'

The voice is awkward but determined, and not entirely unexpected.

Bhavani looks up. He has been sitting on the red plastered bench cemented into The Hub's courtyard, frowning at the fallen flowers of the parijat tree for quite a while now.

'Hello, Jhoomji.'

She walks up slowly. Her usually vivid face is pale, her hair lank and there are purplish smudges under her eyes. She sits down beside him heavily, without any trace of her usual springiness.

In *three*, Bhavani counts internally. In *two*. In *one*.

'I heard Mrs Tomar is dead.'

'Yes.'

'Do you know...' she begins uncertainly, then trails off. 'Has there been any...' She stops again, then raises her chin and asks steadily, 'I mean, do you know why she died?'

He shakes his head gravely. 'She took an injection. Something she had been taking regularly, but we suspect the ampoule inside the packaging had been switched. It arrived by SpeeDart freshly that day.'

'Oh.' She gives a strangled gasp.

He looks at her more carefully.

'Do you have something to tell us, Jhoomji?'

She swallows. 'Well, first of all, I'd like to apologize for my random outburst that day. Murder is murder, you are just doing your job and I acted like a judgy, self-righteous cow.'

'Do nat call cows judgy and self-righteous,' he says genially. 'The right-wingers will get after you.'

Jhoom continues to look wretched.

He leans forward.

'What is it, Jhoomji?'

She takes a deep breath and says all in a rush, 'There's a combination of drugs I use for euthanasia of old or sick animals. Ketamine and xylazine. It's given intra-muscularly and you don't need to be medically trained to administer it.'

Bhavani's face changes. 'We see.'

'I used it to put down an old golden retriever two days ago. He was a big boy, so I had procured a fairly large dose. But when he came to the clinic he had grown so frail that I didn't end up using too much. Anyway, there was a largeish amount of ketamine and xylazine left in my clinic cupboard.' She swallows hard and raises fearful eyes to meet his grave ones. 'And now it's missing.'

'We see.' Bhavani is quiet for a while, waiting to see if she will say anything more.

She doesn't.

'You did the right thing by coming to us,' he says finally. 'This is very important information. One moment please, while we send a message. How do you spell keta…?'

'Here, let me do it.' She takes his phone, types out the name and watches while he sends it.

'Now tell us everything, Jhoomji,' Bhavani says, stowing his phone away. 'Take your time. There is no hurry.'

She pushes her heavy hair off her forehead, her eyes traumatized.

'The trouble is that my mother decided to throw an impromptu party that night, so there were many people in my house and the store cupboard is en route to the loo…'

'Haule-haule, Jhoomji. Tell us about the whole evening— how it began, how it unfolded, in sequence, do nat rush ahead.'

Jhoom nods, draws a deep calming breath and closes her eyes. She is quiet for a moment, then she opens them again and begins to speak. Bhavani listens silently, his entire being radiating sympathy, rather like a three-wick Bath & BodyWorks candle radiates fragrance, Jhoom thinks, with a random rush of affection for the homely old man.

She censors her conversation with Hadi a little, but is otherwise faithful in her retelling.

'So Mehtab bhai lectured about carpets having a light side and dark side, just like life, and Mr Tomar talked about the *Anupama* serial, and everybody urged Pooja Kedia to make margaritas with the lemons life had given her?'

She nods. 'Pretty much.'

'And they all knew the party was #RIPMacho, so they could assume that the medicines you used on him were at hand?'

'Yes,' she says wretchedly.

'How did your mother suddenly get the idea to throw this party?'

Jhoom knits her strong brows.

'It happened while I went in to bathe. Amma said Ayesha Sait phoned and asked to drop in, and when amma mentioned that I was low about putting down a childhood friend's dog, Ayesha auntie suggested staying over for dinner to cheer me up. And then amma decided to invite a few other people as well.'

'We see. So it could have been Ayeshaji's suggestion to have this little memorial dinner.'

She raises troubled eyes to his.

'Yes.' Jhoom nods.

'When did you realize the meds were missing, Jhoomji?' Bhavani asks.

'I do a daily stocktaking before I lock up at night. So I noticed last night itself. But amma had gone a little crazy cleaning up the place for her party and could've shoved it somewhere. Then, this morning, Saraswati came wailing down the road lamenting Mrs Tomar's death, and I don't know, I had a sick sort of feeling, so I came here to tell you about it, in case it proves to be...' she pauses, swallowing hard, 'I don't know... relevant?'

'Thank you. You have done the right thing.'

She looks relieved. 'So you don't think it is him, then? Hadi, I mean?'

He leans forward. 'What do *you* think?'

'I don't know what to think!' She throws up her hands. 'Sushi Kedia was not a nice person, I mean, his *widow* attended amma's party and got happily wasted in white chikankari! Doesn't that tell you something?'

'And Charu Tomar?'

'Also not a likely winner of a popularity contest. Oh God!' She looks horrified. 'I sound like a murderer myself!'

He twinkles. 'And your motive would be?'

'Oh, just his general obnoxiousness, I guess. His behaviour towards the dogs, *and* his family.'

'Jhoomji.' Bhavani's eyes are kind. 'We may be from Delhi but we do have local police working on this case, you know.'

Multiple expressions chase each other across her expressive face.

'What do you mean?' she falters.

He leans forward and says gently, 'We know Sushil Kedia was your mother's go-to jeweller for years and was, to use her own words, "A nauseating kiss-up!" But recently, he barely gave her the time of day when she visited the flagship Kedia Store to try and exchange the pieces she had bought from him over the years for 926-grade gold coins. It all got quite nasty, we heard.'

'*What?*' Jhoom's eyes narrow. 'What happened?' she demands. 'That snake Sushil Kedia had the guts to get uppity with my *mother*?'

He nods. 'Apparently. According to our informant, when he refused to budge from the price he quoted, she accused him of being a fair-weather friend and he told her, with perfect politeness, that that they had never been friends, just business associates.'

'The *fucktard*!' Jhoom breathes hard. 'He was an absolute *nobody* when amma and appa gave him so much business! He had *one* small shop! And what *really* hurts,' her voice breaks, 'is that amma never told me he was rude to her! She came back home and said she didn't have the heart to sell her pretty jewels! And she tells me *everything*. I mean, she never used to before—before the divorce, I mean—but now we're friends more than parent and child, and she treats me like an adult. Now she's going around swallowing insults silently from a piece of *shit* like that Sushi. What the hell, amma!'

She sits staring at the parijat tree in a state of utter shock.

Bhavani remains silent, absorbing the vehemence of this little speech. For all her protestations, Jhoomar's humility and the cheerfulness with which she has embraced her new poverty, both she and her mother unconsciously retain the entitlement and snobbery that come with their class. *And* caste.

'Who told you all this?' she asks him abruptly. 'She did? Someone at the store? Or her therapist? She cannot betray client confidentiality like this!'

'So your mother has a therapist,' Bhavani says gently.

Jhoom colours. 'So what? She's been through a lot—the divorce, the bankruptcy, the break-up of my engagement! On top of that, she's menopausal and working a job for the first time in her life! She needs to look after her mental health!'

'We did nat meet her therapist,' Bhavani reassures her. 'The information came from the salesgirls at the big Kedia Jewellers store on Commercial Street.'

'Oh.'

Bhavani continues matter-of-factly, 'Jhoomarji, you should realize that if this missing medication turns out to be what finished Mrs Tomar off, then it could be argued that your mother threw a party in order to lengthen the list of the people who had easy access to it.'

Her eyes widen. 'Why would I come over and tell you the name of the drugs if that was the case?'

'Because she did nat take you into her confidence. Or perhaps she did, and you are intelligent enough to know that we would discover the names of the drugs eventually.'

She stares at him for a moment then gives a short disbelieving laugh.

'Dude, that's so convoluted!'

He spreads out his hands. 'Who throws a spontaneous party in order to cope with the trauma of putting down an old dog? After not throwing a party for three whole years?'

Jhoom rises to her feet, her expression stricken.

'So you suspect amma. You think *she* picked up the shotgun and put down Sushi Kedia. And Charu Tomar saw amma, so amma neutralized her with a dose of Macho's meds. My *mother*—an absent-minded, single working woman and reluctant academic who struggles to correct forty term papers and submit them in time.'

'It is our job to investigate everybody,' he says gravely. 'Haider Sait, his mother, your mother, you. So do nat feel too singled out. And thank you again for your information.'

'It's the veterinary preparation only,' Dr Krishnan says briskly. 'Ketamine and xylazine. Death would have occurred about twenty minutes after it was administered, followed by a voiding of the bladder. Who put you on the right track?'

'The local veterinarian. Her supplies had been plundered.'

'So somebody who wanted the hefty lady dead switched her water-loss furosemide with the ketamine-xylazine mix, is it?'

'That is our theory, yes.'

'Because she had seen or heard something?'

'Yes.'

'And what did she see?'

'That is a question she is no longer around to answer. But we will find out.'

'You don't think it's this actor fellow?'

'Nat for the motive that is being touted by the media, definitely. Certain other motives are suggesting themselves, however.'

'So what are you thinking, Bhavani?'

'We are thinking, duck sa'ab, that we will begin this phase of the investigation with a heart-to-heart chat with the grieving widower.'

Tomar Tools and Hardware is a medium-sized shop, indistinguishable from the many similar shops that line both sides of the mosque-end of Dispensary Road. Half the hardware sits upon the shelves inside, while the rest is piled up on the pavement, watched over by two scruffy young helpers who perch on electric-blue aluminum painter stools, alternately chatting and scrolling on their phones.

They look up when ACP Bhavani and Inspector Naik greet them, their faces curious but untroubled, and tell the policemen, without getting up, that the owner is inside.

Soon, Bhavani and Naik are seated before the newly minted widower. Bhavani has been provided with a dusty stool, while Naik sits upon an upended twenty-litre Asian Paints drum, an arrangement which makes Naik recall, humiliatingly, the excerpt from his class six English chapter that dealt with the eccentric knight Don Quixote and his faithful sidekick Sancho Panza.

Mr Tomar accepts their condolences with a murmur and a shake of the head. His wispy grey hair is in disarray, his kurta-pyjama crumpled, but he seems calm enough otherwise. His eyes, when he finally makes eye contact, are vaguely worried, but only, it seems, about playing host.

'Will you take tea?'

Bhavani shakes his head. 'We have taken.'

'Oh.' Mr Tomar looks relieved for a moment, then grows anxious again. 'A cold drink, then? Or I can ask the boys to bring biscuits.' His eyes brighten. 'The coconut-cream ones are very good.'

'No, thank you.'

There is a small garlanded photograph of Charu Tomar in the small wooden temple behind Mr Tomar's head. She looks young and soft and classically beautiful. It is a pre-Chengez-era photograph.

'I didn't know what to do at home,' Mr Tomar says after a while. 'My son and daughter-in-law have arrived from Bhopal and taken charge of the funeral proceedings, and Saraswati is there… and I just felt useless!'

His pudgy chin wobbles. Outside, on the blue aluminum stools, his two assistants are still fiddling with their phones but perfunctorily now, having clearly tuned in to the conversation within.

Naik shifts his buttocks about to get more comfortable on the upturned drum and asks, 'Why did your wife contact the news channel, Mr Tomar? What did she want to tell them? Did she confide in you?'

Mr Tomar shakes his head slowly, deliberately, from side to side. Naik finds himself thinking of bull elephants shaking off flies.

'Let me tell you something about my wife. She craved attention. It was food and drink to her. So one thing I do know, and that is the thing I am drawing strength from at this sad, sad time, is that she would have been highly gratified by the attention her death is getting from the press.'

Young Naik is rather taken aback by this statement, but Bhavani nods in understanding.

'She has gone out in a blaze of glory,' he murmurs. 'With the eyes of the whole nation upon her. She has become a personage, a celebrity.'

'Yes!' The mild eyes gleam in acknowledgement of being so quickly understood. 'Now let me tell you one more thing—in complete confidence, because while I do want the murderer to be caught, I do not want my wife to be publicly labelled a liar either. Here is the thing, and I swear on my one and only granddaughter that it is the truth and nothing but the truth!'

He edges forward. Bhavani edges forward too.

They might as well kiss, Naik thinks upon his drum.

Mr Tomar states softly but emphatically: '*Charu never went out into the balcony on Karwa Chauth night. She slept right through the storm.* I woke up, I saw the thunder and lightning and I lay awake, hoping the squirrels were safe. But Charu did not stir. She never saw or heard *anything*.'

He sits back.

Bhavani sits back slowly too.

'So these interviews she gave to the news channels?' he murmurs.

'Made-up stories,' Mr Tomar replies with a quiet shake of the head. 'Lies!' Then he grows more agitated. 'Pure fabrication! Arrey, what-what to tell! *How* to even explain to you!'

Bhavani bows his head and utters a gentle encouraging sound, the kind a loving mother might make to coax her toddler, seated upon a potty, to try harder.

Mr Tomar tries harder.

'You see, my Charu had an inferiority complex. Because we aren't as rich as the ladies she wanted to be friends with, and we aren't as English-medium, and we aren't as good-looking either.'

He pauses expectantly.

Bhavani hurries to supply the required objection. With an admiring glance at the framed photograph, he says, 'Mrs Tomar was beautiful, sir. Like a black-and-white-era heroine.'

Mr Tomar nods, gratified.

'The Nose. She had a beautiful Nose. Nowadays all the actresses get plastic surgery to achieve that Nose. I said yes to her after seeing the Nose in the matrimonial photo, only! And with that gold hoop—*kamaal*!'

Bhavani bows his head in homage. 'It was classic.'

Mr Tomar sighs.

'The actress is *Anupama* is also pretty, but in her heyday, my Charu was prettier. She put on a lot of weight after the children. The C-section operations, you know, they thickened her middle.'

'She was unhappy because she felt she was losing her looks?'

'Yes, but it wasn't just that. She was also unhappy because she had come to realize that while I had started out life at the same level as say, Sushil Kedia, I simply do not have it in me to become rich. There was going to be no chain of Tomar Tools and Hardware, no building of a corpus to invest in the stock market.'

He pauses, his eyes seeing things they cannot.

Is there jealousy at work here, Bhavani wonders. Could this simple man with the mild inoffensive eyes behind the thick glasses have been stirred to madness and committed two murders because of his wife's admiration for Sushil Kedia, a far more successful man?

Almost as if he can read Bhavani's thoughts, Mr Tomar says, 'My son used to say ki how come you are not jealous, papa! But I know my Charu loved me.' He shoots a loving glance at the garlanded photograph. 'She kept her KC also, and so beautifully this year!' His voice breaks. 'She died with rich dark mehendi blooming on her hands!'

Tears fill his eyes.

'Get tea for all of us,' Bhavani calls out to the lounging assistants.

They jump up immediately and peep into the shop.

'And coconut-cream biscuits?' one of them asks hopefully.

Bhavani nods, reaches for his wallet and hands over some money. 'Go, quickly.'

Revived at the thought of the biscuits, Tomar wipes his tears.

'But Charu wasn't one to be defeated. If she couldn't be financially important, then she would become socially important. So she hit upon a fine idea.' Mr Tomar looks up at them, his face suddenly animated. 'Do you understand marketing?'

'A little,' Bhavani replies.

'Marketing says ki you need something to stand out from the clutter. Charu decided to reposition herself by making bhakti or *devotion* her USP!'

'Unique selling point,' supplies Naik, not without a little pride.

'Ah!' Bhavani nods.

'It was not conscious, I think. Matlab she did not sit down one day and say, oho, wealth is taken, beauty is taken, wit is taken, I might as well grab holiness before some other lady does. But she...'

'... had a vision of Matarani, perhaps?' Bhavani suggests.

Mr Tomar gives a small indulgent smile.

'A dream. In the dream she was fast asleep but was roused by the strange sensation of a raspy tongue licking her cheek. She opened her eyes to meet the magnetic gaze of a huge lion, with a golden coat and hot fetid breath. On his back, holding her trident, her sword, her lotus and her conch, sat Matarani herself! She put down a free hand to Charu, Charu grasped it, Matarani pulled and Charu sprang up to sit behind her, on the lion's back! And away they rode through the three worlds, granting boons, performing miracles, while the world applauded and bowed!'

'Byooodiful!' breathes Bhavani. 'Ah, here is the tea!'

Bright orange, extremely sweet tea in tiny plastic glasses is handed around solemnly. Bhavani gets to his feet, opens the packet of coconut-cream biscuits and places it before the bereaved man.

'Tomarji, you say that Mrs Tomar slept soundly and did nat see anything that night. Is it possible that she had seen something earlier or later? That could have scared the murderer so much that he/she decided that she had to be silenced? Can you tell us how she spent Karwa Chauth day?'

Mr Tomar crunches steadily through three coconut-cream biscuits.

'She ate the pre-dawn meal with Sona and Pooja Kedia,' he says. 'Then she came back home and went back to sleep. Later, she applied mehendi and sat in the balcony to dry it in the sun. She sat there for a few hours, I think, listening to devotional songs on her phone.'

An admirable place to see the comings and goings in the neighbourhood, thinks Bhavani. Aloud, he says, 'So she sat in the balcony all mornings? Did you both speak while she was sitting there?'

'Yes. It was Karwa Chauth, after all, and a slow day at the shop, for some reason. We spoke a couple of times. The first time she was wondering which film she and the Kedia ladies should watch at the mall. And she told me that Jaishri Rao had just walked by eating pink candyfloss, so clearly she wasn't keeping the KC. And that Sparsh was off to play pool at The Hub again, despite his father forbidding him from doing so. And the second time she mentioned that Bhagyalakshmi had brought Dondi bai down for a walk in her wheelchair and the dogs were barking at her quite viciously. And then she said,' his voice grows a little unsure, 'that somebody had been throwing stones in the street.'

'At the dogs?'

'I'm not sure.' He shakes his head. 'She said there was a stone, and it had broken something. A vase or something like that.'

The policemen absorb this.

'What about yesterday?' Bhavani asks. 'Did she behave differently yesterday, or the day before yesterday?'

'She was quieter than usual,' Mr Tomar says slowly. 'Like, she did not want to hear all about the party at the Rao mansion. Usually she would have been very interested. But she was not. That was definitely odd.'

'There was something on her mind,' Bhavani murmurs. 'Perhaps she had realized that she had seen something important and she was wondering what to do about it.'

'I think so, yes,' Mr Tomar agrees. 'It hurts that she did not confide in me, but then again, she did not have a very high opinion of my intelligence.'

'Did she meet anybody or reach out to anybody yesterday? Besides the NationNow! people?'

Mr Tomar shakes his head.

'Not that I know of. But on the afternoon of the day of Jaishri Rao's party, she visited Pooja Kedia. Nothing unusual about that. They were best friends, you know.'

'Well, Mrs Kedia, the lady you were sure was the murderer has come to a sticky end herself. What do you say now?'

Mrs Pooja Kedia does not respond at once to Bhavani's deliberately combative greeting. Naik, young and judgemental enough to disapprove of new widows imbibing vast quantities of alcohol, wonders if she is still suffering from an acute hangover and feels that, if so, her suffering is justified.

Finally she blinks, sits up, gestures towards the squashy loveseat and murmurs, 'You were right and I was wrong, Bhavaniji. Please be seated.'

Once they are settled, and supplied with tea and buttery home-baked cookies, Naik says, 'We know Mrs Charu Tomar came to see you in the afternoon before Jaishri Rao's party, Poojaji. What did you two talk about?'

She sighs. 'Poor Charu.'

Bhavani sips his tea calmly and waits for more.

Finally, Mrs Kedia says, 'Charu and I met decades ago, on a ladies-only temple-tour of south India. Some of the temples were on beaches, some were in the hills; we did sightseeing and praying and mocktails, and played dumb charades and sang antakshari in the bus and she seemed nice enough. Please understand that I say this without any vanity: we were both equally beautiful, lived near each other, had children the same age, husbands with small businesses, and so I decided to be her friend.'

She pauses, her eyes faraway.

'Over the years, Sushil's business picked up, but Tomar bhaisaab's didn't. Also, Charu became... how to say this kindly? There is no way to say it kindly—she became *fat*. Which is okay, I am not that lookist and one–two fat friends should be there in a group also, to add variety, like ganthiya inside a packet of Bikaneri bhajia-sev.'

'How true, how true,' Bhavani murmurs while Naik struggles to keep a straight face.

Pooja Kedia's hand gestures grow agitated.

'But the trouble is that being fat as well as poor made her unhappy, so she became holy, and being holy made her narrow-minded, judgemental and bossy. So now there were no longer any beaches or dumb charades but only satsangs and pujas and dreams of Matarani! And then our sons got married.'

'Your son's wedding was grander than her son's, perhaps?'

'Hain?' She shakes her head. 'No no, nothing like that. The thing is ki she fights with her daughter-in-law. I don't.

I like young blood in the house, young girls with new decor ideas, fresh fashions, hatke jewellery! I like cooking shortcuts from Instagram reels that save time and effort, but Charu… She was so horrible to her DIL that the poor girl grabbed her hubby and zoomed off to Baroda in the first year itself, and now even their Diwali puja happens on Zoom!'

Bhavani makes small distressed sounds.

'Yours is the correct attitude, Poojaji. One should move with the times.'

'Yes, but how to explain that to people who do not want to understand? Anyway, then came the biggest challenge to our old friendship, which we discussed on that day you are asking about, when we met for the final time.'

'She came here to meet you?'

'We sat in this very room. And as I have already admitted, you were right and I was wrong. She told me she did not shoot my husband dead. Far from it! She confessed that she was *in love with him*!'

'What!' Naik cannot quite suppress a scandalized gasp.

Bhavani's reaction is more nuanced.

'Oho.'

'All the bonding and discussion on the stray dog menace had led to it, she claimed. And she felt her love had been reciprocated. Personally I find it hard to believe my husband could love anybody but himself, but Charu insisted he had been quite enamoured by her beautiful nose and whatnot!'

She sighs.

'At least this explains why she was so angry with me for breaking my fast early—because doing so endangered the life of the man she loved! To cut a long nightmare short, she said she loved him, he loved her, and she suspects that Mr Tomar shot him out of jealousy. And when I asked her why she was telling me all this, she said it was because she had no one else to turn to, and (this is the best bit!) because I was her best friend. What a joke! And now she was worried Mr Tomar might end *her* life also.'

'And then he doctored her water-retention pills?'

Pooja Kedia shrugs.

'Who else but a husband could have a better opportunity to do it? And what a clever weapon to choose. I tell you, that woman was obsessed with her weight! She acted all devout, but Tomar bhaisaab clearly knew that she would have eaten the beef of Vrindavan cows if somebody had said it would cure her water retention!'

'He understood her psychology well.'

'Yes!' Pooja Kedia says fretfully. 'Anyway, she told me all this, and honestly, I feared for her sanity! But I just told her to go to the police if she had such suspicions. Instead, she decided to call those clowns at NationNow!.'

'But would she really call the police on her own husband?'

'I do not know. Perhaps she was planning to spin them some other story altogether. I am not responsible for the actions of my self-appointed best friend, or her peculiar husband!'

She sits back, all talked out and clearly exhausted.

'Do you believe her, sir?'

Bhavani puffs out his cheeks sceptically.

'Would Charu Tomar have called the NationNow! team and accused her own husband on national television, Manju? Even if she suspected him of murdering the man she loved? And how would she have explained away the fact that she tried to blame Haider Sait first? That bit would nat have tied up easily!'

'Indeed, sir. So Pooja Kedia is lying? To protect somebody in her family, must be! Harsh, perhaps, or Sona?'

'Yes, probably... Manju!' Bhavani's voice sharpens suddenly. 'Mehtab bhai had mentioned that on the day he barged into the Kedia Jewellers store on Commercial Street, Sushil Kedia was entertaining an important man—some white man, he said. Find out who it was.'

'Yes, sir.'

Much to his distaste, Bhavani also has to question the NationNow! anchor. He lets Naik do the talking.

'What did Charu Tomar say to you in her message?'

In a tone far removed from the dramatic accents he adopts on television, the anchor says tiredly, 'Just that there was a brand new khulasa she had to make that would tilt the search for Sushil Kedia's killer in a whole new direction.'

'What is khulasa?' Naik asks. 'I do not speak Hindi.'

'Disclosure.'

'And she did not elaborate beyond that?'

'No.'

'A whole new direction? Means away from Haider Sait?'

'Like I *said*,' the anchor repeats petulantly, with a rather frustrated toss of his famous kiss-curl, 'she did not elaborate.'

> Jhoom.
> Hello? Jhooooom
> Please pick up
> *4 p.m.*

> Can't. I have a line of sick animals in my office. And zero bandwidth.
> *4:15 p.m.*

Relief floods Hadi as he stares down at this message. At least she's speaking to him! The TV channels have been hurling accusations at him all day and cooking up the most convoluted of conspiracy theories. He quickly types:

> 1) I DID NOT COME TO YOUR HOUSE TO STEAL YOUR MEDS.
> 2) I DID NOT KILL CHENGEZ.
> *4.17 p.m.*

A pause during which he stares at the 'Jhoom is typing' notification, sick with anxiety, and then sick at the amount of anxiety he is feeling.

> Okay
> *4.18 p.m.*

Huh? Hadi stares down at his phone in disbelief. That's it?
That's all she has to say on the topic? No demands for proof
or explanations? No recriminations?

And then another message blooms on his screen.

> Why did you come to my house that night, then?
>   4.20 p.m.

Wow, what a girl. Straight to the point.
  He grabs the phone and types:

> I wanted to see you.
>   4.21 p.m.

> Why?
>   4.23 p.m.

Wow, well, to be fair, it is a pertinent question. What is he
supposed to say in reply? Because I've been obsessed with you
half my entire life?

> I don't know. I just did. I was acting on impulse.
>   4.24 p.m.

> And when you pulled me into your lap and held me? Was
> that also impulse?
>   4.25 p.m.

Tenderness floods his muscles, making him almost drop the
phone. He draws a deep breath and types:

Yes.
4.26 p.m.

Eyes closed, he holds on tight to his phone, willing it to vibrate. The gap lengthens, so much that he starts to wonder if she's gone offline. Then the phone buzzes and his eyes fly open.

You know that old Billy Joel song 'Honesty'?
'Honesteee… is mostly what I need from you…' Should I send a link?
4:45 p.m.

I know it.
4.47 p.m.

They should make a 2023 version called 'Clarity'.
'Clariteee… is mostly what I need from you.'
4.48 p.m.

Now, what to even say to this? He thinks for a couple of minutes, typing and deleting several times, then finally sends a message.

If I had clarity, I would give you clarity.
But I don't, so I can't.
4.55 p.m.

Her reply is grudgingly impressed.

> Damn, you're glib.
>
> *4.56 p.m.*

This makes him laugh out loud. And then another message flashes.

> Anyway, just so you know, your wordless cuddling technique, while very toe-tingling, has rendered me completely mindfucked.
>
> *4:58 p.m.*

Hadi is suddenly, idiotically happy.

> Your toes tingled?
>
> *4.59 p.m.*

> Yes.
> And my mind fucked.
> I mean, I got mindfucked.
>
> *5.05 p.m.*

He stares at the screen for a long time, then shakes his head to clear it, and quickly types:

> I didn't dare speak because I would've definitely said something dumb and ruined the vibe.
>
> *5.10 p.m.*

> That is probably true.
>   All in all, I think it's good you didn't say anything then.
>
> *5.11 p.m.*

A zipped lip emoji blooms on his screen, followed by a wink face. He shakes his head, smiling.

Jhoom, I'm... His thumbs hover helplessly over the phone, then drop away.

Another message arrives.

> If you couldn't talk to me, at least you could've kissed me.
>
> *5.12 p.m.*

Hadi gives a small incredulous laugh. Then he rolls over onto his stomach and quickly types:

> I can come over and kiss you now.
>
> *5.14 p.m.*

> I'm BUSY now.
>
> *5.15 p.m.*

He groans and flops back into his bed, feeling both ecstatic and frustrated.

On the muted TV screen before him, anchors gesticulate silently as lurid subtitles accuse him of double murder.

Some perverse instinct makes him type:

> Not afraid of getting cozy with a man who may have killed two people?
>
> *5.16 p.m.*

She takes a while to reply.

Hello, maybe I killed two people! In the words of ACP Bhavani: 'EVERYONE IS A SUSPECT.'

5.25 p.m.

Hadi laughs.

I'm not afraid of you.

5.26 p.m.

It is only fair to warn you that I am a bruised and defective piece. I no longer possess a functioning heart. Or perhaps even functioning private parts.

5.28 p.m.

Hadi knows a green flag when he sees one.

Let's find out.

5.29 p.m.

Her reply is almost instantaneous.

Come home after seven.

5.30 p.m.

Peter Pais has not been able to prevail. His sisters have spoken from across the Atlantic and the Pacific, the Fathers at St Joseph's Church have backed them wholeheartedly and old Dondi bai, thanks to what the daughters are referring to in appalled whispers as 'poor mummy's latest tamasha', is finally being shifted to a five-star assisted-care facility. The news spreads like wildfire through the Mangalorean Catholic community.

'That Peter is an angel, ba,' people say to each other outside the church, after the nine a.m. Sunday mass. 'But he is getting older too. How long can this Queen Elizabeth–Prince Charles situation continue?'

'The fellow never even got married because of her! He made a vow to his papa on his deathbed that he would always look after mummy, it seems. So sad, poor chap. He's become like that Bheeshma pitahmah, Christian version.'

'Na re, saiba, he never got married because he is a gay.'

'*I* heard he doesn't care for his mummy at all. He just wants to look holy like anything. And be morally superior to his sisters! They are both more intelligent than him, no, with grand jobs and families and all! This is his *solo* scoring point, that he looks after mummy. He keeps that servant girl to look after her, makes the sisters pay her salary from abroad and hogs all the credit for being not just plain Peter but *Saint* Peter. Bluddy dhongi.'

'See, he lives in that house for free because of her. If she shifts to assisted living then the sisters will want to sell the flat and split the money three ways. Then where will he go to live with his one-third share?'

'What rubbish you're telling, men! He has a five-hundred-acre estate in Sakleshpur and no dearth of money. A single fellow like him, what are his expenses even? He just has a special relationship with his old mother and he doesn't want to be separated from her. But those witches are bent on breaking up the mother–son bond! It galls them to see him so close to her, and being praised for his dutifulness by the whole community. They toh don't go for confession, even! And their children are walking around unconfirmed at the age of twenty-plus! So sad and shameful, ba!'

'I heard the whole family had booked a luxury villa in Goa! They're going to wine and dine the old lady nicely, take her to the beaches and the casinos and the Basilica of Bom Jesus, and then leave her in the old-age home and run back to their lives abroad!'

Inspector Manjunath Naik, dressed in his estimation of what constitutes 'Sunday best', lingers by the church steps, listens in on all the conversations and takes careful notes.

Back at the flat, Dondi Pais, unaware of all these developments, including her role in the death of Sushil Kedia, is supervising the packing of her bags in the small living room full of crucifixes and mounted animal heads, and chatting happily with an unexpected visitor.

Fearing that seeing either him or Naik again may upset her, Bhavani has deputized Shalini to visit the Pais' home and engage the old lady in a freewheeling chat.

The pretext for the visit is a recipe. Shalini has explained that both her husband and she love the soft fermented rice cakes they've been eating for breakfast at The Hub every morning. Krish Chetty has told her it's a Mangalorean Catholic specialty; would Mrs Pais be generous enough to share the recipe?

'They're called sannas, I believe,' Shalini concludes.

Old Dondi bai utters a dismissive snort.

'Dat Chetty cherdo's sannas are rubbish!' she says. 'He uses dis-one to ferment de idku rice and urad dal, instead of toddy. A fresh strong toddy gives de batter so much bubble, you know. *Den* dey come fluffy, firm yet springy, like a sixteen-year-old's bosom.' She cackles. 'As my husband used to say! But with dis-one dey come like old hot water bottles, so hard and rubbery.'

Shalini says regretfully that Mangalorean toddy will be tough to come by in Delhi, and is there something else one can use instead of the despised dis-one?

'Some people use dat-one,' Dondi Pais says doubtfully. 'Sprite, you know. And some people use dat-udder-one, what is it called now… antacid Eno! Some buggers use beer also, but a *strong* beer, mind! What a day you've come to ask me all dese questions! I'm busy like *anything* with all my packing.' She raises her voice and calls quaveringly, 'Bhagyalakshmi, did you put in my swimming costume?'

'Yes, bai!' a voice replies from the other room. 'I put the one-piece and the two-piece both. And your swimming caps.'

'Swimming caps, naka baba. Don't want.'

'But auntie, you must wear a swimming cap to protect your lovely hair!' Shalini protests. 'Most older ladies tend to thin out at the crown, yours is so glossy and thick it looks like candyfloss! In Delhi the vendors call candyfloss budiya-ke-baal, do you know? That means old lady's hair.'

'My daughter Liza sends me lovely shampoos and conditioners from Boston.' The old lady pats her curls complacently. 'And of course I have a high-protein diet, with plenty of meat and fat! What will you eat your sannas with, my girl?'

Shalini, who considers herself quite venerable at sixty, is slightly taken aback at this form of address, but recovers quickly.

'What do you suggest, auntie?'

Dondi Pais wriggles her shoulders. 'Drumstick sambhar. Or tendli... or...' The beady eyes grow speculative. 'You're vegetarian or wort?'

'Oh, no!' Shalini laughs. 'We eat everything.'

A gleam illuminates Dondi Pais's eyes.

'Prawn pickle. Beef chilly fry. But *beshtu* is dukra maas.' She smacks her lips. 'Wild boar, you know. Wonderful it comes—de taste of Christmas, like! Dis fellow's big square shoulders,' she nods at the head of a large wild boar mounted on the wall behind them, 'were cubed into dukra maas for a grand Christmas celebration in de twenty-fifth year of my marriage! You have to make it with Bafat powder, of course. And ginger, garlic, tomato, vinegar! And if you want to eat it today, den cook it yesterday. The flavours fully soak into de meat den—lovely it comes! Oh, how much dukra maas I will eat in Goa. Nobody can *dare* to stop me!'

She lapses into what seems like a pleasant reverie, the bright white curls partly obscuring her half-closed eyes.

Shalini leans in a little and murmurs, 'I heard Jaishri Rao served dukra maas at her party.'

Dondi Pais's eyes flicker.

Shalini says, a little louder, 'She put it into a rice stew. We heard it was deep maroon in colour. With tomato and red wine vinegar and all the Italian spices and plenty of local chorizo—Goan sausage, we mean—to enhance the hearty flavour. Goan sausage is dukra maas only, no, auntie?'

Dondi bai lets out a low betrayed moan.

'Aiyyo, what a liar dat Peter is! He told me she served pishpash tomato rice, dat's why he didn't bring me back any leftovers!'

Shalini makes a small comforting sound.

'Maybe he forgot.'

'He didn't forget!' Dondi bai snaps, sitting up. 'Dat nice Jaishri invited me also, but of course he dint take me along. Dint want to push my wheelchair down one flight of stairs and across de road, too much work for de grand man!'

'But auntie, he's taking you to Goa now…'

She snorts.

'My *daughters* are taking me! Peter doesn't even *like* me!'

'Why do you say that?'

'He doesn't let me eat chocolate!'

'Because you'll get loose motions, auntie.'

'He doesn't let me wear sleeveless! Bloody Taliban!'

'Because you may catch a cold, auntie.'

'He makes popcorn and chicken nuggets and watches movies but he doesn't let me watch with him!'

Shalini, feeling like she's enacting a weird version of Little Red Riding Hood, says, 'Because he's scared you'll get nightmares, auntie.'

'Nightmares.' Dondi bai moves around agitatedly. 'I'll tell you what my nightmare is!' Her old face crumples. 'Assis… assis…'

'Assisted living,' Bhagyalakshmi says as she enters the room with a tray of tea and biscuits. 'Dondi bai don't wants that. Because they won't let her take Sarr Francis Bacon and all the others there. She'll have to give away her good things. Her China teapots and her curios and her Mamma Mary icons and all.'

'I won't give away my good things,' the old lady says tightly. 'And I won't leave my home. Peter and I are happy here, even though he is a useless fellow, he promised my husband he would look after me, he *promised*—'

She gulps, overwhelmed, and grinds to a halt.

Bhagyalakshmi spoons sugar into the cup, dips a biscuit into the hot sweet fluid and holds it up to the wrinkled, quavering mouth.

Dondi bai bites.

'Tension tugol beda, bai!' Bhagyalakshmi pats the old back competently. 'Drink your tea and eat your biscuits.'

'I'm not a mad old woman—am I, Bhagya?'

'Dondi bai is very sharp,' Bhagyalakshmi replies, continuing to pat the agitated back. 'Dinalu she is doing Sudoku, reading newspaper, checking her Whatsup and telling me what to cook! And after taking breakfast and hot bath, she is sitting at the window and observing the coming and goings on Habba Galli sooo nicely!'

'That sounds lovely. And a walk perhaps also, auntie? In your chair? For some fresh air?'

Bhagyalakshmi sniffs. 'Earlier Peter saar used to carry bai down the stairs, put her in the wheelchair and push her all the way down and up the road.'

'I used to like my walks,' Dondi bai says. 'We went gate-to-gate, shop-to-shop, stopping to exchange greetings and get all de news. *All* used to look forward to my visits—de Kedias, dat Rao cherdu, dat Chetty cherdo and Musa Sait and his daughter and all!'

'She's his *wife*,' Bhagyalakshmi corrects the old lady. 'Not his daughter. His widow, now.'

'Yes, yes.'

'But den, one day, dat bloody darkie sharkie bitch started showing me her yellow eyes and barking at my wheelchair! And she taught her whole wretched pack to bark at me too! *Every time* we went down the road, dey would bark! Peter was worried dey would bite me, so we stopped our walks.'

'How troubling…' Shalini thinks of Ayesha Sait's serpent. 'Mrs Pais, was the mongrel situation always so bad on this street or has it become worse recently?'

'Oh, it's become *much* worse lately, my girl!' Dondi bai's milky old eyes grow huge with earnestness. 'Because dese pilla party people feed dem, you know, so dey've become entitled. Dey think dey rule de street! And dey eat small children and babies—eat dem whole! *And* dey give everybody rabies! It's all on de Whatsup. Dat jeweller fellow posted the videos. Now he's dead, poor chap, had a sudden heart attack, it seems. Cheh cheh, deese vegetarians always die young, dere's no strength in deir diet, no!'

'Mrs Charu Tomar was also vegetarian,' Shalini puts in.

'Eh, what's that you say, my girl? Charu Tomar? Dat fat one? Too holy by half, she was! And a total idol worshipper. De Bible says people like her will burn in purgatory till de second coming! She'll burn well.' The old lady chuckles. 'Lot of fat on her bones.'

The two Hindus roll their eyes over the gently bobbing curly white head.

'So are you going to bring back presents for your friends from your Goa trip?' Shalini inquires.

The old lady's jaw drops. 'Aiyyo, why to bring back presents?'

'Don't be stingy, bai!' Bhagyalakshmi chuckles. 'Bring a present for me! And for all your young friends!'

'You're popular amongst the youngsters, auntie?'

Dondi Pais cocks her head to one side. The old eyes look suddenly very sharp. 'Dey like me,' she says. 'Sparsh, Krish, even dat dog-loving Sona and dat animal-crazy Jhoom. Dey visit me, take my advice, cut my nails and bring me ice cream. All of dem.'

'Mehtab bhai also visits auntie,' Bhagyalakshmi says. 'With bones to boil into a nourishing stew. And my older sister Saraswati comes to massage her feet. Her massage is much better than mine, Dondi bai says!'

'How lovely.' Shalini gets to her feet. 'Well, have a good trip, auntie!'

She leans in to hug the old lady, feeling suddenly very fond and protective of her. 'And come back soon!'

'Oh, I'll be back,' the old lady speaks indistinctly through a fresh mouthful of biscuit. 'I'll gunny boy any bastard who stops me from coming home. Let dem try. *Let* dem *try*, men! I'll take dem all down!'

'You and your serpent,' Shalini tells Bhavani when she returns to The Hub. 'From what we can tell, every blessed person in the galli had a chance to instigate Dondi bai against the dogs. And the dogs also seem to be doing an excellent job of it themselves!'

Bhavani looks up sharply.

'How?'

'They bark at her wheelchair, apparently. Very aggressively.'
Bhavani frowns.

'Is that a recent phenomenon?'

'Yes.' Shalini nods. 'They didn't used to do it till about, say, three months ago. But now it happens every time she goes down, so she's stopped going down altogether.'

He looks thoughtful. 'We would like to examine this wheelchair.'

'Too late.' She shakes her head. 'It—and she—must be in Goa by now.'

9

Herringbone Links

'Hellllo.' Hadi's eyes are dancing.

'Oh,' Jhoom says faintly as she leans on the door. 'It's you.'

'I have a kiss coupon. I've come to redeem it.'

She rolls her eyes. 'Oh God, okay, come on in.'

She leads him through the tiny enclosed garden, through the living room and up the stairs to an oatmeal-and-honey-hued bedroom that smells faintly of wildflowers and vanilla.

'No smell of bacon anywhere,' she says, gesturing towards a massive battered-looking pale-pink velvet couch. 'Sit, na.'

'This is super comfy,' he tells her as he throws himself down on it. 'Do you lure all potential lovers-who-live-down-the-lane here and give them a test drive?'

She doesn't reply, but sits down beside him. He lays an arm around the back of the sofa and turns towards her.

'Ai.' She wards him off.

His eyebrows shoot up in amusement.

'I wasn't going to jump into kissing right away, chill.'

Relief floods her face.

'Good!'

Is she trying to rattle him? Because if she is, it's working.

'We can take kissing right off the agenda, if you like,' he offers, just a little stiffly. 'Seriously. It's all good, if you'd rather not.'

Her face falls.

'You don't want to kiss me?'

Do I? Hadi asks himself. It's been a much-loved fantasy for so long, can it ever live up to the hype? Or am I just setting myself up for a massive anticlimax? Also, what kind of chootiya question is this? It's Jhoomar Rao, of course I want to kiss her.

He leans in and grasps her hands in his strong brown ones. 'I do.' His gaze is intense. 'But only *if* you want to, and only *when* you want to, and only *where* you want to.'

'Oh wow, thanks!' She flops back on the couch, discouraged. 'Lump the entire onus on *me*! Kill me with agency!'

'Arrey.' Hadi's eyes widen in surprise. 'How do you want this to work, then?'

'I don't know,' she says crossly. 'In a mutually agreed upon, mutually enjoyable manner, which is half relaxed trust, and half edgy, passionate spontaneity.' She stares at him defiantly at the end of this little speech, clearly expecting him to laugh.

'That's a tall order,' he replies seriously. 'I'm no expert, but I think we should try and achieve trust first. Relaxation will follow once trust is achieved, and from there we can move on to the good stuff. Why are you looking at me like that?'

'Like this?' She tilts her head. 'I'm just taking in the fact that your eyes are rather like Darponk's—sweet and playful and like you're kinda hoping I'll throw you a ball.'

'I'm definitely not hoping you'll throw me a ball,' he assures her. 'But I'm relieved you like my eyes. Because I've been told, several times, that they aren't half as effective without background music.'

She touches his cheek.

'I'm also wondering if *you're* wondering whether I find you attractive simply because you're famous. Are you?'

He grins.

'Nah. You find me attractive because I *am* attractive.'

This draws a smile and a decided nod.

'Yes. You are. And I'll tell you what makes you so attractive. It's—'

'My eyes.'

'Yes. And—'

'My jaw.'

'Yes, but—'

'I was voted best booty of 2022 by *People* magazine,' he offers. 'Across all of Asia-Pac.'

She shakes her head.

'*Listen* to me. The most attractive thing about you is that you work hard, you live clean and you're self-made—at the ripe old age of twenty-eight. Do you know how rare that is? All the guys I went to school with are lying around in some over-furnished, over-air-conditioned room, getting drunk or snorting cocaine.'

'Jhoom.' Hadi gathers up her hands and looks down at them. 'I do *drink*, you know. Sometimes.'

She shrugs. 'Sure, I get that. My mom drinks too. And I've been there, done that.'

'Cool.' He comes a little closer. 'What else is on your mind?'

'Well…' She pauses to draw a long, ragged, breath. 'No offence, promise, I know I replied "okay" to your WhatsApp message, but I can't shake the thought that you have been to my clinic exactly three times. The first time was when I was operating on Rogu and you saw where I kept everything, including my anaesthetics. The second time you visited, you specifically asked me if I had CCTV cameras and I told you I couldn't afford them. And the third time you came over, you knew, just like everybody else, that I had just put an old dog down and would probably have those meds in my store cupboard—arrey, why'd you do that?'

Because he has leaned down and blown out the scented three-wick candle.

'It's the wrong prop for this situation,' he explains lightly. 'What we need is a single naked light bulb. Because this isn't a seduction scene, is it, it's an interrogation scene. Is ACP Bhavani hiding in the cupboard, by any chance?'

'Haha!' Jhoom gulps, torn between relief and disappointment. 'Of course he isn't. Uh, are you pissed off?'

Hadi's eyebrows rise. 'Because you're accusing me of being a double murderer like the rest of the world is? Why would I be that petty?'

Her eyes grow large with dismay.

'You *are* pissed off.'

'Wow, Jhoomar.' He is standing up now, and to her he seems to be on the brink of walking out. 'Just wow.'

The intensity of the disappointment that grips her at this possibility appalls her.

And then, suddenly, she is angry too.

Nobody can put her in the wrong if she *isn't* wrong.

'Look, I'm just trying to be honest,' she says steadily. 'Things turn to shit otherwise. You should be aware that these are the thoughts going on in the head behind the lips you claimed you wanted to kiss—like it or lump it!'

He stares down at her, exasperated. 'Has it ever occurred to you that there's a reason why we can't all read each other's unfiltered thoughts? Because that way lies complete and total communication breakdown!'

She stands up as well, laying her hands on her hips and confronting him straight up. '*Why* are you pretending to like me?'

He throws up his hands.

'I'm not *pretending* to like you! In fact,' he pauses, 'when did I even *say* I liked you?'

She colours, looking embarrassed and then unapologetic. Her nostrils flare.

'Well, you're a guy, so of course you didn't come out and *say* it,' she says witheringly. 'But you totally *acted* like you did!'

'Because I do.' Hadi is breathing hard. 'I like you, Jhoomar Rao, okay? And I didn't murder anybody!'

She looks at him, her eyes huge and skittering and wild, and then suddenly crumples on the couch.

'Maybe my mother did,' she whispers.

'What the…' He drops to the floor beside her, squatting on his heels. 'Don't be idiotic!'

He tries to get her to look at him, but she shakes her head, turning away and curling up, foetus-like, with her back to him.

'Amma's mental health isn't the best,' she whispers shakily. 'She's doing pretty good, all things considered, but she… she's got the zeal of a new convert and she takes unreasonable dislikes to people, *especially* to men she considers weapons of the patriarchy, and Sushi Kedia was a prime example! Bhavani seems to think that's enough reason for her to have picked up a gun and done him in.'

Suddenly, she whirls around and looks at him.

'When you left the clinic… when you were on the road, going home in the storm, did you…' she draws a deep breath but cannot bring herself to say the words, 'did you see anything?'

Hadi is silent. For so long that tears sting Jhoom's eyes.

'No, Jhoom,' he says firmly. 'I didn't.'

She sags a little.

'You're sure?' she whispers.

He nods. 'Yes. *And* your mum's mental health looks absolutely fine to me.'

She is clearly relieved but all she says is, 'It's not. Believe me, I know.'

He frowns.

'Have you talked to your mother? About these thoughts going on in the head behind the lips I want to kiss?'

She flushes slightly and shakes her head.

'No, I have not. Because that way lies complete and total communication breakdown!'

He says sombrely, 'Jhoom, just talk to her.'

She turns to look at him with huge fearful eyes.

'Why did you say it like that?'

Hadi looks suddenly wary. 'Like what?'

'Like you *know* something about it?'

He laughs. 'Relax! I know nothing! Just *talk* to your mother, Jhoom!'

She shakes her head, utterly panicked.

'I can't! Suppose she says she did it? What will I do then?'

'She didn't do it,' he tells her gently. 'She loves you too much to mess up your life by saddling you with a jailbird mom on top of a bankrupt dad.'

'Ouch,' Jhoom winces. 'Harsh.'

'Sorry.' He grins. 'I was just trying to be clear, as per your preference!'

They sit side by side quietly for a while, and then her hand reaches out for his. She slides her fingers through his, and he curls both their hands shut. She sighs.

'*This* is my aukaat. Hand-holding. Pathetic.'

Hadi looks rueful.

'The new definition of first base. Second base is probably this.'

He raises her hand to his lips and kisses it.

'Oh!' Her cheeks pinken. She stares down at the back of her hand, rubbing the place where his lips have just been with her thumb, then raises suddenly shy eyes to meet his. 'And what's third?'

'Third… is…' He looks around her room. 'How do you pass time most evenings in this lair of yours? I see you don't have a TV. D'you read, call up friends, work out, listen to music?'

Her face brightens. She crosses her legs under her bum, pulls open a crocheted quilt, drags a laptop closer and says eagerly, 'I've been watching *Clinic Makeovers* on YouTube! It's this amazing DIY show on how to make your clinic more animal-friendly, so pets don't panic when they visit. Apparently, you need to put in these massive exhaust fans that basically suck out the stale air, which smells of fear and medicine and faeces, and push in fresh air from the outdoors constantly. They don't cost much but they're hugely effective in calming animals down. They have tons more ideas like that!'

'Awesome.' Hadi drags the quilt over his chest and settles down more comfortably into the couch. 'So third is watching this amazing documentary together. Hello, what's this?'

Because a set of scrupulously clean toes are nudging hesitantly against his thigh. 'Maybe third-and-a-half is a foot massage,' she suggests. 'On a GOGO basis, of course. Give one, get one.'

'What is this, bro?' Krish Chetty demands, disappointed. 'You saw some chootiya documentary and bounced? You should've stayed and pounced!'

'Don't talk like a choot, ya, Chetty.' Hadi's gorgeous eyes are glowing softly. 'Jhoom's been so badly bruised, I have to make it up to her. She wants slow, she's gonna get slow. And why were you creeping on Sona that evening? Just leave the girl alone.'

'I wasn't creeping.' Krish flushes. 'I just talked to her a little... politely. It would've looked odd otherwise.'

Hadi doesn't look convinced.

'Just leave her alone,' he repeats.

Krish throws up his hands. 'Okay, okay, I get it!' Then he smiles knowingly. 'I know why you're putting it off with Jhoom. You're scared that after all these years of hankering it's gonna be nothing spesh.'

Anger flares in Hadi's eyes. 'Define spesh.'

'Ai no, I'm not going to walk into that trap!' Krish shakes his head. 'I'll say fireworks and shooting stars and you'll immediately shit on me and say all that stuff is superficial and what really counts is respect and trust.'

'And I would be right,' Hadi maintains steadfastly. 'I'm done riding the roller coaster for feels. I want something solid.'

'The only thing solid here,' Krish says darkly, 'is the case against the Rao ladies, mother and daughter! You're playing with fire, Hadi.'

At Kedia Kutumb, Sona is in the atelier, efficiently going through the papers, files and albums in her father-in-law's desk. Jhoom watches her, leaning against the desk.

'Everybody else claims it's too painful a task for them to do!' Sona complains as she sorts through photographs of Sushil Kedia from infancy to late middle age. '*So* convenient! The truth, of course, is that Sparsh is too lazy and mummyji and Harsh don't care enough. Ugh, look at this—pics of my dad-in-law in his youth—thank God Harsh looks like his mother… How much I hate this man!'

'Hated,' Jhoom corrects her gently. 'He's gone now, Sona. You can relax.'

Sona's face works. 'Well, he doesn't *feel* dead!' she mutters. 'He's reaching out from beyond the grave to mess with my marriage. Hey, who's this hot lady? Mummyji?' She holds up a photograph and scrutinizes it carefully. 'What do you think, Jhoom?'

'Sona,' Jhoom says plaintively.

Sona glances up, immediately repentant. 'Sorry, sorry. I'll pay attention now. Something else happened with Hadi?'

Jhoom nods, grinning.

Sona grins back.

'Tell!'

Photographs forgotten, they settle down on the sunlit wooden floor and Jhoom gives her friend the lowdown.

Sona isn't particularly impressed. She fidgets right through the narrative and says fiercely, as soon as Jhoom finishes speaking, 'Jhoom, you idiot, be careful! What are you doing? The whole country has damned him as a murderer, he was on the spot both times, he obviously *used* you to access those drugs, how can you get involved with him?'

Jhoom's glowing face grows stubborn.

'My mother has just as good a motive as he does. In fact, better. And anyway, we're *all* suspects—you too! He's trusting me, so I have to trust him.'

'Accha?' Sona's eyes sparkle militantly. 'Trust him, matlab? Are you guys exclusive now? Or at least foot massage exclusive?'

Jhoom draws back. 'Sona! It's too soon for all that!'

Sona starts sorting through the photographs again.

'I don't know, bro,' she says dubiously as she stacks them into piles. 'If he's anything like his bestie Krish, you could end up getting super mindfucked. Be careful, Jhoom!'

Jhoom throws up her hands. 'He's not in the least like Krish!' she says indignantly.

But Sona has gone back to scrutinizing the photographs.

'Who *is* she?' she murmurs. 'She isn't mummyji… but she looks so familiar.'

Jhoom snatches the pic from her.

'Stop trying to change the subject!'

'Jhoom.' Sona sighs. 'Look, somebody has to ask the hard practical questions. Your mom seems to have turned into a complete romantic hippie flower child, so I have to—'

Jhoom cuts her off. 'I just like him, okay? And he seems to like me and…'

'Yes, yes, *but*…' Sona shakes her head fervently, '… don't just surrender to this giddiness, okay? Even if he isn't the murderer, or an asshole, all this is happening too fast. His life has so many many people in it, it's so fast-paced and grand-scaled—and you, well, you're amazing, but you live a quiet life in Habba Galli. It'll take you ages to move on if it doesn't work out. So protect yourself, please. Wear a metaphorical condom.'

'Too late.' Jhoomar sighs. 'I'm in over my head and metaphorically unprotected. I'll just shatter like a chandelier if it turns out badly, I guess. And all of Bangalore can have a good laugh at me. Again.'

Bhavani's pool game is unusually off the next day. A delighted Sparsh Kedia beats him three times in a row, then leans on his cue stick and addresses him chattily.

'What's it like being a cop?' he inquires. 'I mean a crime branch cop, not those noobs who do routine passport clearances and all? Is it like the TV shows?'

'We do nat watch the TV shows so we cannat say.' Bhavani smiles at the gawky lad.

'We do—I mean, I do,' Sparsh replies. 'I always guess the murderer long before the cop does.'

'In that case, perhaps you should consider joining the IPS.'

Sparsh snorts. 'I'm fleeing this shitty country as fast as I can, dude. No offence, but this is not the life I want.'

'What sort of life do you want, Sparshji?'

A wistful light animates the adolescent eyes. 'I wanna get an engineering degree and actually *do* shit with it. Like crack simple, simple solutions to complex problems, you know?'

'We heard it was your idea to design the Airbnb around this tree. It's a superb idea.'

'Yeah, well, I like using what's already lying around. It's a lighter load on the planet.'

'We are sure you will get into a good college. Now tell us, how well did you know Mrs Charu Tomar?'

Sparshu shudders. 'Personally, not at all, bro. I knew she made damn good dal-kachoris, but that was our entire relationship.'

'Did she visit your home often?'

'Almost every day. She's ma's besto. Or at least she was till Sona bhabhi came along, now *she's* ma's besto.'

'Did she ever make up stories? Or wildly exaggerate them?'

'Uh, I guess so. Like I said, we didn't talk much.'

'She visited your mummy the day before she died. Did you happen to overhear what they talked about?'

The boy pulls himself up and looks at him reproachfully. 'No, dude, I'm not a snoop. Besides, I was probably asleep.'

'Let us talk about the party at the Rao residence. Were all of you invited?'

'Just Sona bhabhi and ma. But bhaiya got a little worried. He disapproves of Sona bhabhi's friendship with the Rao women. He thinks they're trouble.'

'And what do you think?'

'They're hot, even the old one. But they're feminists. I don't like feminists coz they don't give blowjobs.'

He looks at Bhavani hopefully, but the old policeman doesn't appear in the least bit scandalized.

'We did nat know that was the definition of a feminist,' Bhavani says interestedly. 'Are you sure?'

Sparsh squirms a little under the placid gaze and is betrayed into an answer that reveals his extreme youth.

'That's what everybody says.'

'You must learn nat to believe what everybody says. Tell us about the party.'

'Huh? Sure. So Harsh bhaiya got triggered coz he could hear them all laughing loudly through the walls, which he felt was inappropriate given the fact that pa has just, you know, popped it—these millennials are wayyyy uptight! So he yanked me out of my bedroom and dragged me over to the Raos' coz he felt awkward going over alone. That's the biggest problem with being so much younger than everybody else in the house—people keep using me like a sort of social lubricant. It sucks.'

'Tell us about the party,' Bhavani urges.

'Well, I think Harsh bhaiya freaked out a bit. There were bottles of wine everywhere, and ma was swearing.' He chuckles gleefully. 'It was damn fun hearing her say "asshole" out loud. Of course, Harsh bhaiya almost had a fit. But then Sona bhabhi gave him a drink and called him "jaan" in this hot voice she has, which makes even me a little randy, to be honest.'

'Who all were there at the party?'

Sparsh counts the names off on his fingers.

'Jaishri auntie. Sona bhabhi. Ma. Harsh bhaiya. Peter Pais, cringing and ogling alternately…'

'How good your English is, Sparshji!' Bhavani says admiringly. 'Our wife is an English teacher, so we know.'

Sparsh smirks. 'I'm prepping for the SATs. But let me finish: the carpet-seller Mehtab, oohing and aahing about some mouldy old rug. Krish Chetty. Ayesha auntie. And *Haider Sait* was in the house, ladies and gentlemen, getting down and dirty with Dr Jhoom in the garden. Of course, they immediately sprang apart when we busted in and acted like they'd only been chatting but, hello, the place was thick with pheromones! And Mr Tomar, who I think is the man whodunnit.'

'Why do you say that?'

Sparsh spreads out his lanky arms. 'He has to *sleep* with Chengez, dude! How could he not slip her a little doggie-killing drug?'

'Do you have any reason to suppose their marriage was nat happy?'

The boy makes a face.

'Well, when you put it like that, with your serious voice and all, then, I suppose, no.'

'Are you aware of where Jhoomji keeps her supplies?'

'Everybody is. The cupboard's on the way to the clinic loo, which was also doubling up as the powder room for the party.' He winks at Bhavani. 'The *powder* room, get it? Krish bhaiya uses, of course. All sorts of edibles. He tried to get me to try some, but I was like, no bro, my body's a temple and my girlfriend's my goddess! Anyway, with the amount of alcohol the Rao ladies were serving, I bet everybody visited the powder room at least once.'

'So you could also have procured this veterinary preparation?'

'What? Zeta Jones and Kylie Minogue? Sure, I could've.'

His tone is carelessly casual. Too casual?

'How is your exam preparation going, Sparshji?'

'Very well,' he replies, looking smug. 'I'm on my third revision.'

'Excellent! You are good in your studies, but we hear that nowadays extracurricular activities count as much as academics.'

'Everybody knows that.' Sparsh rolls his eyes. 'I want to study abroad, so naturally I have to tutor orphans, replant an acre of rainforest with my bare hands, restore a historic home and play several musical intruments nobody has even heard of.'

'Tell us more about your lady friend.'

'Devi?' His young face lights up. 'Devi's the coolest. I never thought she'd waste so much of her time on a chaman like me, but there's no accounting for taste, is there?'

'Hers is clearly good.' Bhavani smiles.

Sparsh flushes.

'She's been with some complete assholes,' he says darkly. 'She says I'm the nicest guy she knows, but she refuses to date me.'

After a pause he continues, with touching awkwardness, 'We're sort-of buddies, really.'

'You are very much like your brother,' Bhavani replies. 'He is a nice guy too.'

But Sparsh doesn't want to talk about his brother.

'I'm hoping she'll date me when I'm older,' he says naively. 'That's kinda the dream.'

'It is a good dream,' Bhavani replies. 'So it is to be an engineering college for you, then? Someplace close to Devikaji?'

'She's studying design in Europe. They have some good colleges there, though pa was keener on the US. Dude, I'll say one thing for pa, he was a strict marker when it came to Harshu bhaiya and me, but he really came through for Devi. He gave her a glowing recommendation letter, so good she called it the crown jewel on her college app! And now she's studying jewellery design in freaking Switzerland on a hundred per cent scholarship.'

'She must be a very talented designer,' Bhavani says as he turns this new information over carefully in his mind. 'Your papaji was looking at one of her designs at the time the bullet hit him.'

Sparsh looks genuinely surprised. 'Really?'

Bhavani nods. 'A bracelet, we think. Platinum and diamonds. Would you have any idea which client she could have been designing it for?'

The boy shakes his head. 'No.'

'How did you two get friendly?' Bhavani asks. 'She is older, no?'

'Not *that* much older. She was at Joseph's only. Father Abreo directed a play and we both had speaking parts. Dude, I like acting! Dressing up and learning lines and pretending to be somebody else. Like Hadi Sait. When are you going to arrest him?'

'Nothing has been proved against Haider Sait yet.'

Sparsh raises his eyebrows. 'Wow, I thought his goose is cooked.'

'And so is lunch,' Krish enters the courtyard to say. 'Come, Bhavani uncle! Sparshu, that's your cue. Beat it, kiddo.'

'And these are actually my cues!' Sparsh says wittily as he gathers his cue sticks, zips them into their hardcase and slings it over his shoulder. Then he grins at Bhavani. 'Say hi to Harshu bhaiya when you grill him, ACP.'

The flagship Kedia Jewellers store stands a good ten feet higher than anything else on Commercial Street. As Bhavani ambles up the highly polished white marble steps to the bevelled glass doors, dressed in his holiday gear of Hawaiian shirt and Bermuda shorts, a pair of matching-matching mustachioed doormen bow to him deferentially. A stately young lady in a fearsomely pleated and pinned sari greets him at the door.

'What can we interest you in, sir? This is the silver floor, but it also stocks simple gold pieces. Antique and jadau gold is on the first floor, while the second floor showcases our diamonds and platinum collection.'

In a low voice, Bhavani explains the purpose of his visit. Blanching a little, she says, 'Of course. Mr Kedia's office is on the third floor, please take this elevator.'

Bhavani ascends to this hallowed level smoothly and is soon peering into a room dominated by a massive blow-up of the now-familiar image of the late Sushil Kedia. Harsh rises from his desk to greet him, his face oddly vulnerable below his freshly shaved scalp.

'ACP! Such terrible news about Mrs Tomar. How can I help you?'

'Thank you for cooperating.' Bhavani's voice is unusually stern. 'Harshji, you do realize that we will have to look into the internal affairs of your business very closely. To see who inherits and what all there is to inherit. Now it is a very clear case of murder and not just one murder, but two.'

Harsh's face pales, but his voice remains calm. 'Our lawyers will be available to answer all your questions immediately. Our auditors as well.'

'Thank you.'

'It's all quite simple, though,' Harsh continues. 'I inherit one-third of all monies and assets absolutely, as do my brother and mother. Sparshu remains mummy's dependent till he is twenty-one, then he attains full charge of his share. Upon her demise, we both inherit fifty per cent of her share.'

'Excellent.' Bhavani's manner grows friendlier. He sits down, signalling that the tough questions are more or less over, and asks conversationally, 'Harshji, everybody has a different working style. And family-run businesses can get tricky. Did you and your father have such issues? Generation gap, creative differences, vagehra?'

Harsh takes his time answering this question, fiddling with the papers on his desk and sliding a coaster to Bhavani's side of the table.

'My father did things his way,' he says finally. 'I was given to understand that it was my job to stay quiet and learn. And that my time would eventually come.'

'And now it has come.'

'It has.' The quiet eyes smoulder. 'In fact, I'm a little surprised to see you here, ACP. Did my mother not tell you about her last conversation with Mrs Tomar?'

Bhavani inclines his head. 'She did. We did nat realize that she had also told *you*.'

'So then?' Harsh's nostrils flare, a sign of combativeness, Bhavani has realized. 'Shouldn't the man be arrested at once?'

'Harshji.' Bhavani adjusts his chair slightly. 'There is the small matter of *proof.* Currently, it is just your mother's word against Mr Tomar's.'

'You're saying my mother is lying.'

Bhavani spreads out his hands appealingly. 'Perhaps Mrs Tomar was lying! Your mother says Charu Tomar was prone to all sorts of fancies, religious and otherwise. Her husband says she was severely complexed! The point is, there is no proof and, pardon us, but your mother did proceed to go out to a party that very same evening and socialize with the very man whom her best friend had just charged with the crime of her husband's murder. You see the problem?'

Several expressions cross Harsh's face throughout this little speech. Before he can speak, Bhavani adds smoothly, 'And this is where we need your help. You are, in fact, a very, very important witness for us.'

The younger man looks surprised. 'I am?'

Bhavani makes himself more comfortable in the well-padded chair.

'The night before Mrs Tomar's murder, Mrs Jaishri Rao invited a small group of friends and neighbours to her home... to commemorate your father—'

'She threw a *party*,' Harsh snaps, his hand rising involuntarily to his tonsured head as if to emphasize his recent bereavement. 'Because a *dog* died! It showed an appalling lack of propriety. I was shocked when I heard Sona had gone *and* taken my mother along!'

'Yes, yes, we understand it was all rather impromptu…'

'*Everything* in Jaishri Rao's life happens impromptu,' Harsh replies dryly. 'The lady staggers from crisis to crisis with no planning whatsoever. Anyway, Sona said she took mummy because she fears mummy is internalizing her grief, which is not good for her health. If I object I am accused of having a low EQ! But why am *I* an important witness, ACP?'

'Because,' Bhavani says, pulling his chair a little closer, 'and please do forgive us for mentioning this, everybody else who attended that party was a little, err…'

'Drunk,' Harsh says bluntly. 'You're right, of course. Even Sparshu attacked the margaritas like a thirsty camel as soon as we entered. That concoction had the kick of a mule! And there was no peg measure in sight!'

'What were your impressions of the party?' Bhavani asks. 'Please don't leave out anything. No matter how unimportant.'

Harsh fidgets with his phone. 'It was *all* unimportant,' he says irritably. 'Some of them were outside when we entered through that old carved door, and let me tell you, I was shocked at the state of the place! The seepage, the weeds! Even in the darkness I could see peepul saplings growing out of the wall in three places!'

'You had nat been in there before?'

'Not since their divorce,' Harsh answers, after thinking about it for a while. 'Anyway, Sait was trying his usual bag of tricks with young Jhoom in the courtyard, but when Sparshu and me showed up, they both came in with us. She offered us a drink and Sait circulated amongst the guests, putting on his "simple, unspoilt, modest" act.'

'You feel it is insincere?'

Harsh gives an incredulous little laugh. 'Yes! We're all Josephites, you know. I've seen Sait and Chetty in action when they were head-banging around town as the Love Sachet. Nothing has changed since then, believe you me!'

'And what did you do?'

He shrugs. 'I found Sona and told her it was time mummy was taken home and put to bed. She refused. Mummy also refused. She said,' Harsh's face spasms, but he overcomes his emotion and continues matter-of-factly, 'she said I was a bloody bore. So I went off and did what boring people like myself do under such circumstances. Found a small knot of men and inserted myself into it.'

Bhavani makes a small sympathetic sound. 'Which men?'

'Mehtab bhai, Peter Pais, Mr Tomar and that idiot Chetty.' He comes to an abrupt halt. 'Oh.'

Bhavani raises an eyebrow inquiringly.

'They were discussing murdering one's spouse,' Harsh continues more slowly. 'Which was hugely insensitive, considering everything. Anyway, it was that kind of party. One of them said it is cathartic, even healthy to fantasize about murdering one's spouse, and that the people who do not even allow their minds to go there and block it because they're too goody-goody or whatever are the ones who one day snap and actually act on the impulse! Oh, and Chetty opined that between the two married men present—Mr Tomar and myself—Mr Tomar was more likely to murder his spouse than me. He said "sau sunhaar ki, ek lauhaar ki" to illustrate his point. Not that Tomar sa'ab is an ironsmith, as such, but he does own a hardware store, and I, of course, am a goldsmith. Typical Chetty smooth talk! And then Jaishri Rao wandered up and stated that she highly recommended divorce and how it is so much kinder than murder.' He makes a small gesture of distaste. 'I told you it was a dreadful party.'

'So young Krish Chetty was actively instigating Mr Tomar?' Bhavani asks. 'Winding him up? Whispering at him? Snakishly?'

Harsh looks confused. 'Snakishly?'

'Like the snake in the garden of Eden,' Bhavani explains. 'Like a troublemaker, you could say.'

'Oh, that snake.' Harsh's face clears. 'Yes, I suppose he was. But then that's Krish Chetty all over, isn't it? It's what he does.'

'Oh really?' Bhavani says invitingly.

Harsh says stiffly, 'Perhaps you're aware that my wife and he dated in the past.'

Bhavani nods. 'Yes.'

'So he's been instigating my brother against me. Slipping him drugs as well.'

'Sparsh does nat exhibit any signs of either drug use or abuse,' Bhavani says positively. 'We know all the signs.'

'Oh, Sparshu's a smart kid,' Harsh agrees at once. 'But Krish is constantly trying to push him down shady paths! Creating trouble in my life because he, the great Casanova Krish Chetty, *lost* Sona to me! His latest is egging Sparsh on to do engineering when he knows very well that we all want him to get a degree in finance.'

'Sparsh has an aptitude for both subjects?'

'I suppose so!' Harsh shifts about restlessly. 'How will an engineering degree help him run a jewellery business? But no, we must all take Chetty's advice because he was such a golden boy before he crashed and burned.'

'Krish Chetty has crashed and burned?'

Harsh shrugs. 'Well, he's just wasting his life away, isn't he, one puff at a time? And he wants to give *my* brother career advice! A man who lives in the past and has only two claims to fame: one, being wealthy for several generations; and two, knowing Haider Sait. How are either of these things accomplishments?'

'They are nat,' Bhavani agrees. 'But tell us, did Krish Chetty have a similar role in the pilla party issue as well? Did you feel he actively drilled away at the fault lines and worsened the tension in any way?'

Harsh is quiet for a long time. 'I really cannot say,' he says finally. 'There, you know, it was more about Tiffinni's puppies, and mummy finding her feminist voice—and why shouldn't she?'

'Why indeed.' Bhavani nods understandingly. 'Krish did nat, for example, admire your mummyji's KLPD collection or speak up in praise of it? The way he spoke up about Sparsh pursuing engineering?'

'That was none of his business.' Harsh's nostrils flare. '*I* spoke up on mummy's behalf—so did Sona—even Sparshu's friend Devika did at the initial stages. Mummy was really chuffed about the fact that Devika liked her designs. She felt it was proof that they were Gen Z enough.'

'What do you think of Devika?'

Harsh's voice grows sharp. 'How is this relevant?'

Bhavani wriggles his chunky shoulders. 'Her drawings were found next to Mr Kedia's body.'

'A coincidence.' Harsh's voice is curt. 'She is Sparsh's first love, naturally the boy is obsessed. My take, sadly, is rather cynical—she's stringing him along, being older and savvier, and it's going to end badly for him. But I could be totally wrong.'

'We see. Harshji, why did your father dislike your mother's collection so much?'

Evasiveness creeps into Harsh's eyes.

'My father had… a huge amount of self-hatred, I think. He did not like the desi patterns, the Indian styles. For him class was always European, Turkish, Persian. In the old days my mother used to joke that he must have had an Irani girlfriend! He preferred whites, blues, purples, the more foreign cuts and settings and—'

'So his dislike of the designs was nothing *personal*? Against your mother, we mean?'

Sparsh stays quiet.

Bhavani changes tack. 'Speaking of foreign, your father had some important visitors recently—Karl Schnieder, the head of acquisitions from Von Matisse AG, Geneva?'

Harsh looks a little surprised. 'Yes, he did.'

'What was that meeting regarding?'

Harsh's eyebrows rise. 'I must say you ask the oddest questions! It was merely a courtesy call. My father and he judged together on the annual Masterpiece awards, so he hit him up when he came to town, I think.'

'We see. Finally, do you regret having your mummyji's collection melted down?'

'Oh, we didn't actually get around to melting it,' Harsh says casually. 'There were some technical issues with the furnace so it couldn't be done. In fact...' He raises his chin, then says, his eyes sparkling quiet defiance, 'we're displaying the entire collection on the first floor, right here in this store. The branding, which had some rather, uh, unfortunate connotations, has been tweaked and it's called The Kedia Pooja Collection now—and it's getting a lot of interest.'

'I really liked Sushi uncle. He was this really austere, hot monk kind of guy. I know he wasn't the most popular, but I think his bark was worse than his bite. And his design sensitivities—brilliant! Of course, his tastes were strictly classical, he didn't like what he called jhig-bhig tutti-frutti ideas, the kind Pooja auntie loves to make, for example, which would sell so well if he would just display them in his stores. But he was too much of a purist for that. I've really started appreciating him since I started classes here, actually. I can see that he really understood the art and the power of expensive classic jewellery.'

Devika Johri is nineteen years old, very pretty and fashionably dressed in a silk scarf bundled over a fitted black puffer jacket. Her cheekbones are exquisite, her eyebrows alarmingly bushy, her large mouth a soft pinky-peach. Her nose is very red—it is clearly freezing where she is.

'So what did you want to ask me, anyway? So exciting, being interrogated by the police!'

'This is more of an informal chat, really.' Bhavani, sitting at a desk in his room at The Hub, and not very well versed with the laptop Krish has provided, ends up displaying rather more of the insides of his nostrils than he intends to. The delicate Devika blanches.

Shalini, eating nippattu on the couch behind him, takes pity on her and comes forward to adjust the screen.

'We just wanted to know what you thought of him,' Bhavani says from a neat frame displaying his head and shoulders. 'Your view seems to be in contrast with what almost everybody else is saying here.'

'What is everybody saying there?'

Bhavani gives her a brief summary. She listens, then leans forward to say emphatically, 'Uncle, I mean ACP, please see the letter of recommendation Sushi uncle gave me! He was so gruff and strict in person, but my God, in that email he was all "Devika has a rare talent, Devika has a perfect eye, faultless taste, audacious freshness coupled with an intuitive knowledge of the earth's ancient traditions of adornment!" I almost started weeping when I read it!'

Shalini raises her eyebrows. 'Sushi had quite a florid style,' she murmurs from her couch. 'Or perhaps a rather fervent crush.'

Bhavani wriggles about a little in his chair to obscure her from Devika's line of sight. 'You are clearly very talented, Devikaji.'

'I guess so.' The girl looks gratified. 'He *did* assign a lot of work to me! Nobody trusts interns with so much responsibility, usually! I designed one *very* expensive bespoke piece—it cost as much as ten lakhs, I think!'

Bhavani holds up some scans to the screen.

'Devikaji, we wanted to ask you about a loose-leafed sketchbook of yours, which was found near Mr Kedia's body.' Intuiting that she may appreciate dramatic detailing, he adds ghoulishly, 'It was spattered with blood.'

'Oh!' Devika looks pleasantly horrified. '*My* notebook! Imagine!'

'Sparshji did nat tell you?' Bhavani asks casually.

She laughs. 'Sparshu thinks I'm delicate and need to be protected from all this gore and killing! It's too cute of him.'

'You two are friends?'

Her face pinkens a little.

'Yes,' she says firmly. 'Just friends. He's got romantic feelings for me, I know, and while I respect that, I've told him that we will not take it to the next level till he's eighteen and maybe not even then, because he may very well fall for somebody else by that time! It's a treasured, *unique* relationship and I won't let anybody label it.'

How these young people *talk* nowadays, Bhavani marvels to himself. Respect, label, treasured… are they all really as mature as the language they use?

'You are a very sensible young lady. Now, please, we have turned on screen sharing—can you identify these sketches?'

She leans in. Shalini, watching from the side, has an opportunity to observe her carefully applied eye make-up: neon-blue eyeliner, white eyeliner, soft smudgy kohl and smoky eyeshadow.

'That's the bespoke piece I was talking about. It was a bracelet made of diamonds, onyx and ordinary Turkish evil eyes, set in the finest platinum with flat herringbone links. Don't you *love* flat herringbone links? They ripple so fluidly, like the vertebrae of a snake. '

'Who ordered it?'

'Oh.' Devika's carefully made-up eyes grow doubtful. 'It was all very top secret, but I suppose I can tell you now.'

'Do tell us, Devikaji. Like we said, the victim was looking at it when he was shot. It could be a vital clue that will help us catch a murderer.'

The girl continues to look conflicted. 'I suppose it's safe enough,' she says hesitantly. 'I mean, it's not like he can come *here*, to Switzerland, and bump me off for telling you…'

'Who?' Bhavani's voice grows sharp. 'Tell us what?'

Devika leans in.

'Well, it's Haider Sait's bracelet, isn't it,' she whispers. 'His mother ordered it for him. It was a birthday present to keep away the evil nazar.'

Bhavani's eyebrows rise.

'Ayesha Sait told you that? Herself?'

Devika shifts into a more comfortable position.

'Mrs Sait wandered into the studio late one evening and we really hit it off. She asked me to design a bracelet, and Harsh sir said I could. My God, I was so excited to be designing such a personal piece for a legit A-list celebrity! I was really happy with it; I even put pictures of the final piece in my portfolio!'

'We haven't noticed any such bracelet on Hadi Sait's wrist,' Bhavani remarks.

'Really?' Devika looks a little disappointed. 'I did wonder if he liked it. I checked his Instagram on his birthday, I was hoping he would post his mother's gift to him and then I could tag myself. But he didn't. Maybe he didn't fancy it.' She rolls her eyes. 'Men are so fussy—fifty times fussier than women!'

On that note, they wind up the call, with Devika promising to make herself available again if Bhavani needs more inputs.

'Well?' says Shalu when he turns to her. 'She's the first person to speak well of Sushil Kedia! Perhaps he was not such a terrible person after all?'

'You're thinking Sushil Kedia was infatuated with this young girl,' he replies. 'She certainly is pretty enough. And she has a fine sense of design too, which is something he would probably have appreciated.'

'One doesn't *like* to think like that,' Shalini grimaces. 'It's so sordid—she's practically a child *and* his son's crush!' But even if he were infatuated with her, how does it connect with our case?'

Bhavani sips his drink quietly.

Shalu gasps and clutches his forearm. 'Bhavani, suppose they were involved, and Pooja Kedia got wind of it, and Sparsh too, and mother and son got together and killed him!'

He puts down his glass.

'And Pooja broke her fast a few hours before killing him? Would that nat be too obvious a giveaway?'

She sits back with a sigh. 'True.'

'And Devika would nat have spoken so highly of him if they had been romantically involved, Shalu. She would have tried to cover it up by being more balanced. But she was openly praising him.'

'It was probably one-sided then,' Shalini says. '*She* was obsessed with *him*. That could have been enough to infuriate Pooja.'

'It could have infuriated her enough for her to break her fast,' he says. 'But not enough to shoot him dead with a shotgun, we feel.'

'Bad Shalu.' Shalini looks guilty. 'A good feminist would work with the assumption that Devika really *is* very talented, and that Sushil Kedia just genuinely appreciated that.'

'There *is* a serpent in the garden, ACP Singh.' Ayesha Sait pulls her pashmina tighter around her shoulders with a shiver. 'Slithering about, poisoning people's minds!'

They are seated in the lawn of her large high-walled villa in Sadashivanagar. It is a cold morning, foggy and damp.

'It was nat Charuji's mind that was poisoned, Ayeshaji, it was her body,' is Bhavani's prosaic reply. 'Serpents don't do that—human beings do.'

Ayesha shifts about restlessly. There are shadows below her eyes, and her usually glowing complexion looks dull in the cold morning light.

'Do you have any suspects?' she asks him. 'Apart from my son?'

He spreads out his hands. 'It is too soon to say, madam, it has been just two days since the fresh murder.'

'*Fresh*.' She shivers again. 'Murder. A fresh murder in Habba Galli. *Two* murders in Habba Galli! It is like that song that used to come on Doordarshan when we were children:

'Ek murder,

Ek aur murder,

Ek-ek karke anek murder!'

Bhavani chuckles. 'That is very well put, Ayeshaji!'

'This is the worst year of my life, I think,' she continues sombrely. 'First Musa died, then Roganjosh got shot, now all this. What makes it worse is that life has been such a fairy tale for the last few years, what with Hadi's career taking off the way it did. I've become unused to sorrow and stress.'

'The universe does deduct its ten per cent TDS annually,' Bhavani replies comfortably. 'Perhaps yours piled up for a few years and had to be paid all at once.'

She smiles wryly. 'Well, I've certainly cleared my arrears now!'

He laughs comfortingly. 'Ayeshaji, we had a few questions for you…'

'Naturally. I assume I am a prime suspect now.'

'Madam.' Bhavani spreads out his hands. 'Everybody who attended that party is.'

'What would you like to know, ACP?'

'How did it come about that you were at Mrs Rao's place that night?'

'Oh! My husband and I have always distributed hampers to all our friends twice a year, once for Diwali and once for Eid. I did consider not sending them around this year, because we are mourning my husband's passing and then Sushil Kedia's horrible accident happened, but it is not an inexpensive hamper, and I know that people look forward to it. So I amended the usual message about having a joyous Diwali to a more sombre one about strength and peace and went ahead. Usually we send them out with the staff, but this year I was missing Habba Galli, so I decided to distribute them myself. When I called to check if people were home, Jaishri mentioned that Jhoom was upset after putting down an old dog, so I suggested that the pilla party all have dinner together to help cheer her up.'

'So when you suggested having a little party, you already knew that the euthanasia medicines would be at hand?'

'That looks bad, I know.' She makes a wry face. 'But yes.'

'Ayeshaji, in the course of the evening, did you pass the cupboard where the medicines are stored?'

'At least twice,' she replies frankly. 'I have the tiniest bladder in the world, plus I was drinking—a lot, to be honest.'

'We see. Did *everybody* pass down that corridor at least once?'

'I think so,' she says. 'Some were going to the washroom, and some were going out into the little open area there to smoke.'

'Ayeshaji, have you ever fired a shotgun? Do you know how to use one?'

She hesitates, then nods. 'I do. Musa was fond of such things. But of course there must be so many different models and brands and all.'

'Yes, yes.' Bhavani produces a neat file and starts to thumb through it. He finds a particular sheet of paper, extracts it and pushes it across the table towards her, face down.

'Ayeshaji, are we correct in assuming that Your Wish works nat just with silver but also with platinum?'

'Yes,' she says, surprised at the change in topic. Her voice growing more animated, she continues, 'I've always loved white metals. They can look gypsy-like and earthy, but they can also give a fine futuristic feel. We work mostly with silver—shined, alloyed or oxidized—and popular Indian gemstones, but for our premium offerings we work with platinum and diamonds.'

'And *yet*,' Bhavani's voice is very casual, very conversational, 'when you had to pick a birthday present for your son, you chose nat to go with your own store but,' he flips over the sheet of paper he has placed before her, 'patronized Kedia Jewellers instead and worked with a young intern nobody has heard of. Why?'

'Oh,' she says rather blankly. 'This. Where did you find this?'

'It was found on Mr Sushil Kedia's desk at the time of his death. Blood-spattered.'

Ayesha flinches. 'Ya Khuda.'

Bhavani continues to study her face steadily.

'You told the young intern who designed it that it was a birthday present for your son. And that you were getting it done at another store so the secret wouldn't leak.'

She nods slightly. 'I did.'

'*Was* he the recipient of this bracelet, Ayeshaji?'

She grimaces. 'Do I *have* to tell you?'

He spreads out his hands.

'It would make our work so much easier. If you refuse then we will have to have your lawyer present, and a proper interrogation with a lady police officer. There could be leaks. Whereas anything you tell us now would remain entirely confidential.'

'You're threatening me, in other words.'

He looks at her steadily. 'Two murders have been committed, Ayeshaji. We have to investigate everybody, properly.'

There is a long pause. Then she says with a tiny shrug, 'It was for Hadi only. It didn't come out too well, but I did not have the heart to tell the sweet little girl that, as she was so excited about designing it. I did not gift it to him.'

'You did nat find her talented?'

'Oh!' She looks torn. 'She was very enthusiastic. A nice girl.'

'So the bracelet is still in your possession. Can we see it?'

She shakes her head regretfully.

'I'm *so* sorry. I had it melted down. In the Your Wish workshop. It no longer exists.'

She doesn't look sorry, though, Bhavani thinks to himself. She looks... defiant.

'Jewellery clearly has no sentimental value for you.'

Her eyebrows shoot up. 'Meaning?'

He spreads out his hands.

'Well, you sold wedding jewellery to start your shop...'

'Oh, that.' She makes a dismissive gesture. 'I didn't like it very much, to be honest. Nor did Musa.'

'Where had your family ordered it from?'

She looks taken aback for a moment, then says composedly, 'Do you know, I have absolutely no idea! My mother just clapped it around my neck a few hours before the nikah.'

Something rustles in Jhoom's pocket when she's taking off her pants that night. She frowns, reaches into it and fishes out a stiff tattered bit of what feels like paper, but turns out to be a photograph.

'Sushi and the mysterious lady.' She recalls her visit to Sona's that afternoon as she uncrumples the photograph. She must've shoved it into her pocket without realizing.

She smoothens it out with her fingers and her eyebrows rise.

Wow, no wonder Sona had been so curious about it—it is remarkably risqué! Young Sushi, bending down to kiss the clasp of an elegant gold choker, placed around the neck of an ethereally beautiful young woman.

I must remember to return it tomorrow, Jhoom thinks as she starts to stow the picture into a thick book to smoothen it out.

And then something about the picture makes her look at it more carefully.

Is that…

No, it can't be.

But it looks *so* much like…

No, impossible.

She snatches up the pic, turns up the lights, studies it closely, more carefully.

The dark, laughing, vivid eyes, so much like the ones that had looked deep into her more ordinary ones only a night ago…

There can be no mistaking those eyes.

10

Palolem

The morning of Chhoti Diwali dawns clear and crisp and cool. In the lush garden of a sarkari bungalow in the heart of town, full of jackfruit trees, bougainvillea and butterflies, DG Gautham sits jiggling one leg impatiently and watching ACP Bhavani Singh work his way leisurely through a plateful of hot, crisp onion bhajjis.

Finally, the old policeman pushes his plate away and reaches for a glass of chilled nimbu-pani.

'What a beautiful garden, sir,' he says. 'The pink Tabebuia, the scents, the bird cries at sundown—you should have had the wedding here only!'

'That's what *I* said,' the DG returns grumpily. 'But it is too small, according to my wife and daughter.'

Bhavani looks sympathetic. 'Do let us know if we can help with any of the preparations, sir.'

'You can help by nabbing this murderer!' is the testy reply. 'With Diwali tomorrow, a Lok Sabha election approaching, rising unemployment and a plunging stock market, one would think people would have something else to think about! But no, all they want to know is if the Bollywood hero is a murderer! Aiyyo, I called up our family priest yesterday, to get a brief on his requirements for the wedding ceremony, and even *he* asked me if Haider Sait dunnit!'

'That is highly unlikely,' Bhavani says calmly. 'And speaking of priests, sir, would it be possible for you to intercede at your level and get an interview with the parish priest in the St Joseph's diocese? We need to speak with somebody who knows the Pais family well.'

'Don't go asking them to break the seal of the confessional, Bhavani.' Gautham's hand hovers over the bhajjis. 'They get bloody worked up about it, you know that.'

'Sir, we just want to chat,' Bhavani assures him.

'You always just want to chat.' Gautham picks up an onion bhajji, holds it tentatively over the bowl of green chilli chutney, then puts it down again. 'I shouldn't be eating these; I'm trying to lose weight for the wedding. I'll look like ragi mudde wrapped in a white paper napkin in my mundu otherwise!'

Bhavani sits forward at once.

'Sir,' he says persuasively, 'we promise you, the daily eleven-minute 5BX workout shows *excellent* results for *all* age grou—'

Gautham hushes him with his hands.

'Too late for all that, Bhavani! I'll speak to the archbishop for you. We have some interesting information on your hero's friend, Krishnan Chetty, by the way. Appears the chap is gunning to be elected as the head of the Habba Galli shopkeepers' association, which is often the first move towards a full-blown political career. His main rival for the post was the late Sushil.'

'Yes, sir. Our superhost Krish Chetty is very much on our mind, sir.'

Gautham utters a short laugh. 'Make sure he doesn't sprinkle some dog killer in your morning cereal! He had some old chakkar with the Kedia daughter-in-law, you said?'

'Yes sir. She is on our list too.'

'Seems like a long list, Bhavani.'

'It is indeed long,' Bhavani replies seriously. 'The Raos, mother and daughter; the Kedias, separately or just one of them playing a lone hand; Mr Tomar; the Saits, separately or alone...'

'Because Haider is playing a killer in his next movie and wanted to get into the skin of the character? Or because of this enmity between his mother and Sushil Kedia? Is it all about dogs or is there something more to it?'

Bhavani nods.

'Perhaps Kedia had ferreted out some secret of hers. Not to extract money—he was rich enough, but just to have a hold of some sort over her. They disliked each other intensely, apparently. Both wanted to be considered the top dog of Habba Galli.'

'There are too many damn dogs in this case.' Gautham sounds fed up.

'And if you really sit down to look at it, there's *nothing* concrete against Haider Sait,' he continues. 'Except for the right wing's desire to punish a humble Muslim boy for having the audacity to become so spectacularly successful.'

'It would seem so, sir. More likely suspects are, as you say, Krish Chetty. And Peter Pais, working alone or with Bhagyalakshmi and Saraswati, who are sisters.'

'His sisters?' Gautham has reached for the bhajjis again.

'No, sir, nat his sisters. They are domestic workers in the houses of the Pais family, the Tomar family as well as Kedia Kutumb.'

'Sounds like they've got a bit of a nexus going?' Gautham gestures with a piece of bhajji. 'These two sisters, both named after goddesses, one working in the home of the murderer, one working in the homes of the victims? Have you explored that angle?'

'We have, sir.'

'And?'

'Nothing conclusive yet but we have one–two ideas. Meanwhile, Peter Pais also has two sisters, named Liza and Suzy. They live in Boston and Sydney respectively, but are currently holidaying in Goa with their brother and mother, who does nat yet know that the holiday is going to end with her being put into assisted living.'

'Poor lady.' Gautham grimaces as he puts down the bhajji and sits back again. 'What has India come to? But I suppose it's the best thing to do under the circumstances—she is clearly suffering from dementia. So you think this Peter did it, do you? Why?'

'To get clarity on the *why* is why we need to speak to his Father Confessor, sir.'

Gautham looks sceptical.

'I'll get you the permission, but you're barking up the wrong tree, I feel, Bhavani.'

'We believe in barking up *all* the trees, one by one, sir,' replies Bhavani with a gentle smile.

'We've all gone barking mad,' the DG says irritably. 'Personally, I think the Saits are out of it—somebody with that much to lose doesn't turn into a mad prince of Denmark just because his frisky ammi may have offed his namazi old abba.'

'We agree, sir. And there was nothing untoward about the father's death, in any case. We have checked it out thoroughly.'

'My money is on the Kedia clan. They saw their chance and they decided to dance! They leapt upon that fallen shotgun, got painful papaji to sit in the hot seat and blew him away for their one-third each—all at the instigation of this new butter-won't-melt-in-her-mouth bride! And then they finished off the fat lady because she figured it out. But it'll be hard to prove, Bhavani, it'll be hard to prove.'

Bhavani maintains a respectful silence.

Gautham finally succumbs to the lure of the onion bhajjis. He picks up the fattest one, dips it into the wickedly green chutney and bites into it with relish. Indistinctly, he gives his final take on the case: 'The family that kills together, sticks together.'

'Ah, the Pais family from Sakleshpur,' says Father Abreo, sighing. 'Two older girls and a younger boy. The usual story—they kept having girls till God blessed them with a boy. The father passed a few years ago—an old-fashioned coffee planter who hated city life. Used to drive down only to bully the officials at the Coffee Board, or to take his boy to task for not doing well in his studies. But Peter was, and *continues* to be, a good son!'

His tone is distinctly less enthusiastic as he adds, 'The daughters live abroad, I believe.'

'Mrs Pais has been in the papers recently, you must have read,' Naik says stolidly. 'The stray dog shooting and the double murder and so on.'

Father Abreo makes a distressed clicking sound. 'Yes, yes, she has stopped receiving communion, alas! I used to visit her every Sunday without fail to give it, but the last couple of times I went, she mocked me for my complexion, called me a black crow in a white frock and waggled her dressing gown in a rather odd manner at me from her window! Poor Peter was thoroughly embarrassed. Truly, she must have done something good before this mental malady claimed her to have such a meek, dutiful son. The daughters are more worldly, I have heard, and somewhat less dutiful, but I must not talk loosely! Anyway, since that incident, I thought it wiser to cease my home visits. I now remember her in my daily prayers and have left the rest in God's capable hands, who,' he adds wryly, 'seems to have seen it fit to make rather a sad hash of things!'

Inspector Naik says firmly, 'Father, we know that things that are told to you in the confession booth are strictly private and not to be shared but we request you to…'

'Oh, but she hasn't come for confession in years.'

'We do nat mean her,' Bhavani steps into the conversation, 'we mean *Peter*. What is the state of his mind, the state of his soul?'

Father Abreo shakes his head, his expression one of genuine regret. 'You cannot expect me to break the seal of the confessional.'

'Father, we have researched you a little bit,' Bhavani says. 'You are a Jesuit. You have spent your entire life drilling the principles of calculus into the heads of reluctant teenagers. You have taught generations of lads, and lately ladies, from the Rahul Dravid batch of Josephites to the Haider Sait batch of Josephites and beyond. What can you tell us, generally, about the several Old Boys associated with these unfortunate deaths? Nat just Peter Pais but also the Kedia brothers, Krishnan Chetty and Haider Sait?'

'You want me to tell you which one of them is most likely to be a killer.' Father Abreo rocks a little in his aluminium office chair. 'Is that it?'

In reply, Bhavani ducks his head and makes a small inviting sound.

The old priest slides a little lower in his chair and stretches out his long legs. The folds of his white cassock rustle.

'I teach middle school, officer. Middle school is a complete warzone because hormones are quickening, voices are thickening, pimples and angst are breaking out. Who has the time to listen to a celibate old man gab about integers and trigonometry and God when the mess and magic of puberty is exploding all around and inside you? Negotiating body hair, sexual stirrings, growth spurts that suddenly make heroes out of zeroes and vice versa is the real syllabus of middle school. Alcohol, pornography, cigarettes, drugs—it's all happening at the Gabba, as the cricket commentators say! And so, as a teacher, one quickly learns to figure out which particular carrot can be waved—judiciously, of course—under the nose of which particular young donkey to coax him along the path of ICSE-prescribed learning... You were saying?'

Bhavani shakes his head in admiration. 'Just that you have it, sir. The power of personality to hold a class of high-spirited youngsters in thrall! You could be a general.'

Father Abreo chuckles. 'Or a drill sergeant! So back in the eighties, Generation X's Peter Pais was motivated by approval. He was the only son, the inheritor of that estate in Coorg or Sakleshpur or Chikmagalur or wherever, and he was anxious to live up to his family's expectations. I think he still is.

'In the early nineties, schoolboy Harsh was motivated by tangible proofs of success. Money, profit, shiny trophies. He still is.

'Around the early two thousands, schoolboy Krish was motivated by adulation. Tall, golden, intelligent, wealthy, he expected it and, back in those days, he always got it.

'His best friend—some would even say sidekick—Haider was motivated by affection. He loved to make people happy and basked in this happiness he had created. He was a team player, deeply empathetic and familial, and I think he still is.

'Coming to the sole Gen Z kid in this tale, schoolboy Sparsh is motivated by sheer intellectual excellence—the purest of all motives, perhaps. He is no trophy collector, like his brother. His highs come from pitting his wits against AI, or simply cracking a tough puzzle, or triumphantly writing "hence solved" at the bottom of a page.'

'So which one of them did it?' Naik asks bluntly.

Abreo turns to him, raising an amused eyebrow.

'Only the Good Lord knows that, young man.'

'Does the motive that has been prescribed to Haider Sait—that he wanted to "feel like a murderer"—feel valid to you?'

Abreo taps his finger on his chin thoughtfully. 'I'm not sure. See, Hadi is a thorough fellow. He actually lived inside an ancient PT-76 tank for a week before he acted in that 1971 war movie, did you know? Ate there, slept there, went to the loo in the bushes just outside! He became great friends with all the soldiers and men at the base. I can imagine him befriending some Mumbai mafia assassins for this role, if such persons actually exist, getting drunk with them even. But murder for such a motive? I don't think so.'

'And his friend Krishnan Chetty?

'Krishnan Chetty has political ambitions. He has been sending out feelers to people with political connections on our Old Boys network. I think he hopes his friend Haider will campaign for him, but is too proud to ask. At the same time, he has opened a door in his heart to drugs, envy and caste-based pride. His poorer, shorter, darker friend from another faith has outshone him. That's the sort of thing that could push a habitual centre-stager like Krish into a dark space.'

Naik stirs excitedly in his seat. 'Sir, Krishnan Chetty's school records show medals for target rifle-shooting!'

'And as the press keeps reminding us, Hadi Sait trained with similar weaponry for the film Father just mentioned.' The ACP turns back to the priest. 'Father, is there anything else you could share with us about Peter Pais—without troubling your conscience, naturally? What is going on in his mind?'

Abreo shakes his head gravely. 'Those are family secrets, believe me, they have nothing to do with Mr Sushil Kedia, alive or dead. *Or* the lady who perished a few days after him.'

Naik leans forward insistently.

'Is he… repressed? Is there any question of homosexuality? Perhaps Sushil Kedia had been taunting him about it?'

Abreo closes his eyes for a moment.

'When he was in school,' he says slowly, 'we put up a production of *The Wiz*—*The Wizard of Oz*, you know.'

He opens his eyes. The policemen nod, waiting for him to come to the point.

'Drama teachers in boys' schools look for plays with all-male characters, but no matter how hard you try, there are always one or two female parts that have to be cast. Peter played Glinda the Good Witch. He seemed to relish it. If not homosexual, then perhaps he is, as the young people say nowadays, gender fluid?'

Early in the morning on Diwali, Bhavani sits on the bench in the courtyard of The Hub@HabbaGalli, soaks up the slanting sunshine and watches Saraswati and Bhagyalakshmi draw an elaborate kolum on the deep red, freshly swept and swabbed courtyard floor.

The sisters have placed a brass Lakshmi–Ganesh statue in the exact centre and are creating an intricate pattern around it, radiating outwards into a steadily widening circle. Their hands move with neat, unhurried expertise: they dip their index fingers into a bowl of thin-as-milk rice paste, then trace whorls and loops and petals and stems and leaves and lamps onto the richly glowing floor. It is a geometric process, but also an artistic one, and clearly they have done it a hundred times before.

Bhavani finds it hypnotic viewing.

Sushil Kedia sits at the centre of my kolum, he muses, just like the statues of Lakshmiji and Ganeshji sit at the centre of theirs. Everything that has happened so far radiates out from Sushil Kedia's death. When the case is cracked, all the seemingly randomly scattered motifs—the petals and sepals and stems and flames and birds and paisleys—will link up and connect perfectly with that. There will be *no* loose ends left.

How to explain this to Manju and DG Gautham but?

Almost from the beginning, Bhavani has been certain about exactly how the first murder was committed. The process of deducing this had been a fairly easy one, but the identity of the killer was harder to establish: Krish Chetty was ruled out right away, as had Haider Sait, Jhoomar Rao, Sona, Harsh and Sparsh Kedia, as well as Mr and Mrs Tomar. Jaishri Rao and Pooja Kedia were the supects he had focused on, along with Mehtab Bhai and, of course, the man against whom most of the evidence is piling up now.

This new evidence includes a key breakthrough made by Manju's team, while scanning the footage provided by the Karnataka Traffic Police cameras.

And a cosy chat in Kannada, which Manju has had with the two girls working so demurely on the kolam now...

All this new evidence seems to indicate most strongly that Bhavani's original theory is the correct one. But what to do about the loose ends that aggravatingly refuse to tie in?

Bhavani had tried to articulate these misgivings to the justifiably excited Manju when they had met at DG Gautham's residence for a debriefing on the Karnataka Police's exciting findings.

They had both heard him out patiently enough, but when he had finished speaking, the DG had shaken his head.

'Maybe you have a point, Bhavani, maybe you have several points, but there's just too much pressure on this case now. Haider Sait's fans are screaming for the murderer's blood, and the right wingers are screaming for Hadi Sait's! For heaven's sake, let's forget about these damn core body temperature readings; they're notoriously inaccurate anyway! I vote we make an arrest and give the press some good news on Diwali day.'

And so, after a little persuasion, Bhavani had agreed. After all, there are some solid pros in following this course of action—poor Shalini's annual honeymoon plan has been quite ruined by the intrusion of this double murder. The least he can do to make it up to her is to go ahead with this arrest.

Now he smoothens the creases on his freshly washed floral Hawaiian shirt, slides his hand into the pocket of his khaki Bermuda shorts, fishes out the pair of rather *Dabangg* sunglasses that are her Diwali gift to him and places them on his blunt brown nose just as she emerges into the courtyard.

Shalini Singh is dressed in a long sleeveless mint-green beach dress that shows off her toned brown body beautifully. Bracelets jingle on her still-slender wrists. A large floppy sun hat of the softest coral is slung upon the back of her shoulders. Her abundant silvery waves of hair gleam in the sunshine and her lively eyes sparkle in anticipation. A quarter of Vat 69 peeks out jauntily from the top of the straw beach bag she is carrying on one arm.

'Arrey bhai, Bhavani, where are you? Manju has called twice. The chopper is waiting! We can't wait to get to Goa!'

Coconut and banana trees sway madly as their helicopter lands on an almost perfectly circular emerald-green helipad. Two Goa Police jeeps stand ready for Bhavani, Naik and the two armed and uniformed policemen accompanying them. As they pile into the jeeps, Shalini's Uber drives up and honks.

She smiles at Bhavani.

'Thank you for gifting us this perfect day!' she whispers. 'Meet us at Palolem beach when you're done and we'll watch the Diwali sun go down together.'

Bhavani's ride to the luxury villa the Pais family has rented is uneventful. When their jeeps drive through the gates, they find a small posse of teenagers playing frisbee in a sparkling swimming pool. Ed Sheeran plays on wireless speakers. The men folk are grouped near a bar, Liza and Suzy are grilling meat on a barbeque and Mrs Dondi Pais, dressed in her hot-pink two-piece, is dipping her feet in the shallows and sipping a pina colada. Her wheelchair is parked behind her.

Everybody looks around when the police jeeps pull up, even though their flashing lights are barely discernable in the daytime. The teenagers wave uncertainly and one smart-alecky lad, clad in Bondi beach surfer shorts, dark glasses and nothing else, exclaims in an exaggerated Broadway accent: 'Lawks, it's the fuzzz!'

He is immediately shushed and dunked into the water by his older sister, and emerges spluttering and subdued to sit shivering at the edge of the pool with his grandmother.

It's a good-looking family, Bhavani realizes. Up till now they have been interacting with its most homely-looking members, but Liza and Suzy are fit, attractive women, with personable husbands and beautiful children. In fact, the cheerleader effect benefits their brother who, for all his bad-mouthing of his siblings, looks happy and almost handsome in their company.

But the moment he recognizes Bhavani the colour drains from his face, leaving it pallid and sweaty. He licks his lips, gulps and comes forward, as the rest of the clan look on curiously.

'Uncle Pete, should I lay your friends a seat?' asks the youngest nephew, all of six years old, who has been entrusted with the important job of setting out plates at the wooden picnic table.

'Uh… no, Derek,' Peter says with rather a ghastly smile. 'Come, let's go inside, shall we?'

'Yes.' Bhavani smiles.

'I'm coming too,' Liza, the older of the two sisters, says determinedly. 'Suze, pour mummy another drink.'

'No, I want to swim first!' Dondi Pais shouts out at once. 'Don't tell me what to do, Miss Lizz-Piz! It's too hot to sit like this, I'm going to take off my clothes and jump in…'

'Uh, grandma, your clothes are already off!' says the littlest little girl.

'Shut up, men!' Dondi Pais scowls at her affectionately. 'And I want to take off my cap also!'

The little girl slaps a hand to her forehead.

'But grandma, you aren't wearing a cap!'

Dondi Pais winks. 'Dat shows how much you know, you silly sausage! Look!'

Reaching up with one shaky hand, she tugs at her thick curly white mop of hair and whips it off with a flourish, revealing a gleaming scalp, bare of anything but a few stringy white strands, to the startled Goan skies.

'We have footage from the highway police that shows your car turning around on the road to Sakleshpur and heading back towards Bangalore at six in the evening, two hours and twenty minutes before the shooting happened,' Naik tells Pais grimly across an ornately carved dining table a little later. 'We also have footage of you crossing a red light two minutes away from Habba Galli at seven-thirty that evening. It's wonderful what you can find once you know what to look for! *And* we have—yes?' He looks up sharply as one of his juniors walks into the room.

The man gives him a thumbs up. Naik smiles.

'*And* we have found a dog whistle fitted into your mother's wheelchair—inaudible to human beings, but very agitating to dogs, liable to make them bark if it is pressed stealthily as the wheelchair rolls past them.'

Manju is in full flow, Bhavani thinks admiringly as he sits back, sips a piping hot cup of tea and watches the scene play out. What a committed young man he is, how much homework he has done! And in a few years, what a fine policeman he will be!

'You made a drama about going to Sakleshpur and left Habba Galli at four p.m.,' Naik tells the cowering Peter. 'You even drove halfway there. Then you turned around, doubled back, parked your car on Dickenson Road—don't bother denying it, we have eyewitnesses—sneaked into the house and, under some pretext or the other, gave your mother a sleeping pill that knocked her out for the night.'

Breathing heavily, he walks to the window, then wheels around and points an accusing finger.

'Then you wore her wig. You wore her dressing gown.' His lips curl scornfully. 'You've always been a good female impersonator, Glinda the Good Witch!'

The drooping Pais straightens up at this. 'Who told you that?' His voice rises, spiralling panickedly. 'Father Abreo! Mujhe Jezu, does the entire congregation know?'

'Nobody knows but us,' Naik replies grimly. 'Now, where was I? Yes. You waited for the moonrise and once it had been sighted, and all of Habba Galli was out on their rooftops, looking at it and taking photos and videos of this exotic north Indian ritual, you loaded up gunny boy, took off his safety catch, pushed up your window pane and, with the theme music of *The Good, the Bad and the Ugly* playing in your ears—metaphorically speaking—you gave the residents of Habba Galli the show of their lives!'

Bhavani's eyebrows rise slightly. Young Manju clearly has a taste for the dramatic.

'It was easy for you to pull it off because you have the same stance and body language as your mother. You sound like her too, and living with her for all these years meant you could mimic her way of speaking successfully. It helped that the lights inside the house were all on, but the street was fully dark outside. You were silhouetted against the light.'

Bhavani, biting into a crisp tea-soaked Goan pao and watching Pais's face narrowly, sees him flinch a little with every sentence Naik utters.

It is like watching an animal being flogged, he thinks, distressed, putting his pao down, suddenly not hungry any more. The delicious snack has turned to dust in his mouth.

Naik continues to build his case.

'Your employees at the estate vouch for what a good shot you are and how well you know that gun! Child's play for you to look above that leafy hedge, spot the hated lamp-lit face of Sushil Kedia and then, like Ajay Devgn said in *RRR*, "Load, Aimmm, Shooooot!"'

Peter's tortured face looks confused at this.

Perhaps, Bhavani thinks to himself as he pushes his teacup away, he is too English-medium to have watched *RRR*.

Naik pauses, panting lightly.

'I'm not sure if you *meant* to drop the gun. Perhaps it fell out of your hands because you suffered a pang of conscience when you saw Sushil Kedia's figure slump sideways across the street. Perhaps the recoil was too much for you. Or perhaps it was both. Either way, you shut the window, removed your disguise, slunk out of the flat and back to your car, still parked on Dickenson road, and made a big show of surprise when Jaishri Rao phoned you a little later.'

Peter Pais sits up suddenly, shaking his head. He tries to speak, to object, to refute something, but the young policeman is in full spate.

'And the *cruellest* thing you did…' Naik's eyes smoulder with fire '… was to ram the butt of the shotgun into the frail shoulder of your sleeping mother so it would look like she had bruising from the recoil!'

Peter Pais covers his face with his hands.

'Yes, that was terrible of me, that was the most terrible thing I did,' he moans. 'God will never forgive me for doing that, even if mummy will!'

'She kept insisting she hadn't done anything,' Naik says bitterly. 'Denying it just like a child who has done something wrong would, is how we rationalized it. But it was just the *plain* and *simple* truth!'

Peter Pais's hands drop away. He raises a ravaged face to them, tears leaking down his cheeks. It is not a pretty sight.

'I just couldn't bear it any more,' he says hopelessly. 'It became too much for me to handle day in, day out, months, years, decades, the smells, the sounds, the bedpans, the rubber mats, the boiled food, the puréed fruit, the hospital reports, the boxes of medicine, and the constant *constant* talking! I wanted my *space*, I wanted my *place*!'

Bhavani makes a small distressed sound.

'And yet...' Peter's face spasms, 'what else is my identity, what else is my achievement, apart from the fact that everybody agrees that I am the good, dutiful son who looks after his *mummy*? I haven't got a big corporate job in the US, I'm not a senior civil servant in Australia, I have no children to show, I have nothing! I just run the estate, and even *that* my manager does really, he's a clever fellow, while I—just look—after—mummy! Father Abreo told me...' his despairing eyes light up, 'he said this was enough to get me a seat in the *highest* place in heaven!' He gives a small mirthless laugh.

'*Heaven! I'll* tell you what heaven is. Heaven is being alone in my flat with the windows open, not shut *because it's so cold, puta*! Heaven is a crisp cleansing breeze blowing through every stuffy room, and *bright white* lighting, not zero-watt yellow bulbs to save electricity! Heaven is a pool table instead of a bloody dining table, heaven is pouring myself a drink without having to pour one for her, heaven is sipping it with my booted feet up on the table, and the comfort of knowing that I can walk around naked, and fart and splash loudly into the pot when I take a piss without having to hear the giggles of those damn cleaning women she insists she can't do without!'

He draws a long shuddering breath. 'So yes, I got tired of carrying her up and down every day, so I used the whistle to stop the damn walks. And yes, I dressed up as her and shot at the dogs, because I wanted to make *such* a nasty public nuisance of Dondi bai that my sisters, the church and the police would have no choice but to intervene. That way I would still be good dutiful Peter who didn't want to send his mother into assisted living, but was *forced* to because she had become impossible to live with!'

He stops, panting, and buries his face in his hands again.

Naik's macho-cop persona wavers a little. He says briskly, 'Take your time. Take your time!'

After a while Pais looks up again. 'Of course, it backfired on me,' he says dully. 'Like everything sinful always does. That bloody jeweller was sitting in his damn office, and I shot the bugger by mistake! My God, when you people came around the next day and told me that had happened, my very soul shrivelled up and sank into my shoes. I felt like Jesus, Mary and Joseph had had the last laugh after all!'

Naik twitches and starts forward at this, but Bhavani lays a restraining hand upon his arm.

Peter Pais continues, now looking a little relaxed at having got the worst over with, 'To be honest, I'd even enjoyed my little performance. I've shot enough animals to know that the strength of Roganjosh's howling indicated that she would survive with not too much harm done, and yes, it was evil of me to strike mummy on the shoulder with the butt of the gun, but it was just a gentle tap and she really does bruise easily, so I thought a nine-month novena of the rosary would be enough repentance for that. But Sushil bloody Kedia was a different kettle of fish altogether! I've been sick as a dog with guilt and regret, but it's hardly like I could come forward and admit I'd been running around in my mother's nightie like Norman fuckin' Bates!'

Bhavani continues hold Naik's arm.

Peter Pais says quietly, his voice now unsure, 'So I shut up and hoped that the nightmare would pass. But then that fat woman dragged Musa Sait's son into the whole mess, so naturally the press came running and everything snowballed crazily and now there's all sorts of conspiracy theories going around! All I want to say really, with my sincerest apologies, is that there's no great big criminal mind striding through Habba Galli! It's just boring old me—I went a little stir-crazy and shot Sushil Kedia, *entirely* by mistake, and even Charu Tomar's death must've been some sort of accident only! Maybe she'd started a cottage industry of killing strays in her free time, God knows she hated them enough to want to do it, and she mixed up the two medications!'

'That is a very interesting theory,' Bhavani says placidly. 'Tell us two things, Peterji. Firstly, did you actually see Sushil Kedia fall over when your bullet hit him? Did you notice the sound of the glass breaking, the sight of a man slumping sideways in his chair? And secondly, how did you come to drop the gun? Was it because you saw Sushil Kedia slump and were horrified at what you had accidently done?'

Pais shakes his head. 'None of the above,' he says miserably. 'I was too busy acting like mummy. I didn't even register Kedia's window. Also, the shots were loud, the recoil was strong and Roganjosh was whining so loudly! That's why I slept so well that night—I had no clue the man was gone till you two came to my house and told me. That's when I got trapped in this endless nightmare.'

'And why did you drop the gun?' Bhavani asks.

'I don't know,' Peter says irritably. 'The damn thing was heavy, and I was just behaving in character, so to speak. I felt in my heart that if it had really been mummy, then hundred per cent the gun would have dropped out of her shaky old hands. So I dropped it. It felt correct and final and dramatic somehow!'

'It was method acting,' Bhavani says. 'You are really a very fine actor, you know.'

Peter reddens. 'Well, thank you, I suppose.'

Naik speaks up. 'You're saying it was an accident, not premeditated murder?'

'Yes!'

The young policeman gives a scornful laugh. 'You can't expect us to believe that!'

'Why?' The question is wrung out of Pais. 'It's the truth!'

Bhavani asks gently, 'But what about the pornography, Peterji?'

Pais blinks. 'The what?'

'The porn you're addicted to, which you watch on the large-screen TV after your mother goes to sleep. Isn't that why you want to be all alone in your flat, with your drink in your hand and your booted feet up on the table?'

Pais's face pales.

'I'm not *addicted*!' He seems revolted by the idea. 'In any case, consuming adult content involving consenting adults; if one is an adult, is not a crime.' The phrase slides off his tongue glibly. He has clearly thought about it a lot and rationalized it to himself.

'It is, in the eyes of Mujhe Jezu,' Bhavani says softly. 'We know you were quite addicted, because Bhagyalakshmi figured out what you were up to and she told her sister Saraswati, and Sushil Kedia overheard them chattering outside his atariya during their lunch hour, and he threw it in your face that day when he came to confront you about being a bad influence on his son Sparsh. Is this nat true?'

Pais sighs. 'It is,' he admits.

'He said he would reveal your shameful secret to your sisters!' Naik says triumphantly. 'And to the community! The entire congregation of St Joseph's! He was about to make you a laughing stock, and you would rather have died than have that come out, so you decided, didn't you, that it would be better if *he* died...'

'I did not!' Peter screams. 'I told him exactly what I just told you—that consuming adult content involving consenting adults; if one is an adult it is not a crime!'

'And a few days later you shot him, by accident?' Naik is openly sceptical.

'Yes!' Peter gives a little moan and covers his face with both hands. 'I did! Oh God, it sounds unbelievable!'

'I believe you, Pete,' Peter's sister Liza speaks up quietly from the back of the room. 'Suze and I speak to both mummy and Bhagyalakshmi on a regular basis, you know. We know you're... troubled.' She turns to look at the policemen. 'Officers, this kind of stupid drama is *just* the sort of thing Pete would pull, instead of just admitting, like a normal person, that mummy has become too much for him to handle.'

He stares at her with wide panicked eyes. 'They're going to arrest me for *murder*, Lizzy!'

She sighs and turns to the policemen.

'Are you here to arrest him?'

Naik nods grimly. 'Yes, madam. We have enough evidence to do so.'

Peter Pais starts to rock back and forth.

'I didn't do it! I mean, I *did* do it but I didn't do it on purpose! You have to believe me!'

Bhavani gets to his feet for the first time. He walks over to the rocking, perspiring man and bends to look him full in the face.

'We believe you,' he says calmly. 'We believe every single word you are saying.'

Naik's jaw drops.

'And now, you have to help us figure out who has phasaoed you into this situation. Because you have been phasaoed, Peterji.'

'You're what they call the patsy,' explains the bare-chested teenager in the surfer shorts, who has stolen into the room. 'The fall guy, or the bakra.'

Peter Pais gulps pathetically.

'You believe me?' he says to Bhavani.

Bhavani nods. 'We do.'

Pais points a quivering finger at Naik. '*He* doesn't.'

Bhavani leans in closer and looks deep into the panicked eyes.

'Peterji, we promise you the *whole world* will believe you. Now tell us this, could anybody have known what you were planning?'

'I don't know!' Pais shakes his head miserably. 'I'm a very private person, I didn't even confess it in *church*. I keep to myself, I don't talk to anyone...'

'That's true enough,' Liza says, rolling her eyes. 'The bugger's an absolute clam.'

'Maybe a mind reader read his mind,' Naik says sarcastically.

Peter continues to shake his head. 'Nobody could have read my mind! Nob—' He pauses abruptly. 'Somebody could have read my diary! I wrote everything down in my diary! My God, that's it!'

'Sir, please!' Naik, still unconvinced, appeals to Bhavani. 'This is all an elaborate cover-up. There is nobody else. And anyway, it's *his* diary, he could go on writing *anything* in it!'

'Don't panic, uncle Pete,' the surfer dude, who is still evesdropping shamelessly, pipes up. 'This is standard good-cop–bad-cop technique.'

'We are both good cops,' Bhavani states firmly. 'Peterji, this is excellent progress. Who could have read this dairy of yours? Where do you keep it?'

'It's on my phone, a one-person group on my WhatsApp, only I can access it.'

Excitement enters Bhavani's voice. 'But Peterji, the *first* thing you mentioned to us when we entered your house on the morning after the shooting was that your phone had been stolen or lost recently! *Where* did you lose it, Peterji?'

'In the market only.' Hope enters Peter Pais's voice for the first time. 'Some shop there… a vegetable thela, a shoe shop—or maybe I just dropped it on the road…' He looks up excitedly. '*Anybody* could have found it!'

'Is Manju very upset?' Shalini asks Bhavani in the evening. 'He was hoping to make a great arrest today!'

They are lounging in twin canvas deckchairs, sipping LIITs on Palolem beach.

Fireworks rise in the skies around them. The waters of the Arabian Sea lap at their toes, a balmy breeze blows and everywhere is the smell, the sound and the sparkle of Diwali.

'He got to make a great breakthrough instead,' Bhavani says with a shrug. 'We found out about the diary, Shalu!'

'That *is* a big one.'

She reaches for the plate of batter-fried calamari between them.

'How were you so sure Peter didn't do it, Bhavani? Everything seemed to add up so well!'

He sips his drink.

'Well, literally the *first* thought we had had was that somebody could have been dancing about in a wig with the gun. But it would have been a very hit-or-miss way to commit a murder. Also, some things just did nat tie up.'

She dips a chunk of calamari into the creamy sauce and bites into it with relish. 'Like what?'

'One. Saraswati's comment that the carpet in front of the row of bulletproof safes in the atariya appeared faded. Which meant that it had been moved—rotated around to face the other way. Why? And by whom?

'Secondly. The core body temperature reading, which indicates that the death happened much later than the time of moonrise, which was when Peter was doing his little act.'

'Speaking of core body temperature.' Shalini spits her calamari into her napkin delicately. 'This batter is hot, but the squid inside is still frozen. Yuck.'

Bhavani goes very still.

Shalini looks up. 'Arrey, it's okay, Bhavani. Don't complain to the waiter or make a scene, please. We're having such a nice evening.'

But Bhavani shakes his head. His eyes are screwed up tightly, and he is rocking back and forth.

Shalini looks alarmed. 'Bhavani, don't overthink, don't strain. You'll get haemorrhoids in the brain.'

His eyes fly open. His face is glowing. It looks almost handsome in the soft beachlight.

'You've solved it, Shalu,' he says simply. 'Saraswati said Sushil Kedia liked the atariya to be really cold. So much so that he used to switch the AC on remotely one hour before he even entered the room.'

Shalini blinks. 'So?'

'So, we have been very, very stupid. And superstitious—which is worse! But we are on the right track now! Manju will just have to confirm two–three things for us…'

11

A Lover Who Lives Down the Lane

Hadi, call me back.

10.30 p.m.

Hadi, it's Jhoom. Call.

5 a.m.

Hello, it's urgent. I can't tell you on WhatsApp.
I need to MEET you. Urgently.

12.30 a.m.

Call.

7 p.m.

Call.

12.30 a.m.

Have you ghosted me?

8 a.m.

Should I save your number as Tatti Sait?

4 p.m.

Wow, you've ghosted me. Okay. Whatevs. But this has nothing to do with whatever was going on between us (if anything even WAS!) so you needn't panic. I have information you need to know. It concerns FAMILY.
Unless of course you know it already.
Cannot say more on WhatsApp.

11.30 p.m.

Fuck this.
I tried.
Have a nice life.

2.30 a.m.

She is drearily starting her day in the clinic, heavy-eyed with lack of sleep and dressed in her sloppiest sweatshirt and vet pants, when they come for her.

Jhoom blinks at her visitors in exhausted awe. In black sunglasses and tight black tees that show off their biceps and pectorals to great advantage, the towering figures of Bheema and Luther are a picturesque sight.

'Whuh… what's all this?' she asks apprehensively. 'Who are you?'

'HS's security detail,' the darker one replies in a deep voice. 'You need to come with us. He wants to talk to you.'

Relief courses through Jhoom's veins, followed swiftly by anger.

'Then why can't he phone me like a normal person?'

The lighter one's eyebrows shoot up. 'Coz his situation ain't normal, innit? He's a goddamn movie star.'

Jhoom flushes.

'I'm not coming with you,' she says coldly. 'I have a full day of work and patients to treat.'

The darker man puts forward a placating hand.

'Ma'am, please, ignore this moron. Listen to me, the cops have HS's phone. In fact, they have all our phones—the entire team's, and his mother's as well. They're reading every message we send and every message we receive. Privacy's a real bitch at the moment.'

Jhoom's heart gives a huge horrid lurch.

'Has he been arrested?'

They shake their heads in unison.

'No, no, he's just cooperating with the police, very quietly.'

'Don't be idiotic,' she snaps, sounding just like her mother. 'We all know what assisting the police in their inquiries means! He's under arrest or about to be arrested!'

Wordlessly, they hand her a motorcycle helmet and a handwritten note.

She's never seen Hadi's handwriting before, yet the sight of it feels like a reassuring embrace.

Jhoom,

Save my number as anything, just keep it saved.
Lots to say, but face to face.
Please come with B and L?
They'll wait till you're free.

Love,
Hadi

They ride through the chaotic Shivajinagar office rush hour tripling on the heavy powerful bike. They turn onto Bellary Road, into the large green bungalows of Sadashivanagar, and stop at a massive Sankey-tank-facing villa surrounded by high barbed-wire-topped boundary walls, eleven news channel vans, two traffic police vans and a horde of perspiring reporters who recognize Bheema and Luther and surge forward hungrily, cameras raised on mechanical arms and clicking like the pincers of some fantastic giant insect.

Behind the reporters is a surging solid mass of angry-eyed people who set up a hoarse hostile chant as a white gate, thick and opaque as a stone wall, slides open soundlessly to admit the bike.

Kolegara!
Kolegara!

Kolegara!
Kolegara!

Jhoom, sandwiched between two reassuringly solid bodies, watches all this unfold through the tinted visor of her helmet with a sense of sick panic and complete unreality. Is this what Hadi's daily life is like?

The gate glides shut behind them, they ride up a deep, shaded driveway flanked by flowering trees and lush hedges and suddenly there is Hadi, springing to his feet from an aesthetically weather-beaten bench set in front of a jade-green lily pond in the lavishly landscaped lawn.

Sweatshirted, tousled and worried-eyed, he holds out his hands to her.

Jhoom ignores them and takes off her helmet slowly.

'Hi.' He sounds unsure.

'Hi,' she returns shakenly. 'Nice house.'

'Thanks for coming.'

She throws up her hands in a helpless, whatever gesture.

'What does *that* mean?' He continues to look uncertain.

'Nothing!' she shrugs and almost laughs. 'Or rather, everything! The texts unanswered for thirty-six hours, the muscled guys on bikes, the gate, the cocaine-smuggler-style fencing, the nutjob crowd outside shouting "murderer", your entire ecosystem. Also, where's Ayesha auntie?'

His face sobers.

'She's sleeping, finally, thank God. Sit, na.'

He gestures towards the bench.

She looks at it rather dazedly, then gives a small jump as a waterfall starts to bubble and splash in the lily pond behind them, making a pleasant rushing, bubbling sound.

'Safer.' He rolls his eyes. 'In case somebody's listening.'

Jhoom's eyes widen in disbelief. '*Bhavani's* doing this to you?'

'We're finally feeling the steel hand within the silk glove, I guess,' he says wryly.

'What's happening, Hadi?'

He shrugs. 'They've decided I dunnit. Something to do with Peter Pais's phone diary... I'm not entirely sure what.'

'Peter Pais's phone?' she repeats blankly.

'Yeah.' He nods. 'I keep telling them I barely knew these two people, why would I kill them, what motive could I possibly have?'

Jhoom swallows, then looks up at him with wary, searching eyes. 'You, uh, you haven't told them anything, have you?'

His troubled gaze, which was turned toward the distant gate as he was speaking, returns to caress her face. 'Jhoom, don't worry. I'll never tell anybody what I saw—your secret is entirely safe.'

'*My* secret?' She is confused. 'I've been messaging you for the last two days to tell you that *your* secret is safe!'

Her hand moves involuntarily to pat the pocket of her pants, then drops away quickly.

It is his turn to look confused. '*My* secret?'

They stare at each other in mutual non-comprehension.

The waterfall falls silent abruptly, and in the resultant quiet, a cheerful voice speaks up from behind them.

'Jhoomarji!'

They look up to find ACP Bhavani Singh smiling down blandly at them.

'Hey, ACP!' Jhoom manages to say lightly, though her heart is thudding like a piston between her eardrums. Shit, suppose he orders his men to frisk her? In the same steady voice she continues, 'You finally switched gears, huh.'

Bhavani nods genially. 'Tough times call for tough measures. Hadiji is being very cooperative. It is so nice of him.'

'He's very nice.' Jhoom's chin rises combatively.

Hadi's arm lands calmingly around her shoulders.

'She was just leaving,' he says firmly. 'We're saying goodbye.'

Bhavani nods and retreats.

They turn back to look at each other.

'He switched off the fountain,' Jhoom says wretchedly. 'We can't talk now.'

'No, we can't,' Hadi agrees with a sigh. 'Perhaps that's just as well.'

'Huh?'

His eyes start to dance below his tousled hair. He takes her hand and gets to his feet, pulling her up with him.

'What do you think of my garden, Jhoomar Rao?' he asks. 'It's quite something for a boy from Habba Galli, isn't it?'

'It's very nice,' she replies sincerely. 'Though I wouldn't call it a garden, it's more of a park, really.'

'It's got really high walls,' he replies. 'And I had to pay a *lot* of money to have it declared a drone-free zone.'

'Good for you. You can succumb to the alpha male's primal urge to pee on your turf in perfect privacy.'

'Spare me the veterinary science lectures. What I'm trying to tell you is that except for ACP Bhavani who, I think, will have the decency to avert his gaze, and Bheema and Luther, whose contracts stipulate that they step away at such moments, nobody can see us.'

Jhoom's cheeks grow hot. If her heart had been thudding earlier, it is now slamming like a sledgehammer.

'You want to kiss me.'

He nods. His eyes are intense and laughing and adorably hesitant.

'A goodbye-for-now kiss,' he says. 'A meet-you-on-the-other-side-of-the-murder-investigation kiss. Do you say yes or do you say no?'

She tilts up her chin and twinkles at him.

'Let's see what you've got, hero.'

He shakes his head, pulling her towards him, sliding his arms down her body to grip her waist as his gaze slips slowly to her mouth. 'No bracing,' he whispers. 'It's not a tetanus shot or an eyebrow threading, you know.'

'You're the one bracing,' she shoots back, looking up at him through half-shut lashes. 'Wow, your eyes *really* look like Darponk's.'

His eyes smoulder.

'Watch who you call Darponk.'

And then his lips mush down softly on hers.

Their mouths move against each other, tentatively, questioningly, then Jhoom gives a small sigh and her palms flutter up to hold Hadi's head in place.

There is silence in the garden for a while.

Birds chirp.

Bees buzz.

In the distance, the crowd continues to chant:

Kolegara!

Kolegara!

Kolegara!

Kolegara!

When he finally pulls away, it is only to cup her head with unsteady hands.

'Jhoom,' he says breathlessly, looking down at her with dazed, unfocused eyes. 'I know this looks like a big deal right now, but it will pass. I'll make everything okay, I'll shut everybody up, nobody will *ever* find out...'

She gives a sudden gasp and pulls away, her hand sliding again to the pocket of her pants.

'I have to go now,' she says abruptly, harshly. 'I shouldn't even have come. Goodbye.'

And as Hadi stares at her, stunned, confused, a thousand questions in his eyes, she whirls around and runs from the garden.

Later that day, Bhavani drops in on Jaishri Rao. He finds her chilling in her straggling little enclosed garden in her maroon dressing gown, her feet up on an old steel cage, her eyes resting meditatively on the weathered terracotta of the courtyard bricks visible through the seepage-plagued cement. Velvety emerald moss coats the chipped bricks, a colony of large black ants marches across an exposed pipe, there is surface dust and deeply encrusted grime, and over everything is the beautifying glow of the early November Bangalore sun.

'Do you know,' Jaishri asks dreamily, 'what the artist Anjolie Ila Menon told the architect who was going to build her a spanking new farmhouse in Delhi?'

He shakes his head silently.

She raises one arm and declaims dramatically: 'Build me a ruin!'

'Ah!' says Bhavani appreciatively.

Jaishri nods. 'As an artist, she understood the beauty of what the passage of time does to a person or a place!' She looks about her crumbling house fondly. 'Personally, I like this place much more now than I did when it was all tiptop! It's gone to seed just like me—no waxing, no roots touch-up, no skin polishing or age-spot removals—just solid, old-fashioned bones, weathering gloriously, without any outside interference!'

'It is a happy home.'

She shoots him an ironic look.

'Housing a happy murderess? That's why you've come to see me, haven't you? You think I dunnit.'

'We think that you certainly have a lot of valuable information, which we would request you to share with us.'

Her eyebrows rise. 'What a perfectly polite request! Ask away. Though I must admit I think this murderer has very good taste. He—or she, one mustn't be sexist—is picking and murdering the exact people whom I would pick to murder if I had to murder someone. You know, like in those hypothetical scenarios where we're all adrift on a raft and one person needs to be sacrificed so the rest of us can eat their flesh in order to survive. Now I've gone and shocked you, haven't I?'

'We think,' he says steadily, 'that you like to shock people, Jaishriji.'

Her eyes gleam. 'Guilty as charged.' She grins. 'I didn't used to be like this, you know, maybe it's the menopause. Or the public shaming that came free-free-free with the bankruptcy and the divorce. I literally have zero fucks to give now.'

'You have become honest to the point of brutality.' He nods in understanding. 'And you demand the same kind of honesty in return.'

'What an intelligent man you are!' she says delightedly. 'No wonder you've made a name for yourself in the nab-the-murderer industry!

'So let me ask you again, d'you think I'm the killer? Because slimy Sushi insulted me in front of half the employees in his vulgarly large shop when I tried to get him to swap some of the trinkets he'd sold me for good ole solid gold? Oh, yes, Jhoom told me what you told her, she tells me everything.'

'*Are* you, Jaishriji?' he asks her simply.

'Well, I can't say I didn't have murderous thoughts when the ungrateful snake offered me a shockingly low rate and no tea/coffee/pomegranate juice.' Jaishri looks genuinely torn. 'And it would be *so* dramatic to fling up my head and say yes! *Yes!* I did it! I kabool karo the gunha, milord, I took down Chengez Charu and sadistic Sushi! Except I *didn't.*' She sighs. 'I have no idea who did. Sorry.'

Bhavani stays quiet. He intuits that there is more to come.

'How sharper than a serpent's tooth,' Jaishri says, sighing gloomily, 'it is to have a thankless jeweller!'

'Serpent?' Bhavani pricks up his ears.

'King Lear,' she explains. 'His daughters were thankless. Except the youngest one, who wasn't, rather like my Jhoom.'

'She is a good girl!' he says sincerely. 'Can you tell us about your party, Jaishriji? Was anybody acting odd or looking on edge?'

She sits up at once.

'Well, I've obviously been thinking about nothing else since we heard the news,' she says candidly.

'And?'

'See, I've never partied with any of these people before—it was the first time we hung out socially—so I can't really say if somebody was being odd. Everybody was dressed up and smelling nice, they'd made an effort... and we all got a bit drunk. People were letting their hair down, that felt nice...' Her face spasms. 'I remember thinking, as I sipped my second glass of sangria, that I had finally passed through a dark phase of my life and emerged victorious into the light...' her face twists, '... and then *this* happened!'

'Did anybody take photographs?'

'Jhoom started to take a few, but I asked her to make drinks instead, and then she went off into the garden to chat with—'

She stops.

'With?'

Her head comes up. 'To chat with Hadi. They sat in the garden for a while, till Harsh Kedia burst in like some heavy-breathing, hyperventilating moral police.'

'We see. Can you show us the pictures?'

Jaishri nods and picks up her phone.

'Here,' she says, scrolling. 'They're mostly pics of me cooking... Jhoom clicked those before people showed up— ah, here's a few. Nodi, ACP. Oh, how nice Ayesha looks here!'

Bhavani studies the vibrant image of Ayesha Sait, bright-eyed, smiling, clad in her usual flowing anarkali. She is sitting next to Mehtab. His hand is raised as he speaks animatedly, and his several metal and bead bracelets are catching the light.

'Jaishriji, Harsh Kedia told us there was a small knot of men discussing the murder of spouses at your party?'

She grimaces.

'Trust Harsh Kedia. Real chip of the old block that boy is!'

'Is it true? Do you recall?'

'Godddd.' She looks mildly guilty. 'Yes, it was discussed, but obviously people were just joking. Because it was a party, and you're expected to be all witty and glittering when you're holding a glass of wine in your hand. It didn't mean anything! It's not like we actively goaded Mr Tomar to bump off ghastly Charu and pressed the euthanasia meds into his hands!'

'You think Mr Tomar murdered his wife?'

She shakes her head confidently.

'No. And I'll tell you why. It's because the man has literally *no* initiative. *None!* He's sat stolidly in that shop on Commercial Street for thirty-five years, and in that marriage for thirty years, and he would've continued to sit in both till he died. He lacks the imagination to visualize a better life for himself, so he stays happy in whatever position he is in. I cannot for the life of me visualize him researching poisons or stealing meds from Jhoom's cupboard and furtively switching his wife's water-retention medication with a lethal one. It's like expecting Roganjosh to walk two-legged into my kitchen, put on an apron and whip up a batch of strawberry muffins.'

'That is a very useful observation, Jaishriji. Who do you think then, among the guests who came for your party, had the initiative and resourcefulness required to pull off these murders?'

'Oh, that's interesting!' She crosses her legs under her bum and gets more comfortable. 'Let me see now, who-who was there? Krish couldn't have done it—he's indolent, smokes too much weed and lives in the past.'

She doesn't seem to be aware of the Krish–Sona relationship, Bhavani thinks. So her daughter doesn't tell her *everything*.

Aloud, he says, 'Mrs Tomar also hinted that there was something unnatural about the death of Musa Sait.'

Jaishri raises her eyebrows. 'What a foul woman. *Was* there something dodgy about it? I bet you put all your best boys on the business of digging up any dirt on that one!'

'Yes we did, and we found nothing suspicious about it.'

'There you go, then.'

'She also seemed to hint that Ayesha Sait is having, or has had, an affair.'

'Really?' Jaishri looks almost envious. 'Since when? Is she just a merry widow or was she also an adulterous wife?'

'She was ambiguous.'

'What did Chengez say about me?' Jaishri wants to know. 'Am *I* having an affair, too? Or aren't I pretty enough?'

He smiles and shakes his head.

'Was the Saits' marriage a happy one?'

Jaishri wrinkles her brows. 'I've never assumed it to be anything but,' she says. 'There weren't any loud quarrels or anything, if that's what you're asking. They seemed well-adjusted. Of course, he was much older than her—by more than twenty years, I believe. Anyway, I didn't get friendly with her till recently, so I can't really say. Did Chengez really have nothing to say about me or Jhoom? I feel almost insulted.'

She falls silent, thinking.

Bhavani doesn't prompt her.

After a while, she says, 'Pooja's been having quite the glow-up recently. Coming into her own, you know? Designing that collection, paying for Tiff's neutering, breaking her fast.' She looks up interestedly. 'Did Chengez say if *she* was also having an affair?'

'She did nat.'

Jaishri looks a little disappointed.

'Pooja could've dunnit,' she pronounces finally. 'Not alone, but with Sona's help. Sona is wonderfully efficient and beautiful, and God-fearing as well. She has really changed the temperature of that house, you know!'

'The *temperature*,' he repeats thoughtfully.

'I suppose I meant atmosphere.' Jaishri smiles. 'Sorry! Anything else?'

He smiles.

'We have no more questions for you.'

'Good.' She looks relieved, then looks up, suddenly hesitant. 'Uh, what about Hadi, ACP? Is he still suspect number one or is he off the hook? I'm not a gossip, I'm asking because he's started coming over a lot, and I... I rather egged Jhoom on towards him, and I want to prepare her if he turns out to be a bad lot.'

'Everybody is on the hook at the moment, Jaishriji,' he replies. 'What is your opinion of Haider Sait, by the way? As a next-door neighbour who has seen him grow up?'

'Well.' She knits her brows. 'Everybody talks about Hadi's eyes and his infectious energy. And it's true, they have the power to simply electrify a room. And I'll tell you why that happens. It happens because it's clean energy. Hadi is inherently a good person and I would say he's incapable of murder. Unless...'

She falls silent.

They sit quietly in the gently-falling-to-ruin mansion for a while.

And then Bhavani completes her train of thought: 'Unless he committed it to protect somebody he loves.'

12

The Favour of the Goddess

The notice in all the daily newspapers is the same, the now-familiar photograph of Sushil Kedia taking up half a sheet of the city news page, along with a simple message:

Tehraveen
The thirteenth-day ceremony of Shri Sushil Kedia will
be held from 11 a.m. today
at Kedia Kutumb, Habba Galli
'Our finest jewel, you will shine bright in our hearts
forever'
Please do pay your respects.
In Grief:
Pooja Kedia
Harsh & Sona Kedia
Sparsh Kedia

'Our finest jewel, you will shine bright in our hearts forever?' Jaishri Rao reads aloud mock-solemnly and then chuckles. 'They turned an obituary into an ad for Kedia Jewellers! Well, that's good old Marwari business acumen for you!'

'Visualize Sushi boi hanging around your neck suspended on a simple gold chain, Jaishri beni!' says Mehtab. He shakes his head and touches his fingers to his ears. 'Hooosh hooosh hooosh, we are being evil. May his soul rest in peace!'

'Are you going for the tehraveen, Mehtab bhai?'

He nods. 'Certainly I am attending. The entire shopkeepers' association is attending, led by Mr Tomar!' He lowers his voice. 'We have appointed him interim president, you know, and he's doing a fine job!'

'Is he not "in grief" himself?' she asks.

He shakes his head and says, in a carefully neutral tone, 'He is keeping himself busy to keep his grief at bay.'

'Ah, well.' The hint of a smile twinkles in her eyes. 'To each his own, who are we to judge?'

'That is Allah's job,' says Mehtab devoutly.

The tehraveen is an elaborate yet efficient affair, planned and executed in perfect Sona-style. After the shantipaath and other rituals, the huge turnout of mourners are served a lavish vegetarian brunch on glossy banana leaves in the garden.

Inside the house, the massive glass-topped dining table has been laid for a select group of people. As and when they arrive, somebody from Kedia Jewellers, who has been supplied with a list, murmurs into their ears and guides them into the house and to their seats.

'You two take the Jesus-and-John seats at the centre of the Last Supper table,' Shalini tells Bhavani and Naik, before withdrawing to sit at one of the several serving tables in the back of the room. 'Happy hunting!'

The table starts to fill up.

Jaishri Rao. Jhoomar Rao. Mr Tomar. Krish Chetty. Mehtab. Ayesha Sait. Haider Sait. Harsh Kedia. Sparsh Kedia. Pooja Kedia. And finally, Sona Kedia.

She looks around at Bhavani as she takes her place and he gives her a small nod of approval. Unobtrusively, two junior members of Naik's team stroll over to stand at the two doors of the large dining room.

And even though all this has been planned and executed with Sona's active involvement, she can't help feeling uneasy and a little trapped. There is something different about ACP Bhavani today. He looks… powerful? Almost charismatic. He is exuding main character energy, Sona realizes with shock. Pudgy, genial halkat Bhavani! Who would've thought?

Bhavani smiles around the room.

'Jaishriji, we have copied your guest list. The same group of people you hosted at your home next door are sitting at this table now.'

'Except Peter Pais,' observes Krish Chetty shrewdly. 'Are you here to tell us hedunnit, ACP? So the soul of Sushil Kedia can finally depart in peace?'

This creates a minor sensation. People murmur and exclaim and consult each other.

'My colleague Inspector Naik and I are definitely here to tell you whodunnit, Krishji.' The quality of Bhavani's voice changes subtly. It is louder, firmer and somehow sterner, and it immediately makes all the fidgeting stop.

The actor in Haider silently acknowledges the star quality on display. Nobody is going to move a muscle till this performance is over, that much is assured.

'One of you will be leaving this table with handcuffs on your wrists.'

'*Not* Peter Pais, then,' Sparsh Kedia muses.

Bhavani acknowledges this with a small nod in the boy's direction.

'You are intelligent, Sparshji. In fact, *all* the denizens of Habba Galli seem to have a quick, intelligent mind. It must be something in the Gadbad! This quickness is an important motif in this case—a tragedy in three acts, which began on the day of Ayudha Puja when Dondi Pais brought gunny boy down to the galli and gave everybody present a show-and-tell lecture on how to use it.

'A week later, on the night of Karwa Chauth, gunny boy had another outing. Dressed up in his mother's wig, dressing gown and flesh-coloured gloves, Peter Pais threw open his kitchen window and, with his face in darkness, silhouetted against the light, and his mother's white wig on his head, hurled a series of "drunken" abuses at the street dogs and emptied a hail of bullets into the galli.'

There are shocked gasps from around the table, and a bewildered voice demanding, 'But… but *why*?'

'Peter Pais is deeply troubled,' Bhavani says gravely. 'He gloried in the praise he received from the community for being such a good son, but he loathed the squalid reality of living with a sick old woman. He decided to hold on to the one but rid himself of the other by staging a scene so ugly that even the strictest old biddy in the congregation would agree that Dondi Pais was past the stage of living at home.'

'That was *him*?' Mr Tomar's mild eyes bug out with incredulity. 'He fooled me completely, and Charu too! We never for a moment suspected! He is a better actor than Haider!'

'How... how sad.' Jaishri Rao looks distressed. 'What a lonely, twisted life he must lead!'

'Yes, Jaishriji. And so we have the scene that unfolded on Karwa Chauth night, a date he chose purposely because so many people would be out on their balconies waiting for the moon and would bear witness to his poor mummy's dramatics.'

'Why not Diwali night?' Harsh Kedia asks. 'More people would have been on the street then.'

'Diwali would have been too loud,' Bhavani explains, 'and all the dogs would have been in hiding because of the fireworks.'

'Dude thought of everything,' Sparsh Kedia says admiringly. 'What a guy.'

'He then shut the kitchen window,' Bhavani continues, 'and sneaked away when everybody was busy with the injured dog, and drove back later in the night, after being summoned by Jaishri Rao, to play the part of the horrified dutiful son.'

'How surprised he sounded when I phoned him!' Jaishri says wonderingly. 'Surprised, and now that I come to think of it, sort of energized, almost like he was enjoying himself!'

Bhavani nods.

'Jaishriji, he was definitely enjoying himself. So much so that, carried away by his own histrionics, he melodramatically dropped gunny boy into the street before slamming the window shut. This was nat part of his original plan.'

He looks around the table at their riveted faces.

'And because of this one small, unplanned dramatic flourish, what Peter Pais had intended to be a simple one-act play became a tragedy in three acts.'

He's a fine one to speak disparagingly about dramatic flourishes, Jhoom thinks a little hysterically. When he himself is putting up more of a performance than poor damaged Peter Pais did.

Bhavani rests one chunky buttock on the edge of the glass-topped table and looks around at all of them gravely.

'A famous writer once said that if you wish for something with your whole heart, the universe will conspire to give it to you! To that we add a corollary: *You just have to be brave enough to seize the given chance—and dance to it!*' His eyes swivel sharply to Haider Sait. 'Would you nat agree?'

Hadi, who is looking rather underslept in his mourning kurta-pyjama, says sombrely, 'Yeah. Be careful what you wish for, though!'

'You are wise,' Bhavani replies. 'That is the crux of it! Anyway, back to the second act of our story. Somebody on the street, with a strong hatred in their heart for Sushil Kedia, saw the shotgun fall. When a storm started to rage later in the night, with thunder loud enough to drown the sound of a gunshot (more cooperation from the universe!), this person, after confirming that Sushil Kedia was still sitting at his desk, picked up the shotgun and shot him through the glass, killing him with a single lucky shot.

'The gun was swiftly thrown back into the leaves; the falling rain was sufficient to get rid of any fingerprints. Any gunpowder residue forensics found on the road could be blamed on the Diwali season firecrackers, which children had already started bursting in the evenings. The trajectory of the bullet would not be perfect, yes, but close enough to pass muster.'

Harsh Kedia slams his palms down on the table. 'This is ridiculous! Peter Pais only must have shot papa! Either purposely or by mistake—my guess is purposely! Sona, why are we allowing this tamasha to unfold inside our house?'

'The last time I checked,' Pooja Kedia's voice carries a serene firmness, 'this was also *my* house.'

Harsh flushes and subsides, but not without throwing a bitter look at his wife.

Bhavani takes up the narrative again.

'So who could our chance-pe-dancer be? The time band provided by our forensics team says that Mr Kedia died between ten p.m. and three a.m. Nat Poojaji, who the CCTV cameras reveal went into her room and did nat emerge throughout this time period. Nat Sparshji, who was on a Zoom video call from eight p.m. to six a.m. that night, talking to recruiters in a US university. And probably nat Sona and Harshji, whose images would have been captured by some CCTV camera or the other if they had left Leela Hotel and returned home—just like Peter Pais's images were captured, thanks to the extensive screening done by Inspector Naik and team. All the Kedias have an alibi, but none of the other people present here do.

'And so we come to motive. Because this was an impulsive murder where the killer succumbed to a sudden, short-lived surge of bloodlust, the motives could be quite minor—even, when thought over later with a calm mind, illogical. But in that moment of madness, they seemed all-important and all-compelling.'

He looks around the long table deliberately.

'So what are these motives? The first one that springs to mind is that of sundered lovers.'

'Ooh, juicy.' Sparsh Kedia rubs his hands together gleefully. Everybody else looks startled, and then uncomfortable.

'Just remember, ACP,' Harsh cuts in a soft, level voice, '*I* phoned the DG—that's how you're even in this room. Given sufficient reason, I can phone him again.'

'I think it's best we keep interruptions to a minimum,' Sona intercedes quickly, 'and not be offended while the ACP goes about his investigation.'

'Thank you, Sonaji.' Bhavani looks unperturbed. 'Murder is a serious business, and it is our humble request to all of you nat to take offence at what we may say going forward. Remember, it is all in the good cause of catching a double murderer who may strike again if allowed to roam free.'

He raises his voice and continues, 'Let us begin with Krishji and Sonaji. They were close in the past but have since moved on and do nat even speak to each other. But what if they did?

And what if Sonaji's father-in-law, who disliked the energy she had brought into the male-dominated home, found out and threatened to tell all to his son? Could this nat have spurred on Sonaji, who theoretically could have wanted the best of both worlds—the economic and social security of her marriage, as well as the emotional satisfaction supplied by her first love—to conspire with Krishji and take down Sushil Kedia?'

'Wow, Bhavani uncle,' Krish drawls, shaking his head at the old policeman, 'what an absolute douchebag you must think me! I take it that Sona was slipping me money too, in this scenario? To shore up my shitty business and finance my drug habit?'

Bhavani shakes his head gently. 'We have made inquiries, Krishji. Your financial situation is rock-solid.'

Krish bows ironically. 'Thank you!'

'But you do want to be president of the shopkeepers' association, a position you hope will jumpstart your political career. A position that has been monopolized, for almost two decades, by Sushil Kedia. Which brings us to…'

His eyes swivel to the mild pudgy man sitting at the end of the table.

'Mr Tomar. As we all know, Mrs Tomar visited Pooja Kedia on the afternoon of the day before she died. Poojaji has made a statement to the police that during that visit, Mrs Tomar confessed that she had feelings for Pooja's husband Sushil Kedia, which he reciprocated, a fact that had driven her husband Mr Tomar mad with jealousy. Poojaji claims that Mrs Tomar told her that it was Mr Tomar who turned the dropped shotgun on Sushil Kedia that night and, given half a chance, would probably kill her too.'

Mr Tomar's jaw sags. '*What?* Lies! I would never hurt my Charu! Why are you telling such lies, Pooja bhabhi?'

Pooja Kedia gives a pained little sigh.

'I'm sorry, Tomar bhaisaab, facts are facts.'

He stares at her in helpless bewilderment.

'But she *wasn't* in love with him! And I wasn't jealous of him!'

'It is possible that part of it was merely her fancy,' says Bhavani softly. 'Perhaps she believed what she wanted to believe, but she did get one thing right. It may nat have been for reasons of the heart, but you *were* jealous of Sushil Kedia. Because he held the post you have coveted silently for decades, the post which you (much to Krishji's disappointment, we are sure) hold today—president of the shopkeepers' association. Congratulations, Tomarji, today *you* are the biggest man in Habba Galli! Were two murders worth it?'

Mild Mr Tomar lets out a soft whimper.

'But I didn't. I *swear…*'

'Shame on you for bullying a helpless widower,' Jaishri Rao says fiercely. 'Disgusting, dissipated *Delhi* behaviour! D'you have proof of any of this?'

'Amma!' Jhoom exclaims, horrified. 'You're right, but don't say *Delhi* and all! Be *nice!*'

Bhavani meets Jaishri's flashing eyes gravely.

'Ah, but Jaishriji does nat believe in pulling her punches.'

Jaishri's chin rises challengingly. 'Meaning?'

'You recently humiliated Sushil Kedia by making cutting remarks about pedigree and class and his lack of it.'

She flushes. 'Yes. I did. The man has no class. His wife, though, has oodles of it.'

'He retaliated by humiliating you when you went to resell your jewellery at his flagship store. It was a nasty scene, wounding to your pride. You are after all, a Rao of Rao Mansion, an old Bangalore family!'

She looks rueful. 'Well, yes, it wasn't very nice. But I've been through worse. Believe me, it wasn't powerful enough to push me over the edge into silencing his sneering forever.'

'Yes.' Bhavani's voice is silky. 'But while working with the Kedia auditors, Inspector Naik's men discovered that Sushil Kedia purchased the mortgage on your home from your bank and was threatening to evict you…'

Jhoom gasps.

Bhavani continues, '… out of sheer spite. You knew his son, no matter what your differences with him, would never do that to an old neighbour. So perhaps *that* was a powerful enough motive for you to impulsively pick up the shotgun that was lying so temptingly on the road on a dark stormy night with no witnesses in sight?'

Jaishri's face pales at this revelation. Her eyes skitter to her daughter's, then come back to meet Bhavani's resolutely.

'You're right,' she admits lightly. 'That *is* a powerful motive.'

'So you took him down, auntie?' Sparsh's eyes are wide with admiration. 'Just like *that*?'

She shakes her head. 'The idea didn't occur to me, puppy,' she says regretfully. 'I didn't even realize that she—I mean, he—had dropped the shotgun. Or that there was still a bullet in it.'

'Really?' Naik speaks up for the first time. 'Because we have a witness who says otherwise.'

He looks towards the serving tables, and a pale-faced Saraswati peeks out from behind a burly Karnataka police constable.

'Jaishri-amma, I'm so sorry,' she sobs in distress. 'You are a *so*-nice olley amma, and you always give soopar tip, not like Peter saar and other peoples…'

'It's okay, Saraswati,' Jaishri, though astounded, manages to say gently. 'Say what you have to…'

'I *saw* you, amma!' Saraswati bawls, heartbroken, tears rolling slowly down her face. 'Standing next to the hedge, in your that maroon dressing gown!' As she sees words rise to Jaishri's lips she wheels to the right. 'Hadi saar, you saw her too! You mustu tell the police! I saw you seeing her when you came out after the operation! *Ask* him, inspector saar!'

Everybody turns to look at Haider.

Anxiety grips Jhoom's stomach like a vice.

Oh God, what is this? Had Hadi lied to her in her room that evening? And is this what he had meant last night when he said that she needn't worry, nobody would ever find out?

Was her mother a *murderer*? A double *murderer*?

She gives a silent sob and holds her breath.

Hadi's beautiful eyes meet Saraswati's without wavering.

'I don't know what you're talking about, Saraswati,' he says steadily. 'I never saw anybody at all.'

And Jhoom can breathe again.

Bhavani smiles genially. 'Is that so, Hadiji? Very well, we will leave it at that for the time being. Saraswati, thank you so much for your statement. You have been very brave.'

Saraswati throws Haider a scornful look as she is led away from the table. He flushes and looks away.

'Bro…' Sparsh Kedia crows softly, almost ecstatically, as his eyes skitter around the room. 'This is better than Netflix. ACP, you're the shit.'

'Now what?' Sona Kedia asks in a stupefied whisper. 'When will we know what actually happened?'

'The honourable ACP said that was the second act, Sona,' Harsh says lightly, though his eyes, resting on Bhavani, glitter with open, hostile dislike. 'The third act is yet to come, and I have a feeling it's gonna be a real banger.'

Bhavani nods, acknowledging this prediction, then turns around to address the riveted room.

'And now we come to the most famous denizens of Habba Galli, Shivajinagar: Haider and Ayesha Sait.'

'Woo-hoo!' Sparsh gives a tiny whoop. Everybody ignores him.

'The motive the newspapers suggested seemed too far-fetched at first, Haiderji, which was that you wanted to get the *feel* of being a killer. In interview after interview, you have stated that you are not an actor, that you simply "feel" your way into a character. This is your simple, intuitive, rather hit-or-miss method. But then you confided in us that you are no longer happy to drink deep from the cup of commercial success, you have secretly started to hanker for serious, critical praise, and validation from people with more refined sensibilities…'

His gaze moves deliberately towards Jhoom.

'… like a certain young lady who has nat seen any of your movies.'

Jhoom gives a guilty start. She is beginning to get a sick, swimming headache.

'Add to that the fact that your mother purchased a bracelet worth ten lakhs from Kedia Jewellers, pretending it was intended as a birthday present for you, and gifted it to her "good friend" Mehtab, that too while your father was still alive. Sushil Kedia recognized it on Mehtab's wrist when he came around gesticulating wildly and making a scene in his store. So Sushil Kedia started making veiled threats to Ayeshaji that he would reveal all to the press…'

'Hooosh hooosh hooosh hooosh hooosh!' Mehtab grabs his earlobes with his fingers, his eyes darting apologetically to Ayesha. 'What are you saying? Ayeshaji bought a carpet from me worth ten lakh rupees, so she paid me with this bracelet!'

'Why then, Ayeshaji,' Bhavani turns to look at her, sitting so still and beautiful in her white anarkali, 'did you tell us that the bracelet—which had not turned out fine enough to gift to Hadi but which you did not have the heart to return as the young girl who had designed it would get into trouble—had been melted down to white gold in your workshop?'

'Because…' Ayesha falters.

Hadi reaches out and grasps her hand. His eyes are curiously expressionless in his pale taut face and a pulse has started at the base of his throat, just above the open button of his white kurta.

Ayesha throws up her head defiantly. 'You tell me, ACP.'

Bhavani smiles.

'You were trying to throw us off the real scent. And the *real* scent was your wedding jewellery—the necklace, bangles and earrings you famously sold to set up Your Wish.'

Ayesha goes very still.

'A lot of people use their jewellery as collateral to set up a business, but they usually do it later in life, not so soon after their marriage when they are still feeling sentimental and proud of it. When we asked you about it, you replied that the jewellery had not been very pretty. And when we asked you which store it had been bought from, you replied that *you didn't remember*—an odd reply from a lady who is clearly interested in jewellery, and who would have had to get it valued in order to sell it.

'We then deduced that perhaps the jewellery itself had not been ugly, but the memories associated with it were. And then our team found this photograph…'

He slides a picture across the table to Ayesha Sait.

Fuck, thinks Jhoom chaotically. Suppressing that ghastly photograph and running away in panic from Hadi last night had been entirely pointless. Bhavani had managed to figure things out anyhow.

She steals a quick glance at Hadi. He is still sitting quietly, with that curiously expressionless look on his face. Noticing Bhavani noticing her, Jhoom quickly looks away.

The old policeman continues musingly, 'A lady from a humble, conventional Muslim home, with a small trousseau budget in the late eighties, who could afford only a struggling jeweller, who visited her home in Haliyaal several times to get the fittings right, before her arranged marriage to a man more than double her age…'

Ayesha holds up a peremptory hand to cut him off and looks across the room at the new widow.

'I'm so sorry, Pooja,' she says sadly. 'For me it was just a mild infatuation, but not for Sushil. He tried to make my married life difficult, and so, taking my courage in both hands, I told my husband the truth. Musa was a kind, supportive man—he forgave me and warned off Sushil. But after Musa died, Sushil returned. Being a total narcissist, he had brooded over my rejection for years, and violently resented Hadi's well-deserved success. For no other reason than to torture me mentally, he escalated the hate on the WhatsApp group, complaining about the dogs constantly, and let me know, through constant veiled threats, that he would leak our old photographs to the press and claim that it had never really ended, that we were still involved, even going so far as to claim that Hadi was his son.' Her voice shakes with revulsion and exhaustion. 'Filth for filth's sake. It was a complete nightmare.'

'Ammi, you idiot.' Hadi has been staring at her in consternation for a while now. 'Why didn't you just tell me? As if I would have given one single fuck.'

'Ayesha, I *like* this son of yours!' Jaishri Rao speaks up decidedly, making the room break into nervous, uncertain laughter.

Ayesha Sait, looking absurdly young and luminous, leans forward to look at Jaishri with glad, meaningful eyes.

'And Jaishri, I *like* your daughter!'

'Oh.' Jaishri looks startled.

She turns to consider Hadi, who is looking across the table at Jhoom with his heart in his eyes.

And Jhoom, thinking about the damning photograph she has squirrelled away in her underwear drawer, feels the vice that has been closed around her heart all this while loosen. A little.

Because what had amma been doing out on the road that night?

Ayesha Sait turns to look at Bhavani.

'ACP, your theory is that I told Hadi, and he impulsively decided to take Sushil down so he could "feel" like a murderer. I'm sorry, but that just did *not* happen.'

'You had better explain who murdered my wife and why.' Mr Tomar has recovered his mojo. In a shaking, aggrieved voice, he continues, 'Going on and on about Sushil Kedia! Arrey, even in *death* my Charu is not being given the importance she craved!'

'Tomarji, please don't get upset.' Pooja Kedia stretches out an appealing hand to the upset man. 'Charu was my best friend and her loss has left a *giant-sized* void in my life.'

But this is the wrong thing to say. His eyes widen in outrage.

'Fat-shaming her even in death!' he splutters. 'You p-people... you bl-bloody people!' His shoulders shake.

'Thank you for your patience, Tomarji,' Bhavani says quietly. 'We are now arriving at the most vital revelation of all.

'Yesterday only we discovered that Peter Pais writes a diary—on his phone. He recorded all his thoughts there, including the details of his plan for Karwa Chauth night.'

'What does that have to do with Charu?'

'We are explaining—patience, please. Now, if somebody read his diary, which is highly possible because one, his phone was stolen two months ago, and two, his unlock pattern is the sign of the cross and extremely easy to guess, then this chance-pe-dance crime turns out to be *nat* spontaneous, heat-of-the-moment insanity driven by a trivial triggering motive, but...' Bhavani pauses before sending his words shooting like gunny boy's bullets across the captivated room, 'a *clear-cut case of pre-planned, deliberate, cold-blooded murder.*'

His words land in a pool of tense, pulsating silence. Even Mr Tomar does not speak. Everybody seems utterly shocked, and on tenterhooks to hear the next revelation. Except for one person, thinks Bhavani grimly, one feral, desperate person, the only person he cares about at this point in time, trapped like a rat, turning this way and that, hoping, or perhaps smugly believing, that the stupid old policeman has been outwitted and is on the brink of making a complete idiot of himself.

'But what about my wife?' Mr Tomar demands finally, though less angrily. 'Why was she killed?'

Bhavani turns to him.

'You have already told us, Tomarji—and we believe you—that your wife slept like a baby right through the storm on Karwa Chauth night. She did nat actually see anything; she merely claimed to have seen Haider Sait picking up the gun on the road because that was what the press wanted to hear and record and air on TV.'

'That's true enough,' Mr Tomar agrees sullenly.

Bhavani leans in.

'In which case, *what was it that Charu Tomar saw, which made it essential for the murderer to eliminate her*? Could she have seen something else at some other time or place? Something she did nat recognize the significance of immediately, but which dawned on her over time, till she knew, without doubt, the identity of the murderer and, fired with religious fervour, confronted him or her about it?'

'My poor Charu.' Mr Tomar shakes his head. 'Always riding a tiger. She had the strength of Matarani.'

Bhavani continues gravely.

'And then we remembered that Charuji had told you on the phone on the afternoon of Karwa Chauth that somebody was throwing stones across the road, and that perhaps a vase had been broken. What if that had not been a stone but a bullet?'

Everybody gasps.

Bhavani nods gently.

'That seems unthinkable, does it nat? We will tell you why. It seems so because of our belief in the Karwa Chauth legend, heard unquestioningly in childhood and reinforced several times over in full technicolour by Bollywood—which is that married women keep the rigorous dawn-to-moonrise Karwa Chauth fast for the long life of their husbands. This pleases the goddess and ensures them a long happy married life. But *if* a wife breaks her fast before the moonrise, *then* the angered goddess immediately strikes down her husband and condemns her to eternal widowhood.'

'I wish!' Jaishri Rao says wistfully. 'If it were only that simple to get rid of an unwanted husband, half the women in India would just start the fast, break it off early and be widowed by sunset!'

'Yes!' Bhavani beams at her. 'But that is what Mrs Charu Tomar consciously believed, that is what we all subconsciously believe, and that is the core reason why we, our team and the hundreds of press people sniffing around our heels trying to solve this case, have never considered the possibility of the murder happening *earlier* in the day, *before* Mrs Pooja Kedia broke her fast. And that, ladies and gentlemen, is *exactly* how Mrs Pooja Kedia wanted us all to think!'

'But the core body temperature—' Hadi starts to say, then trails off uncertainly. 'I mean—that's what all the news reports said.'

Bhavani turns to address him.

'Sushil Kedia, who was obsessed with really chilled air-conditioning, had a remote that allowed him to change the temperature of the atariya without even entering it. Which made us wonder if somebody could not have killed him as early as the afternoon of the previous day, then turned the AC up to maximum heat to warm the body all the way to its core, then turned the AC to maximum cooling at around four a.m. to quickly chill the room down again? This way, the core body temperature would still give a warmish reading at the time of police examination, which happened around six-thirty a.m., which would make it appear as if death had occured at around the time of moonrise, or even late night, but definitely not as early as the previous afternoon, much before Mrs Pooja Kedia had actually desecrated her fast by consuming steamed chicken momos and jammy doughnuts.

'We had the forensics team examine the memory chip on the AC remote, and the records checked out exactly as anticipated. And once we shifted focus from ten in the night to the previous afternoon, guess what happened?

The alibis of the entire Kedia family, which, until then, had seemed watertight, immediately went up in smoke!'

He looks towards Pooja Kedia, sitting like she is carved out of stone at the head of the table, flanked by Harsh on one side and Sona on the other. 'Poojaji, is what we are saying correct?'

'Mummy, you don't have to reply,' Harsh says swiftly, but Pooja Kedia cuts him off with a tiny wave of her hand.

In a colourless voice, she says, 'It's your story, Bhavaniji. Please complete it.'

'Poojaji's motive is clear enough. She was nat happy in her marriage, her contribution was constantly belittled, her jewellery designs, her looks and language were mocked at—she was nat even allowed to feed the street dogs! The examples set by two gutsy females inspired her to rebel—one was her fiery daughter-in-law Sona, and the other was the independent old matriarch Roganjosh.'

He looks around the table quietly.

'Meanwhile, things were nat going too well at the store between father and son. We got in touch with Karl Schnieder, head of acquisitions from Von Matisse AG, Geneva.' Bhavani pauses, puts on a pair of reading glasses and reads from his phone. 'A leading name in the world of fine crafted jewellery, patronized by eleven Royal Houses from Europe, Africa and the Middle East, and undoubtedly the industry benchmark in quality, reliability and design.'

He stops reading and looks up.

'In an email to me, Schniederji confirmed that his visit to the flagship Kedia store had nat been a mere courtesy call, as claimed by Harsh Kedia.'

He reads from his phone again:

For the last six months we have been in a series of (highly confidential) conversations with the family-run Kedia Group regarding a possible merger. While family elder Sushil Kedia was very keen on the idea and was driving the negotiations to a speedy conclusion mutually beneficial to both parties, he had confided in me that his son Harsh was vehemently opposed to the idea of a merger.

Apparently Harsh Kedia preferred to 'go it alone', rather than 'get into bed with the first hot blonde who'll have us'.

Naturally I am embarrassed to use such intemperate language. But you are the top official in charge of investigating this case and I feel it is nothing short of my duty to let you have this background on the inner workings of the Kedia family.

Bhavani removes his glasses and puts his phone away.

'Frustrated, angry, not knowing whom to turn to, Harsh confided all this to his wife and mother. And mother-in-law and daughter-in-law, whose bonding is truly exemplary, decided that enough was enough.'

He looks around the table.

'Somehow, Peter Pais's lost phone had ended up in Sonaji's hands. The situation around the stray dogs had become so nasty after Tiffinni's puppies were born that the pilla party lived in daily fear of the mongrels being poisoned or removed to a remote location, so Sonaji was anxious to know what the dog-hater faction was planning. Guessing Peter Pais's unlock pattern, she opened his WhatsApp to check the messages between her father-in-law and him—and found the diary.

'And so, the plan was laid. Sonaji dropped in on Dondi Pais one rainy afternoon when Peter was out and smuggled the shotgun across the road to Kedia Kutumb, camouflaged inside her umbrella. On the afternoon of Karwa Chauth, Pooja Kedia, who knew the code to the atelier even though she pretended not to, opened the door, entered and shot her husband from the doorway, at a distance of about thirty feet, as he sat at his desk. Then she walked across the room, turned his revolving chair around to make it face the window, carefully lifted the papers that had got splattered with his blood and placed them on the other side, and cranked the AC remote to its highest heat setting.

'Then MIL and DIL slid one of the bulletproof steel cupboards lined up against the back wall onto the Persian carpet, dragged it across the smooth wooden floor so as to leave no marks and placed it with its back facing the street in front of the glass window.

'At three in the afternoon, Sonaji carried the gun back across the road, again neatly camouflaged in her umbrella. And, as the old lady slept in the next room and Charu Tomar sat in her balcony with henna on her hands, she shot a bullet from the shotgun, aiming for the grey bulletproof cupboard in the atariya window.

'Poojaji, waiting in the atariya, heard the sound of the bullet breaking through the glass and lodging safely into the back of the bulletproof safe. She then dragged the safe back, using the carpet, and slid it back into place in its usual position.

'But when she replaced the carpet, she ended up rotating it, which later drew the comment that it looked faded. This comment is what drew our attention to the carpet and the row of safes behind it in the first place. And then she left the room again, using the code she pretended nat to know the next morning.

'All that was left for Poojaji to do, at four a.m. the next day from the comfort of her bed, was to turn the atariya remote to the coldest possible setting, in order to cheat the core-body-temperature test. And then, of course, act surprised when the body was discovered. All was well.

'But then Charuji, thinking things over in her busy mind, realized that what she had seen and heard on Karwa Chauth afternoon had actually been a bullet. *That* is what she came over to tell Poojaji in the afternoon of the day of Jaishriji's party! She accused her friend's family of cold-blooded murder and threatened to reveal all to NationNow! Perhaps she asked for money? We do nat know. But by revealing this knowledge, she signed her own death warrant.'

Bhavani sums up grimly, 'There can be no doubt, ladies and gentlemen, that Pooja Kedia and Sona Kedia went to Jaishri Rao's party with murder in their hearts, and returned from it with ketamine and xylazine in the pockets of their white chikankari kurtas.'

There is a stunned silence when Bhavani finishes speaking. Harsh has his shorn head in his hands, Pooja Kedia sits straight as a statue and Sparsh's jaw is childishly agape.

Jaishri Rao is the first to speak. In a shaking voice she says, 'All this… the bullet… in the atelier safe… you're not making it up? You have *proof*?'

'Yes,' Naik says grimly. 'We do. We found the bullet lodged in the back wall of the safe.'

Sona gasps. Her eyes go to her husband's, then her mother-in-law's. 'What?' she exclaims.

So do the eyes of every single other person in the room.

Pooja Kedia's head comes up proudly.

'Sona had nothing to do with it,' she says simply. 'Saraswati found the phone lying on the road, and being very honest, asked me to click a picture of it and post it on the neighbourhood WhatsApp group. But I had seen a similar phone in Peter's hands and I was worried for the dogs, so I kept the phone and read his messages…'

Her voice trails away.

The stunned silence continues to hold.

'I did it all myself,' Pooja Kedia says. 'I'm very fit— pushing the cupboard was easy for me. And I've always been a good shot.'

'Mummy…' Harsh says brokenly. 'Mummy, what was the need? I was there, I would have handled everything, we would have persuaded papa to back your collection!'

But Pooja isn't looking at him, she is looking at Sparsh.

'Sparshu?' she appeals to him tremulously. 'Make a joke, na. Maybe a big American college will give you admission on compassionate grounds now?'

But he shakes his head silently, refusing to even look at her.

'Mummyji, don't say anything more!' Sona says urgently. 'We'll get you the best possible lawyers, clearly there is a mental health issue at play here. *Harsh*…' she pleads, 'make some phone calls!'

Jaishri Rao gets to her feet swiftly. 'We should give them some privacy,' she says. 'Really, ACP Bhavani Singh, did this have to be done in public, like this? C'mon, everybody, let's move out—'

'*Sit down*, Jaishriji.' Bhavani's voice is steely. 'We are nat finished yet.'

Jaishri blinks and obeys.

Sona looks worriedly at Bhavani. 'What happens now? Are you going to arrest mummyji? How long… oh God, how horrible to be asking this—how long is the sentence for something like this, typically?'

'Sona, shush, we need to get in some expert opinions.' Harsh turns to look, with some difficulty, towards his mother. 'Mummy, you know I love you... I know you haven't had a very easy life—and I suppose what you did is even justifiable... But why *Charu auntie*, mummy? I know she irritated you many times, but she was your friend! I don't understand, papa was bad, yes, but you... you are... you were my *good* parent, mummy!'

His face works, he is almost in tears. With his bald head, chubby cheeks and stubble, he looks faintly ridiculous.

Bhavani, watching closely, decides that he needs to give the unfolding drama a little nudge in the right direction.

'Well, that's it then,' he says briskly. 'We have the warrants all ready—Manju?'

Inspector Naik rises impressively. 'Mrs Kedia, you're under arrest for the murders of Sushil Kedia and Charu Tomar. You have the right to remain silent and consult a lawyer, as your son suggests.'

Pooja Kedia gets slowly to her feet.

'My son?' she says, breathing thickly. 'Don't call him my son! Worthless, thankless, selfish, entitled! Shoots his father, poisons his auntie and doesn't even bat an eyelid when the police are arresting his mother for a crime he *knows* she didn't commit? Expecting me to protect him *as usual* and cover up his sins! I *spit* on such a son!'

There are gasps from all around the room. Sona stands frozen, turned to stone.

Harsh's face blanches. He starts to stammer, his eyes skittering from his wife to his mother and back again.

'Mummy?' he says weakly. 'Wha… what are you saying? Why would I? Please don't… you're not well, mummy.'

But Pooja Kedia is beyond reason now. She whirls around to appeal to the table.

'Where's his love for me? Where's his *duty*? Isn't it enough that I cook his food and shield him and cajole his father to forgive his mistakes? I must walk into a boiling hot room and find a dead body, I must break my holy fast early to confuse the police, I must send WhatsApp messages from my dead husband's phone and hide what has happened for a whole night, and now go to jail for the murders he committed? *Why* should I? Why *should* I?'

Harsh sinks to his chair, tears streaming down his cheeks.

Pooja continues speaking, in a wild, lifeless voice.

'I was a fool and a criminal to cover up your crimes, my son, but I will no longer do it. You *will* own up to your deeds and you will *get* your punishment, because if I let you treat me like dirt today, you'll treat any woman who loves you like dirt tomorrow! *And I would rather die than let that pattern repeat itself!*'

Saying which, she takes a deep breath, walks across the room, drags the cringing Sparsh to his feet by the collar of his shirt and shakes him till his glasses fall off.

'Here's your murderer,' she tells the unsurprised Bhavani in a quick hoarse voice. 'Take him away.'

'But he's a *child*.'

Jhoom's horrified whisper echoes in the suddenly silent room.

Sparsh bends to retrieve his glasses with a trembling hand and straightens up, shoving them back up his reddened cheeks. He looks around the room, his young face twitching oddly.

'No, I'm not,' he says unevenly. 'I'm not a child, I'm the bravest person in this family—I'm the bravest person in all of Habba Galli, actually! You *all* wanted frikkin' Sushil dead, all of you, but none of you had the guts to actually *do* it. Honestly, you noobs should all be queuing up to suck my dick.'

'Sparsh!' Harsh Kedia roars, rising to his feet, his face pale.

Sparsh gives a short, high giggle. 'Wow, I didn't mean that *literally*, Harshu bhaiya. Chill. But then you never understand these things; you never understand *anything*, you wouldn't even be *married* today if I hadn't intervened and done all your chatting for you!'

Harsh sits down again slowly, looking sick with horror.

Sparsh looks at his mother now, his expression one of complete exasperation mixed with affectionate contempt.

'Ai ma, don't looked so shattered. KLPD's gonna fly off the shelves now. And honestly, there was no need for you to panic or do all that fast-breaking drama or "cover up" for me! I had the whole thing under control all the time! And, anyway, this is all your fault—if you'd taken a harder line with pa from the beginning instead of being so meek and letting him boss you around, he would never have turned into such a kosmopolitan, kultured, kreative kunt with a K in the first place, and I wouldn't have had to end him.'

'Keep *quiet*, Sparsh.' Sona's voice is shaking. 'You're being cruel and crude, and you're compromising yourself. You need to keep quiet and get a lawyer.'

Sparsh doesn't seem to hear her. His gaze is travelling slowly across the room.

'Yeah, whatevs, it all seems to have gone tits-up now. I figured out pretty early that old Pete was a horndog, so I scanned his WhatsApp code to my laptop and used it to watch some paywall-protected porn now and then—just for time-pass. I'm not a sad incel like him, of course. I've got Devi.'

'Yes, you have Devikaji,' Bhavani murmurs in agreement. 'And then you discovered his diary on the phone—'

'It made for fun reading,' Sparsh says, 'and then I read *all* about his desperate, pathetic little plan.'

A long rather stunned silence falls over the room as everybody absorbs this statement and all of its ramifications.

'I'm not sorry about pa.' Sparsh shrugs finally. 'And I'm even less sorry about Chengez—all she was good for was dal-kachori and a miserable five-hundred-rupee note on my birthday every year. They were both *horrible* people. Besides, I'm a minor—and a school topper—and I did it all just to help my family and friends…'

He grins lopsidedly at the old ACP. 'I'll get off easy, won't I?'

Bhavani gets to his feet.

'We should continue this conversation privately, Sparshji,' he says in a gentle matter-of-fact voice. 'And your sister-in-law is right. You do need a lawyer. Come.'

'Of course he didn't do it to help family and friends,' Bhavani tells Jhoom and Jaishri later. 'He did it all for Devika Johri.'

'But she's in Europe,' Jhoom says, bewildered. 'How does she come into this?'

'They share a special friendship—she is very aware of the fact that he is still a minor, the child protection squads in Dilli Police would say that she is grooming him, while the ladies who watch Star Plus serials would argue that it is a pure platonic bond. Never mind all that. The point is that she asked him to ask his father to give her a recommendation letter to her college in Geneva. Sparshji asked, but Sushil Kedia was entirely unimpressed with Devikaji and refused point-blank. Sparsh couldn't bear to say no to his goddess, so he broke into the link the college had provided and sent off a glowing recommendation. Devika got the admission and wrote to Sushil, thanking him. Sparshji couldn't intercept the mail on time, and Sushil saw it. He was furious and told Sparshji he was going to write to the college and say the recco letter was a scam. Devikaji's admission would have been revoked at once. Sparsh couldn't bear to let that happen.'

'So he did it for love,' Jaishri says slowly. 'And *also* for family and friends. And now he's trying to keep that part of it quiet so she doesn't get expelled?'

Bhavani nods. 'That's the deal his lawyers will try and push.'

'But what made you suspect him, ACP?'

'Several things,' Bhavani replies. 'One, while everybody on Habba Galli was unanimously in agreement that Sushil Kedia was a horrible person, Devikaji seemed to be dwelling in a la-la land where he was a wonderful man with a heart of

gold whose bark was much worse than his bite. Our initial
thought was the very obvious one that perhaps Sushilji was
besotted with her, but then we realized that that was nat
the case.

'The second clue was that Ayeshaji was nat at all impressed
with Devikaji's work. At that point in time we thought she
was making excuses to cover up the fact that the bracelet
had been commissioned nat for her son but for a lover,
but it turned out that she was just speaking the plain truth.
Devikaji's work had been shoddy, so Ayeshaji, who didn't
want to hurt the young girl's feelings or career, traded it with
Mehtab bhai for a carpet. Which raised the question ki how,
if she was *so* untalented, did she manage to secure such a
glowing letter of reccomendation from a finicky perfectionist
like Sushil Kedia?

'Both these things prompted us to do a thorough exam
of Sparshji's phone and emails. And we uncovered the fake
recommendation mail.

'The third clue was the fact that Peter Pais's diary was
written in a one-person WhatsApp group. Sparsh is very
comfortable breaking into other people's WhatsApp chats.
He did it to get Sona and Harsh together and he could have
easily done it again.

'The fourth clue was the school principal's assessment
of him, echoed by Krish Chetty—that Sparsh is extremely
ingenuous. He prides himself on working with whatever
material is already available to achieve stellar results. These
crimes were a classic example of on-the-fly jugaad. He
worked with the elements that were already on the table—the
arguments about the stray dogs, Dondi bai's eccentricities,

Peter Pais's wild scheme, the ketamine and xylazine—it was all about using what was already there, organically, to achieve his outcome.

'And finally, there was the clue that Charu Tomar also cracked. Sparsh's personal pool cue stick case. The killer would have needed to carry the shotgun across the road and back without anybody suspecting, and a cue stick case would have been the perfect camouflage. Charuji saw him carrying it across the road that afternoon and then, a few minutes later, she saw the bullet fly across the road and pierce the window. And then Sparshji crossed back again.'

Jhoom wrinkles her forehead.

'Why didn't he just shoot him through the window?'

'That would have been too hit-and-miss, Jhoomarji. For one, his father may nat have even been sitting in the chair at that time! Sparsh did nat want to take any chances. He shot his father at closer range, while he was sitting in the chair. The shot through the window was just to cheat the trajectory and make the correct sort of puncture mark through the glass. And that is why that bullet had to be intercepted by the bulletproof safe. Otherwise there would have been two bullets—one inside the corpse and one somewhere in the atariya!'

'In his own way, he is as big a perfectionist as his father,' Jhoom says thoughtfully.

'And as big a psycho,' Jaishri says decidedly.

'Perhaps, Jaishriji. In all fairness, he did nat plan on committing a second murder! But when he overheard Mrs Tomar telling Poojaji what she had guessed, he knew he had to take her out, and fast.'

'Karwa Chauth fast,' Jaishri says, rather whimsically. 'So in a way, Pooja was a good goddess-fearing wife. She never broke her fast, did she? She only broke it after her husband was dead.'

'Yes. She did her best to protect her son. We were hoping we could guilt him into confessing by pretending to arrest her, but he was too hardened for that. Finally, *she* only cracked because of his lack of gratitude!'

'Has he gone over totally to the dark side, ACP?' Jaishri asks. 'Do you think there is any scope for repentence and redemption? He is so young, after all!'

Bhavani's years in the crime branch have taught him that a leopard remains spotted till the day it dies. But people always need a ray of hope to cling onto in such situations.

He smiles encouragingly at the Rao women.

'Be there for your friends,' he says. 'That is why we are telling you all this. They have supported you through your dark times, now it is your turn to support them.'

'Oh, I'm super impressed with Pooja Kedia,' Jaishri assures him earnestly. 'I am *totally* gunning for the position of new besto!'

Jhoom glares at her. 'Amma, what were you doing on the road at ten o'clock that night in your wretched maroon dressing gown?'

Jaishri looks guilty. 'I snuck out for a wee vaping session,' she confesses.

'I hate you.' Jhoom's voice throbs with pure loathing.

'No, you don't.' Jaishri cackles. 'Nobody hates their Cupid and I *am* yours, you know.'

13

Phoenix

'I never actually got a look at that photograph of Sushi with ammi.'

They are lying in the big saggy bed in her room on the top of the stairs, watching the fan spin in wonky circles in the seepage-infested ceiling. Outside, the setting sun is touching the stacked fruit and the snoozing mongrels and the fabric bales of Habba Galli with molten gold.

Jhoom lifts her head off his chest.

'You wanna see my copy?'

He looks conflicted, then nods slowly.

She grins, clambers off the bed, runs across the room in just her pretty shortie pyjama bottoms and sits cross-legged in front of her dresser. A flurry of undies come flying at Hadi and then she returns, holding out the tattered photograph to him with a grimace.

'Nodi at your own risk.'

But he shakes his head and pulls her to him, so she tumbles into the bed, falling against his chest.

'You're *really* good at that!' she says happily.

'Years of dance practice,' he replies, nuzzling her neck. Then he hugs her to him and squares his shoulders. 'Okay, show it to me.'

They stare at the picture in silence.

'Ugh,' says Hadi finally.

Jaw set, he tears it up into tiny pieces. Then he looks around the room consideringly. 'Should we eat it?'

'Yuck!' She gurgles with laughter. 'It'll make us ill.'

'I'm gonna flush it down your pot.'

She throws out her arm in a grand gesture. 'Be my guest!'

When he comes back, she's still lying on her stomach on the bed. He flops down beside her, rests his chin on her shoulder and whispers: 'Hey.'

She tilts her face.

'I'm not the Sushi Kedia of your life, am I? Just some mild, passing crush you wanna forget?'

Her eyes are serious, so his grow serious too.

'You know the two-hundred-word essay you wanted all prospective lovers who-live-down-the-lane to write?'

She nods. 'You got one?'

He hands her his phone. 'Here, read it. It's more of a flashback than an essay, though. Bongo helped me write it all down like a story, but the experience is all mine.'

It was the day before his class five maths final exam and abba had locked him up in his room to study. But the lure of the (rarely) empty galli and the perfect weather had been too much for Hadi. He had clambered through the window and joined his friend Krish in a game of galli cricket.

They hadn't meant to hurt the dog. Hadi's bat had dispatched Krish's ball with an incredibly sexy *thwaaaackkk*, it had risen in the air in a perfect arc, and as they both watched, their delight turning to horror, it had crashed into the skull of a mangy, slumbering mongrel, sleeping curled up in a sand pile close by. The ugly black-white-and-brown patched creature had given one terrifyingly loud squeak and then gone abruptly quiet.

Hadi and Krish had raced over at once, but abba's scooter had turned into the lane just then, causing them to duck for cover in the dry nallah.

'Shit shit shit!' Hadi had cursed. 'Is it dead?'

'I think so,' Krish had replied solemnly. 'You hit its head, it's bleeding so badly! You're a murderer.'

'It's moving.' Hadi had felt almost weak with relief.

And yes, the mutt was trying to open its eyes. It was whimpering. Small, breathless, agonized sounds that smote Hadi's heart and made his stomach roil with guilt.

'Shouldn't we try and save it?' he'd whispered uneasily even as he eyed his father dismounting from his scooter and wheeling it through the small gate into the porch of their small single-storey home.

Krish had shaken his head violently. 'Chhee, my amma says all street dogs have rabies. And this one is filthy. Touching it will kill us.'

Hadi had stared from the nallah at the bleeding dog. It *was* filthy, yes, with scum in its eyes and muck in its paws and ticks crawling along its patched skin, but its ribs were sticking out like Mahatma Gandhi's and its eyes were full of dumb agony and it didn't look like it could kill anyone...

He bent down impulsively to touch it and it snarled, showing teeth dripping with frothy saliva.

'Haaaadi!!!' Abba was thumping through the tiny house to bang on the locked door of Hadi's room. 'Finished your syllabus?'

'Go!' Krish pushed him. 'I'll take care of it!'

With a last guilty glance at the dying cow-dog, Hadi had turned around and clambered back through the window, his ears burning with shame and guilt.

And then that traitor Krish, instead of running back to the puppy, had retrieved his ball, turned around and marched off home!

Watching this happen out of the corner of his eye, even as abba interrogated him about his preparedness for the paper, Hadi hadn't been able to do much. But when abba finally left the room, he had rushed to the window.

The sight below had made him sag against the bars in blessed relief.

A young girl was sitting cross-legged in the middle of the muddy galli, her dark hair spilling in waves around the injured dog cocooned in her lap against her bare thighs. God knows how she had manoeuvred around those snarling teeth! The dog was still shivering and gasping against her PE shorts—Hadi recognized the uniform of that snobbish school in Yelahanka—but it was also steadily lapping up water from her cupped palm. Her water bottle and school bag lay discarded carelessly beside her on the road.

As Hadi watched, guilt-ridden, the girl got gingerly to her feet, almost doubled over with the weight of the dog, staggered across the road and elbowed open the massive carved doors of the huge house opposite Hadi's. He caught a glimpse of a lush rose garden, a marble fountain and creeper-festooned pillars.

'Ammaaaa…' the girl called.

The massive door shut behind her, but Hadi strained to hear what was being said inside.

A husky older female voice said, 'Jhoomar Rao, what in God's name?'

'Somebody hit a dog! Let's save it!'

'Aiyyo, it looks pretty done for. I don't think it's gonna make it…'

But the mutt made it. It took Jhoomar Rao several months, but she managed to restore the cow-dog, whom she named Phoenix, to full and blooming health. With consistent care, physiotherapy, medication and nutrition, Phoenix got tall and strong and glossy and cocky and except for a very slight limp, there was nothing to betray the fact that he'd ever made contact with Hadi's cricket ball.

But now, it was Hadi who was hurting.

Humbled by how she'd come through when he had failed to act, blown away by how she had unhesitatingly righted a wrong of his making, watching her nurse the ugly, tiny creature with single-minded dedication, he lost his eleven-

year-old heart to the ten-year-old Jhoom and never really
got it back.

'Of course it helped that as she grew older, she grew more and
more beautiful,' he whispers in her ear now.

Jhoom blinks back tears, groans and bangs her head
repeatedly against his chest.

'God, I hate it when my mother's right!'

He pulls away a little, confused.

'Andre?'

'Nothing,' she says, yanking him back and hugging him
tight. 'Look, I'm not gonna mince my words—it was shitty
of you to abandon Phoenix, but you did a much better job
with Roganjosh.'

He looks at her uncertainly. 'I did, right?'

She hugs him again. 'Yes!'

'Phew.' He hugs her back, relieved. Then he frowns.
'Bongo made Krish sound like a total douche, though. He
isn't that bad.'

'Oho, never mind your bros and their beef!' Jhoom pulls
away a little to look at him seriously. 'Hadi… I just want to
say… I'm so so sorry I took so long to see you!'

He kisses the top of her head.

'As long as you see me now.'

'Oh, I do,' she assures him fervently. 'I do.'

'I've cracked Scene 52 for that fool Bongo,' Krish Chetty announces to Bhavani and Shalini as they check out of The Hub@HabbaGalli. 'I'm thinking of visiting Bombay for a while, hanging around at his shoot and giving him more inputs. Anyway, Tomar uncle has pipped me to the post at the shopkeepers' association. Maybe it's time I expanded my horizons.'

'That is excellent news, Krishji.' Bhavani beams at him. 'We will definitely watch *Bittoo: From Lover to Lootera* with great interest.'

'Zero extras?' exclaims Shalini, who has been examining the bill Krish has just handed them. 'But we ate so much chicken ghee roast! And drank so much alcohol!'

Krish grins sheepishly, looking extremely handsome.

'Please don't embarrass me—it's obviously all on the house, Shalini auntie.'

'And this Tree-of-Life carpet is not exactly on the house, but it is yours at a very *special* discount!' announces Mehtab as he comes puffing up to the portico, red-faced and lugging a bulky parcel. 'Full thirty-five per cent!'

Bhavani's homely face wavers between consternation and gratitude. Gratitude wins. 'Thank you, Mehtab bhai!'

'And we wish you luck with your pursuit of the lovely Jaishri Rao,' Shalini says knowingly.

Mehtab grimaces. 'Alas, Shalini beni! She seems to be developing a fondness for that sad-faced Tomar. It is her soft heart and her love for underdogs, you know!'

'Tomar uncle really seems to be winning the day!' Krish says, shaking his head. 'Ah well!'

'Your car's here!' Harsh Kedia says as his driver reverses Sushil Kedia's Mercedes outside The Hub. 'Ready to go, ACP?'

Seated next to the driver on the front seat of the car he has only ever peed against is young Darponk, very smart with a turquoise-blue bow around his tawny neck.

'We've adopted him,' Harsh says wryly. 'Tiffinni and he can live happily ever after now.'

His eyes look sad, Bhavani thinks, and he has lost weight. But there are two loving women in his life and a flourishing business to run. And he will definitely look more attractive when his hair grows back.

'This is for you,' Sona says with a soft smile, handing Shalini a velvet box emblazoned with the four golden entwinned Ks logo of Kedia Jewellers. 'A complete set of The Pooja Kedia Collection. Please don't say no, or mummyji will be heartbroken.'

'Than you so much,' Shalini says warmly as she stacks the velvet box on top of the *Complete Book of Mangalorean Cooking* and the two packets of Bafat powder that had been dropped off by Bhagyalakshmi in the morning. 'You are all too, too generous!'

'As a first annual honeymoon that was quite a success, wasn't it, Bhavani?' Shalini says sentimentally as they drive out of Habba Galli, waving in a gracious, almost royal manner to Hadi and Jhoom, standing hand-in-hand on the balcony of Rao mansion, and to Pooja, Ayesha and Jaishri, who are sipping chilled (spiked?) lemonade on the terrace of the Sait house opposite.

A gentle smile spreads over ACP Bhavani's homely brown face.

'Yes, Shalu, yes.'

Acknowledgements

To my sister Nandini Bajpai, doggie benefactress from Boston, who has fostered and placed more than thirty desi strays into carefully vetted homes in New England, and who continues to keep the KC vrat with full faith and rigour while we in India have long fallen off the fasting wagon—thank you for inspiring this book!

To all past, present and future members of PAWSS—my real-life pilla party right here in Holly-Swiss Town. From our early halycon days when we ran about madly, 'nai hinde' with our dog-catcher nets, feeding mommies, fixing pappies and getting puppies adopted, to these current quieter times, to hopefully better days ahead, it's always so joyous and energizing working with you.

To Amma-Tipu and Gigi-Sonali and Ringo-Rico and Haaru-Cookie-Ginger-Whity-Darponk—much cuddles and treats!

To Dr Gowda at Sudeeksha Pet Clinic, who looks after all our pets, and to Dr Karthik, who helped me with the technical aspects in this book—many thanks.

So much love to my daughters Nika and Tara, my fellow adventurers into the gallis and goochas of Shivajinagar—how much twistato and chunked pineapple and tandoori chicken we have consumed and how many many clips and jhumkis and scrunchies and lehengas we have bought!

To Nika and Tara again, as well as my son Daivik, for their beta (and beti!) reading, rereading, pointing out flaws and missing bits and bloopers of all sorts.

Much love to my Mini didi for her usual overnight speed-read and enthusiastic (though highly biased!) double thumbs-up.

To Suprotim Sengupta, Sharada Karki and everybody at Maddock Films who is working to bring ACP Bhavani Singh to life on Netflix. Thank you for your faith in my work.

To my mother, who loved street dogs and who narrated the Karwa Chauth katha so beautifully to us every year. To my Kannada tutor Shilpa, for her sweetness and patience. To my effervescent friend Mehreen and the precious memory of her mum, Ayesha auntie. Also, in very special memory of Dr Martin Pais, fellow PAWSS member, whose sudden passing stunned us all. And to my friend Mina, whose family name I stole for Dondi bai.

To my husband, Niret, who *always* reads my manuscripts one day before they absolutely HAVE to go, and then starts dishing out feedback which is as aggravating as it is vital—thank you for said feedback and also, thank you for bringing

Josephites and dukra maas and Pink Trumpet trees and, most importantly, namma 'Uru into my life.

Many thanks to Neelini Sarkar for her (always) meticulous editing. To everybody at HarperCollins, Ananth, Poulomi, Swati, Shabnam, Bonita and Rahul, thank you for your support through all my hyperventilating and nitpicking.

Fervent thanks to you, dear reader, for reading!

And finally, to the divine spark that ignites us all—human and animal alike—all my love and gratitude.

About the Author

Anuja Chauhan worked in advertising for over seventeen years and is credited with many popular campaigns, including PepsiCo's Nothing Official About It, Yeh Dil Maange More, Mera Number Kab Aayega, Oye Bubbly and Darr ke Aage Jeet Hai. She is the author of six bestselling novels (*The Zoya Factor, Battle for Bittora, Those Pricey Thakur Girls, The House that BJ Built, Baaz* and *Club You to Death*), the screen rights for all of which have been acquired by major Bombay studios. She lives outside Bangalore in an empty nest with her husband, Niret Alva, with whom she shares three valiantly adulting children and a varying number of dogs and cats.

Also in the Series

CLUB YOU TO DEATH

'Her ear for dialogue is one of Chauhan's strengths.'
INDIA TODAY

When a hunky personal trainer is found asphyxiated to death under an overloaded barbell at the posh Delhi Turf Club, on the eve of the club elections, it is first thought to be a freak accident. But soon, it becomes clear that one of the members of the DTC—all pickled-in-privilege Dilliwallahs—is a cold-blooded killer. As the capital bristles with speculation and conspiracy theories, Crime Branch veteran ACP Bhavani Singh is appointed to investigate the case. Together with his able deputies—ex-lovers Akash 'Kashi' Dogra, hottie crusader for human rights, and Bambi Todi, wealthy girl-about-town—ACP Bhavani sets out to solve a crime that seems simple enough at the surface, but turns out to have roots as deep and spreading as those of New Delhi's famous Neem trees... Anuja Chauhan returns with a bloody good romance set in the pulsating heart of Lutyens' Delhi.

Other Books by Anuja Chauhan

THE ZOYA FACTOR

'[India's] funniest and most entertaining novelist.' MINT

When the younger players in India's cricket team find out that advertising executive Zoya Singh Solanki was born at the very moment India won the World Cup back in 1983, they are intrigued. When having breakfast with her is followed by victories on the field, they are impressed. And when not eating with her results in defeat, they decide she's a lucky charm. The nation goes a step further. Amazed at the ragtag team's sudden spurt of victories, it declares her a Goddess. So when the eccentric IBCC president and his mesmeric, always-exquisitely-attired Swamiji invite Zoya to accompany the team to the tenth ICC World Cup, she has no choice but to agree.

Pursued by international cricket boards on the one hand, wooed by Cola majors on the other, Zoya struggles to stay grounded in the thick of the world cup action. And it doesn't help that she keeps clashing with the erratically brilliant new skipper who tells her flatly that he doesn't believe in luck...

BATTLE FOR BITTORA

'Fun. Fearless. Fabulous.' COSMOPOLITAN

Twenty-five-year-old Jinni lives in Mumbai, works in a hip animation studio and is perfectly happy with her carefree life. Until her bossy grandmother shows up and announces that it is Jinni's 'duty' to drop everything and contest the upcoming Lok Sabha elections from their sleepy hometown, Bittora.

Jinni swears she won't, but soon ends up swathed in cotton saris and frumpy blouses, battling prickly heat, corruption and accusations of nymphomania as candidate Sarojini Pande, a daughter of the illustrious Pande dynasty of Pavit Pradesh. And if life isn't fun enough already, her main opposition turns out to be Bittora ex-royal Zain Altaf Khan—an irritatingly idealistic though undeniably lustworthy individual with whom Jinni shares a complicated history.

Enlivened by Anuja Chauhan's characteristic brand of wicked humour and sexy romanticism, this is a rollicking new tale of young India.

THOSE PRICEY THAKUR GIRLS

'If there's one word that describes [Anuja's] writing, it's chic.'
THE TELEGRAPH

In a sprawling bungalow on New Delhi's posh Hailey Road, Justice Laxmi Narayan Thakur and his wife Mamta spend their days anxiously watching over their five beautiful (but troublesome) alphabetically named daughters.

Anjini, married but an incorrigible flirt; Binodini, very worried about her children's hissa in the family property; Chandrakanta, who eloped with a foreigner on the eve of her wedding; Eshwari, who is just a little too popular at Modern School, Barakhamba Road; and the Judge's favourite (though fathers shouldn't have favourites), the quietly fiery Debjani, champion of all the stray animals on Hailey Road, who reads the English news on DD and clashes constantly with crusading journalist Dylan Singh Shekhawat, he of shining professional credentials but tarnished personal reputation, crushingly dismissive of her 'state-sponsored propaganda', but always seeking her out with half-sarcastic, half-intrigued dark eyes.

Spot-on funny and toe-curlingly sexy, *Those Pricey Thakur Girls* is Anuja Chauhan writing at her sparkling best.

THE HOUSE THAT BJ BUILT

'Delightful. Wickedly accurate.' INDIA TODAY

'I'll make my sisters squirm like well-salted earthworms. I won't sell. Even my jutti won't sell. And if I die na, then even my gosht won't sell!' The late Binodini Thakur had been very clear that she would never agree to sell her hissa in her Bauji's big old house on Hailey Road. And her daughter Bonu is determined to honour her mother's wishes. But what to do about her four pushy aunts who are insisting she do just that?

One is bald and stingy, one is jobless and manless, one needs the money to 'save the nation' and one is stepmother to Bonu's childhood crush – the brilliant young Bollywood director Samar Vir Singh, who promised BJ upon his deathbed that he would get the house sold, divvy the money equally and end all the bickering in the family. The first word baby Bonu ever spoke was 'Balls' and, indeed, she is ballsy, bullshit-intolerant, brave and beautiful. But is she strong enough to weather emotional blackmail by the spadefuls? Not to mention countering shady builders, wily politicians, spies, lies and the knee-buckling hotness of Samar's intense eyes?

BAAZ

1971. The USSR-backed India-Mukti Bahini alliance is on the brink of war against the America-aided Pakistani forces. As the Cold War threatens to turn red hot, handsome, laughing Ishaan Faujdaar, a farm boy from Chakkahera, Haryana, is elated to be in the IAF, flying the Gnat, a tiny fighter plane nicknamed 'Sabre Slayer' for the devastation it has wreaked in the ranks of Pakistan's F-86 Sabre Squadrons.

Flanked by his buddies Raks, a MiG-21 Fighter, Maddy, a transport pilot who flies a Caribou, and fellow Gnatties Jana, Gana and Mana, Shaanu has nothing on his mind but glory and adventure - until he encounters Tehmina Dadyseth, famed bathing beauty and sister of a dead fauji, who makes him question the very concept of nationalism and whose eyes fill with disillusioned scorn whenever people wax eloquent about patriotism and war...

Pulsating with love, laughter and courage, Baaz is Anuja Chauhan's tribute to our men in uniform.

HarperCollins *Publishers* India

At HarperCollins India, we believe in telling the best stories and finding the widest readership for our books in every format possible. We started publishing in 1992; a great deal has changed since then, but what has remained constant is the passion with which our authors write their books, the love with which readers receive them, and the sheer joy and excitement that we as publishers feel in being a part of the publishing process.

Over the years, we've had the pleasure of publishing some of the finest writing from the subcontinent and around the world, including several award-winning titles and some of the biggest bestsellers in India's publishing history. But nothing has meant more to us than the fact that millions of people have read the books we published, and that somewhere, a book of ours might have made a difference.

As we look to the future, we go back to that one word— a word which has been a driving force for us all these years.

Read.

Harper Collins

HARPER PERENNIAL

HARPER BUSINESS

HARPER BLACK

हार्पर हिन्दी

HarperCollins *Children'sBooks*

HARPER DESIGN

HARPER VANTAGE

Harper Sport